'Jack Vance is a peerless creator of strange landscapes, and in *Night Lamp* he conjures up a kind of Asia among the stars. Buy it. It's cheaper and at least as exotic as two weeks in the sun' *Financial Times*

'Rush out and buy this glorious book' *Interzone*

'*Night Lamp* yields rich rewards in its humorous complexities' *Publishers Weekly*

Also by Jack Vance

NOVELS

The Space Pirate (also titled Five Gold Bands and The Rapparee, 1953)
Vandals of the Void (1953)
To Live Forever (1956)
Big Planet (1957)
Take My Face (as Peter Held, 1957)
The Isle of Peril (as Alan Wade, 1957)
The Languages of Pao (1958)
Slaves of the Kau (also titled Planet of the Damned and Gold and Iron, 1958)
The Man in the Cage (1960)
The Dragon Masters (1963)
The Four Johns (as Ellery Queen, 1964)
The Houses of Izm (1964)
Son of the Tree (1964)
The Star King (1964)
The Killing Machine (1964)
A Room to Die In (as Ellery Queen, 1965)
Monsters in Orbit (1965)
Space Opera (1965)
The Fox Valley Murders (1966)
The Madman Theory (as Ellory Queen, 1966)
The Blue World (1966)
The Brains of Earth (1966)
Last Castle (1966)
The Eyes of the Overworld (also titled Cugel the Clever, 1966)
The Pleasant Grove Murders (1967)
The Palace of Love (1967)
City of the Chasch (also titled The Chasch, 1968)
The Deadly Isles (1969)
Emphyrio (1969)
Servants of the Wankh (also titled The Wankh, 1969)
The Dirdir (1969)
The Pnume (1970)
Bad Ronald (1973)
The Anome (also titled The Faceless Man, 1973)
The Brave Free Men (1973)
Trullion: Alastor 2262 (1973)
Morreion (1973)
The Asutra (1974)
The Gray Prince (also titled The Domains of Koryphon,1974)
Marune: Alastor 993 (1975)
Showboat World (also titled The Magnificent Showboats of the Lower Vissel River, 1975)
Maske: Thaery (1976)
Wyst: Alastor 1716 (1978)
The House on Lily Street (1979)
The Face (1979)
The Bagful of Dreams (1979)
The Book of Dreams (1981)
Lyonesse: Suldrun's Garden (1983)
Cugel's Saga (also titled Cugel: The Skybreak Spatterlight, 1983)
Lyonesse: The Green Pearl (1986)
Amanita Station (1987)
Green Magic (1988)
Lyonesse: Madouc (1990)
Ecce and Old Earth (1991)
Throy (1992)
Night Lamp (1996)
The Laughing Magician (1997)
Ports of Call (1998)
Lurulu (2004)

SHORT STORY COLLECTIONS

The Dying Earth (1950, originally titled Mazirian the Magician)
Eight Fantasma and Magics (1969)
The Worlds of Jack Vance (1973)
The Moon Moth and Other Stories (1976)
The Best of Jack Vance (1978)
Green Magic (1979)
Galactic Effectuator (1980)
Lost Moons (1982)
The Narrow Land (1982)
Rhialto the Marvellous (1984)
The Complete Magnus Ridolph (1984)
Light from a Lone Star (1985)
The Dark Side of the Moon: Stories of the Future (1986)
Demon Prince: the Dissonant Worlds of Jack Vance (1986)
Bird Isle and Take My Face (1988)
Chateau d'If and Other Stories (1990)
When the Five Moons Rise (1992)
The Jack Vance Treasury (2007)
The Jack Vance Reader (2008)
Wild Thyme, Green Magic (2009)
The Men Return (2009)

SF MASTERWORKS

Night Lamp

JACK VANCE

This edition first published in Great Britain in 2015 by
Gollancz
An imprint of the Orion Publishing Group
Carmelite House, 50 Victoria Embankment, London EC4Y 0DZ
An Hachette UK Company

1 3 5 7 9 10 8 6 4 2

A CIP catalogue record for this book is available from the British Library

ISBN 978 1 473 20892 6

Printed in Great Britain by
Clays Ltd, St Ives plc

www.orionbooks.co.uk
www.gollancz.co.uk

Dedicated to:

Alexia Schulz
Danae Schulz
Eric Fedrowisch

INTRODUCTION

by Adam Roberts

Jack Vance lived a long life and wrote steadily through all of it. He started publishing in the 1940s, and his last published book (a memoir) won a Hugo Award in the 2010s. When he died in 2013 he was three months away from his 97th birthday. His list of publications is one of those that make bibliographers throw up their hands in despair: something like 90 novels and many hundreds of novellas and short stories. What is most remarkable here is Vance's consistency. Pretty much without exception all his books are elegant, off-kilter, gorgeous, intricate and marvellous. Jack Vance's writing has rarely been imitated and never been bettered.

It is natural to want to find a way of orienting ourselves with respect to so large a body of work, and one way of doing this is group Vance's best novels by their shared worlds. *The Dying Earth* series (the first volume appeared in 1950) comprises a clutch of novels set in a very far future version of Earth, where science has become magic, and both landscape and society are faded and mellowed with immense age. Also High Fantasy in flavour are the superlative *Lyonesse* books (1983–85). The five books in the revenge-themed *Demon Princes* series (1964–81) and four books in the *Planet of Adventure* series (1968–70) contain more conventionally science-fictional elements, although always with Vance the aura and charm of a more beguiling Fantasy idiom informs the writing.

From the 1970s through to the end of his life Vance tended to write novels set in his 'Gaean Reach', a large region of space (including 'Old Earth', from one of whose alternate names, 'Gaea', the area takes its name) containing an apparently inexhaustible supply of human-colonised planets. Trade, research and tourism links most, though not all, of these worlds. Some are defined by advanced technology, others – like the planet 'Alastor', about which Vance published three novels – are nature reserves. There are democracies, aristocracies, feudal and anarchic, systems of society both eccentric and familiar. Vance set more than a dozen novels and many stories here. 'Never has the human race been less homogenous,' says the narrator in *The Gray Prince* (1975).

Night Lamp (1996) is a deeply characteristic Gaean Reach novel, and may be the best of them. Two rather stiffly formal academics, the Faths, adopt an orphan they find being beaten to death on a planet they are visiting. Something terrible has traumatised the boy, and his mental wounds are even more life-threatening than his physical injuries. To save him, the Faths have the boy's memory artificially wiped. This lad, Jaro, grows to manhood not knowing his origins, haunted by mysterious voices, an outsider on the ornately hierarchical world of is adoptive parents.

It is a common, though lamentable, habit amongst readers to 'read for the plot'. By this I mean 'reading *only* for the plot', concentrating your attention, as you read, on *what is happening* by way of wondering *what will happen next.* There's nothing wrong with this, of course, provided only it doesn't supersede the other foci of your reading enjoyment. It's natural to want to find out what will happen. But you need not fret about this, because, if you read on, you will.

You can certainly read Jack Vance's novels for the story, for his plots are full of incident and variety and generally move quickly. This, though, is more a surface feature than a deep one; structurally speaking, as it were, Vance tends to tell the same core story over and again, and to deploy similar kinds of characters in all his many novels. The protagonist is often a self-contained and resourceful young man, who moves through a landscape of peril and glamour, weirdness and charm. There will be elderly mages, thuggish bravos, beautiful women – sometimes sensually alluring, sometimes frigid. There will also be imposing dames, strange siblings and alien life-forms often humanoid-insectile in form, whose behaviour is more or less baffling to human observers. Plots are often powered by revenge, by the uncovering of a secret, or both. Vance is fascinated by the larger structures of law and finance – in *Night Lamp* both play a large part, and when (in his Fantasy novels) he writes about magic and spells they are defined by an actuarial or lawyerly need to pay precise attention to the details before agreeing to anything.

As a writer of speculative anthropology Vance finds both endless variety and unlikely consonances in the myriad societies and cultures he invents, ranging across scores of colourfully distinguished ethnicities – never more so in his Gaean Reach novels. What they all share is an intricately rigid logic of social stratification: code and modes of behaviour that restrict individual freedom of action. Several societies in *Night Lamp* share this, from the hydrophobia of the gypsies of Camberwell, to the various arid hierarchies of 'societies', 'clubs' and 'ledges' which defines the world of Jaro's upbringing and in which he refuses to accede, to the more traditional aristocratic sense of absolute entitlement that defines the slave-society of Night Lamp itself. In all cases, rules absolutely determine human existence. We may think, especially when we are young, that rules are nothing more than the bars of a prison. But Vance understands that rules are the necessary scaffolding for elegance, and elegance is his dominant aesthetic passion. 'Society without ritual,' he notes early in *Night Lamp*, 'is like music played on a single string with one finger.' Like all his books, *Night Lamp* is a multi-stringed performance of tremendous grace and skill. And as is so often the case with Vance, the greatest pleasure is to be found not in the main tune, but in the many grace notes, the ornaments and curlicue of Vance's capacious imagination. His books are never the transcript of mere facts and events. This is why it is a mistake to read him hurriedly for the plot. Rather Vance creates a sense of infinite variety as determinative of human existence in all its infinitely varied forms.

The edifice of Vance's genius was supported by three great pillars: wit, variety and style. He was an immensely witty writer, something perhaps overlooked by some on account of the fact that his wit was extremely dry. That fact, though, seems to me an advantage rather than anything else. Wit differs from broader comedy in requiring shared structures of manners and values properly to bite, and Vance's world is one where villains, no matter how murderous and rapacious, respect properly drawn-up contracts and protocols. It means that there is an enduring dignity to Vance's characters, even as his characters are betrayed, demeaned, sold into slavery, thrown into captivity with barbarian aliens, or exiled to the furthest reaches of the cosmos. That dignity is one of the most immediate impressions a Vance novel creates for the reader, and it is a rarer thing in writing nowadays than it once used to be. The grimmer and darker modern Fantasy gets, the less charm and dignity it possesses, and the more refreshing it is to pick up Vance again.

The *variety* in this novel is a matter of fineness of apprehension rather than brute ingeniousness. Don't get me wrong: Vance is often a brilliantly ingenious writer. He likes to invent grotesque and striking creatures, odd social codes, and his plotting delights in unexpected twists and reversals. But this isn't what makes him unique as a writer. He sees the world as almost endlessly surprising and varied and fresh and beautiful, but always in controlled and expressive ways, never as pure gush or enthusiasm. If we had to pick one word to capture his vision of the truth of things, we might light upon *elegance*: and his novels are brimming with the beauties of elegance, from speech and manners to descriptions of the natural world and that emotional state known in Portuguese as 'saudade', for which there is no real English translation. In the long run this reveals itself as a fineness of truth, or what we might call 'style'. And truly he was the most stylish of writers.

Adam Roberts

One

1

Toward the far edge of the Cornu Sector of Ophiuchus, Robert Palmer's Star shone brilliant white, its corona flaring with films of blue, red and green color. A dozen planets danced attendance, like children careening around a maypole, but only the world Camberwell knew that narrow range of conditions tolerant to human life. The region was remote; the early explorers were pirates, fugitives and fringers,* followed by miscellaneous settlers, to the effect that Camberwell had been inhabited for many thousands of years.

Camberwell was a world of disparate landscapes. Four continents with intervening oceans, defined the topography. The flora and fauna, as always, had evolved into forms of unique particularity, the fauna having attained such a bizarre variety, with habits so startling and destructive, that two continents had been set aside as preserves where the creatures, large and small, biped or otherwise, could hop, pounce, lumber, run, rumble, pillage and grind others to bits, as met their needs. On the other two continents the fauna had been suppressed.

*From "fringe," such as the "fringes of society." "Fringer": a human sub-class impossible to define exactly. "Misanthropic vagabonds" has been proposed as an acceptable approximation.

The human population of Camberwell derived from a dozen races which, rather than merging, had clotted into a number of stubbornly discrete units. Over the years the differentiation had produced a picturesque tumble of human societies, so that Camberwell had become a favorite destination for off-world xenologists and anthropologists.

The most important town of Camberwell, Tanzig, had been built to the dictates of a precise plan. Concentric rings of buildings surrounded a central plaza, where three bronze statues a hundred feet tall stood facing away from each other, arms raised in gestures whose purport had long been forgotten.*

2

Hilyer and Althea Fath were Associate Professors at Thanet Institute on the world Gallingale. Both were associated with the College of Aesthetic Philosophy. Hilyer's special subject was the Theory of Concurrent Symbols; Althea studied the music of barbaric or semi-barbaric peoples, typically performed on unique instruments using unconventional scales to produce bizarre harmonies. Such musics were sometimes simple, sometimes complex, usually incomprehensible to alien ears, though often fascinating. Many times the old farmhouse where the Faths lived had resounded to strange sounds, along with impassioned argument as to whether the word "music" might truly apply to such extraordinary noises.

While neither Hilyer nor Althea would have described themselves as youthful, still less would they have admitted to middle age. Hilyer and Althea were both conservative in their natural tendencies, though not necessarily conventional, both subscribing to the ideals of pacifism and both indifferent to social status. Hilyer was slight if sinewy of physique, sallow, with mouse-gray hair thinning back from a high forehead, and a manner of cool urbanity. His long nose, lofty eyebrows, a thin drooping mouth, gave him a faintly disdainful expression, as if he were noticing an

---

*Early chronicles declared that the three statues represented the same individual, the fabled justiciary and law-giver David Alexander, depicted in three typical poses: summons to judgment, quelling of the rabble, and imposition of equity. In this latter pose he carried a short-handled axe with a broad lunate blade, possibly no more than an object of ceremonial import.

unpleasant odor. In sheer point of fact, Hilyer was mild, carefully polite, and disinclined to any sort of vulgarity.

Althea, like Hilyer, was slender, though somewhat more brisk and cheerful. Without herself noticing the fact, she was almost pretty, by reason of bright hazel eyes, a pleasant expression, and a head of chestnut brown curls, worn without reference to style. Her temperament was cheerful and optimistic, and she had no trouble dealing with Hilyer's occasional small irascibilities. Neither Hilyer nor Althea took part in the earnest striving for social prestige which dominated the life of most folk; they belonged to no clubs and commanded no "comporture"* whatever. Their areas of expertise dove-tailed so neatly that they were able to undertake joint offworld research expeditions.

One such expedition took them to the semi-civilized world Camberwell beside Robert Palmer's Star. Arriving at the dilapidated Tanzig spaceport, they rented a flitter and set off at once to the town Sronk, near the Wyching Hills, at the edge of the Wildenberry Steppe, where they planned to record the music and study the lifestyle of the Vongo gypsies, eighteen tribes of which roamed the steppe.

The gypsies were fascinating folk, on many levels. The men were tall, strong, with long legs and arms, intensely active and athletic, proud of their ability to leap over thornbushes. Neither men nor women were well-favored. Heads were long and meaty, with dull pinkish-plum complexions, coarse features, shocks of varnished black hair and short spade beards also varnished. The men painted white circles around their eye-sockets to emphasize the glare of their black eyes. The women were tall, buxom, with round cheeks, large hooked noses and hair cut square at ear level. Both men and women wore picturesque garments to which were sewed the teeth of dead enemies: the booty of intertribal vendettas. Water was considered an enervating, even despicable, fluid, to be shunned at all costs. No gypsy allowed himself or herself to be bathed, from infancy until death, for fear of rinsing away a magic personal unguent which, oozing from the skin, was the source of mana. A rank beer was the drink of choice.

The tribes were hostile in accordance with intricate formulae involving murders, mutilations and gleeful scarification of captured children, to make them vile in the eyes of their parents. Often these children were banished by their horrified parents to

*See footnote on page 25.

wander the steppes alone, where they became assassins and musicians expert in the playing of a tandem flute, forbidden to all other musicians. This musician-assassin caste included both men and women, and all were required to wear yellow trousers. The women, on becoming pregnant and giving birth, stealthily abandoned the child in the crêche of their native tribe, where it was tolerantly raised in proper style.

The gypsy tribes gathered four times a year at specified encampments. The host tribe provided the music, pridefully attempting to awe the musicians of rival tribes. The rival musicians, after jeering at the music of their hosts, were in due course allowed to play, along with assassins and their tandem flutes. Each tribe played its most secret and powerful music, which the musicians of the other tribes attempted to duplicate, in order to gain dominance over the souls of the tribe from whom the tune had been stolen. Such being the case, anyone discovered recording the music was instantly throttled. The Faths, in order to record the music in safety, wore small internal devices which could not be detected by external inspection. Such were the desperate exigencies to which the dedicated musicologist must submit, the Faths told each other, with wry grimaces.

For an off-worlder to visit a Vongo encampment was, at any time, an unnerving experience, but the tribal camp meetings were even more intense. A favorite pastime of the young bucks was to kidnap and rape the girls of another tribe, which caused a great hubbub, but which seldom came to bloodshed, since such exploits were considered juvenile pranks, at which the girls had probably connived. A far more serious offense was the kidnap of a chief or a shaman, and the washing of him and his clothes in warm soapy water, in order to deplete him of his sacred ooze. After the washing, the victim was shorn of his beard and a bouquet of white flowers was tied to his testicles, after which he was free to slink back to his own tribe: naked, beardless, washed and bereft of mana. The wash water was carefully distilled, finally to yield a quart of yellow unctuous foul-smelling stuff, which would be used in tribal magic.

The Faths, upon making gifts of black velvet fabric, were allowed to visit such a convocation, and managed to avoid trouble, the threat of which seemed to curdle the air around them. They watched as at sundown a bonfire was set alight. The gypsies feasted upon meat boiled in beer along with ramp and soursaps. A few minutes later, musicians gathered by one of the wagons and began to produce odd squeaking noises, apparently tuning and warming their instruments. The Faths went to sit in the shadow of the wagon and started their recording machines. The musicians began to play strident insistent phrases, which gradually diverged into harsh permutations and apparently irrelevant squeakings provided by a yellow-trousered assassin on his tandem flute. Reacting to the clang of gongs, the process repeated itself. Meanwhile, the women had started to dance: a graceless waddle in a slow counter-clockwise circle around the fire. Black skirts swept the ground; black eyes glittered above a curious black demi-mask, covering mouth and chin, upon which a great leering mouth had been painted in white pigment. From each depicted mouth hung a simulated tongue six inches long, painted bright red. The tongues swung and lolloped as the women jerked their heads from side to side.

"This will haunt my dreams," Hilyer croaked under his breath.

"Maintain your strength, for the sake of science!" Althea told him.

The dancers sidled forward, dipping and advancing first the right leg, bending it and wallowing the massive right buttock around, drooping the right shoulder forward to catch the movement, then repeating the process from the left.

The women's dance ended and they went off to drink beer. The music became louder and more emphatic; one by one the men stepped out to dance, kicking first forward, then backward, then performing odd contortions with arms akimbo and shoulders shuddering, followed by a leap forward, and then more of the same. At last they too went off to drink beer and boast of their leaps. The music started once again and the Vongo men started a new dance, cavorting about at random, inventing wonderful combinations of kicks, jumps and acrobatics, each crying out in triumph as he completed a particularly difficult evolution. At last limp with fatigue they went off to the beer tubs. They were still not finished. After a few moments the men returned to the edge of the firelight, where they engaged in the curious practice of "louthering."* At first they stood drunkenly reeling, peering up at the sky, pointing to the constellations they intended to disparage. Then, one after another, they threw clenched fists high, and shouted taunts and challenges toward their distant oppo-

*Literally, "defiance of the constellation-heroes," and by transference, the IPCC.

nents. "Come, all you washed rats, you parvenus and soap-eaters! Here we stand! We are ready for you; we will eat your gizzards! Come, bring on your fat-cheeked warriors; we will tear them into bits! We will douse them in water! Fear? Never! We defy you!"

Almost as if on cue, a bolt of lightning flashed out of the sky and rain pelted down in a sudden deluge. Croaking and cursing, the Vongos dashed for the cover of their wagons, and the area became deserted, save for the Faths who took the opportunity to run to their flitter. They returned to Sronk, happy with the night's work.

In the morning the Faths wandered the Sronk bazaar, where Althea bought a pair of unusual candelabra to augment her collection. They found no musical instruments of interest, but were told that at the market village Latuz, a hundred miles to the south, gypsy instruments of all kinds, some new, some antique, were often to be found at the back of the market stalls. No one wanted such junk, so the prices would be low, except for the Faths, who would be recognized as off-worlders, and the prices would instantly become high.

On the following day the Faths flew south, skimming low over the road which followed the desolate Wyching Hills, with the steppe extending away to the east.

Thirty miles south of Sronk they came upon an unsettling scene. In the road below four gangling peasant youths armed with cudgels were carefully clubbing to death a squirming creature which lay in the dirt at their feet. Despite oozing blood and broken bones, the creature tried to defend itself and fought back with a desperate gallantry which transcended bravery and seemed to the Faths sheer nobility of spirit.

Whatever the case, the Faths dropped the flitter down upon the road, leapt to the ground and thrust the youths back from their limp victim, who they now saw to be a dark-haired urchin five or six years old, emaciated as if from hunger and dressed in rags.

The peasant boys stood resentfully to the side. The oldest explained that the creature was a wildling, no better than an animal, who would, if allowed, grow to become a robber or a depredator of crops. It was sensible to exterminate such vermin when the opportunity offered, as of now, so—if the travellers would be good enough to step aside, they would get on with their work.

The Faths scolded the slack-jawed peasant lads, then with great care lifted the battered child into their vehicle, while the peasant lads looked on in baffled disapproval. Later they would regale their parents with the weird conduct of the odd folk in funny clothes, probably off-worlders, to judge by the way they spoke.

The Faths took the semi-conscious body to the clinic at Sronk, where Doctors Solek and Fexel, the resident medical officers, nurtured the boy's flickering vitality, until finally the boy's condition had stabilized, and he seemed to be out of danger.

Solek and Fexel stood back, shoulders sagging, faces drawn, but gratified by their success. "A hard pull," said Solek. "I thought we'd lost him."

"Give the boy credit," said Fexel. "He doesn't want to die."

The two surveyed the still form. "A handsome fellow, even with all the bruises and bandages," said Solek. "How could anyone abandon a child like that?"

Fexel examined the boy's hands, teeth, and touched his throat. "About six years old, I'd say. He might well be an off-worlder, upper class at a guess."

The boy slept. Solek and Fexel went off to take some rest, leaving a nurse on duty.

The boy slept on, slowly growing stronger. Inside his mind fragments of memory began to renew broken linkages. The boy stirred in his sleep, and the nurse on duty, looking into his face, was startled by what she saw. She immediately summoned Doctors Solek and Fexel. They arrived to find the boy straining against the devices which held him immobile. His eyes were closed; he hissed and panted, as his sluggish mental processes quickened. Oddments of memory fused into strings. The old synaptic nodes reformed and the strings became blocks. Memory produced an explosion of images too awful to be borne. The boy went into hysteria, causing his broken body to grind, squeal and convulse. Solek and Fexel stood aghast, but only for an instant. Then, throwing off their shock, they administered sedation.

Almost immediately the boy relaxed and lay quiet, his eyes remaining closed, while Solek and Fexel watched uncertainly. Was he asleep? Apparently.

Six hours passed, during which the doctors took time to rest. Returning to the clinic, they cautiously allowed the sedation to dissipate. For a few moments all seemed well, then once again the boy erupted into a raging fit. The sinews of his neck corded; his eyes bulged against the restraints. Gradually, the boy's struggling became more feeble, like a clock running down. From his throat came a wail of such wild grief that Solek and Fexel jerked into motion and applied new sedation, to forestall a fatal seizure.

At this time a research fellow from the Tanzig Central Medical Facility was at hand, conducting a series of tutorial seminars. His name was Myrrle Wanish; he specialized in cerebral dysfunctions and hypertrophic abnormalities of the brain in general. Seizing upon opportunity, Solek and Fexel brought the injured boy to his attention.

Doctor Wanish looked down the list of breaks, fractures, dislocations, wrenches and contusions which had been inflicted upon the boy, and shook his head. "Why is he not dead?"

"We have asked the same question a dozen times," said Solek.

"Up to now he has simply refused to die," said Fexel. "But he can't hold out much longer."

"He's had some sort of terrifying experience," said Solek. "At least, that is my guess."

"The beating?"

"Possibly, but my instincts say no. When he remembers, the shock is too much for him. So—what have we done wrong?"

"Probably nothing," said Wanish. "I suspect that events have welded a loop, with feedback bouncing back and forth. It gets worse instead of better."

"And the remedy?"

"Obvious! The loop must be broken." Wanish surveyed the boy. "There's nothing known of his background, I take it?"

"Nothing."

Wanish nodded. "Let's have a look inside his head. Keep him sedated while I set up my gear."

Wanish worked for an hour connecting the boy to his apparatus. At last he finished. A pair of metal hemispheres clasped the boy's head, exposing only the fragile nose, mouth and chin. Metal sleeves gripped his wrists and ankles; metal bands immobilized him at chest and hips.

"Now we begin," said Wanish. He touched a button. A screen came to life, displaying in bright yellow lines a web which Wanish identified as a schematic chart of the boy's brain. "It is obviously topologically distorted; still—" his voice dwindled as he bent to examine the screen. For several minutes he studied the twining networks and phosphorescent mats, meanwhile uttering small exclamations and sharp hisses of astonishment. At last he turned back to Solek and Fexel. "See these yellow lines?" He tapped the chart with a pencil. "They represent overactive linkages. When they tangle into mats, they cause trouble, as we have seen. Needless to say, I oversimplify."

Solek and Fexel studied the screen. Some of the linkages were thin as spider webs; others pulsed with sluggish power; these latter Wanish identified as segments of a self-reinforcing loop. In several areas the strands coiled and impacted into fibrous pads, so dense that the individual nerve was lost.

Wanish pointed his pencil. "These tangles are the problem. They are like black holes in the mind; nothing which touches them escapes. However, they can be destroyed, and I shall do so."

Solek asked: "What happens then?"

"To put it simply," said Wanish, "the boy survives, but loses much of his memory."

Neither Doctor Solek nor Fexel had anything to say. Wanish adjusted his instrument. A blue spark appeared on the screen. Wanish settled himself to work. The spark moved in and out of the pulsing yellow tangles; the luminous mats separated into shreds, which faded, dissolved and were gone save for a few ghostly wisps.

Wanish deactivated the instrument. "That is that. He retains his reflexes, his language and his motor skills, but his primary memory is gone. A wisp or two remain; they may bring him random images—no more than glimpses, enough to unsettle him, but nothing to give him trouble."

The three released the boy from the metal sleeves, bands and hemispheres.

As they watched, the boy opened his eyes. He studied the men with a sober expression.

Wanish asked: "How do you feel?"

"There are pains when I move." The boy's voice was thin and clear, carefully enunciated.

"That is to be expected; in fact, it is a good sign. Soon you will be well. What is your name?"

The boy looked up blankly. "It is—" He hesitated, then said, "I don't know."

He closed his eyes. Up from his throat came a low growling sound, soft but harsh, as if produced by extreme effort. The sound formed words: "His name is Jaro."

Wanish leaned forward, startled. "Who are you?"

The boy sighed a long sad sigh, then slept.

The three therapists watched until the boy's breathing became regular. Solek asked Wanish: "How much of this will you report to the Faths?"

Wanish grimaced. "It is queer—if not uncanny. Still—" he reflected "—it probably amounts to nothing. I think that, so far as I am concerned, I heard the boy give his name as 'Jaro,' and nothing more."

Solek and Fexel nodded. "I think that is what we heard too," Fexel said.

Doctor Wanish went out to the reception area where the Faths awaited him.

"Rest easy," said Wanish. "The worst is over and he should recover quite soon, with no complications other than gaps in his memory."

The Faths pondered the news. Althea asked, "How extreme is the loss?"

"That is hard to predict. Something remarkably terrible caused his distress. We were forced to blot out several nodes, with all the side linkages. He'll never know what happened to him, or who he is, other than that his name is 'Jaro.' "

Hilyer Fath said weightily: "You are telling us that his memory is entirely gone?"

Wanish thought of the voice which had spoken Jaro's name. "I wouldn't dare predict anything. His schematic now shows isolated points and sparks, which suggest the shape of old matrices; they may provide a few random glimpses and hints, but probably nothing coherent."

3

Hilyer and Althea Fath made inquiries at places along the Foisie River valley, but learned nothing either of Jaro or his origin. Everywhere they encountered the same shrugs of indifference, the same perplexity that anyone should ask such bootless questions.

Upon the Fath's return to Sronk, they complained to Wanish of their experiences. He told them: "There are only a few organized societies here, and many small groups, clans, and districts: all independent, all suspicious. They have learned that if they mind their own business no one makes trouble for them, and so goes the world Camberwell."

Jaro's shoes and clothing suggested an off-world source, and with Tanzig, an important space terminal, close by the river, the Faths came to believe that Jaro had been brought to Camberwell from another world.

At the first opportunity Althea attempted a few timid questions but, as Doctor Wanish had predicted, Jaro's memory was blank, except for an occasional shadowy glimpse, which was gone almost before it arrived. One of these images was exceptional: so intense as to cause Jaro a great fright.

The image, or vision, came to Jaro without warning late one afternoon. Shutters screened the low sunlight and the room was comfortably dim. Althea sat by the bed, exploring as best she could the bounds of Jaro's mental landscape. Presently he became drowsy; the conversation, such as it was, lapsed. Jaro lay with his face to the ceiling, eyes half-closed. He made a sudden soft gasping sound. His hands clenched and his mouth sagged open.

Althea noticed at once. She jumped to her feet and peered down into his face. "Jaro! Jaro! What's wrong? Tell me what's wrong?"

Jaro made no response, but gradually relaxed. Althea tried to keep her voice steady. "Jaro? Say something! Are you well?"

Jaro looked at her doubtfully, then closed his eyes. He muttered, "I saw something which frightened me." Althea tried to control her voice. "Tell me what you saw."

After a moment Jaro began to speak, in a voice so soft that Althea was forced to bend low to hear him. "I was standing in front of a house; I think it was where I lived. The sun was gone, so that it was almost dark. Behind the front fence a man was standing. I could see only his shape, black against the sky." Jaro paused, and lay quiet.

Althea asked, "Who was this man? Do you know him?"

"No."

"What did he look like?"

In a halting voice, assisted by Althea's promptings, Jaro described a tall spare figure silhouetted against the gray sky of dusk, wearing a tight coat, a low-crowned black hat with a stiff brim. Jaro had been frightened, though he could not remember why. The figure was austere, majestic; it turned to stare at Jaro. The eyes were like four-pointed stars gleaming with rays of silver light.

Fascinated, Althea asked: "What happened next?"

"I don't remember." Jaro's voice drifted away and Althea let him sleep.

4

Jaro was lucky that the memory had been blanked from his mind. What happened next was terrible.

Jaro went into the house and told his mother of the man standing beyond the fence. She froze for an instant, then made a sound so stern and dismal as to transcend fear. She moved with decision, taking a metal box from a shelf and thrusting it into Jaro's hands. "Take this box; hide it where no one can find it. Then go down to the river and get into the boat. I'll come if I can, but be ready to push off alone if anyone else comes near. Hurry now!"

Jaro ran out the back door. He hid the box in a secret place, then stood indecisive, sick with foreboding. At last he ran to the river, made the boat ready and waited. The wind blew in his ears. He ventured a few steps back toward the house, stopped and strained to listen. What was that? A wail, barely heard over the wind-noise? He gave a desperate little moan and, despite his mother's orders, ran back to the house. He peered through the side window, and for a moment could not understand what was happening. His mother lay on the floor, face up, arms outspread, with a black satchel to the side and some sort of apparatus at her head. Odd! A musical instrument? Her limbs were tense; she made no sound. The man knelt beside her, busy, as if playing the instrument. It looked to be a small glockenspiel, or something similar. From time to time the man paused to put questions, as if asking how she liked the tune. The woman lay stony and still, indicating no preferences.

Jaro shifted his position and saw the instrument in full detail. After a single startled instant his mind seemed to move aside, while another, more impersonal if less logical, being took control. He ran to the kitchen porch and took a long-handled hatchet from the tool box, then ran light-footed through the kitchen and paused in the doorway, where he appraised the situation. The man knelt with his back to Jaro. His mother's arms had been fixed to the floor by staples through her palms, while heavier bands clamped down her ankles. At each ear a metal tube entered the orifice, curved down through the sinal passages to emerge into the back of the mouth and out through the lips to form a horseshoe-shaped hook which pulled her lips into a grotesque rictus. The horseshoes were connected to the tympanum of the sound-bars; they tinkled and jingled as the man hit them with a silver wand, apparently sending sound into the woman's brain.

The man paused in his playing and asked a terse question. The woman lay inert. He hit a single note, delicately. The woman twisted, arched her back, subsided. Jaro crept forward and struck down at the man's head. Warned by a vibration, he turned; the blow grazed the side of his face and crushed into his shoulder. He uttered not a sound, but rose to his feet. He stumbled upon his black bag and fell. Jaro ran through the kitchen, out into the yard, around the house to the front door, which he cautiously opened. The man was gone. Jaro entered the room. His mother looked up at him. She whispered through contorted lips: "Jaro, be brave now, as never before. I am dying. Kill me before he returns."

"And the box?"

"Come back when it is safe. I have put a guidance upon your mind. Kill me now; I can tolerate no more gongs. Be quick; he is coming!"

Jaro turned his head. The man stood looking through the window. The oblong opening framed his upper torso as if he were the subject of a formal portrait. The design and chiaroscuro were exact. The face was stern and rigorous, hard and white, as if carved from bone. Below the brim of the black hat was a philosopher's brow, a long thin nose and burning black eyes. The jaw angled sharply; the cheeks slanted down to a small pointed chin. He stared at Jaro with an expression of brooding dissatisfaction.

Time moved slowly. Jaro turned to his mother. He raised the hatchet high. From behind him came a harsh command, which he ignored. He struck down and split his mother's forehead, burying the hatchet in an instant welter of brains and gore. Behind him he heard steps. He dropped the hatchet, ran from the kitchen, down through the night to the river. He pushed off the boat, jumped aboard and was carried out upon the water. From the shore came a cry, harsh, yet somehow soft and melodious. Jaro cringed low into the boat, even though the shore could not be seen.

The wind blew in gusts; waves surged around the drifting boat and from time to time washed up and over the gunwhales. Water began to slop heavily back and forth across the bilges. Jaro, at last bestirring himself, bailed out the boat.

Night seemed interminable. Jaro sat hunched, feeling the gusts of wind, the wallow of the boat, the splash and wetness of the water. This was proper and helped him in his perilous balance. He must not think; he must manage his mind as if it were a brooding black fish, suspended in the water deep below the boat.

Night passed and the sky became gray. The broad Foisie curved, sweeping away to the north beside the Wyching Hills. With the sun's first glare of orange-crimson light, the wind pushed the boat up on the beach. Directly at the back of the foreshore the landscape sloped up in bumps and hollows to become the Wyching Hills. At first glance they seemed mottled or even scabrous, overgrown as they were with a hundred varieties of vegetation, many exotic but most indigenous: blue scruffs of tickety-thicket, copses of black artichoke-tree, bumblebee-plant. Along the ridges stood rows of orange-russet scudhorn, glowing like flame in the low sunlight.

For several days, or perhaps a week, Jaro wandered the hills, eating thornberries, grass seeds, the tubers of a furry-leaved plant which smelled neither bitter nor sharp, and which, fortuitously, failed to poison him. He moved listlessly, in a state of detachment, aware of no conscious thoughts.

One day he came down from the hills to gather fruit from trees growing beside the road. A group of peasant boys from along the Wyching Belts took note of him. They were an unlovely lot, squat, sturdy, with long arms, thick legs and round pugnacious faces. They wore black felt scuttle-hats, with tufts of auburn hair protruding through holes above the ears, tight trousers and brown coats: proud formal garments, suitable for the weekly Cataxis, which was their immediate destination. Still, they had time for good deeds along the way. With hoots and whoops they set out to exterminate this nibbler of roadside fruit. Jaro fought as well as he could, and quite amusingly, so that the boys were encouraged to invent variations upon their methods. Eventually it was decided to break every bone in Jaro's body, in order to teach him a smart lesson.

At this point the Faths arrived on the scene.

5

In the hospital at Sronk Jaro's hurts had mended and the protective devices had been detached from his frame. He now lay easy on his bed, wearing the soft blue pajamas the Faths had brought him.

Althea sat beside the bed, surreptitiously studying Jaro's face. The cap of black hair, washed, trimmed and brushed, lay sleek and soft. The bruises had faded, leaving clear dark olive skin, long dark lashes shrouded his eyes, the wide mouth drooped at the corners as if in wistful reverie. It was a face, thought Althea, of poetic charm, and she fought the impulse to snatch him up, hold him close, pet him and kiss him. It would not do, of course; first, Jaro would be shocked by the outrage. Second, his bones, still fragile, might not withstand the kind of hugging she would like to give him. For the thousandth time she wondered at the events which had brought Jaro to Pagg Road, and how distressed his parents must feel. He lay quiet, eyes half-closed: perhaps drowsy, perhaps preoccupied with his own thoughts. He had described the silhouette as best he could; there was no more to be learned in this quarter. She asked, "Do you remember anything about the house?"

"No. It was just there."

"Were there no other houses nearby?"

"No." Jaro lay with jaw set and hands clenched.

Althea stroked the back of his hand and the fist gradually relaxed. "Rest now," she told him. "You are safe and soon you will be well."

A minute passed. Then, in a dreary voice Jaro asked, "What will happen to me now?"

Althea was taken by surprise, and responded with the hint of a stutter, which she hoped Jaro might not notice. "That depends on the authorities. They will do what is best."

"They will lock me away in the dark, down where no one knows."

For a moment Althea was too astonished to speak. "What an odd thing to say! Who put such a wicked idea into your head?"

Jaro's pale face twitched. He closed his eyes and restlessly turned away.

Althea asked again, "Who told you such an awful thing?"

Jaro muttered, "I don't know."

Althea frowned. "Try to remember, Jaro."

Jaro's lips moved; Althea bent to hear, but Jaro's explanation, if such it had been, went past her ears unheard.

Althea spoke fervently: "I can't imagine who put such a notion in your head! It's utter nonsense, of course."

Jaro nodded, smiled and seemed to fall asleep. Althea sat watching him, pondering, wondering. It seemed as if the surprises would never end! Someday, mused Althea, Jaro's fragmented memory might again be made whole—quite possibly a sad day for Jaro.

Doctor Wanish, however, had indicated that the baneful recollections had been destroyed, which, if true, would be good news. Otherwise, Jaro's prognosis was favorable, and he seemed to have suffered no permanent damage other than what Wanish had called "a mnemonic void."

The Faths were childless. When they came to visit Jaro at the hospital, he greeted them with obvious pleasure which tugged at their hearts. Arriving at a decision, they filled out a few documents, paid as many fees, and when they returned to Thanet on Gallingale, Jaro accompanied them. Presently he was legally adopted, and began to use the name Jaro Fath.

TWO

1

Society without ritual is like music played on a single string with one finger." Such was the dictum of Unspiek, Baron Bodissey in his monumental *LIFE*. He pointed out further: "Whenever human beings join to pursue a common objective—that is, to form a society—each member of the group will ultimately command a certain status. As all of us know, these status levels are never totally rigid."

At Thanet on the world Gallingale, the quest for status was the dominant social force. Social levels, or "ledges," were exactly defined, and distinguished by the social clubs which occupied and gave character to that particular ledge. Most prestigious of all the clubs were the so-called Sempiternals: the Tattermen, the Clam Muffins, the Quantorsi; membership in such clubs was tantamount to the prestige of high aristocracy.

The stuff of social advancement—"comporture"—could not easily be defined. Its main components were aggressive striving up the ledges, gentility, wealth and personal mana. Everyone was a social arbiter; eyes watched for uncouth behavior; ears listened to hear what should not have been said. A moment's lapse, a tactless remark, an absent-minded glance might negate months of striving. To presume to a status one had not earned was met with instant rebuff. The perpetrator would incur wondering contempt, and might well be branded a "schmeltzer."*

Hilyer and Althea Fath, though well respected at the Institute, were "nimps," and lived without knowing either the joys of "comporture" or the even more intense pangs of rejection.**

2

The Faths lived four miles north of Thanet, in Merriehew, a rambling old farmhouse situated on five hundred acres of rough countryside, where Althea's grandfather had once engaged in experimental horticulture. The tract was now considered wilderness, and included a pair of forested knolls, a river, a high pasture, a water meadow and a copse of dense woods. All evidence of the horticultural experiments had been lost under the forest mold.

Jaro was assigned living quarters at the top of the high-ceilinged old house. His early troubles faded from memory. Hilyer and Althea were affectionate and tolerant: the best of parents. Jaro, in his turn, brought them pride and fulfillment; before long they could not imagine life without him, and they were haunted by an insidious worry: was Jaro truly happy at Merriehew?

For a time Jaro showed a tendency toward introversion, which accentuated their worry, but which they finally ascribed to his frightening early experiences. They were reluctant to ask questions for fear of intruding upon his privacy, though Jaro was not naturally secretive and would have answered their questions without restraint, had they asked.

The Faths had supposed correctly. The moods derived from Jaro's past. As Doctor Wanish had predicted, a few shreds of the shattered mnemonic clots had rearranged themselves along the

---

*Schmeltzer: one who attempts to ingratiate himself, or mingle, with individuals of a social class superior to his own.

**On Gallingale, the attainment of status was an exciting and often desperate quest. Those who refused to participate in the striving were "nimps," and in general commanded no respect, even though many had won reputations for themselves in their own fields.

A person's status was determined by the prestige of his club and by his 'comporture': that dynamic surge which generated upward thrust, and was similar to the concept of "mana."

old matrices, to generate an occasional image, which swirled away before Jaro could focus upon it. The two most vivid of these images were of quite different sorts. Both were heavy with emotion. One or the other might appear whenever Jaro's mind was passive, or tired, or half asleep.

The first, possibly the earliest, induced a sad sweet ache which brought tears to Jaro's eyes. He seemed to be looking over a beautiful garden, silver and black in the light of two pale moons. Sometimes there was a shudder of displacement, as if Jaro might be someone else. But how could this be? It was himself, Jaro, who stood by the low marble balustrade looking over the moonlit garden, out to the tall dark forest beyond.

There was nothing more to the recollection; it was brief and dreamlike, but it afflicted Jaro with longing for something, or somewhere, forever lost. It was a scene of tragic beauty, rife with an odd nameless emotion: the humiliation of something innocent and gorgeous, so that the throat choked with sorrow and the pain of lost grandeur and pity.

The second of the images, more powerful and vivid, never failed to strike terror into his soul. The gaunt shape of a man stood silhouetted against the luminous twilight sky. The man wore a flat-crowned hat with a stiff brim; a tight black magister's coat. He stood with legs apart, brooding across the landscape. When he turned his head to stare at Jaro, his eyes seemed to glitter like small four-pointed stars.

As time passed, the images came ever less frequently. Jaro became more confident and his periods of reverie waned and were gone; Jaro was everything for which the Faths might have hoped, unusual only in that he was neat, orderly, soft-spoken and dependable.

This halcyon time seemed as if it might go on forever. Then one day Jaro became aware of something he had not noticed before: an uneasy weight at the edge of his consciousness, as if he had forgotten something important. The feeling went away, leaving Jaro in a mood of depression, for which he could find no explanation. Two weeks later, after he had gone to bed, the sensation returned, along with a near-inaudible sound, like the mutter of distant thunder. Jaro lay stiffly, looking up into the dark, tingling to the nearness of something eery. After a minute the sound was gone and he lay limp, wondering what might be happening to him.

Spring became summer. One evening, with the Faths out attending a seminar, Jaro heard the sound again. He put down his book and strained to listen. From far away he thought to hear a low-pitched human voice, expressive of grief and pain. There was no articulation of words.

At first Jaro was puzzled rather than concerned, but the sounds became distinct and ever more woeful. Could they represent a simple seepage from his dead memory: the aftermath of dark deeds mercifully forgotten? A theory as reasonable as any. He listened to the sounds with as much detachment as he could muster, until they drifted away into silence.

Jaro sat in a state of bafflement. Without conviction he told himself that the sounds were no more than a minor nuisance which sooner or later would dwindle to nothing.

This was not the case. From time to time Jaro continued to hear the woeful sounds. They wavered in and out of definition, as if originating in a place sometimes near, sometimes far. It was most confusing, and Jaro presently gave up any attempt at analysis.

As time passed the sounds became more immediate, as if they were deliberately challenging Jaro's composure. Often they intruded into his mind when he could ill afford the distraction. He thought to detect malice and hatred, which made the sounds frightening. Jaro finally decided that they were telepathic messages from an unknown enemy: an idea no less far-fetched than any other. A dozen times he started to confide in the Faths; as many times he held back, not wishing to excite Althea.

Who could be causing such a dreary nuisance? The voice came and went without regularity. Jaro grew resentful; no one else suffered such persecution! It clearly derived from the occluded early years of his life, and Jaro made a resolve he was never to abandon: as soon as possible he would explore all the mysteries and learn all the truths. He would locate the source of the voice and release it from its torment.

Questions marched across his mind. Who am I? How did I come to be lost? Who was the gaunt man who stood so dark and ominous against the twilight sky? His questions, clearly, would never be answered on Gallingale, so that only one course lay open. Despite the certain opposition of the Faths, he must become a spaceman.

When Jaro thought these thoughts, he felt an eery tingling of the skin, which he took to be a presage of the future—whether for good or for bad he could not guess. Meanwhile, he must find a means to deal with the nuisance which had invaded his mind.

As time passed, he found that the most effective strategy was simply to ignore the voice and let it drone on unheeded.

Still, the voice persisted, as dreary as ever, returning at intervals ranging from two weeks to a month. A year passed. Jaro applied himself to his schoolwork and ascended the levels of Langolen School. The Faths provided him everything but what they themselves had renounced: high social status, which could only be gained by "striving" up through a series of ever more prestigious social clubs.

At the tip of the pyramid the three Sempiternals maintained a precarious stability. These were the mysterious Quantorsi—so preferential that the membership was limited to nine—the equally exclusive Clam Muffins and the Tattermen. The Sempiternals were unique in that their members enjoyed hereditary privileges denied the common ruck. Next below were the Bon-tons and the steady old Palindrome. The Lemurians asserted equal status but were considered a bit recherché.

To the ledges an iota below clung Bustamonte, Val Verde and the Sasselton Tigers. Claiming equal status were the Sick Chickens and the Scythians: both considered a trifle extravagant and hyper-modern. At the bottom layer of the "Respectables" (though indignantly asserting otherwise) were the four Quadrants of the Squared Circle: the Kahulibahs, the Zonkers, the Bad Gang and the Naturals. Each claimed pre-eminence, while half-jocularly deriding the deficiencies of the others. Each expressed a particular character. The Kahulibahs included more financial magnates, while the Zonkers tolerated unconventional types, including musicians and artists of a decent sort. The Naturals were dedicated to the refinements of decorous hedonism, while the Bad Gang included a contingent of top level Institute faculty. Still, all taken with all, there was little difference between any of the quadrants, despite the sometimes rather shrill claims to supreme status, and a few incidents of hair-pullings, slapped faces, and the occasional suicide.

The Quadrants of the Squared Circle, like all middle-status clubs, were anxious to recruit high-quality new members, but even more anxious to exclude outsiders, schmeltzers and bounders.

For Jaro it came as a surprise and a shock to learn that both his beloved foster parents and he himself were considered "nimps." Jaro was shamed and indignant. Hilyer only laughed. "It makes no difference to us. It's not important! Is it fair? Probably not, but what of that? According to Baron Bodissey: 'Only losers cry out for fair play.' "*

To this day the most erudite thinkers of the Gaean Reach ponder the significance of the remark.

Jaro quickly learned that, like Hilyer and Althea, he had no inclination for social striving. At Langolen School he was neither gregarious nor socially aggressive; he took no part in group activities and competed in no sports or games. Such conduct was not admired, and Jaro made few friends. When it became known that his parents were nimps and when he showed no comporture of his own, he became even more isolated, despite his neat garments and well-scrubbed appearance. In the classroom, however, he excelled, so that his instructors considered him almost on a par with the notorious Skirlet Hutsenreiter, whose intellectual prowess was the talk of the school, as were her haughty and imperious mannerisms. Skirlet was a year or two younger than Jaro: a slender erect little creature so strongly charged with intelligence and vitality that, in the words of the school nurse, she "gave off blue sparks in the dark." Skirlet carried herself like a boy, though she was clearly a girl, and far from ill-favored. A cap of thick dark hair clasped her face; eyes of a particularly luminous gray looked from under fine black eyebrows; flat cheeks slanted down to a small decisive chin, with a stern little nose and a wide mercurial mouth above. Skirlet seemed to lack personal vanity, and she dressed so simply that her instructors sometimes wondered as to the solicitude of her parents—all the more surprising, since her father was the Honorable Clois Hutsenreiter, Dean of the College of Philosophy at the Institute, a trans-world financier, purportedly of great wealth, and—more importantly—a Clam Muffin, at the very apex of the status pyramid. And her mother, Espeine? Here there seemed to be hints, if not of scandal, at least of some high-status irregularity, very spicy, if the gossip could be believed. Skirlet's mother now resided in a splendid palace on the world Marmone, where she was Princess of the Dawn. How and

---

*Unspiek, Baron Bodissey, a philosopher of Old Earth and elsewhere and creator of a philosophical encyclopedia of twelve volumes, entitled *LIFE*, was especially scathing in regard to what he called "hyper-didacticism," meaning the employment of abstractions a half-dozen stages removed from reality to justify some pseudo-profound intellectualism. Toward the end of his life he was excommunicated from the human race by the Assembly of Egalitarians. Baron Bodissey's comment was succinct: "The point is moot." To this day the most erudite thinkers of the Gaean reach ponder the significance of the remark.

why this should be no one seemed to know, or dared to ask.

Skirlet made no attempt to gain the approval of her classmates. Some of the boys grumbled that she was sexless, cold as a dead fish, because she ignored their routines. During the lunch period, Skirlet often went out to sit on the terrace, where she would attract a group of acquaintances. On these occasions, Skirlet was sometimes gracious, sometimes moody, and sometimes she would jump to her feet and walk away. In the classroom she tended to complete her work with insulting facility; then, flinging down her stylus, she would look around at the other students with patronizing amusement. She also had the unsettling habit of glancing up sharply should the instructor carelessly make a mistake, or indulge in some lame facetiousness. The instructors were non-plussed, especially since Skirlet never spoke with other than cool politeness. In the end they treated her with wary respect. When they gathered in the faculty lounge during the lunch hour, Skirlet often came under discussion. Some disliked her with bitterness and spite; others were more temperate, and pointed out that she was still barely adolescent, with small experience of the world. Mr. Ollard, the erudite sociology instructor, analyzed Skirlet in terms of psychological imperatives: "She's intellectually vain and even intolerant—to a degree which transcends simple arrogance, to become an Elemental Principle: a real achievement for a person so young and slight of physique." He thought it best not to say that he found her captivating.

"She's not a bad girl," said Dame Wirtz. "There's nothing vicious or mean in her nature, though of course she can be quite exasperating."

"She's a little snip," said Dame Borkle. "She needs a good spanking."

Since Skirlet was a Clam Muffin by birth, while Jaro, a nimp, commanded no prestige whatever, there was small chance for communication between the two, and even less for any social connection. Jaro had already discovered that some girls were prettier than others. At the upper end of the list he included Skirlet Hutsenreiter. He liked her taut little body and the swagger with which she conducted her affairs. Unfortunately, it was not Skirlet, but Dame Idora Wirtz, the middle-aged mathematics instructor, who found Jaro a charm and a delight. Jaro was so handsome, so clean, so innocent that she could barely restrain herself from seizing him and hugging him until he squeaked like a kitten. Jaro sensed her inclinations and kept out of reach.

Idora Wirtz lacked physical appeal; she was small, thin, energetic, with sharp features and a barbaric ruff of brick-red ringlets. She wore garments of gaudy, purposely discordant, colors and always a dozen or more jangling bracelets, often on both arms. She had achieved the Parnassians, a society of the middle range, but could not escape; despite her most earnest efforts, she had been denied ascent into the clever Safardips, and the even more avant-garde Black Hats.

One day she took Jaro aside. "A word with you, if you please. I must gratify my curiosity."

Dame Wirtz led Jaro into an empty classroom; then, leaning against the desk, studied him a moment. She said, "Jaro, you must be aware that you do excellent work—in fact, sometimes it is truly elegant."

"Thank you," said Jaro. "I like doing my best."

"That is evident. Mr. Buskin says that your compositions are very well done, though they always deal with impersonal subjects, and that you never express your own point of view. Why is that?"

Jaro shrugged. "I don't like to write about myself."

"I realize that!" snapped Dame Wirtz. "I asked for your reasons."

"If I wrote of myself everyone would think I was vain."

"Well, what then? Skirlet Hutsenreiter writes the most scurrilous things imaginable, and doesn't care a fig whether anyone likes it or not. She lacks all inhibition."

Jaro was puzzled. "And this is how I should write?"

Dame Wirtz sighed. "No. But you might consider changing your point of view. You write like a proud recluse. Why are you not out there in the swim, breasting the social currents?"

Jaro smiled. "Probably because I truly am a proud recluse."

Dame Wirtz made a sour face. "Naturally you know what those words mean?"

"I think it is someone like a Clam Muffin who has never paid his subscription."

Dame Wirtz went to look out the window. When she turned back, she said, "I want to explain something very important. Please give me your attention."

"Yes, Dame Wirtz."

"You cannot go out into life without giving your best effort to the striving."

Jaro remained patiently silent. Idora Wirtz resisted the impulse to ruffle his hair. If she had one like this for her very own, how she would dote on him! She said, "As I recall, your parents are faculty folk at the Institute?"

"Yes."

"I believe that they are nimps, as well. Mind you," she hastened to say, "there's nothing wrong with that! Though I myself prefer the social slope, for all its intricate nonsense. But of yourself? Naturally you do not intend to remain a nimp, and now is the time to set your foot on the ladder. The first rung is usually the Junior Service League. Anyone can join, so the prestige is small. Still, it's a useful springboard up to more important clubs, and everyone starts somewhere."

Jaro smilingly shook his head. "For me it would be a waste of time. I intend to be a spaceman."

Dame Wirtz was scandalized. "What's all this?"

"It should be an exciting life, looking for new planets at the back of the galaxy. Spacemen don't need to join clubs."

Idora Wirtz compressed her lips. A typically boyish ambition, she supposed—if more than a little callow. "That's all very well, and exciting it might be, but it's a lonely anti-social life, away from family and all your wonderful clubs! You wouldn't be able to go to parties, or political rallies, or march in parades with banner held high, and you'd never be elected up-slope to fine new memberships if you weren't on hand to press your case!"

"I'm not interested in that."

Dame Wirtz became excited. "You are saying all the wrong things! Reality is communal interaction! Space flight is an escape from the problems of life!"

"Not for me," said Jaro. "I have important things to do that I can't do on Gallingale."

Dame Wirtz seized Jaro's shoulders and gave him a little shake. "Go, Jaro! I have heard as much as I can tolerate! You are a maddening person, and will no doubt infuriate every girl unlucky enough to fall in love with you."

Jaro gratefully went to the door. Here he turned and said: "I'm sorry if I said something to disturb you. I meant no harm."

Dame Wirtz grinned at him. "I know all about people like you! Now go, and do something nice to surprise me!"

Jaro told Althea of his conversation with Dame Wirtz. "She wants me to join the Junior Service League."

Althea shook her head in vexation. "So soon? We had hoped to avoid the problem for just a little while longer." They went to sit at the kitchen table. Althea said, "At Thanet almost everyone strives. A few climb the ladder: from Parnassians to Black Hats to Underwoods, to Squared Circles, then perhaps to Val Verdes or Sick Chickens, to Girandoles and finally to Clam Muffins. Of course, that's just one of a dozen routes." She peered sidewise at Jaro. "Does this interest you?"

"Not very much."

"As you know, your father and I belong to no clubs. We are 'Non-orgs,' or 'nimps,' and we have no social status. You are the same. Think about it. Then if you feel that you want to mix with the others, you can join the Junior Service League and then, when you are ready, strike for the next level: the Persimmons, for instance, or the Zouaves. You'll never be lonely; you'll make many friends and play at a dozen sports, and no one will call you 'nimp.' Also, you'll spend hours being nice to people you don't like, which perhaps is good training. You'll pay high subscriptions, wear the club token and speak the club jargon. You may enjoy this; many people thrive on it. Others think it's easier to be a nimp."

Jaro nodded thoughtfully. "I told Dame Wirtz that since I wanted to be a spaceman, joining a club would be a waste of time."

Althea tried to hide her amusement. "And what did she say?"

"She became rather cross. She told me I was running away from the realities of life. I said no, that wasn't it; that I had things to do which could not be done on Gallingale."

"Really!" Althea was startled and alarmed. "What things are these?"

Jaro looked away. This was a private subject which he did not want to discuss. He said slowly, "I suppose that I'm interested in learning about where I came from, and what happened during the years I can't remember."

Althea's heart sank. Both she and Hilyer had hoped that Jaro would have lost interest in his past and would never think seriously of it again. Evidently, this was not the case.

Jaro left the room. Althea brewed a pot of tea and sat pondering over the unwelcome news. She definitely did not want Jaro to become a spaceman; he would go off into space and leave Merriehew and the Faths behind, and who knows when they would see him again. It was a dreadfully lonely thought!

Althea sighed. Clearly she and Hilyer must use their best persuasive powers to guide Jaro along the academic career they had planned for him at Thanet Institute.

THREE

1

Dame Wirtz made a final attempt to enlist Jaro into the Junior Service League. "It is the best possible training! And enormous fun! When you march in formation, the slogan that you shout is:

'UP THE LEDGES! UP!
DON'T BE A NASTY PUP!
BUMBLE DE BUMBLE! HOOT HOOT HOOT
AND A TWEAK IN THE PUNGLE
FOR SCHMELTZERS.'

There! Doesn't that sound like fun? No? Why not?"

"It's a bit noisy," said Jaro.

Dame Wirtz sniffed. "It's ever so jolly, swinging along in formation! The secret password is 'comporture.' "

"Then what happens?"

"It's a surprise!"

"Hm. What kind of surprise?"

Dame Wirtz smiled bravely. "A bit of this, a bit of that."

Jaro shook his head. "Only an idiot would want to find out."

Dame Wirtz pretended not to hear. "A wonderful magic stuff is comporture, and your stringbooks make it all so easy. You record favors you have done for others against the favors you have received: the so-called 'Outs' and 'Ins.' Their ratio is your social buoyancy, and you must keep a careful balance sheet. This will help you with your strivings, and you'll be up the Persimmons in a trice! Just like Lyssel Bynnoc, who stormed up through the League like a spanked baboon. Her father is a Squared Circle. That lubricates many a tight corner and Lyssel is quite a charming creature, but the fact remains that she's a striver and has comporture in her bones." Dame Wirtz giggled. "It is said that in frosty weather when Lyssel breathes, instead of steam she blows two plumes of comporture from her nostrils."

Jaro raised his eyebrows. "Surely that can't be true!"

"Probably not, but it only goes to demonstrate the temper of her striving."

Jaro was aware of saucy golden-haired Lyssel Bynnoc, though she had never so much as looked in his direction. Lyssel was already flirting with older boys of upscale clubs and had no time to waste on nimps. Jaro asked: "What about Skirlet Hutsenreiter?"

"Aha! Skirlet was born a Clam Muffin and already commands the full scope of prestige, above all the other aristocracy of Gallingale! Skirlet need never fret about status, and she might not in any case, since she does everything with great éclat." Dame Wirtz looked away. "Well, well, we can't all be Clam Muffins like dear little Skirlet, and now we must see about enrolling you in the Junior Service League. Naturally, you'll start in the Buddykins Ward."

Jaro hung back. "I have no time for such things!"

Dame Wirtz gave an incredulous caw. "That is absurd! You are almost as bright as Skirlet; she rolls through her schoolwork as if it were a dish of ripe cheese, and then she has time for every caprice that enters her mind. How do you spend your spare time?"

"I study manuals of space mechanics."

Dame Wirtz threw her arms into the air. "My dear boy, you mustn't waste your time with fantasy!"

Jaro made his escape as gracefully as possible.

About this time Skirlet was transferred into Jaro's class, and whether they liked it or not, the quality of their work was constantly compared. It soon became evident that Jaro surpassed Skirlet in basic science, mathematics and technical mechanics; also he was rather more deft at draughting, where his hand was fluid and accurate. Skirlet excelled in language, rhetoric, and musical symbolism. They did equally well in Gaean history, the geography of Old Earth, anthropology and biological science.

Skirlet was surprised to find herself inferior to anyone, in anything, to any degree whatever. For several days her conduct was subdued. In anyone other than a Clam Muffin, it might have been said that she sulked. At last she shrugged. The circumstances, though bitter, were real. Had Jaro been a misshapen freak, or a bizarre genius, she would have accepted the situation with no more than an uninterested jerk of the chin. But Jaro was quite normal, clean, nice looking, something of a loner, and even more indifferent to her than she to him—or so it seemed. Too bad he was a nimp, and so could not be taken seriously. She wondered what would become of him. Then, thinking about her own case, she gave a sardonic little grimace. What, indeed, would become of Skirlet Hutsenreiter?

Skirlet at last accepted the presence of Jaro philosophically. After all, it was an excellent thing to be born a Hutsenreiter and a Clam Muffin! Unfair? Not necessarily. Things were the way they were; why make changes?

One afternoon, halfway through the term, Skirlet sat in a group and heard Jaro's name mentioned by a certain Hanafer Glackenshaw. Hanafer was a large boisterous youth with rich blond curls and emphatic overlarge features. Hanafer considered himself decisive and masterful: a maker and shaper of enterprises. He liked to stand with head thrown back, the better to display his prideful high-bridged nose. He felt himself gifted with great inherent comporture, and perhaps it was so; he had thrust and wheedled and shouldered his way up the ledges, surmounting the Persimmons, up past the Spalpeens and into the Human Ingrates. Now the time had come to re-establish his social buoyancy and make new entries into his stringbooks.

Hanafer was captain of the Langolen School roverball team, which found itself in need of several strong agile forwards ready for a mix-up. A loose-limbed tomboy of a girl named Tatninka indicated Jaro, at the other side of the yard: "Why not him? He looks strong and healthy."

Hanafer glanced toward Jaro and snorted. "You don't know what you're saying! That's Jaro Fath, and he's a nimp. Further, his mother is Professor Fath at the Institute and she's a pacifist, and won't allow him to wrestle, or box, or compete in any violent sport. So: he's not only a nimp, but a total and absolute moop."

Skirlet, on the periphery of the group, heard the remarks. She glanced toward Jaro; by chance their eyes met. For an instant there was communication between them; then Jaro looked away. Skirlet was unreasonably annoyed. Did he not realize that she was Skirlet Hutsenreiter, autonomous and free, who tolerated neither criticism nor judgment, and went where she chose?

It was Tatninka, rather than Skirlet, who bore the news to Jaro. "Did you hear what Hanafer called you?"

"No."

"He said you were a moop!"

"Oh? What's that? Nothing good, I suspect."

Tatninka giggled. "I forgot; you're really off in the clouds, aren't you? Well, then!" She recited a definition she had heard Hanafer use only the week before: "If you come upon a very timid nimp who wets the bed and wouldn't say 'peep' to a pussycat—you have found a moop."

Jaro sighed. "Very well; now I know."

"Hmf. You're not even angry," said Tatninka in disgust.

Jaro reflected. "Hanafer can be carried off by a big bird, for all I care. Otherwise, there is no return message."

Tatninka spoke with annoyance, "Really, Jaro, you should not act with such insouciance when you can't show an itch of status, nor so much as a place to scratch it."

"Sorry," murmured Jaro. Tatninka turned and marched off to join her friends. Jaro walked home to Merriehew.

Althea met him in the downstairs hall. She kissed his cheek, then stood back and inspected him. "What is wrong?"

Jaro knew better than to dissemble. "It's nothing serious," he growled. "Just some of Hanafer Glackenshaw's talk."

"What kind of talk," demanded Althea, instantly brittle.

"Oh just names: 'nimp' and 'moop.' "

Althea compressed her lips. "That is not acceptable conduct, and I shall have a word with his mother."

"No!" cried Jaro in a panic. "I don't care what Hanafer thinks! If you complain to his mother, everyone will laugh at me!"

Althea knew that he was right. "Then you'll just have to take Hanafer aside and explain in a nice way that you mean him no harm and that he has no reason to call you names."

Jaro nodded. "I may do just that—after punching his head to attract his attention."

Althea uttered a cry of indignation. She went to a couch and pulled Jaro down beside her. He became stiff and uncomfortable, and wished that he had guarded his tongue, for now he must listen while Althea explained the tenets of her ethical philosophy. "Jaro, my dear, there is no mystery about violence. It is the reflexive act of brutes, boors and moral defectives. I am surprised that you use such words even as a joke!"

Jaro moved restlessly and opened his mouth to speak, but Althea seemed not to notice. "As you know, your father and I think of ourselves as crusaders for universal amity. We are contemptuous of violence, and we expect you to live by the same creed."

"That is why Hanafer calls me a 'moop.' "

Althea spoke serenely, "He will stop as soon as he sees how wrong he is. You must make this clear. Peace and happiness are never passive; they are flowers in a garden which must constantly be worked."

Jaro jumped to his feet. "I don't have time to work in Hanafer's garden; I have other things on my mind."

Althea stared at him, all thoughts of Hanafer dismissed, and Jaro saw that he had made another mistake. Althea asked, "What 'other things' are these?"

"Just things."

For perhaps half a second Althea wavered, then decided not to pursue the matter. She reached out and hugged him. "Whatever the case, you can always discuss it with me. We can straighten things out and I'll never urge you to do anything harmful or wrong! Do you believe me, Jaro?"

"Oh yes. I believe you."

Althea relaxed. "I'm glad you're so sensible! Now then, go make yourself look nice; Mr. Maihac is coming for dinner. As I recall, you and he get along well together."

Jaro gave a guarded response. "Yes; well enough." As a matter of fact he liked Tawn Maihac very much, which caused him to wonder about his parents, since Maihac was not typical of their usual set of acquaintances. Maihac was an off-worlder who had evidently traveled far and wide across the Gaean Reach and had known many odd adventures. He had made an immediate impression upon Jaro though, from the Fath's point of view, for all the wrong reasons. Maihac was neither a pacifist nor a savant nor yet the exemplar of an avant-garde art form.

Tawn Maihac's adventures had not left him unscathed. His face displayed a broken nose and his neck was marked by a scar. Otherwise, Maihac lacked conspicuous characteristics, and on first acquaintance seemed placid and mild. He was younger than Hilyer; lean and strong, with a weathered dark skin and a black mat of hair. Althea thought him almost handsome, since his features were well shaped. Hilyer, who was more critical, found these same features graceless and hard, perhaps by reason of the broken nose, which suggested violence.

Hilyer took little pleasure in Maihac's company, suspecting that Maihac might have been a spaceman, which brought him no credit in Hilyer's eyes. Spacemen were customarily recruited from the ne'er-do-wells and vagabonds at the fringes of society. As a class, their values and patterns of behavior were incompatible with Hilyer's own, and those which he wished to sponsor in Jaro.

From the first Hilyer had felt deeply suspicious of Maihac. When Althea scoffed, Hilyer claimed darkly that his instincts were never wrong. He felt that Maihac, if not a blackguard, had much to hide, to which Althea said: "Oh piffle. Everyone has something to hide."

Hilyer started to declare, "Not I!" in a decisive voice, then thought of one or two shrouded episodes in his past and merely gave a noncommittal grunt.

During the next few days he took the trouble to make discreet inquiries, then went triumphantly to Althea with his findings. "It's about as I thought," said Hilyer. "Our friend is using a false name. He is actually someone named 'Gaing Neitzbeck,' who for reasons of his own is using the name 'Tawn Maihac.' "

"This is incredible!" declared Althea. "How do you know?"

"Just a bit of detective work, and an iota of inductive reasoning," said Hilyer. "I glanced over his application for admission at the Institute. I took note of his stated date of arrival at Thanet spaceport, along with the ship on which he arrived, which was the *Alice Wray* of the Elder Line. When I looked over the list of arrivals aboard the *Alice Wray* upon the cited date, there was no 'Tawn Maihac,' but only a 'Gaing Neitzbeck,' who gave his occupation as 'spaceman.' I searched the list of arrivals for the entire year and I found no 'Tawn Maihac.' The conclusion is inescapable."

Althea stammered, "But why should he do such a thing?"

"I could form a dozen hypotheses," said Hilyer. "He might be trying to dodge creditors or avoid an importunate wife, or wives. One thing is clear, however: when folk use false names, they are concealing themselves from someone." Hilyer quoted one of Baron Bodissey's choicest maxims: " 'Honest folk do not wear masks when they enter a bank.' "

"I suppose not," said Althea doubtfully. "What a shame! I did so like Tawn Maihac, or whatever his name."

On the evening of the next day, Hilyer noticed an air of suppressed excitement, or mirth, or some such emotion in Althea. He ignored the signals, aware that she could not hold her news to herself for very long. He was right. As she served their usual goblet of Taladerra Fino, she burst out: "You'll never guess!"

"Guess what?"

"I've solved the mystery!"

"I wasn't aware of any mystery," said Hilyer stiffly.

"Of course you are!" said Althea teasingly. "You're aware of a hundred mysteries! This one concerns Tawn Maihac."

"I suppose you are referring to Gaing Neitzbeck, and, truly, Althea, I'm not interested in the man's peccadillos, or whatever has caused him to deceive us."

"Very well! I promise: no peccadillos! What happened was this: I went to the telephone and put in a call for Gaing Neitzbeck. I reached him at his place of work, the machine shop at the space terminal. His face appeared on the screen; it was definitely not Tawn Maihac. I told him that I was calling from the Institute in regard to Tawn Maihac's application, in which he stated that he had arrived at Thanet aboard the *Alice Wray*."

"Well what of it?" said Neitzbeck.

"He arrived on the same day as you did?"

"Certainly."

"Then why does not his name appear on the terminal records?"

Gaing Neitzbeck laughed. "Maihac was at one time an IPCC officer. He is now inactive, but that means nothing. When he arrives at a spaceport, he merely shows his card and walks through the gate. I could do the same, but I forgot to carry my card."

Althea leaned back in her chair and drank from her goblet of wine.

Hilyer put on a rather sour expression. "It was of no great moment. No need for stirring up a tempest in a teapot. The fellow is as he is; that's enough for me."

"Then you'll be nice to him? He's always quite well-behaved."

Hilyer agreed somewhat glumly that Maihac's conduct could not be faulted. Maihac was quiet and correct; his clothes were more conservative than Hilyer's own. He spoke little of his past, except to remark that he had taken up residence at Thanet in order to top off his previously deferred education. Althea had met him at the Institute, where Maihac was a student in one of her advanced graduate courses. He and the Faths had discovered a mutual fascination with peculiar musical instruments. Maihac during his wanderings had acquired a number of these unique artifices, including a froghorn, a pair of tangletones, a wishdreams, a wonderful tudelpipe—four feet long, inlaid with a hundred silver dancing demons; a full set of Blori needlegongs. They caught Althea's attention and before long Tawn Maihac had become a regular visitor at Merriehew.

On this particular occasion Hilyer had not known that Maihac would be a dinner guest until his own return from the Institute.

He was further irritated when he took note of what seemed to be special preparations. "I see you are using your Basingstoke candlesticks. Tonight is evidently a signal occasion."

"Of course not!" declared Althea. "I have these beautiful articles and they should be put to use. Call it 'creative impulse,' if you like. But these are not the Basingstokes."

"Certainly they are! I remember the transaction distinctly! They cost us a small fortune!"

"Not these—and I can prove it." Althea lifted one of the candelabra and studied the label on the underside of the base. "The label reads: 'Rijjalooma Farm.' These come from that farm on Rijjalooma Ridge; don't you remember? It's where you were attacked by that peculiar hedgehog-like thing."

"Yes," growled Hilyer. "I remember very well. It was absolutely unwarranted and I should have sued that farm woman for irresponsibility."

"Well, no matter. She let me have the candelabra at quite a decent price, so your suffering was not in vain. And here we are, enjoying the recollection at our dinner!"

Hilyer muttered something about his hope that Althea's "creative impulse" did not extend to the cuisine. Here Hilyer alluded to the anomalous dishes which had resulted from Althea's previous attempts at experimental or avant-garde cooking.

Althea turned away, smiling to herself. Hilyer, so it seemed, was a bit jealous of their rather fascinating guest. "By the way!" she said. "Mr. Maihac is bringing his silly froghorn. He may even try to play it, which should be great fun!"

"Ha hm," Hilyer growled. "So Maihac, among his other talents, is also a skilled musician!"

Althea laughed. "That remains to be seen. He won't prove it on the froghorn."

Jaro had come to realize that during Maihac's visits the topic in which he was most interested: namely, the lore of spacemanship, was not considered appropriate and would be discouraged. Since the Faths intended an academic career for Jaro in the School of Aesthetic Philosophy, they gingerly encouraged Jaro's interest in Maihac's odd instruments, while pretending to ignore the picturesque methods by which they had been obtained.

Tonight, as Hilyer had noted, Althea had set a beautiful table. From her collection she had chosen a pair of massive candelabra forged from rude bars of blue-black cobalt alloy, to complement a service of old faience, glazed a dim moonlight blue, in whose depths submarine flowers seemed to float.

Maihac was suitably impressed, and complimented Althea upon her arrangements. The dinner proceeded, and in the end Althea felt that it had been tolerably successful, even though Hilyer, in connection with the devilled landfish in pastry shells, had found the pastry too tough and the sauce too sharp, while the souffle, so he pointed out, had gone limp.

Althea dealt politely with Hilyer's comments, and she was pleased with Maihac's behavior. He had attended Hilyer's sometimes rather pompous opinions, and he had said nothing of space or spaceships, to Jaro's disappointment.

After the group had moved to the sitting room, Maihac brought out his froghorn, perhaps the most bizarre item of his collection, since it comprised three dissimilar instruments in one. The horn started with a rectangular brass mouthpiece, fitted to a plench-box sprouting four valves. The valves controlled four tubes which first wound around, then entered, the central brass globe: the so-called "mixing pot." From the side opposite the mouthpiece came a tube which flared out into a flat rectangular sound bell. The four valves were controlled by the fingers of the left hand, to produce the notes of an exact if irrational scale, each tone an unctuous disreputable gurgle. Above the mouthpiece, a second tube clipped to the nostrils became a screedle flute, fingered by the right hand to play intervals with no obvious relationship to the tones of the horn. The right foot pumped air into a bladder which was controlled by movements of the left knee to produce a heavy diapason of something over an octave. Clearly, to play the froghorn with mastery would require endless hours of practice: even years or decades.

Maihac told the Faths: "I can play the froghorn, but am I playing it well? You will never know, since good sounds much like bad, so far as I can tell."

"I'm sure that you play splendidly," said Althea. "But don't keep us dangling! Play something frivolous and delightful!"

"Very well," said Maihac. "I will play 'The Bad Ladies of Antarbus,' which is the only tune I know."

Maihac took up the instrument, adjusted its straps and buckles, and blew a few introductory glissandos. The nose-flute produced a shrill warble. Tones from the big-bellied horn seemed to gurgle up through syrup, to produce a sound so raucously indecent as to make both Hilyer and Althea wince. The air-bladder droned and moaned along a delicate if rather dreary set of intervals.

Maihac explained the salient features of the instrument. "The great virtuosos of the froghorn presumably played with total control over the half tones, the hoots, gurgles, thumps and squealing. Well, here I go: 'The Bad Ladies of Antarbus.' " Jaro, listening carefully, heard: "Teedle-deedle-eedle teedle a-boigle oigle a-boigle moan moan da-boigle-oigle moan teedle-eedle moan teedle-eedle-eedle a-boigle a-boigle-oigle moan moan teedle-eedle teedle da-boigle."

"That's the best I can do," said Maihac. "What did you think?"

"Very pretty," said Hilyer. "With a bit more practice, you'd have us all compulsively dancing."

"One must be careful with froghorns," said Maihac. "They are said to be built by devils." He pointed to symbols carved on the flare of the brass horn. "Notice these marks? They read: 'Suanez has done this thing.' 'Suanez' is a devil. According to the shopkeeper, each horn is impregnated with a secret song. If the human musician chances to play part of this song, he is trapped and must continue playing until he drops dead."

"The same song?" Jaro asked.

"Yes; no variations allowed."

Hilyer put a sardonic question: "It was the shopkeeper who authenticated the provenance of the horn?"

"He did indeed, and when I asked for documentation, he gave me a picture of the devil Suanez, then added a surcharge of twenty sols to the price of the horn. He knew I wanted the horn; I could either haggle another two hours or pay the twenty sols—which I did. These shopkeepers are all irredemptible rascals."

Hilyer chuckled. "We have learned this backward and forward, up and down, on our own account."

Althea said, "When I found my copper candelabra I had an experience much like your own. It happened during our first off-world field trip, which was truly a saga in itself!"

"Now then," said Hilyer smiling. "We must not wax overdramatic! Mr. Maihac after all is surely accustomed to exotic places."

"Tell me about it," said Maihac. "I haven't been everywhere: that's for certain."

Hilyer and Althea together told the tale, with many interpositions and interpolations. Shortly after their marriage they had gone off on a field trip to the world Plaise, in a small local swarm not far from the edge of the galaxy. Like many other worlds, Plaise had been located and settled during that first great explosion of humanity across what would ultimately become the Gaean Reach. The Faths had gone to Plaise on what they now knew to be a foolhardy mission: to record the so-called "Equinoctial Signs" of the Kindred Mountain folk. This feat had never before been attempted, much less accomplished, for a good reason: it was considered suicidal. The Faths, blithe as songbirds, arrived at Plaise spaceport and took lodgings at the resthouse at Sern, in the foothills of the Kindred Mountains. Here they learned of the difficulties which made their program impossible—namely, that they would be killed on sight.

Brash and foolish rather than courageous, the Faths ignored the warnings and contrived ruses to defeat each of the difficulties in turn. They rented a flitter and two nights before the equinox, flew down into the Kouhou Chasm and affixed thirty-two recording devices to stations along the vertical walls. By great good luck they evaded detection, whereupon the flitter would have been netted and dragged to the floor of the chasm, where the Faths would have been subjected to deeds too horrible to bear mentioning. "It makes my blood run cold whenever I think of it!" Althea shuddered. "We were young fools," said Hilyer. "We thought that if we were caught we could simply say that we were Thanet Institute faculty, and they would make no further complaint."

The night of the equinox the mountain folk performed their ceremony. All night long pulses of sound reverberated up and down the chasm. On the next day the folk performed their penitential rite, and the cries so elicited rose like sad-sweet warbling.

The Faths meanwhile laid low in Stern, passing themselves off as agronomists. While they waited, Althea had gone to rummage through a ramshackle old shop, where oddments of this and that were offered for sale. In a casual pile she noted a pair of massive copper candelabra, from which she hastily averted her eyes and went to examine what seemed to be a dented old pot. "A valuable piece," the shopkeeper told her. "That is genuine aluminum."

"I'm not really interested," said Althea. "I already have a pot."

"Just so. Perhaps you like those old candle-holders? Very valuable: pure copper!"

"I don't think so," said Althea. "I already have a pair of candelabra, as well."

"Very handy if one of them broke," argued the shopkeeper. "It is not good to be without light."

"True," said Althea. "What do you want for the dirty old things?"

"Not much. About five hundred sols."

Althea merely turned him a scornful look, and went to study a stone plaque, highly polished and intricately carved with glyphs. "What is this thing?"

"It is very old. I can't read it. They say it tells the ten human secrets: very important, I should think."

"Not unless you can read this odd script."

"Better than nothing."

"How much?"

"Two hundred sols."

"Surely you're joking!" cried Althea indignantly. "Do you take me for a fool?"

"Well seventy sols then. A great bargain: seven sols per secret!"

"Bah. Those secrets are old and useless, even if I could read them. My price is five sols."

"Aiee! Must I give valuables to every crazy woman that walks into the shop?" Althea haggled long and devoutly, but the shopkeeper held to a price of forty sols.

"The price is reprehensible!" stormed Althea. "I'll pay it only if you include some extra pieces of lesser value: let us say, this rug and, well, why not? those candelabra."

Again the shopkeeper showed distress. He patted the rug which was woven in stripes of black, russet and russet-gold. "This is a fecundity rug. It is woven from the pubic hairs of virgins! The candlesticks are six thousand years old, from the cave of the first Hermit King Jon Solander. I value the three items at a thousand sols!"

"I will pay forty sols for all."

The shopkeeper handed Althea a scimitar and bared his throat. "Kill me first before you dishonor me with such robbery!"

In the end, somewhat dazed, Althea walked from the shop, carrying candelabra, plaque and rug, after having paid a price which Hilyer later reckoned to be about double what she should have paid. Nevertheless, Althea was happy with her acquisitions.

On the next day they took the flitter aloft and flew high above Kouhou. The area was deserted; the mountain folk had trooped to Pol Pond for their ablution rite. The Faths hastily retrieved their recording devices, returned to Plaise spaceport and departed by the first appropriate packet. The results of their reckless mission were highly satisfactory; they had recorded an amazing sequence of sounds: surges of—what? Melody? Dynamic projection? Soulforce made audible? No one could find a proper place in the taxonomy of music where the Kouhou Chants—as they came to be known—could be filed.

"We'd never go off on such a hare-brained venture again," Althea told Maihac. "Still, if nothing else, it started me collecting candelabra. But now—enough of me and my ridiculous hobby. Play us another tune on the froghorn."

"Not tonight," said Maihac. "I am snuffling around the nose-flute. It is a matter of embouchure at the nose-piece. It takes years to develop a really good nasal embouchure. If I ever achieved it well and truly, I would have the look of a vampire bat." Maihac packed the instrument away in its case.

"Next time you must bring your four-twanger," said Althea. "That is a far gentler instrument."

"True! I risk neither Suanez the devil, nor a sore nose."

"Still, you should work up a repertory on the froghorn. If you played weekly concerts at the Centrum, you'd attract no end of attention and command quite a decent fee, or so I should think."

Hilyer chuckled. "If you are yearning for fame and comporture, there is your chance. The Scythians would sign you into their membership before you could say 'knife'; they love to flaunt eccentricity."

"I'll consider your suggestion," said Maihac politely. "However, I no longer look to the froghorn as a solution to my financial problems. In fact I've taken on a part-time job, at the spaceport machine shop. It pays me rather well, but after classes at the Institute, I'll find little time for froghorn practice."

Noting Jaro's enthusiasm, Hilyer and Althea were restrained in their congratulations. Like Dame Wirtz, they felt that Jaro's fascination with space might distract him from the academic career which they hoped he would pursue.

A month passed. The term at Langolen School approached the spring recess. Jaro's work, meanwhile, had suddenly deteriorated, as if Jaro had been afflicted by a fit of absent-mindedness. Dame Wirtz suspected that Jaro had been allowing his imagination to rove too freely among the far worlds, and one morning, just after his first class period, took him into her private office.

Jaro admitted the shortcomings and undertook to do better.

Dame Wirtz said that was all very well—but not enough. "Your work has been excellent, and we have all been proud of you. So now—why this sudden lethargy? You just can't drop everything and go off to chase butterflies! Surely you agree?"

"Yes, of course! But—"

Dame Wirtz refused to listen. "You must put aside your daydreams, and attend to your future."

Jaro despairingly tried to deny the imputations of sloth. "Even if I explained, you still would not understand!"

"Try me!"

Jaro muttered: "I don't care a fig for comporture. As soon as I can, I'll be gone into space."

Dame Wirtz began to wonder. "All very well, but why the frantic urgency?"

"I have a good reason."

As soon as Jaro had spoken he knew that he had gone too far. Dame Wirtz pounced.

"Indeed. And what is this reason?"

Jaro spoke in a numb monotone: "There is something important I must do, to save my own sanity."

"Indeed," said Dame Wirtz again. "And what must be done?"

"I don't know just yet."

"I see. Where will you go to do what needs to be done, and what will you do?"

"I don't know that either."

Dame Wirtz carefully controlled her voice. "Then why go to such lengths if you don't know what you are doing?"

"I know well enough."

"Tell me how you know, if you please."

"Because of things I hear in my mind! Please don't ask me anything more!"

"I want to get to the bottom of this. Are you telling me that you hear instructions when you dream at night?"

"You have it all wrong! They are not instructions, and I don't hear them during dreams, and not always at night. Now please, may I go?"

"Yes, Jaro—after I find out what is going on. This is not at all normal! You hear voices which give you directions?"

"They don't give me directions. There is just one voice and it frightens me."

Dame Wirtz sighed. "Very well, Jaro. You may go."

But Jaro, aghast at what he had let slip, lingered and tried to convince Dame Wirtz that nothing really serious was going on, and that, truly, he had everything under control, so that she was to ignore what he had told her.

Dame Wirtz smiled and patted his shoulder, and said that she must give the matter thought. Jaro slowly turned and went his way.

Althea was busy in her office at the Institute. The communicator on her desk sounded a chime. Glancing at the display, she recognized the nested blue and red rectangles of the Parnassian Club. A tap on the desk brought the face of Idora Wirtz to the screen.

"I'm sorry to call you, but something has come up which I think you should know."

Althea was instantly alarmed. "Is Jaro all right?"

"Yes. Are you alone? May I speak freely?"

"I am alone. I suppose Hanafer Glackenshaw has been acting badly again?"

"As to that, I can't say. In any event Jaro simply ignores him."

Althea's voice rose in pitch. "What else could he do? Call the Glackenshaw boy a bad name in return? Attack him with his fists? Kill the boy, perhaps? We have taught Jaro to avoid rough and competitive games, which encourage bellicosity and which in fact are small wars!"

"Just so," said Dame Wirtz. "But that's not why I called. I fear that Jaro is suffering nervous problems, which may well be serious."

"Oh come now!" cried Althea. "I can't believe this!"

"It is true, I'm sorry to say. He hears inner voices which give him directions—probably to go out into space to perform some adventurous deed. I extracted this information only with difficulty."

Althea was silent. For a fact Jaro had recently made some very odd remarks. She asked, "What exactly has he told you?"

Dame Wirtz reported what she had heard. When she finished, Althea thanked her. "I hope you will say nothing of this to anyone else."

"Of course not! But we must set things right with poor Jaro!"

"I will see to it at once."

Althea called Hilyer and repeated what she had learned from Idora Wirtz. At first Hilyer was inclined to skepticism, until Althea insisted that she herself had heard similar statements, and that there was no question but what Jaro needed professional help. Hilyer at last agreed that he would make relevant inquiries, and the screen went blank.

Half an hour later Hilyer returned to the screen. "Health Services speaks well of a group called FWG Associates at Buntoon House in Celece District. I called, and we are to go out immediately for an interview with their Dr. Fiorio. I take it that you can get away?"

"Of course!"

4

Mel Swope, Director of the Institute Health Services, had informed Hilyer in regard to FWG Associates. The senior staff consisted of three notable practitioners: Doctors Fiorio, Windle and Gissing. Their reputations were good; they were said to be solidly based in orthodox science, but willing to consider innovative procedures, if need arose. Away from Buntoon House, all three enjoyed high social status, and their clubs were havens of high comporture. Dr. Fiorio was with the Val Verde; Dr. Windle, the Palindrome. Dr. Gissing belonged to several clubs, the most notable being the Lemurians, who were considered both daring and unpredictable. In their physical characteristics, the three were dissimilar. Dr. Fiorio was portly, punctilious and pink as a well-scrubbed baby. Dr. Windle, the oldest of the group, seemed all lank arms, sharp elbows and bony shanks. The yellowish dome above his forehead nurtured several brown moles and a few wisps of nondescript hair.

In contrast, Dr. Gissing was airy, mercurial, slight of physique, with a fine fluff of white hair. He had been described in a trade journal as "much like a dainty little garden dryad, who may often be found hiding among the pansies, or laving his pretty feet in the birdbath." The same trade journal had described FWG Associates as "a most peculiar synergism, stronger in every way than the sum of the separate parts."

Hilyer and Althea arrived at Buntoon House within the hour. They discovered an impressive structure of pink stone, black iron and glass, in the shade of seven langal trees.

The Faths entered the structure and were conducted into the office of Dr. Fiorio. He rose to his feet: a large man, wearing a crisp white jacket. He inspected his visitors with amiable blue eyes. "The Professors Hilyer and Althea Fath? Dr. Fiorio here." He indicated chairs. "If you will be so good."

The Faths seated themselves. Hilyer spoke. "As you know, we have come on behalf of our son."

"Yes; I have seen the notation. Your statements were a bit vague."

Hilyer was sensitive to any criticism of his literacy, and so was immediately rubbed the wrong way. He said shortly, "Our own information has been vague. I tried to communicate this fact with clarity; evidently I have failed."

Dr. Fiorio saw his mistake. "Of course, of course! I intended no innuendo, I assure you."

Hilyer acknowledged the remark with a formal nod. "Jaro has reported some peculiar occurrences which we can't explain. We have come to you for professional advice."

"Quite so," said Dr. Fiorio. "How old is Jaro?"

"I had better tell you the whole story." Hilyer outlined the salient events of Jaro's life from the time he had been rescued under the Wyching Hills to the present moment. "You must keep in mind the six-year gap in Jaro's memory. I can't help but feel that this so-called 'voice' is a relict of that period."

"Hm," said Dr. Fiorio. "So it may be." He pulled at his round pink chin. "I'd like to call in my colleague Dr. Gissing. 'Multiple personalities' is one of his specialties."

Dr. Gissing appeared: a slight, rather jaunty, man with an alert inquisitive face. As Dr. Fiorio had predicted, he was instantly interested in Jaro's case. "Do you have records describing the treatment Jaro received at the Sronk Clinic?"

"No." Hilyer felt as if already he had been put on the defensive by the crafty Dr. Gissing. "Things were most hectic; we were trying to save the boy's life; niceties of record-keeping perhaps were neglected."

"Understandable!" declared Dr. Gissing. "I'm sure you did as well as any other frightened layman might have done."

"Quite so," boomed Dr. Fiorio. "New schematics will be needed, in any event."

"It is an interesting case," said Dr. Gissing. Smiling pleasantly at both Hilyer and Althea, he left the office.

"Then that's settled," said Althea hastily. "When should we bring Jaro in?"

"Tomorrow morning about this time will do quite nicely."

Althea stated that the time was convenient. "I can't tell you how relieved we are to put the case into your hands!"

"One matter remains," said Dr. Fiorio. "I refer to our fee, which we are as anxious to collect as you are to minimize. We are neither inexpensive nor magnanimous, and it is well to part on a note of mutual understanding."

"No fear," said Hilyer. "As you know, we are faculty at the Institute in the Department of Aesthetic Philosophy. You may submit your invoices to the Health Services Bursar."

Dr. Fiorio scowled. "They are over-scrupulous at the Bursar's office," he said with a sniff. "On occasion they make peevish difficulties over a sol or two. But no matter! We will see Jaro in the morning."

FOUR

1

Late in the afternoon, when Jaro returned from school, he found Hilyer and Althea waiting for him in the living room: an unusual situation. Althea jumped to her feet and poured three small glasses of the special Altengelb and gave one to Jaro. This was the wine of occasion, and Jaro sensed that something significant was afoot.

After a perfunctory sip, Hilyer cleared his throat. When he spoke, his discomfort caused him to sound far more pompous than he would have liked. "Jaro, your mother and I were very much surprised to learn of your problems. It's a pity you did not confide in us sooner."

Jaro heaved a small private sigh. The matter had entered that inevitable phase which he both dreaded and welcomed. Now he wanted to explain everything in a great spate of communication—all his awe, fear, confusion, his spasms of claustrophobic panic; his dread of the unknown. He wanted to express in a single burst of words all the love and gratitude he felt for these two kindly folk, who now might be troubled or even damaged on his account—but when he spoke, the words sounded stiff and artificial. "I'm sorry that this thing has worried you. I didn't want it to happen that way; I thought I could work it out by myself."

Hilyer gave a crisp nod. "That's all very well, but—"

Althea broke in. "To make a long story short, we think that

you should consult with specialists. We have arranged an appointment for you with Dr. Fiorio of FWG Associates. He is well thought of, and we hope that he will be able to help you."

Jaro sipped the wine, though he did not like it very much. "How long will it take?"

Hilyer shrugged. "As to that, we can't be certain, since no one knows what is causing the trouble. Your first appointment, by the way, is tomorrow morning at Buntoon House in the Celece. It's a very nice place."

Jaro was startled. "So soon?"

"The sooner the better. Your school has started spring recess; the time could not be more convenient."

"I suppose not."

Althea stroked Jaro's shoulder. "Naturally, we will be with you. There is no reason to worry."

"I'm not worried."

2

Not long after dinner Jaro bade Hilyer and Althea goodnight and took himself off to bed. For a long time he lay staring into the dark, wondering what sort of therapy would be inflicted upon him. It could not be too ferocious; otherwise, FWG Associates would soon find themselves short of repeat customers.

One thing seemed certain: they would try to resolve the mysteries of his early years, which was all to the good. Jaro could offer few clues: the image of a gaunt man, silhouetted against the twilight of a distant world; a glimpse across a romantic garden, illuminated by a pair of large pale moons. And then: the voice!

A great mystery! Where did the voice originate? Jaro knew a few superficial facts regarding telepathy; perhaps here was the answer. He might have become the receptor for someone else's tragic emotions!

Jaro often had started to confide in the Faths, but each time he had drawn back. The Faths, so kind and loving, tended to overreact. Hilyer dealt with emergencies in a rather impractical way, meticulously organizing every detail of the necessary countermeasures. Althea would alternately swoop back and forth across the room, then hug him until he was breathless, meanwhile reproaching him for his secrecy. Together, they would extract promises to report every future malaise, ache, pang, twinge and itch, no matter how trivial, since they knew best what was good for him. At least, thought Jaro, the affair would be out of his jurisdiction, and who knows what might eventuate.

Now he would find out.

3

Hilyer could not alter his work schedule, so that Althea accompanied Jaro on his first visit to Buntoon House. They arrived at the stipulated hour and were immediately taken to Dr. Fiorio, who looked Jaro over, from head to toe. "So this is the boy with the problems? He looks to be a healthy young specimen. How are you today, Jaro?"

"Very well, thank you."

"Ah! That's the way to talk! Straight from the shoulder!" Dr. Fiorio indicated a white wicker chair. "Sit there, if you please, and we'll have a little discussion."

So far, so good. Dr. Fiorio seemed pleasant enough, if perhaps a trifle boisterous.

"Now then, Jaro! Just wait patiently a moment or two. I must conduct some business with your mother." He took Althea to an outer office, where, so he explained, she must endorse a standard packet of legal documents. The door remained half open; Jaro could hear them discussing the papers.

"Very good," said Dr. Fiorio at last. "That ties up all the loose ends. Now, if you please, refresh my memory regarding Jaro's troubles. How did they start?"

Althea collected her thoughts. "As to the voice itself, Jaro can tell you more than I can."

"Has he suffered any recent injuries to his head? Any falls, knocks, collisions?"

"None that I know of."

"And his health? Is he as sound as he looks?"

"Yes indeed! He has never been one to ail. We mentioned that when he was six he was almost killed by a gang of thugs, who were breaking all his bones. We rescued him but he was near death. In the hospital he went into spasms of hysterical emotion, which were draining what small vitality he had left. Something in his mind was driving him to distraction. As a last resort the therapist deleted a segment of his memory, and this is all that saved his life, though most of his first six years of memory were lost."

"Interesting! Where did all this happen? Not on Gallingale, surely?"

"No," said Althea. "It was—" she stopped short. A curious sort of silence ensued—furtive and secretive, not at all like Althea. The door was gently closed and he could hear no more.

Strange! Jaro had never known where these early events had taken place. When he had asked, he was given vague answers: "Oh, just off on some minor little world where we were doing a bit of research. It's all in the past; of no great importance, really."

Odd, such evasions!

The door opened; the two entered the room where Jaro waited. Althea was making the point that Jaro would feel more comfortable if she were present during the initial examination. Dr. Fiorio would hear none of it. "Absolutely not! Your presence would make Jaro self-conscious. You might like to take tea in the canteen just across the court."

With poor grace Althea went off to the canteen. Dr. Fiorio ushered Jaro to an examination chamber, with gray-green walls exuding a subaqueous light. He indicated a chair for Jaro and settled himself at his desk. Jaro waited, his mood fatalistic.

Dr. Fiorio was ready. He slapped his palms down on the desk. The therapy had begun. "Well then, Jaro, here we are! Our first job is to get acquainted. If I may say so, you seem a fine bright chap, and no doubt a real social scrambler. You're well above the Junior Service? I don't see any emblems, still I'd guess you were well up into the Persimmons or maybe into the Zouaves, or perhaps the Golliwogs."

"I am nothing. Not even a nimp."

"Ah yes! Hm ha!" Dr. Fiorio raised his eyebrows. "Just so! Everyone must strive to his own altitude; comporture is a mask of many guises. But that is a complicated truth, and we won't take it up now. Agreed?"

"Yes, sir."

"That's the spirit! Now then, what about these mysterious voices? Tell me about them, and they'll be crying for mercy in jigtime."

Jaro spoke slowly, "It's rather more serious than what you would like to make out."

Dr. Fiorio looked at him a moment with eyebrows raised, the cheerful smile slowly fading. "Indeed!" He considered. "I see that I have mistaken my man. Sorry; I'll try to make the adjustment. Tell me about the voice. Do you hear it often?"

"At first, not often—once a month, and then it barely seemed worth noticing. During the last year I've heard it several times a week, and now it is disturbing. It seems to come from inside my head and I can't get away from it."

Dr. Fiorio grunted softly. "This voice—is it male or female?"

"It is male. What frightens me most is that sometimes it sounds like my own voice."

"Hm. That is possibly significant."

"I don't think so," said Jaro. "I decided that it was not my voice." He went on to describe the voice as best he could. "In the end I had to tell someone, and now I'm here."

"You have given me a great deal to think about," said Dr. Fiorio. "This is something I've never encountered before."

Jaro asked anxiously: "What causes the voice?"

Dr. Fiorio shook his head. "I don't know. I could guess that your previous therapy had welded some unnatural loops together, which finally started to pick up energy. If so, the upshot may well be wrong. We'll know more after we examine you. Our first task is to isolate the source of the voicc. We will begin at once." Dr. Fiorio rose to his feet. "This way, if you please, into the laboratory. I want you to meet my colleagues, Dr. Windle and Dr. Gissing. We will work together on your case."

Three hours later Dr. Fiorio and Jaro returned to the waiting room. Althea looked from one to the other. Jaro was composed, if a trifle ruffled. Dr. Fiorio seemed to have sagged and had put aside the ebullient mannerisms which earlier had enlivened his conversation. He told Althea, "We've made a start, using mild hypnosis and fact enhancers, but we have learned nothing significant. That's about all I can tell you, except that it will be best if Jaro takes up temporary residence in one of our garden suites, where he will be conveniently situated for therapy."

Althea protested. "All very well, but he will be separated from his family and friends! We will want to discuss his therapy with him, and offer our counsel, if it seems to be needed. If Jaro stays here, this will be impossible!"

"Exactly so," said Dr. Fiorio. "That is why I suggested it."

Althea reluctantly conceded to the arrangements. "But don't worry," she told Jaro. "You will not be abandoned! I'll drop by every day, and keep you company for as long as I can!"

Dr. Fiorio cleared his throat and raised his eyes to the ceiling. "It will be better for all of us if you restrict your visits to a reasonable minimum: let us say an hour every third day."

"But Doctor Fiorio!" cried Althea. "That is hardly reasonable! Jaro needs my support and I want to know every detail of his therapy!"

Dr. Fiorio spoke rather testily. "We prefer to issue no regular progress reports. If there have been no changes, which is usual, we are forced to invent a set of cheerful platitudes. This is tiresome. When we have something consequential to announce, you will know at once."

"It is difficult to live in a vacuum of information," Althea complained. "Especially when one is anxious."

Dr. Fiorio relented. "We'll try to keep you abreast of what we are doing. Today, for instance, we put Jaro under hypnosis, hoping to stimulate the voice, without success. We then started to prepare schematic analogs of Jaro's brain, which will allow us to trace synaptic routes. We have the most modern autoflexes and information processors; still it's a slow delicate job, and there are always surprises."

Althea hesitated, then asked: "Do you think that you can set things right?"

Dr. Fiorio stared sadly at Althea as if in wounded pride. "My dear lady, of course! That is the basis of our comporture!"

Althea had taken her leave and the housekeeper was showing Jaro his room. The three colleagues retired to the refectory to refresh themselves. Dr. Gissing commented upon Jaro's somber self-possession. "I had the uncanny feeling he was watching us more carefully than we were watching him."

"Nonsense," said Dr. Windle. "You are suffering from a guilt neurosis!"

"True enough, but is this not the seminal force which drives us all?"

"Allow me to pour you some more tea," said Dr. Fiorio and the topic was put aside.

4

The therapeutic sessions at Buntoon House became the total substance of Jaro's life. Work went methodically. Plotting mechanisms traced the principal schema of his brain, in both two and three dimensions. He was fitted with monitors. Should the voice manifest itself, the area of the brain affected could now be identified. The voice, however, remained silent, which Dr. Windle, the most skeptical of the three therapists, considered a significant indication in itself. "The boy no doubt had a bad dream or two," he told his colleagues. "He is a nimp and thinks the sky is falling. We have known a hundred cases of such hysteria."

The three sat in the library, holding their daily conference, at which it was their custom to take a dram or two of smoky old malt tonic. They occupied their usual places: Dr. Fiorio, with the face of an aging cherub, leaned against the central table. Dr. Windle, erudite and sardonic, sat leafing through a journal, while Dr. Gissing lounged in a careless pose upon the sofa, his face serene and enraptured, as if he listened to a strain of delightful music. It was this particular expression, which Dr. Windle unkindly compared to the face of "a bewildered rat."

Dr. Gissing now chided Dr. Windle for his skepticism. "Come now! The boy is transparently honest. He surely can't enjoy what we are doing to him. He has had some bad experiences and he wants no more."

Dr. Fiorio said slowly: "We are definitely faced with something uncanny. This case is bizarre beyond all my prior experience. I refer, of course, not only to the voice, but to the moonlit garden and the dark shape against the twilight. I can't help but wonder what else is lost in the boy's memory. There may be stuff there to curl our eyelashes!"

"Perhaps some of this shattered memory can be recovered," suggested Dr. Gissing.

Dr. Windle was emphatic. "The possibility is remote. The gaps are clear on his schematics!"

"True! But did you not notice the broken matrices? I counted a dozen at a single glance. They are, admittedly, in various stages of degradation."

Dr. Windle dismissed the topic with a grunt. "They mean nothing! They are only points of reference, and have no mnemonic function. They are not truly significant."

"Significant, no. Intriguing, yes."

"To you, perhaps. But we cannot waste time chasing down each of your vagaries, like mad scientists with butterfly nets running through the swamp."

"Puff and nonsense!" declared Dr. Gissing in high good humor. "Have you forgotten my comporture? We Lemurians eat pepper with our cheese! If necessary, I will carry on alone!"

"My dear fellow," droned Dr. Windle, "we know your predilection! Your bent for the arcane and aberrant may yet lure you into a sad miscalculation!"

"I am grateful for your warning," said Dr. Gissing. "In the future I will use my curative powers with all caution."

5

A week later, the Faths were notified that Dr. Fiorio wished to discuss Jaro's case. At the stipulated hour the Faths arrived and were ushered into Dr. Fiorio's consultation office. The doctor appeared, greeted the Faths, saw to their seating in cushioned chairs, then went to lean back against his desk. He looked from Hilyer to Althea, then said, "What I have to tell you is neither good news nor bad. It is simply an overview of our activities to date."

The Faths had nothing to say, and Dr. Fiorio continued. "We are making progress, of a sort, as I will presently explain. There has been no recurrence of the voice. If it were truly a sentient thing, it might have taken alarm and gone to hide in some far corner of Jaro's mind."

Althea cried out in dismay: "Is that what you believe?"

"In the absence of evidence I believe nothing," said Dr. Fiorio. "Still, we now strongly suspect that the voice exists."

Hilyer decided that it was time to introduce cold logic into the discussion. He said, "You are surprisingly definite on this point."

"I can well understand your skepticism," said Dr. Fiorio. "The rationale behind my opinion will not be intuitively clear to a layman. I will express myself in basic concepts. The resultant ideas will be neither elegant nor precise, but they should lie within your range of understanding. Are you with me so far?"

Hilyer gave a curt nod. "Proceed."

"Start, if you will, from this perspective. Jaro heard the voice and stored the memory in his mind. On the next occasion, the same thing occurred; likewise on the next, until a group of mnemonic strings had been recorded. Here, then, would be information which we wish to chart upon our schematics. First, we tried overt present-time stimulation to find the so-called 'kickoff button,' without success. Next, we tried light hypnosis, but did no better.

"So then, to our next option: the drug Nyaz-23, which facilitates deep hypnosis. We discovered a barrier, but were able to attack it from the flank, so to speak, and finally found the 'kick-off button.' We made contact and asked Jaro to duplicate the voice as best he could. He obliged by giving vent to some very strange sounds indeed, which we recorded. The moans, outcries, inarticulate curses are exactly as he described them. This, generally, is the substance of our findings to date."

Hilyer pursed his lips. "If I understand you correctly, the sounds you have recovered are not the original sounds but, rather, Jaro's attempts to reproduce what he thinks he has heard: in short, a re-creation of what might have been hallucinatory in the first place?" Dr. Fiorio studied Hilyer a moment, his expression no longer innocently cherubic. "That is generally correct, yes. But I am puzzled as to the apparent thrust of your remarks."

Hilyer smiled frostily. "It is simple enough. You are citing what, in legal parlance, is known as 'hearsay evidence.' It has little probative force."

Dr. Fiorio's face cleared. "I am grateful for your insights! No more need be said. We shall take it as read that I am a dupe and a numbskull. So now, with these caveats in mind, let us proceed."

"I would not presume to use such words," said Hilyer primly. "I pointed out only that your evidence was flawed."

Dr. Fiorio sighed. He circled his desk and seated himself. "Your comments, I am sorry to say, indicate only that you have not yet grasped the direction of our inquiry. The fault is mine. I must present my ideas more carefully."

"To repeat: using methods of great sophistication, we were able to stimulate memory of certain events, which in turn established significant vectors on our schematic charts. Subject matter, of course, was inconsequential."

To Dr. Fiorio's relief, neither of the Faths asked to hear the recorded sounds, which they would surely find harrowing.

"Now then," said Dr. Fiorio. "This is our thesis: Jaro's memories of the sounds are lodged at various addresses on his cortex. They did not arrive by the usual conduits—that is to say, his aural nerves—but by another route. The flow of messages leaves a trail which persists for an indeterminate period. With our remarkable equipment, we can stimulate a memory, then trace the line of synaptic lineages back to its source. The procedures are indescribably delicate and produce vectors upon schematic charts. Am I clear so far?"

"It seems a most elaborate procedure," Hilyer grumbled. "Do

you have a goal in view? Or will you be satisfied with the first hare to leap from the thicket?"

Dr. Fiorio chuckled. "Be patient, sir, and I will continue."

Hilyer nodded crisply. "Please do; in our poor way we will try to keep pace."

Dr. Fiorio approved. "That's the way! Dogged does it, every time!"

"Now then, where do we go from here? In the broadest sense, we collect data and watch for a pattern to emerge. This pattern will dictate the direction of our treatment."

Althea put a tentative question, "What is the difference, if any, between 'treatment' and 'therapy'?"

"Only a matter of degree. But remember, as of now we are still in the diagnostic stage."

Hilyer spoke in his most nasal drawl, "We hope that no other segments of Jaro's intelligence will be damaged by therapy."

Dr. Fiorio ticked points off his fingers. "First, the previous therapy interfered only with Jaro's memory, not his intelligence. The two functions are separate, though they work in tandem. Second, there is no reason to repeat such therapy. Third, we are not as irresponsible as you may fear. Jaro is safe from any reckless trampling about in his head. Do you have any further questions?"

Hilyer was by no means daunted by Dr. Fiorio's three points. "How does Jaro react to all this probing?"

Dr. Fiorio shrugged. "His composure is superb. He complains of nothing; even when he is tired, he cooperates to his best ability. He is a fine boy. You can be proud of him."

"Oh we are!" cried Althea. "We are, a hundred times over!"

Dr. Fiorio rose to his feet. "I won't have anything more to tell you until the next stage of our work is completed. It may be as long as a week."

6

Four days later, toward the end of the afternoon, Dr. Fiorio joined his colleagues in the conference chamber. A young woman wearing the smart blue and white uniform of a nurse's aide, served tea and nut cakes. For a few moments the three savants sat relaxed in their chairs, almost limp, as if resting after strenuous exercise. Gradually their tensions eased. Dr. Fiorio sighed, reached for his teacup and said, "If nothing else, we are no longer working at random. This is a great relief."

Dr. Windle snorted. "We cannot exclude the possibility of a hoax."

Dr. Fiorio sighed. "That is the most incredible suggestion of all."

"What do we have left?" cried Dr. Windle. "Willy-nilly we are forced to propose that a more or less rational intelligence controls this phenomenon!"

Dr. Gissing wagged his finger at Dr. Windle in mock reproach. "That is like saying we must, willy-nilly, invoke the presence of sidereal equations to explain the morning sunrise."*

"The implication of your remarks eludes me," said Dr. Windle coldly.

Dr. Gissing kindly explained. "This 'directive agency,' if internal, would indicate a multiple personality. If external, we would be forced to consider a telepathic provenance, which is a bit beyond our scope, or so I believe."

Dr. Windle's voice took on an edge. "You have provided us some helpful nomenclature. My comment is this: to name a malady is not to cure it."

Dr. Fiorio spoke testily. "All this is irrelevant. Our vectors point to a specific location, namely Ogg's Plaque."

Dr. Windle made a sound of disapproval. "You are taking us into the trap of mysticism. If that albatross is hung around our necks, it will cost us dearly, both in working efficiency and in prestige!"

Dr. Gissing said, "If truth is to be our goal, we should not slam the door on all but purely mechanistic theories."

Dr. Windle demanded: "So what then is your opinion?"

"I feel there is more here than simple dementia."

"In this regard, we are agreed," said Dr. Fiorio heavily.

A chime sounded. Dr. Fiorio rose to his feet. "The Faths have arrived. We must give them the facts; no help for it."

Dr. Windle glanced at his watch. "Today I cannot participate; I am already late for my meeting. Simply make a factual report, without your usual pontificating, and all will be well."

Dr. Fiorio laughed, if somewhat painfully. "My 'pontificating,'

*Those familiar with the works of Baron Bodissey may remember his tale of the guest at a dinner party who, anxious to impress the company, asserted that he had only just arrived from an extraordinary world where the sun rose in the west and set in the east.

as you put it, is no more than good public relations—lacking which, you would be tapping old ladies on the knees with rubber mallets."

"Yes, yes; just so," said Dr. Windle. "Do the job any way you like." He departed the room.

"I also must leave you in the lurch," said Dr. Gissing ruefully. "I've been trying to get my elbow under the skirts of the Girandole, and today is the day: what they call their 'Quelling of the Innocents' and I must be on hand to be quelled. Who knows? You might find yourself affiliated with a Girandole before the month is out."

"Very well!" growled Dr. Fiorio. "Go! Be quelled! I'll deal with the Faths alone—which is probably all for the best, in any case."

7

Dr. Fiorio joined the Faths in the reception chamber. They sat quietly, their faces somber. Today Hilyer wore loose trousers of brown-gray twill, a dark brown pullover with black sleeves. Althea wore a dark green skirt, with a white blouse and a jacket of dark orange nubble. Dr. Fiorio absent-mindedly noted that they displayed no emblems defining their status; then he remembered that they were nimps, which was all very well, but they would hardly flaunt emblems advertising the fact. He slipped into his usual chair behind the desk and extended perfunctory greetings. The Faths responded in kind, watching him carefully, sensing that he had news to impart.

Dr. Fiorio said, "We have made definite progress in your son's case. The mysteries remain, but finally we can come to grips with them."

Althea asked tremulously, "Is the news good, or bad?"

"It is neither. You must judge its significance for yourselves."

"Very well," said Hilyer. "Tell us what you have learned."

"As you know, we have been systematically studying Jaro's mind; in the process, logging vectors upon the schematic charts. To our surprise, they pointed to an inconspicuous little nodule of twisted nerve tissue known as Ogg's Plaque, at the back of the medulla. Today as we studied the area in detail, Jaro began to make occasional sounds. They were of no particular interest, but we recorded them nonetheless. Then the probe apparently stimulated a special area, and you will now hear what ensued."

Dr. Fiorio put a small black box upon the table. "After some ordinary noise and a warning chime, you will hear Jaro's voice. It will sound strange. I warn you, take a grip on yourselves; you may be disturbed." He touched a button, then turned and waited, watching the Faths.

Sounds issued from the box: the rustling of papers, thumps, Dr. Fiorio muttering to his aide, a scrape, a small chime, then a voice, harsh and heavy. It had been formed in Jaro's throat; otherwise, none of Jaro's characteristics could be discerned. The voice called out, soft and forlorn: "Oh my life! My precious life; it passes and I am helpless in the dark! I am a lost soul, while my life seeps away; seep, seep, seeping! Away it seeps! I am forgotten, dark and deep, while my wonderful life seeps." The voice broke into a sob, then spoke again, even more desolate than before, "Why must it be me, to be lost in the dark, forever and ever?" There was the sound of muffled sobbing, then silence.

Dr. Fiorio's voice, tense and sharp, came from the box. "Who are you? Tell us your name!"

There was no response. No further sounds issued from the box; only the singing stillness of solitude and nothingness.

Dr. Fiorio touched a button on the box to halt the recording. He turned to find himself staring, not at the Faths, but at two strangers, with white emaciated faces and great round eyes like puddles of black mud. Dr. Fiorio blinked; the spell was broken; reality returned. He heard himself saying, "For the first time we come to grips with a fact. For us this is good news; it is a relief to learn that we are not groping for a will-o'-the-wisp."

Althea cried out softly, "Where is the voice coming from? Is it Jaro?"

Dr. Fiorio held his arms wide and let them flap to his sides. "We have not had time to form sensible opinions. At first glance it seems a classic case of multiple personality, but such a diagnosis is suspect, for a variety of technical reasons, which I will not develop now."

Hilyer asked hesitantly, "What other possibilities might there be?"

Dr. Fiorio replied with caution, "At this stage I could only speculate, which might mislead you."

Hilyer smiled sourly. "I don't mind listening to speculation, if it is clearly labeled as such. For instance, at Sronk a block of Jaro's memory was erased. Is it possible that by miscalculation, an entire lobe was isolated from the rest of his mind, and deprived of sensory input? We might be hearing cries from this isolated lobe."

Dr. Fiorio reflected. "It is a clever idea, and superficially plausible. But any such isolated segment would have revealed itself on the schematic charts. Therefore, this cannot be the solution, despite its appealing simplicity."

"But something very similar must be happening!"

"Well—perhaps."

Althea ventured a question, "Will you be able to help Jaro?"

"Yes—though I am not quite sure where to start. If we knew the truth of Jaro's past, perhaps we could exorcise the sad ghost which haunts his mind."

"I suppose that's reasonable," said Althea, "though it doesn't sound very practical."

"Not practical at all," declared Hilyer. "Such a program would mean far travel, much time and expense, with a very cold trail to follow, and small prospects of success."

"I'm afraid that's true," said Dr. Fiorio.

Althea spoke wistfully, "You're not really optimistic about Jaro, are you?"

Dr. Fiorio grimaced. "I want neither to inflate you with false hopes, nor send you away in despair. The simple truth is that we are still collecting data."

Hilyer inspected him skeptically. "And that is all you can tell us?"

Dr. Fiorio reflected a moment. "Ordinarily we do not like to disclose raw data until it has been fully analyzed; still, I see no harm in mentioning an item which may interest you."

Dr. Fiorio paused to arrange his thoughts. Hilyer became impatient. "Well then! What is it?"

Dr. Fiorio gave Hilyer a look of reproach, but said, "During our work sessions, monitors detect the small neural currents which indicate brain activity. While the voice was speaking the monitors recorded no activity. If the voice had been driven by memory, such activity would be expected at characteristic locations. This was not the case."

"Which means?"

"Subject to review and analysis, it indicates that the source of the voice was external to Jaro's mind."

After a pause, Hilyer said stiffly, "I find that hard to credit. The concept leads to mysticism."

Dr. Fiorio shrugged. "That is not my responsibility. I can only cite evidence."

The Faths rose to their feet and went to the door. Dr. Fiorio accompanied them out into the entry hall. "You were interested in speculation," he told Hilyer. "Now you have the facts, and may speculate to your heart's content. I will do the same, after I have bathed, changed into my fine linen lounge suit and settled myself into the saloon bar at the Palindrome, where I will instantly be served one or more gin pahits."

8

A week later, when Dr. Fiorio once again conferred with the Faths in the reception room, he was accompanied by Jaro. Althea, thought that Jaro looked pale and somewhat drawn, but also relaxed and confident.

Jaro went to sit on the couch between Hilyer and Althea. Dr. Fiorio leaned back against the table. He said, "This has been a puzzling case—although we know somewhat more now than we did at the start. For a fact we have put an end to Jaro's problems; at least, it seems so at the moment."

"Then that is glorious news!" cried Althea.

Dr. Fiorio nodded without enthusiasm. "I am not altogether satisfied. Our technique has neither been elegant, nor a piece of brilliant improvisation, nor yet even dictated by classical theory. Instead, we used a crude and nasty pragmatism, whose only virtue was its success."

Althea laughed in happy excitement. "But isn't that enough? I think you are far too modest!"

Dr. Fiorio shook his head sadly. "Our goal was to solve the mystery, which is of a fundamental nature. In essence, was the voice produced internally, by Jaro's memory, or externally, by an agency like telepathy? During our research we more or less incidentally happened to cure Jaro's affliction. The voice no longer groans and curses, so now we must turn off our equipment and declare a great victory."

Hilyer compressed his lips. Dr. Fiorio's ponderous levity—if such it were—no longer seemed appropriate, and in fact had started to grate on his nerves. "Sorry," said Hilyer. "I'm not sure that I grasp what you are trying to tell us."

"It is quite simple, when translated into layman's language."

"Do so, by all means," murmured Hilyer.

"Of course, of course!" declared Dr. Fiorio, never suspecting that the meek and non-status academician might feel anything other than awed admiration for himself, his expertise and his association with the Palindrome. "As I mentioned, we located an area which seemed to be the seat of the problem: a pad of spongy tissue at the back of the medulla known as Ogg's Plaque. A chance stimulation of this area had been followed by the voice which you heard. We attempted new stimulations, with varying results. We never answered the basic question of origination, since it had become moot."

"How so?"

Dr. Fiorio paused to consider, then said, "To make a long story short, we isolated Ogg's Plaque from its input of nervous impulses, sheathing it in pannax film and totally surrounding it with an insulating capsule. On that instant, the noise associated with the Plaque disappeared. Jaro at once noticed a sensation of liberation. He feels that the voice has been quieted and he is much relieved. Am I right, Jaro?"

"Yes," said Jaro.

Hilyer's attention was caught by a hesitancy in Jaro's response. He asked sharply, "What is wrong? Are you uncomfortable with what has been done?"

"No! Of course not! I'm only afraid that if the therapy wore off, the voice might come back."

Althea asked, "You feel, then, that the voice comes from outside yourself?"

"Yes."

Althea shivered. "It is an eery thought."

Hilyer spoke with cool and rational detachment. "If the voice were part of what is called a 'multiple personality,' it would also sound like someone else."

Dr. Fiorio smiled with that complacency which already had exasperated Hilyer. "Are there any other points you might want illuminated?"

"There are indeed," said Hilyer crisply. "For instance, the matter of side effects. You have isolated an organ of Jaro's brain; is that not a serious matter?"

"Probably not. Ogg's Plaque has been studied at length; it is generally considered a vestigial redundancy."

"Still, are you not interfering with something you do not completely understand?"

Dr. Fiorio said patiently, "The short answer to your question is 'yes.' We intend to keep Jaro under observation. His problems have been controlled; now we must wait to see what happens, if anything."

Althea asked, "Is Ogg's Plaque active during hypnosis? Does it control hypnotic suggestion?"

"The answer is: definitely not. Hypnosis operates across quite different areas of the brain. So then—what else? Nothing more? Then I will make an observation on my own, in regard to Jaro. During this work he has gained our affection and also our respect. He has shown us persistence, courage and grit: traits of which he can be proud. He's also good-natured, cheerful and polite. I realize that you are non-orgs, but if Jaro set his mind to the striving, he'd go fast up the ledges, since he has a natural comporture which will ultimately take him high."

Althea gave Jaro a quick hug. "Did you hear that? Dr. Fiorio is talking about you! Now perhaps you'll buckle down and apply some of that persistence to your schoolwork, and put aside your daydreams of wandering space."

Dr. Fiorio gave an indulgent laugh. "At Jaro's age, we're all romantics! I wanted to be the ace roving plunger for the Kaneel Roverball Club." He addressed Jaro: "Listen to your mother, Jaro; she's got the right of it. There's precious little status to be gained in space, and while there is nothing truly wrong in being a nimp, it's best to suck the sweetest juice from the melon! And strive toward the top!"

"Hmf," said Hilyer. "Jaro has his sights set on an academic career, and perhaps he will prefer not to be distracted by nursing comporture, and suffering a thousand deaths every time his application to an up-status club is rejected."

Dr. Fiorio smiled benignly. "That, of course, is an alternate philosophy, and no doubt quite valid. Well then; I wish you all a pleasant day!"

FIVE

1

Jaro's time at Buntoon House coincided with the spring recess at Langolen School, so that he returned to his classes without discontinuity. Nevertheless, everything seemed different. His new liberation put him into a mood close to euphoria. He was sure of his competence; nothing could prevent him from undertaking his quest! He might learn unpleasant facts, or worse; already he had experienced inklings of the evil which lurked in his past and which might be groping forward into the present. Somewhere the voice still groaned and howled into a place now dark and empty.

Where?

Why?

What to look for?

Jaro had questions but no answers. The Faths refused to speculate upon or even discuss the voice. Hilyer had officially declared it a "queer little kink" in Jaro's mental processes, now happily repaired. They had always been reticent in regard to his early years. When he asked questions, they had responded with absent-minded generalities. The nameless urchin was gone from mind and memory; there was only Jaro Fath, with a distinguished academic career in prospect. They meant no harm, of course; they wanted only that he be like themselves, which was the prerogative of all parents. Dame Wirtz greeted him with a sharp glance of appraisal and a pat on the head. She asked no questions, but Jaro was sure that she had communicated with Althea and that the two had discussed him at length. Jaro cared little, one way or the other. He looked around the room, seeing his classmates from a new perspective. He felt more detached from them than ever. Almost all were strivers. About half wore the blue and white Junior Service emblems. Others had been accepted into the Persimmons, and a few had arrived among the Zouaves. There were two nimps, sitting quietly at the back of the room. The boy, like himself, belonged to a family of Institute academics, the girl had only recently arrived from off-world and was said to have peculiar eating habits. There was a single Clam Muffin in the class: Skirlet Hutsenreiter.

Jaro's survey of the group reinforced his own sense of singularity. His classmates considered him not only a nimp but a solitary person who shunned class activities and perhaps indulged in mysticism of one sort or another. On several occasions Jaro had explained his intention to become a spaceman, for whom striving up the social ledges of Thanet could only be wasted effort. No one had troubled to listen to him. It made no great difference. Next year he would enter the Lyceum, where he would concentrate on space studies: astronomy, the history and geography of Old Earth, the morphology of the Gaean Reach, space technology, the locators and the ever more remote frontier which separated the Reach from Beyond. He would try to read all twelve volumes of Baron Bodissey's *LIFE*, which might well meet with Hilyer's approval. On second thought, perhaps not; the Baron was closely identified with space exploration, while for many folk, including the Faths, the Gaean Reach was quite large enough, and there was no need for any more spacemen. The Faths had already established a program for Jaro's future, consonant with their own ideals. Jaro's plans would surely meet resistance at home. The idea saddened him, inasmuch as he loved Althea and Hilyer, who had devoted so much of themselves to his well-being. But it could not be helped. He wanted no part of an academic career, any more than he yearned to become a Tatterman or a Clam Muffin. Jaro thought of Tawn Maihac, who could be relied upon for discreet advice.

A week had passed since Jaro had last seen Maihac. On this occasion, with the reluctant permission of the Faths, Maihac had taken Jaro to the space terminal. After crossing the main lobby, they entered a long hangar and sauntered along a line of space-yachts, of many sizes and varieties. They moved slowly, studying each of the gleaming shapes in turn, appraising qualities of comfort, strength, and that peculiar air of dauntless magnificence which could be found in no other human construction.

In the machine shop Maihac introduced Jaro to Trio Hartung, the shop foreman, and to a ferociously ugly mechanic named Gaing Neitzbeck, who acknowledged the introduction with a curt nod.

Upon leaving the machine shop, Maihac took Jaro to an outdoor cafe at the side of the plaza. Over tea and a dish of cream tarts Maihac asked Jaro his opinion of Hartung and Neitzbeck. Jaro gave the matter consideration, then said: "Mr. Hartung seems very steady, and quite friendly. I found that I liked him."

"Fair enough. What about Gaing Neitzbeck?"

Jaro knit his brows. "I don't know what to think. He looks a bit grim."

Maihac laughed. "He is not altogether what he seems. One thing for certain, he is not diffident."

"You've known him a long time, then?"

"Yes. Let me ask you this: when the Faths brought you to Thanet, you could remember nothing of your past?"

"Nothing of consequence."

"And you don't know where they found you?"

"No. They won't tell me until I am graduated from the Institute."

"Hmf. Tell me what you remember."

Jaro described the inklings and images he had brought to Thanet.

Maihac listened intently, his eyes fixed on Jaro's face as if he could read more than words in Jaro's expression. "And that is all you remember?"

Jaro looked off across the plaza. "Once or twice—I don't know how many times—I dreamt of my mother. I could barely make out her shape, but I heard her voice. She said something like, 'Oh my poor little Jaro! I am so sorry to put this burden upon your shoulders! But so it must be!' Her voice was sad, and when I awoke I felt very sad, too."

"What did she mean 'burden'?"

"I don't know. Sometimes, when I think of her, I feel that I ought to know, but when I try to remember, it slips away."

"Hmm. Interesting. And that's all you remember?"

Jaro grimaced. "There is something else. I think it's connected with the garden under the two moons." Jaro told Maihac of the doleful voice which had caused him so much anxiety. He described the therapy at Buntoon House and the harsh blurted words on the recording. "The doctors had no explanation except telepathy," said Jaro. "Even then, they could not agree. But at least, I have no more trouble with the voice."

As Jaro spoke, a change came over Maihac. He leaned forward, tense and rigid, as if the account held a dreadful fascination. Jaro wondered if Maihac had suffered a similar intrusion into his mind.

Maihac finally said, "That's a remarkable set of events."

Jaro nodded. "I'm glad that they have ended."

Maihac leaned back in his chair and looked off across the plaza. He asked: "You don't hear this voice anymore?"

"I don't think so. Sometimes I feel a tingle in the air, like coming into a room where someone has just spoken."

"That's good news," said Maihac. He rose to his feet. "I must be getting back to work."

Maihac left the table. Jaro watched the erect figure cross the plaza and disappear into the terminal. For a time Jaro sat pondering Maihac's strange conduct. It was more than simple surprise; Maihac had been shaken.

Jaro returned to Merriehew thoroughly surfeited with mystery.

Time passed, and Jaro had no further word from Maihac, nor

had Maihac shown himself at Merriehew. Perhaps he had not been invited? Jaro thought he knew what had happened. Maihac, from the Fath's purview, was no longer identifiable either with esoteric music or arcane instruments. Maihac now worked at the space terminal; he had cruised far and wide through space, and the Faths feared his influence over Jaro. If a role model were needed, they preferred that it should be Hilyer Fath, not Tawn Maihac, who was not only a spaceman but far from a pacifist.

Jaro smiled a thin sad smile. It was all quite clear. The Faths, benevolent and loving though they might be, were impressing upon him the guidance he neither needed nor wanted. Jaro knew that Maihac liked him; as soon as possible he would seek him out and try to probe deeper into the tantalizing mysteries of which Maihac was now a part.

In the morning he returned to school, and focused his mind upon his studies, as if invoking a hermetic discipline upon himself. During the lunch hour he passed Hanafer Glackenshaw in the central courtyard. Hanafer glanced at him, his mind elsewhere, but not so far that he could not spare a sneer and a sniff, to indicate the persistence of his old disdain. Jaro went his way without change of expression.

It was an unpleasant situation. Hanafer's contempt might dissipate, or it might prompt him to actions which Jaro could not ignore. What then? What if Hanafer became so offensive that Jaro felt impelled to fight? It would not accord with the teaching of the Faths. They would remind him that no law compelled him to strike another human being and hurt him, no matter what the provocation; high ethical doctrine required that Jaro politely announce his abhorrence of violence, excuse himself and walk away from the unpleasant affair. In this fashion, said the Faths, he would inculcate shame and contrition in his adversaries, and bring to himself the joy of a deed well done. Once again Jaro's mouth twitched in that sad half smile. The Faths had never allowed him to undertake physical education courses involving pugilism or combat of any sort; as a result, in the event of attack, he would be at considerable disadvantage, and Hanafer no doubt would thrash him soundly.

Jaro was annoyed by this notion. His deficiency might cause him serious embarrassment, if it were not repaired.

During the afternoon of the first day of the new term, Jaro visited the library, where he borrowed a volume describing various methods of hand-to-hand combat. He left the library and went to sit on a concrete bench in the courtyard, to peruse his acquisition. He became aware that someone had settled upon the far end of the bench. It was the notorious Skirlet Hutsenreiter, whose status as a Clam Muffin was so exalted that she gave not a thought to comporture. She sat sidewise, one leg tucked up under the other, one arm along the back of the bench, the other in her lap, achieving a negligent elegance which Jaro could not help but notice before returning to his book.

A moment passed. Jaro glanced aside, to find Skirlet studying him intently, bright gray eyes alight with intelligence. A casual tangle of short dark locks framed her face; and as usual, she wore whatever had been closest to hand: today a blue peasant's jacket, a size too large, trousers of offwhite duck which lovingly fit the curves of her round rump. Jaro sighed and again went back to his book, nerves tingling to a not unpleasant excitement. In the past Skirlet had barely noticed him; now she watched his every movement. Odd! What was going on in her mind? If he spoke to her and suffered a rebuff—as was to be expected—he would become annoyed and waste time thinking bitter thoughts. He decided to have nothing to do with her.

Skirlet seemed to divine his thinking and allowed herself a rather lofty smile.

Jaro gathered all his dignity and sat stiffly erect. His plan was a good one: he would ignore her totally, until her attention wandered and she ran off to amuse herself elsewhere. She was mercurial; it would be two or three minutes at the most. Skirlet called out: "Hoy! You there! Hello!"

Jaro appraised her without change of expression. She must be regarded as unpredictable, and treated with immense caution.

Skirlet spoke again. "Are you alive or dead? Or simply comatose?"

Jaro responded with stiff formality: "I am alive, thank you."

"Well said! Your name is Jaro Fath; am I right?"

"Not altogether."

Skirlet was annoyed by Jaro's evasiveness. "How so?"

"The Faths are my foster parents."

"Oh? You have other names?"

"Very likely." Jaro looked her over. "Who are you?"

Skirlet was taken aback. "Surely you know of me! I am Skirlet Hutsenreiter."

"I remember your name; it's quite unusual."

Skirlet said evenly: "My name is short for 'Shkirzaksein' which is my mother's country estate on Marmone, and where her palace Piri-piri is situated."

"That sounds very grand."

Skirlet nodded, rather bleakly. "It is, after a fashion. I stayed with her two years ago." Skirlet compressed her lips, and looked off down the length of Flammarion Prospect. "I learned things I never would have learned at Thanet. I'll never go back."

Skirlet slid closer along the bench. "At the moment I'm interested in you."

Jaro could hardly believe his ears. He stared at her dumbfounded. "You are interested in—me?"

Skirlet nodded primly. "In you and in your conduct." Jaro relaxed. Skirlet's manner was amicable, and while he must guard against complacency, it was hard not to speculate as to what she had in mind. Could she suddenly need an escort for some unexpected social function? Or perhaps, out of sheer caprice, might she wish to introduce him into the exalted ranks of the Clam Muffins? Or could she conceivably—Jaro's mind faltered at the edge of ideas wild and unthinkable, then cautiously drew back. Of course, such things happened. He eyed Skirlet dubiously. "You show very good taste. Still, I am puzzled."

"No matter. Do you mind if I watch you rather closely for a time?"

"It all depends. How closely, and for how long?"

Skirlet answered briskly, "No longer and no more closely than necessary."

"What about privacy?"

"At the moment, none is needed. Now then!" Skirlet held out her hand, touched her thumb to each of her fingers in turn. "Can you do that?"

"Of course."

"Show me."

Jaro performed the feat. "How was that?"

"Quite good. Do it again. Again. Again."

"That is enough for now," said Jaro. "I don't want to form an annoying nervous habit."

Skirlet clicked her tongue in vexation. "You've broken the sequence. Now we'll have to start all over."

"Not unless I know why."

Skirlet made an impatient gesture. "It is a clinical test. Deranged people start making characteristic mistakes at specific counts. I heard that you had been declared, well, just a bit crazy by the psychiatrists, and I wanted to try the experiment as soon as possible."

After an interval of dead silence Jaro uttered a soft syllable. Then he looked toward the sky. All was well; the world was sane again; Skirlet had not succumbed to a sudden amorous obsession. Too bad, in a way. He could use the practice.

"I now understand your interest," said Jaro. "For a time I suspected that you had fallen in love with me."

"Oh no," said Skirlet airily. "I have no interest in that sort of thing. In fact, I don't even like you very much."

Jaro gave a rueful grimace. After a moment he said: "May I offer you some valuable advice?"

Skirlet's expression became haughty. "From a nimp? Of course not."

"I'll do so anyway. If you hope for a successful career in psychotherapy, you must learn to be charming and sympathetic. Otherwise you'll annoy all your clients and they won't come back for a second session."

Skirlet laughed scornfully. "That's sheer doodle-whisker! Have you forgotten? I am a Clam Muffin; I plan no career! The idea is a vulgarity."

"In that case," Jaro began, but Skirlet interrupted.

"The facts are simple. I am interested in human personality and its deviations. This is a casual interest—what the Clam Muffins call 'dancing with toys.' When the chance arose, I decided to make a quick survey of you and your abnormalities."

"Good thinking," said Jaro. "There's just one flaw. I am not crazy."

Skirlet stared at him with eyebrows lifted. "Then why did you visit the psychiatrists?"

"That is my own affair."

"Ha hah! Perhaps you are crazy, after all—what the trade calls a 'croque-couvert.'"

Jaro decided to reveal at least part of the truth. "The first six years of my life are a mystery. I know nothing of my father or mother or where I was born. The psychiatrists were trying to recover some of the lost memory."

Skirlet was impressed. "Did they succeed?"

"No. The first six years are gone."

"Odd! Something terrible must have happened to you."

Jaro nodded somberly. "The Faths found me during one of their off-world expeditions. I had been beaten so severely that I was dying. They saved me but my memory was gone, and no one could tell them where I had come from. They brought me back to Thanet, and here I am."

"Hmm. This is material for the start of a really unusual case history!" Skirlet reflected a moment. "I expect that the trauma has loomed large in your life?"

Jaro agreed that this was probably so.

Skirlet asked, "Would you care to hear what I think?"

Jaro opened his mouth to reply, but Skirlet took his interest for granted. "You tell a pathetic tale—but, whatever your distress, it is no excuse for self pity! This is a crippling emotion! In the worst cases comporture is reduced to a stagnant puddle. You should take stock of yourself, even though you may not like what you find. You are still a nimp while others storm past you, up the ledges into the Zouaves or even the Bad Gang! The contrast causes inner shame, which degenerates into a truly defeatist loop, and ultimately takes you up Buntoon Hill to the psychiatrists."

Jaro considered the analysis then nodded. "I see what you mean. It is a very sound judgment—though I can't imagine whom you are judging; certainly not me."

"Oh?" Skirlet scowled. This was not the abject murmur she had expected. "Why do you say that?"

Jaro laughed—an impolite, mocking laugh, thought Skirlet. "Isn't it clear? I don't care a twitch for all your clubs: Clam Muffins, Lemurians, Sasselton Tigers or nimps. They are all the same to me! I'll be off into space as soon as I can, and you'll never see me again."

Skirlet's jaw dropped. Jaro had disparaged herself, the Clam Muffins, and the whole gorgeous panoply of cosmic order in one fell swoop! His insolence was amazing! She finally found her voice, but before speaking paused to select words of proper impact. The job must be done well and truly, but no fear as to that: she was Skirlet Hutsenreiter; using no instrument other than her glorious intelligence, she would overwhelm this prideful though rather nice-looking youth! She would conquer him and befuddle him until he stood before her abject and submissive, and there could be no thought of clemency until he had cried for mercy. After that—well, she would see, and might even consider a kindly pat on the head.

So then: these were the goals. How to proceed? She must establish a foundation of irrefutable logic, so as not to alarm him. She made herself speak gently. "You just can't go off into space by yourself. You need passage vouchers. They are expensive. Do you have money?"

"No."

"What of the Faths? Will they give you money?"

"Never, nor would they tell me where to start looking."

"But that's unkind!"

Jaro shrugged. "They're afraid that I'll become a vagabond, searching forever across the back worlds of the Reach. They don't want to pour money into a wild goose chase, and they are quite right. If I can't pay my own way I'll ship out as a spaceman."

"That's still no solution. If you're a spaceman you go where the ship takes you."

"I agree that it's a problem. My only solution is to marry someone with money. What about you? Can you finance a quest for six lost years? If so, I'll marry you this instant. I'm sure you are wealthy, being a Clam Muffin."

Skirlet could hardly speak for outrage. The joke was cruel and vindictive, and one which she would not have expected from Jaro. She said frigidly: "Apparently you have heard the rumors. Your jokes are in poor taste."

"I've heard no rumors, and I'm not joking."

Skirlet saw that she had made a mistake. "If you don't know, you're the only one who doesn't."

"I have no idea what you are talking about."

"Why do you think I'm enrolled at that grubby Langolen School instead of Aeolian Academy? Have you wondered why we lack fine gardens at Sassoon Ayry?"

Sassoon Ayry, on Lesmond Hill, so Jaro knew, was home to the Hutsenreiters. He said: "By preference, I suppose."

"Right! The bankers prefer not to lend my father more money. The gardeners prefer to be paid for their work. We live on the edge of poverty!"

"Strange!" said Jaro. "I thought all Clam Muffins were wealthy."

Skirlet laughed. "My father considers himself a brilliant financier, but his speculations are always too early or too late. He still owns a few bits of property, all more or less worthless, including Yellowbird Ranch, out near where you live. He thinks he can sell it to Mildoon the promoter, but Mildoon won't offer more than the land is worth, and my father is too vain to sell at a loss. He took the money from my trust fund to buy shares in a traveling menagerie. The animals died and my money is gone."

"Too bad."

"Very much so. I can't finance your quest, and you are liberated from your proposal of marriage."

Jaro studied her sidelong. She sounded almost serious—which of course was most unlikely.

Skirlet now coroborated his thinking. She rose to her feet. "All else to the side, the idea is tasteless—even if you intended no more than a jocularity."

"Quite correct," said Jaro. "My sense of humor is coarse. A space vagabond has no need for a wife."

Skirlet turned and looked off over the balustrade, and away down the long Flammarion Prospect. Jaro watched her in fascination, wondering what she was thinking.

The sun had drifted down upon the hills. The light was already fading. A puff of wind ruffled Skirlet's hair. For a fleeting instant the world seemed to shift into a new mode. Jaro thought to see a thin-cheeked waif: a lost trifle of tragic humanity.

Skirlet moved; shadows shifted; the illusion broke; she was as before. Slowly she turned and looked at Jaro. "Why are you blinking so foolishly?"

"It's hard to explain. For an instant I saw you as you might have been, if you were not a Clam Muffin."

"What an odd thing to say! Was there any difference?"

"I'm not sure."

"Poof. There's no difference. I've tried both ways. No difference whatever." She set off across the court, ran up the wide stone steps beside the library and was gone.

2

A week passed. At school Jaro saw Skirlet but kept his distance, and she took no notice of him. One evening Jaro asked Althea why they had seen so little of Tawn Maihac. Althea pretended absentmindedness, but the effort was unconvincing. "Who? Tawn Maihac? Oh yes, of course! The funny froghorn man! He is no longer in my class. He told someone that his new work kept him much too busy, and he could find no time for social occasions."

"Too bad," said Jaro. "I liked him."

"Yes, he was quite a talented fellow," said Althea vaguely.

Jaro went to his room and tried to call Maihac on his telephone, only to learn that Maihac was not listed in the exchange.

On the following day Jaro left school early and rode out to the space terminal by public transport. To the right of the terminal building a long high hangar flanked the field, protecting a row of space yachts from the weather; many were for sale. Jaro had come this way before with Maihac, and they had discussed the yachts along the line in loving detail. The least expensive were for the most part the evolutionary versions of the ancient Model 11-B Locator, now produced by numerous builders and sold as Ariels, Cody Extensors, Spadway Hermits and the like. They were broad-beamed craft of compact contour, all about fifty feet long, with only cosmetic differences from their rugged if spartan prototypes. Prices for such craft started at something over twenty thousand sols,* depending upon age, condition and furbishments. Maihac had told Jaro that sometimes at remote spaceports such craft could be had for ten thousand, or five thousand, or even two thousand sols, depending upon exigencies of the moment. Often, said Maihac, title to such vessels passed across the gambling tables of spaceport saloons.

"I don't know much about gambling," Jaro had said wistfully.

"I know enough to avoid it," said Maihac.

Other vessels ranged the gamut in size, quality, elegance and price, culminating in a magnificent Golschwang 19 and a Sansevere Triumph, neither for sale, though each, according to Maihac, would probably command a price of over two million sols. The Golschwang 19 belonged to a Tatterman banker; the other to a Val Verde magnate whose source of income was obscure. Jaro's special favorite was a splendid Fortunatus of the Glitterway series, named the *Pharsang*, currently offered for sale by a Kahulibah banker. The sign at the bow explained that the owner lacked the time to give this fine yacht the utilization it deserved, and so he might sell at the right price to a buyer of appropriate status; no others need apply. The asking price was unstated, but Maihac had suspected that it was well over a million sols. The craft was enameled a lustrous black, with trim of scarlet and mustard-ocher. Jaro was entranced with the vessel, as was Maihac. "I know where I will spend my first million sols," Maihac had said. "It is exactly the right size, either for living aboard or for hauling passengers out on excursions or to unscheduled ports. It would pay for itself in five years."

Jaro had said that it must cost a great deal to operate.

---

*Sol: monetary unit, about equal to $8 in contemporary terms.

"It all depends," Maihac had continued, "the present owner probably uses a full crew: captain, chief mate, first and second engineers, cook, two stewards and perhaps a spare hand. First class cuisine for owner, guests and crew could be very expensive. In short: large outlay. On the other hand, a single man could operate the yacht. His expenses would be negligible."

As Jaro passed down the line on his way to the machine shop, he came to the *Pharsang* Glitterway, and as usual paused to admire its massive yet graceful lines. The "For Sale" sign was no longer in evidence; had someone of adequate status purchased the vessel? Jaro noticed movement in the forward saloon. A girl passed by the observation pane. Jaro instantly recognized the flowing blond hair of Lyssel Bynnoc. She seemed to be talking and laughing with great animation, which of course was her normal style. Jaro rather admired Lyssel, who was very pretty, but he did not want her to see him staring with what she would think to be envious longing at the *Pharsang*. Too late! She turned and looked down at him where he stood staring at her. She turned away; Jaro suspected that she had failed to recognize him, which was more annoying than if she had done so.

Jaro had the grace to laugh at himself. He had encountered her years before at Langolen school in a science laboratory. Even then he had been favorably impressed, though with detachment, since at the time he had been preoccupied with his own affairs. Lyssel, in her turn noticed the tall dark-haired youth with the pensive expression. She felt his attention and turned away, expecting him to approach on one pretext or another, but when she looked around he was busy with his work.

Hmm, thought Lyssel. She appraised him covertly. In a quiet and unobtrusive way he was quite attractive. His features were well shaped, even rather aristocratic. She wondered whether he might be an off-worlder. It was quite possible, she thought. Rather a romantic notion! Lyssel liked romantic notions. Of course, like all the other boys she knew, he'd be putty in her grasp—once she got her hands on him. It seemed a good idea; Hanafer Glackenshaw would be annoyed.

Hanafer was indeed irked when she mentioned Jaro and described his virtues. "He has a very interesting look, as if he were a landed grandee, or perhaps one of the Overmen from Dambrosilla. There's some sort of mystery about him. At least, that's the rumor."

"Bah!" sneered Hanafer, a large, rather heavy youth with bold features, including a long nose which, in his opinion, lent him a commanding profile. He wore his blond hair after the new and daring fashion, sweeping over his fine broad forehead then back and off to the side. He scoffed at Lyssel's reference to Jaro. "That's sheer bullypup. There's no mystery about the fellow! First of all, he's a nimp!"

"Oh really?"

"Yes, really. His parents are nimps; they are academic types at the Institute, and pacifists to boot. So in the future, confine your rapturous theories to me! Let's take up where we left off."

"Stop, Hanafer! Someone will see us."

"Would that bother you?"

"Of course!"

"I wonder. Did you hear what Darsay Jechan said about you?"

"No."

"It was down by the fountain. He was rhapsodizing that you were like the pure and delicate flower of the legend, which fades and collapses after pollination."

"That's a very sweet compliment!"

"Kosh Diffenbocker also had a compliment. He said that it was a beautiful thought, but that you were probably more durable than the flower of legend, and if any such pollination had occurred, you seemed none the worse for it."

"Those are odd compliments, Hanafer Glackenshaw; I am not amused, least of all with you, and you may leave as fast as your fat little legs will take you!"

3

Jaro arrived at the machine shop, and went directly to the supervisor's office. Here he found Trio Hartung, who greeted him cordially. "Well, Jaro, what's for it today? Are you ready to take over my job?"

"Not yet," said Jaro. "I wish I qualified, however."

"Come see me when you are ready," said Hartung. "We'll start you up the ladder. Believe me, there is lots to learn."

"Thank you," said Jaro. "I'll come as soon as I can find time from school. Is Mr. Maihac around?"

Hartung looked at him in surprise. "Maihac has been gone—let me see. It's been two weeks now. He shipped out aboard the *Audrey Anthe*, of the Osiris Line. You did not know?"

"No."

"Odd. He said something about leaving you a message."

Jaro cast his mind back over the preceding weeks. "I had no such message." Then he asked, "When will he be back?"

"That's hard to say."

Jaro gave a dubious shrug. He left the machine shop and walked back along the line of space yachts. There still seemed to be folk aboard the *Pharsang*, but no one stood by the forward vantage panes.

Jaro passed through the terminal and came out upon the plaza. At open-air cafes folk sat enjoying the fresh air. Jaro seated himself at a table and was served a goblet of iced fruit juice. Feeling hollow and unsettled he sat looking across the plaza. Folk passed in front of him, coming and going from the terminal—persons of many sorts, from many worlds. Jaro paid them no heed.

If a message had arrived at Merriehew, what then? Might the Faths have decided not to distract him during this trying period? And then had either lost or forgotten the message?

If Jaro actively pursued the inquiry, in the end he must look to the Faths for information—which would grate upon Hilyer's composure and hurt Althea's feelings. He had no choice but to let the matter drop.

Jaro brooded for half an hour. The basic fact, by itself, was puzzling. Maihac had suddenly departed, leaving no clues as to his reasons. Perhaps, thought Jaro, he was not a man for farewells and preferred to slip quietly away into oblivion.

Perhaps.

One thing was certain: when someone searched into secret places, he often came up with things he would rather not have found.

SIX

1

The property behind Merriehew House at one time had included three thousand acres of wild terrain, and was known as the Katzvold Ranch. Over the centuries the property had dwindled, parcel after parcel, to a mere five hundred acres; still it included a cluster of forested hills, a small river, several meadows, a deep woods, some rolling parkland and, near the house, the area where Henry Katzvold, Althea's grandfather, had conducted his horticultural experiments. Henry Katzvold was a diligent man of expansive temperament, with a system of tantric theories he stubbornly sought to impose upon reality. He met no success, and produced only freaks and sports, pulpy rots, green slimes and stinking muddy messes. He was killed by a lightning bolt as he marched across his lands; and some said that as he fell he made a last furious gesture, as if to hurl the lightning back at the sky.

Henry's son Ornold, a poet and Fellow of the Institute, had been accepted into the Scrivener's Club, though he was a nimp by natural instincts. He transmitted this tendency to his daughter Althea, bequeathing her as well a substantial sheaf of conservatively invested securities, Merriehew House and the five hundred acres of hinterland. The house lacked all fashionable distinction, and everyone agreed that it was suitable for habitancy only by nimps. The acreage was roughly trapezoidal in shape, averaging close to three miles wide and almost four miles in length. The landscape was broken by small gulches, vales and ravines and scarred by decaying stony outcrops. It had often been declared useless for agriculture: both Althea and Hilyer were content to let the land remain a wilderness. Twenty years before there had been rumors that Thanet might expand northward along Katzvold Road, and speculators had hastened to buy up tracts of land at premium prices, among them Clois Hutsenreiter, Skirlet's father. Thanet, however, had expanded to the south and east. The bubble collapsed and the speculators were left holding large tracts of remote and useless wasteland. The Faths' daydreams of owning valuable property also collapsed.

At this time Merriehew was an eccentric construction of dark timber and stone, with a complicated roof of many dormers, gables, and ghostchasers. Every year Merriehew seemed a trifle more worn and shabby and in need of loving care. It was also roomy, comfortable and generally cheerful, thanks to Althea's ebullient personality, along with her flower boxes, gaudy wall hangings and imaginative dinner settings. In the beginning Althea had collected candelabra of every size, shape and material, and each night had illuminated her dinner table with different sets, or groupings. This, she presently decided, was not enough, and began to collect service settings to enhance the beauty of her table. During the years when her enthusiasm was at its peak, Althea created a romantic new adventure in the dining room each night. Hilyer dutifully admired her arrangements, though privately he wished she would channel more of her energies into the production of the cuisine itself. "Let it be fine and let it be ample!" Hilyer muttered to himself.

Hilyer was less attached to Merriehew than was Althea. At times he expressed himself tersely: "Rustic, yes. Bucolic, yes. Picturesque, yes. Convenient, no."

"Oh Hilyer, come now!" Althea protested. "This is our wonderful old home! We're used to its jolly little quirks!"

"For 'quirks' substitute the word 'aggravations,' " growled Hilyer.

Althea paid no heed. "We can't dismiss tradition out of hand. Merriehew has been in the family so long that it's become part of us!"

"You're the Katzvold, not me."

"True, and I can't bear to think of anyone living here but us."

Hilyer shrugged. "Sooner or later someone other than a Katzvold will own Merriehew. That, my dear, is a certainty. Even Jaro is not a true Katzvold, by bloodline."

At such remarks, Althea could only sigh and admit that Hilyer, as usual, was right. "Still, what can we do? Move into town, with all the noise? We'd get nothing for the property if we tried to sell."

"It's peaceful out here now," Hilyer agreed, "but I've heard talk that one of the local magnates wants to develop the area hereabouts into an enormous complex of some kind. I don't know the details, but if it ever happened, we'd be in the middle of worse clutter than if we lived in a small convenient place near the Institute."

"It probably won't happen," said Althea. "Remember? There was talk of such things before and nothing came of it. I like this tumbledown old house. I'd like it even more if you would fix the windows and splash on some paint."

"I'm not gifted in these skills," said Hilyer. "Ten years ago I fell off a ladder and I was only on the second rung."

So Merriehew continued to function as before, with only airy space, light, privacy and comfort to commend it.

During his years at Merriehew, Jaro had frequently gone off to explore the country behind the house. Althea at first had been reluctant to let him stray so freely, but Hilyer had insisted that the boy be allowed to wander as he liked. "What can happen to him? He can't get lost. We have no savage beasts, and even fewer Gihilite Perpatuaries."*

*Gihilites: a sect of mystics based in the Uirbach Region at the far side of the continent. The Perpatuaries were roving missionaries who purportedly stole children and conveyed them back to Uirbach for unpleasant purposes.

"He might fall and hurt himself."

"Not likely. Let him do as he likes: it will develop his self-reliance."

Althea made no further protest and Jaro was allowed to wander as he saw fit.

Years before Althea had explained to Jaro the source of the house name "Merriehew," Jaro had learned that in its original meaning the merriehew was a supernatural creature of delicate beauty, something like a fairy, with gauzy hair and webs between its fingers. If one captured a merriehew and nipped one of its ears, the merriehew became bonded to the person who had done the nipping, and must serve as his slave forever. Jaro was assured as to the validity of this legend by the Faths, and saw no reason to disbelieve so pleasant a possibility, and whenever he went walking in the forest or along the meadow he moved silently and stayed on the alert.

2

A line of steep-sided knolls, partially wooded, marked the southern boundary of the Katzvold acreage. Halfway up one of the slopes, on a flat area beside a rill and shaded under a pair of monumental smaragd trees, Jaro for several years had been building a hut. He used stones, carefully fitted and chinked with mortar, for the walls; saplings of flagstaff pine for the roof beams; layers of broad sebax leaves for the thatch. During his last year at Langolen School he had started a fireplace and a chimney, but slowly he realized his hut had become too small, a toy he had outgrown; to continue the project a counter-productive exercise. He still frequented the area but now he came to read, to draw in his sketch-pad, to paint watercolor landscapes and for a period he tried to teach himself the craft of tying decorative knots, using instructions found in a volume entitled: *COMPENDIUM OF 1,001 KNOTS, Both Plain and Fancy*.

One day Jaro went to the site of his hut, sat on the turf, his back against the trunk of a smaragd tree, his strong brown legs thrust out in front of him. He wore pale dust-colored shorts, a dark blue shirt, low ankle boots; he had brought a book and a sketch-pad, but he put them aside and sat contemplating the events of his own strange and turbulent life. He reflected upon the voice and the psychiatrists of Buntoon Hill. He thought of the Faths, who no longer seemed absolutely wise and infallible. With a pang of desolation he thought of Tawn Maihac and his sudden departure from Gallingale. Some day he would see Maihac again; of this he was sure, and then there would be explanations.

Jaro became distracted by the sound of distant calls and shouts, which came drifting over the hill from the property to the south. The noise intruded upon the primitive silence of the countryside. He grumbled a bit to himself, then picked up his sketch-pad and began to draw: a space yacht, sleek yet massive and powerful, not unlike the *Pharsang* Glitterway.

A new sound came to his ears. He looked to see someone half sliding, half scrambling down from the ridge. It was a girl: slim, jaunty and somewhat reckless, to judge by the manner in which she descended the slope. She wore dark gray shorts and a red-and-white-striped skirt, a dark green pullover, dark green knee-length stockings and gray ankle boots. In slack-jawed surprise Jaro saw the newcomer to be Skirlet Hutsenreiter, who could no longer be mistaken for a boy.

Skirlet jumped down upon the flat, paused to catch her breath, then crossed to stand gazing down at Jaro. "You look very placid—almost sleepy. Have I startled you?"

Jaro grinned. "Even I must rest."

Skirlet thought that Jaro looked even nicer when he smiled. She glanced down at his sketch-pad. "What are you drawing? Space ships? Is that all you have on your mind?"

Not altogether. "I'll sketch you, if you care to pose."

Skirlet curled her lip. "I suppose you mean in the nude."

"That would be nice. It depends upon the effect you'd like to produce."

"What foolishness! I never try to produce an effect! I am myself, Skirlet Hutsenreiter; that is effect enough for anyone! Your notion is absurd."

"Most wonderful ideas are absurd," said Jaro. "Mine especially. What are you doing here?"

Skirlet jerked her thumb toward the south. "My father and Forby Mildoon are looking over the Yellowbird property, along with a surveyor."

"What's the occasion?"

"My father wants to sell. He thinks he has a hot prospect in

Mr. Mildoon, who is very sharp, and probably unscrupulous. Worse, he belongs to one of those vulgar Square Circles: the Kahulibahs, I believe."

"I had forgotten that your father owns the property."

Skirlet said bitterly: "He doesn't own much else, which is tragic." She dropped to the ground, to sit beside Jaro. "A Clam Muffin needs wealth to maintain proper grandeur. I lack that wealth."

"But you still have your grandeur."

"Not for long."

"What of your mother? Isn't she wealthy?"

Skirlet made a dismissive gesture. "She is an interesting case—but wealthy? No." She studied Jaro sidelong. "I won't tell you unless you want to know."

"I've nothing better to do."

Skirlet pulled up her knees and hugged them. "Very well. Listen at your own peril. My mother is very beautiful. On Marmone she belongs to a social class known as the 'Sensenitza,' the 'People of Grace.' She is Naonthe, 'Princess of the Dawn,' which is quite important, and she can't be bothered with us poor provincials at Thanet. She lives at Piri-piri, which is a palace half in and half out of a garden. Every day there are festivals and banquets. The folk who come to rejoice wear remarkable costumes, and no expense is too great in the pursuit of pleasure. This goes on for half the year: the 'High Season.' Then comes the 'Low Season': the other half of the year, when the Sensenitza toil to pay off their debts. The noble People of Grace will now do anything for money. They cheat, they steal, they pander their bodies. They are avaricious beyond belief. When I visited my mother, I arrived halfway through the Low Season, and so I worked three months tending berry vines on the side of Flink Hill. It was hard work, and one of my mother's friends, the Lady Mavis, stole all my money. No one cared. Then, at the Rite of Renewal, the High Season returned. My mother was once again the Princess of Dawn, and we went to live at Piri-piri, among the flowers and pools. The Sensenitza wore their splendid new costumes and pursued joy with passionate emotion. At night there was a special music that was supposed to express both the rapture of joy and the pathos of heartbreak. I did not like the music. It was too rich and too disturbing. Beneath all the splendor, there was still the strain and yearning and avarice; though now it was concealed by elegant postures and amorous ardor. The Bal Masque was the strangest of all, so strange that I began to doubt my senses. The essence of dreams hung in the air."

Skirlet grimaced as she recalled the Bal Masque. "In the Pageant of Idylls I was assigned the role of a naked nymph skipping about a meadow. I went to hide in the forest, but some young men chased me."

"And they caught you?"

"No," said Skirlet coldly. "I climbed a tree and struck at them with branches and twigs. First they pleaded with me to come down and frolic with them, then they threw clods of dirt and cursed me and called me a freak and a virgin. Finally they went away."

"That must have been a bad experience, you a Clam Muffin and all."

Skirlet looked at him, but Jaro seemed solemn and concerned for her safety.

Jaro asked, "So, in the end, what happened?"

"Halfway through High Season, before everyone's money was gone, I stole all Lady Mavis' money. It was enough for passage back to Gallingale, so I came home. I don't think my father was pleased to see me. I wanted to go to the Aeolian Academy at Glist, which is a private school for high-caste students; my father said that we lacked money to pay the fees, which were high. He sent me down the hill to Langolen School, among the Junior Strivers and the nimps, but it was still better than Piri-piri. Now then, to answer your question: I can't expect any money from my mother."

"And you won't be going back to Marmone?"

"Most unlikely."

Jaro turned to listen, as once again the sound of far shouts drifted over the hill. He asked Skirlet, "Are they calling you?"

"No. The surveyor is shouting to his rod man." She indicated a small black disk clipped to the shoulder of her pullover. "They will call me through this button when they are ready to go."

"I thought you might be helping with the survey—taking notes, vamping Mr. Mildoon and so forth."

Skirlet looked at him incredulously. "Of course not! I just came along for the outing, and I thought I might find your hermit's den."

"This is not a den. I am not a hermit. I come here for peace and quiet."

"Aha! Would you like me to leave?"

"Now that you're here, you might as well stay. Who told you where to find me?"

Skirlet shrugged. "Dame Wirtz worries about you. She doesn't want you flinging yourself off into space. She says it's not wholesome for you to come out here to brood when you could be striving. By the way, what's in that packet?"

"Lunch. There is enough for us both."

"Naturally, I will pay for what I eat," said Skirlet proudly. "Although, now that I think of it, I'm not carrying any money."

"No matter. I will feed you free."

Skirlet had nothing to say and accepted Jaro's largesse without comment.

Jaro began to reminisce: "When I was little, I liked to think of this place as part of a magic realm, divided into four kingdoms, each with its own magic. This was the Kingdom of Daling, where I was a prince, very handsome and gallant."

"Much as you are now," said Skirlet. Jaro tried to decide whether or not she was joking. He continued. "Over yonder is the Land of Coraz, which is ruled by King Tambar the Unpredictable. Tambar owns a wardrobe where shelves support a thousand faces. Each day he goes about Coraz in a different guise, prowling the streets and listening in the market. If he hears disloyal talk, the offender loses his head on the spot. He is an amateur of magic, and knows just enough joss to make everyone's life miserable. His court seethes with intrigue, and one day the Princess Flanjear comes to Daling. The prince finds her charming, but wonders if she has come to do him harm."

Skirlet asked: "Is she beautiful?"

"Of course; in fact, you can be Princess Flanjear if you like."

"Indeed! What are my duties?"

"That hasn't been decided yet. Whatever your plans, wicked or not, you fall in love with the prince."

"And this is Prince Jaro?"

"Sometimes it has to be me," said Jaro modestly. "Often I am the only one available."

"I suppose you fall in love with Princess Flanjear?"

"Only if I can break the spell which makes all maidens seem to have long red noses. It is one of Tambar's mischiefs, of course, and goes to explain his general unpopularity."

Skirlet thoughtfully touched her nose, but said nothing. There was silence for a period. Jaro finally asked cautiously, "Will you be at Lyceum next term?"

"Nothing is settled yet."

"How so?"

"When my father sells Yellowbird Ranch, he wants to travel off-world for a year. If this came about he would close up Sassoon Ayry and send me back to Marmone."

"What do you say to that?"

"I say no. I prefer to stay at home. He said that I'd be alone in the house except for the servants. It would not be considered genteel, since, as a Clam Muffin, I must uphold high standards. I asked what he thought of the standards at Marmone; he said that was different, and whatever happened there was my mother's responsibility; also it was more economical to close up the house." Skirlet's voice became flat. "No matter what, I will not go back to Marmone."

"Doesn't your father have friends? What of the Clam Muffin Committee? Or the Academic Council? Surely there's someone who would look after you for a time. I'd do so myself, if I could."

Skirlet glanced at him sidelong. "Remarkable," she murmured to herself. Then after a moment: "I thought you were anxious to leave Gallingale yourself at full speed. What then would happen to me?"

Jaro spoke as if to a child: "I can't go anywhere or do anything until it becomes practical. That means: not soon. But, sooner or later, it must be done."

Skirlet gave a flippant gesture. "Your mindless fervor confuses me."

Jaro spoke patiently. "Someday, when you are in a serious mood, I'll tell you about it."

"I'm serious; tell me now." Jaro was not ready for another session of psychoanalysis. "It's too nice a day."

"Tell me this, at least. How do you know what you must do, or where to go?"

Jaro shrugged. "The knowing is there."

"What kind of knowing? Dates and places?"

Jaro had already said more than he had intended. Still, he went on. "Sometimes I can almost hear my mother's voice—but I can never understand the words. Sometimes I seem to see a tall gaunt man wearing a magister's coat and a black hat. His face is pale and hard, as if it were carved from bone. The thought of him makes me shiver—I suppose with fear."

Skirlet sat hugging her knees. "And you intend to find this man?"

Jaro gave a short laugh. "If I go looking, I will find him."

"And then?"

"I haven't planned that far ahead."

Skirlet rose to her feet. She spoke not unkindly: "Do you care to hear my opinion?"

"Not particularly."

Skirlet paid no heed. "It's clear that you are suffering from a severe obsession, which might be close to dementia."

"You may discard that analysis," said Jaro. "The psychiatrists said I was sane. They admired my strength of character."

"No matter. These so-called mysteries have no urgency to them. If you rush off into space, what can you hope to find? A man wearing a hat? Face facts, Jaro! You are victim of what psychiatrists call a 'fixed idea.' "

"If you please, Skirlet, I am neither unbalanced nor insane."

"Then you should act correctly. Prepare for a degree at the Institute, as the Faths suggest! Give thought to your comporture and start striving up the ledges!"

Jaro gazed up at her in wonder. Surely she could not be serious! "All very well," said Jaro, "but I don't want to do any of these things. I don't want to be a Zonker or a Sick Chicken or a Palindrome, or even a Clam Muffin."

Skirlet spoke with disgust. "It is sad! Despite all the Faths have done, you still are at heart an off-worlder! You don't respect anything or anyone—not the Faths, nor the Clam Muffins, nor any of the faculty, nor even me!"

Jaro scrambled to his feet, grinning. Finally it was all clear! "I know why you are angry with me."

"Ridiculous! Why should I be angry?"

"Do you really want to know?"

"I'll listen, certainly."

"The answer comes in two parts. The first is that I am too complacent and don't notice any of the really important things, such as how wonderful it is to be a Clam Muffin and at the same time so marvelously pretty and so intelligent! But I do notice! I am startled by the person of Skirlet Hutsenreiter and her accomplishments! Her vanity is justified!"

"What nonsense!" scoffed Skirlet. "I am not at all vain. What is the second part?"

Jaro hesitated. "It's so secret I can only whisper it into your ear."

"That is not reasonable! Why must it be?"

"Those are the rules."

"Oh very well." Skirlet tilted her head; Jaro bent toward her ear. Skirlet cried out: "Ooh! You bit my ear! That's not what you were supposed to do."

"No," said Jaro. "You are right. I made a mistake and it was wrong of me. Let's try again."

Skirlet looked at him skeptically. "I'm not sure that I trust you."

"Of course you can! Your ear is safe. I won't blow, pant, or nip."

Skirlet came to a decision. She shook her head. "It's quite absurd! You should be brave enough to tell me to my face."

"Very well, if you think that's the best way. Close your eyes."

"Whyever for?"

"So that I won't be embarrassed."

"I can't imagine why you need such preparations." Skirlet closed her eyes and Jaro kissed her. On the second time she kissed him back. "Now! You've got that out of your system! So tell me."

"I'd rather kiss you."

"No," said Skirlet breathlessly. "Once is enough."

"It was twice."

"Still it makes me feel funny, and I don't think I'm up to it. Not yet."

The call-button at Skirlet's shoulder sounded a small tinkling chime. A voice uttered peremptory instructions. Skirlet responded, hesitated, looked toward Jaro, but quickly turned away. She studied the slope, picked out an expeditious route, gave Jaro a wave of farewell, then was gone.

Jaro watched until she had disappeared over the ridge, then gathered his belongings and returned to Merriehew House.

3

Skirlet was absent from school the first three days of the week. When she returned, she seemed moody and conducted herself with none of the old gallant derring-do which had provided the thrust for so many unpredictable exploits. She ignored Jaro, and looked away when he approached. Jaro was not pleased with her manner and conducted himself with lofty indifference, while watching her from the corner of his eye. She seemed not to notice and went her way at her usual half trot, her nondescript catch-as-catch-can garments magically transformed into raiment of dramatic flair, because it was she, Skirlet Hutsenreiter, with her taut little body which animated them.

Jaro was troubled on other accounts. His old easy relationship with the Faths had clouded over with a trace of reserve, induced principally by their refusal to inform him of his past. They were not about to encourage any reckless forays into space; when he had taken his degree they would tell him everything they knew. Jaro tried his best to put aside hurt feelings, but a residue remained.

Hilyer and Althea were aware of the changes. Rather hollowly they told themselves that Jaro was growing up and no longer could be considered a little boy. "He is defining autonomy for himself," was Hilyer's rather ponderous comment. "Such are the facts of life."

Althea was less objective. "I don't like such facts! They come too fast, just when I'm getting used to the old ones!"

"Ah well," said Hilyer. "There's nothing we can do about it, except encourage him in the right direction."

"But he is so single-minded! He told me he wants to work at the space terminal this summer!"

Hilyer shrugged. "He's still very young. Give him time to grow up and learn the ways of the world; he'll see reason after a bit."

The thought that he might be hurting the Faths caused Jaro frequent twinges of conscience. Hilyer, despite his occasional crustiness, was gentle, patient and generous; Althea overflowed with love. Still, Jaro's intentions were fixed and the estrangement would persist until Jaro had accomplished what needed to be done. Jaro wondered how many years would pass, what adventures would befall him, how many dangers he must overcome, before he achieved his goal. The idea was daunting. Somewhere along the way, he was likely to meet the man in the black hat, with the glitter of four-pointed stars in his eyes. What of Skirlet? The darling, reckless, proud, fascinating, tart and pungent, sweet and sulky Skirlet! Marvel of marvels! He had kissed her and she had kissed him! Would they ever come together again? And then there was Tawn Maihac, who might return as abruptly as he had gone. Jaro hoped so. He needed a friend.

Two days before the end of the school term Skirlet once more absented herself from school, nor did she appear at the matriculation ceremonies. She had been designated the class spokesman, both by reason of her status and her near-perfect scholarship ratings. Her absence caused distress and confusion, and the authorities decided that a substitute must be selected. Jaro Fath was considered one of the possibilities, since his ratings were also of a high order and his so-called 'citizenship record' was unblemished. However, he was a nimp and could not be considered a suitable exemplar for a class of strivers, and in the end a youth named Dylan Underwood, who had already been accepted into the Bad Gang, was selected. Jaro could not have cared less. During the evening he was approached by Dame Wirtz, who first shook his hand, then hugged him. "I'll miss you, Jaro, very much! You're a pleasure to have in the class—even though you are a wrong-headed young renegade, and I can only hope that you don't come to a bad end."

"I hope so, too. By the way, what happened to Skirlet? Why isn't she here?"

Dame Wirtz gave a rueful laugh. "Her father is Dean Hutsenreiter; he's a Clam Muffin, but still he is as wild as the wind. He never approved of Skirlet's association with Langolen School, since it brought her into contact with the most vulgar and importunate striving. He definitely did not want her representing the class; such an office diminished her dignity, and there you have it."

"Hmf. What of next term? Is she going on to Lyceum?"

Dame Wirtz gave her head a dubious shake. "Who knows what will happen to her? There was talk of a private school, Aeolian Academy at Glist, on Axelbarren: a very fine school, but very expensive."

Jaro stoically attended graduation ceremonies, and stood by in embarrassment as both Dame Wirtz and Althea wept tears of sentiment. Never again, Jaro told himself, if I can possibly avoid it.

The summer recess began. Before a week had passed, Jaro received a rather mysterious call from Skirlet. He spoke cautiously, wondering what would be required of him. "Jaro here."

Skirlet's voice came back crisp and edgy, as if she were nervous. "What are you doing?"

"At the moment nothing much. What about you?"

"The same."

"Where were you during graduation?"

Skirlet's tone became even more crisp. "I stayed home, naturally. For once I agreed with my father. He told me that as a Clam Muffin, my excellence was taken for granted; that if I accepted honors at commencement, I would seem ostentatious and not at all dignified. He was, of course, right."

"Wrong. Dignity is when you do not care, or even notice, one way or the other."

"No matter!" snapped Skirlet. "It is quite irrelevant. I want you to come here at once, while my father is gone."

"Where is here?"

"At Sassoon Ayry, of course! Come to the garden entrance, beside the south lawn. Be discreet."

Jaro obeyed instructions, and with some trepidation made his way through the gardens which surrounded Sassoon Ayry to the door Skirlet had designated. She was waiting, and took him to a room which she identified as her father's private study. Cases lined the walls, displaying curios, objects of virtu, including a fine collection of ritual dolls. A desk beside the window supported a litter of pamphlets, documents, brochures, proposals, smartly bound in blue paper.

"This is where my father achieves his financial successes," said Skirlet sardonically. "His ledger is yonder." She picked it up and showed Jaro the last page. He saw a massive block of numbers printed in red. Skirlet tossed the ledger back on the desk. "Very sad. It is the reason for this meeting of the Mediators."

" 'Mediators'? Mediating what?"

"Injustice, avarice, inequity. For the moment, these details need not concern you."

Jaro moved toward the door. "In that case I'll leave, and you can sort out the details by yourself. If the truth be known, I'm not all that comfortable here."

Skirlet ignored his qualms. "Please listen carefully. The Mediators are an exclusive club, whose members enjoy a very high prestige. By comparison, the Sempiternals seem inept and insipid, though we acknowledge their existence. Our goals are inspiring. We explore regions of grandeur and beauty, which others have ignored, and we right wrongs whenever they lie within our scope."

"All very well," said Jaro, "but doesn't this take up a great deal of time?"

"Just so," said Skirlet. "For this reason the Mediators occasionally recruit new members."

"How many members are now active?"

Skirlet frowned, as if calculating. "Up to this moment, the

Mediators have been fanatically exclusive. In fact, the only member is myself. All other applicants have been rejected."

"Hmf. The standards must be strict."

Skirlet shrugged. "To some extent. Persons of free spirit are not excluded on that basis alone. Applicants must be clean, polite and intelligent. Also, they should not be sluggish, vulgar or talkative."

Skirlet went on to say that, while musing over admission requirements, the name 'Jaro' had surfaced into her mind and he was welcome to apply for membership, if he so desired. "Prestige, of course, is automatic," she told him, "since I am involved and we are fearfully exclusive."

Jaro agreed that there was nothing to lose. He applied for membership on the spot and was accepted.

To celebrate the occasion, Skirlet went to a cupboard and returned with a bottle of Dean Hutsenreiter's most expensive liquor. She poured out two tots. "This liquor, so I am told, is over two hundred years old, and in mythical times was used to appease the Gods of Thunder."

Skirlet cautiously tasted the dark red liquor. She winced. "It is strong but palatable. Well then, to our agenda. The Mediators on hand make up a quorum, so that we can get about our principal business."

"And what is this business?"

"The most immediate problem concerns half the membership, which is to say, me. My father is soon to be off on a grand junket, first to Canopus Planet, and then to Old Earth. He will be gone at least a year and he always travels first class. In order to conserve funds, he wants to close up Sassoon Ayry, and bundle me off to my mother on Marmone. I prefer to stay at home, even if it means that I must attend Lyceum. He says this is impossible. I said in that case he could send me to Aeolian Academy at Glist. This is a very enlightened school. The students are lodged in private suites, where they are served their meals to order. They study topics of their own choosing, at their own pace and are encouraged to cultivate social relationships as they see fit. The academy overlooks the Greater Kanjieir Sea, and the city Glist is nearby. I explained to my father that I would be happy to attend Aeolian Academy, but he said that it was far too expensive, and that it was time my mother took responsibility for my education. I said that at Piri-piri I would be taught more than

I wanted to learn, and that I would be happy either at Sassoon Ayry or at the Aeolian Academy. He became quite short, and told me that I could apply to the Clam Muffin Committee and they would put me into what is called 'supervised habitancy,' which would be depressing. Money, of course, is the main problem and this is the deficiency which the Mediators must repair."

Skirlet rose to her feet. "Another half-gill or so of this liquor might stimulate our thinking."

Jaro watched in fascination as Skirlet replenished his goblet. "You have thought how best to acquire these funds?"

"Blackmail may be best," said Skirlet. "It is quick and easy and special skills are unnecessary."

There was the sound of footsteps. The door opened; Dean Hutsenreiter burst into the room: a thin man, wearing a natty suit of pearl-gray silverstrack. He was pale, with skin stretched taut over the angular bones of his face; soft brown hair flowed back from a receding forehead and down to the nape of his neck. He seemed in a state of nervous emotion; his eyes darted about the room and finally came to rest on the bottle which Skirlet still held poised over Jaro's goblet. Hutsenreiter cried out in a fury: "What is going on here? Some sort of drinkfest, with my priceless Bagongo?" He snatched the bottle from Skirlet's grip. "Explain yourself, if you please!"

Jaro gallantly stepped forward and spoke with formal politeness. "Sir, we were engaged in a calm and interesting conversation; your agitation is out of order!"

Dean Hutsenreiter's jaw dropped. Then he threw his hands wildly into the air. "If I must accept insolence in my own house, I might as well go out and lie in the street, where the cost is less." He turned to Skirlet. "Who is this fellow?"

Jaro again responded. "Sir, I am Jaro Fath. My parents are members of the Institute faculty, in the College of Aesthetic Philosophy."

"Faths? I know them. They are nimps! Is this your license for entering my house, sorting through my papers, drinking my choice liquor, and preparing to seduce my daughter?"

Jaro started to protest, but Dean Hutsenreiter became more agitated than ever. "Do you realize that you are lolling in my favorite chair! Up with you and out! Never return to this house! Out with you, this instant!"

Skirlet said wearily: "You had better go, before he becomes angry."

Jaro went to the door. He turned, bowed to Dean Hutsenreiter and departed.

A week passed, during which Jaro heard nothing of Skirlet. One afternoon Dame Wirtz dropped by Merriehew to recruit Althea's help at a horticultural exhibition. Jaro chanced to pass through the room. He greeted Dame Wirtz and during their conversation, he asked in regard to Skirlet. Dame Wirtz was surprised. "Didn't you hear? Dean Hutsenreiter found it necessary to close his house for the summer, so he sent Skirlet off to a private school: Aeolian Academy at Glist, on Axelbarren, I believe. It's a fine school, and Skirlet should consider herself lucky. I wish the best for her, but the Reach is wide and we may never see her again."

"I'm not so sure," said Jaro. "Here she is a Clam Muffin; anywhere else just a Hutsenreiter."

4

During the summer recess Jaro worked at the space terminal machine shop. Trio Hartung posted him as assistant to the squat and burly machinist, with a stubble of gray hair, weather-darkened skin and an evil leer, named Gaing Neitzbeck. Jaro recalled that Tawn Maihac had introduced them.

Hartung took Jaro aside. "Don't be deceived by Gaing's appearance. He is not as kind and patient as he looks."

Jaro glanced dubiously toward Gaing, who, so he thought, looked anything but kind and patient. His face was a tragic mummer's mask, with glinting eyes and a heavy low nose which had been broken either so badly, or so often, that it splayed first one direction, then the other. Gaing's shoulders and chest were deep; his arms long; his legs heavy and strong. He stood at a crouch and moved by hops and lurches.

Hartung said: "For a fact, Gaing is an ugly lump, but he knows all there is to know about spaceships and space. Just obey orders, speak only when necessary, and you'll get along well enough."

Jaro approached Gaing. "Sir, I am ready to work whenever it is convenient."

"Very well," said Gaing. "I'll show you what needs to be done."

Jaro discovered that Gaing's procedure was to assign work,

then go away and leave Jaro to his own devices until the job was done, and then subject the work to careful scrutiny. The procedure left Jaro untroubled and even grimly amused, since he already had determined to do the work perfectly if not better. Jaro therefore incurred few reprimands, and these were perfunctory grumbles, as if Gaing were disappointed not to find real reason for complaint. Jaro gradually relaxed. He meticulously followed instructions and spoke only when Gaing spoke first, which obviously suited Gaing well. Jaro was assigned all the dirty jobs Gaing himself wished to avoid. Jaro set upon each new job with energy and zeal, trying to complete it both efficiently and well, if only as a challenge to Gaing to do his worst.

Jaro found Gaing impossible to dislike. Gaing was neither small minded nor unfair, and when necessary he spared himself no more than he did Jaro. Further, Jaro began to discern complex traits in Gaing's character which Gaing did his best to conceal.

Jaro soon understood that if he attended to business and learned whatever Gaing could or would teach him, he would ultimately become a most excellent and versatile mechanic.

Halfway through the summer Trio Hartung chanced to meet Jaro in the corridor. Halting, he asked how affairs were going.

"Very well," said Jaro.

"And how are you getting along with Gaing?"

Jaro grinned. "I do my best not to annoy him. I'm beginning to understand what a remarkable man he is."

Hartung nodded. "He is that, well enough. He has led an eventful life, traveled far and wide: Beyond, and who knows where else? I'm told that he worked for the IPCC, teaching combat skills to recruits, but I think that IPCC neatness and order wore him down."

"That's amazing," said Jaro. "I would not like to come upon him in the dark if he were annoyed with me."

"Small chance of that," said Hartung. "Gaing likes you. He says you are a good worker, that you don't shirk and are more stubborn than he is himself; also, that you don't bother him with foolish talk. From Gaing, this is high approval, and he'd never tell you himself."

Jaro grinned. "I'm glad at least to hear the news from you." Hartung started to turn away, then paused. "You are starting Lyceum, I think you said?"

"In about a month."

"If you like, I'll find part-time work for you, whenever it fits your schedule."

"Thank you very much, Mr. Hartung."

SEVEN

1

Jaro's first two years at Lyceum passed in relative tranquility. He opted for a basic curriculum, emphasizing the sciences, mathematics and technics. During his first year he also undertook three electives, which he hoped might please the Faths: Elements of Harmony; A Historical Survey of Music, and instruction in the playing of the suanola. This was an instrument based upon the ancient concertina, with a pump supplying the air flow and toggled keys controlling both upper and lower registers. The Faths considered the suanola a trivial, or even vulgar, instrument but refrained from criticism, so as not to demean Jaro's efforts to please them. Jaro, however knew his limitations: he was accurate but over-meticulous in his phrasing and lacked the wild, slightly discordant, passion which distinguished musicians from practitioners. His skills were adequate to playing with a small orchestra, the Arcadian Mountebanks, where he wore the costume of a Gitanque sheepherder. The group played casually at parties, picnics, fiestas and riverboat excursions.

The Faths, in general, approved of Jaro's schedule, which was challenging; they could almost hope that he verged toward the Institute and the College of Aesthetic Philosophy. This hope was diminished when Jaro, by dint of early rising, was able to work at the spaceport terminal four hours each weekend morning.

As Jaro had expected neither Hilyer nor Althea was pleased. Hilyer adopted his most pedantic manner: "The time you waste in that shop could be put to more constructive use."

"I'll be learning how to repair and perhaps operate a spaceship," said Jaro mildly. "Don't you think that's useful knowledge?"

"No. Not really. It's a job for specialists. Space is the void between civilized environments. Space is not a destination in itself. Any romance you apply to this sort of work is factitious."

Jaro grinned. "Don't worry; if I can't keep up with my schoolwork, I'll let the job drop."

Hilyer knew that Jaro would do all that was required without apparent effort. Still, he was not defeated. "From what you tell me, they are fobbing off the most menial jobs upon you: sorting out bits of this and that, cleaning up slops, running errands for a surly mechanic."

"Unfortunately this is true," said Jaro. "Still, someone must do these jobs. Since I'm new, I do them. Also, Gaing's not so bad when you get to know him. He likes me well enough; when he sees me now he grunts instead of pretending I don't exist. Meanwhile, little by little, I'm learning what makes a spaceship fly."

"I still don't understand it," said Hilyer peevishly. "What good is that sort of knowledge to someone with your prospects! Nor can you be attracted by the wages, which are not excessive. You don't even spend your allowance, according to your mother, but scuttle it away in a jam jar."

"True! But I want to earn money for a special purpose."

"What purpose is this?" demanded Hilyer coldly, though he already knew.

Jaro nevertheless answered politely. "I want to learn the truth about myself. It's a mystery which I can't get out of my mind, and I won't rest until I unravel it. But I won't ask you to finance what might be a wild goose chase. I'll try to earn money of my own."

Hilyer made an impatient gesture. "For the present you must ignore this mystery; a degree at the Institute is prerequisite to a secure life. Without it, you are a will-o'-the-wisp or a vagabond."

Jaro remained silent and Hilyer continued, his voice stern: "I strongly urge that you postpone this quest—which in any event is likely to be futile. First things must come first. Your mother and I will help you without stint to gain a proper education—but we will resist any other course as being against your better interests."

Althea came into the room. Neither Hilyer nor Jaro wished to pursue the subject and it was dropped.

2

For Jaro the first three years at Lyceum slipped by so smoothly that, later, when he cast his mind back, they merged indistinguishably, one with the other. They were the last of the halcyon times, and never again would life be so tranquil.

Still, the years were not without event; there were a hundred gradual changes. Jaro grew several inches, to become an erect square-shouldered youth, moderately muscular, though lacking in bulk through chest, flanks, arms and legs, quiet and self-contained in manner. When girls gathered to discuss their affairs, they generally agreed that Jaro was handsome, in an austere way, like the fairy barons of romantic legend. How distressing and sad that he was a nimp!

During the recess following Jaro's third year he was allowed to work full time at the terminal machine shop. One day he undertook an especially complicated job. Things went right for him and he finished in what he considered good time. He tested the mechanism with meters and field gauges; all seemed well and he signed the worksheet. Turning, he found Gaing standing nearby, his corded face unreadable. Jaro could only hope that he had performed the procedures properly. Gaing glanced at Jaro's worksheet, then spoke, using a soft husky voice Jaro had not heard before. "That's a nice bit of work you've done, lad. You did it nice; you did it fast, and you did it right."

"Thank you, sir," said Jaro.

Gaing went on: "From now on you may regard yourself as 'assistant mechanic,' and there will be a corresponding increase in your salary." He reached up to a shelf and brought down a gnarled jug formed of lavender-gray stonemelt. He pulled away the stopper and poured dollops of amber liquid into a pair of squat stoneware cups. "The occasion calls for a taste of the Old Particular, which you may be sure is not offered around freely." He pushed one of the cups toward Jaro. "Let us salute your new status!"

Jaro eyed the sultry liquid dubiously. The sharing of Old Particular had the force of a ritual, so he understood, and he must play his part properly. He turned to face Gaing. Joining valor to stoicism, he raised the cup and said: "Your good health, sir."

Gaing lifted his own cup, nodded and drank from it. Standing stiffly, Jaro lowered the draught to his mouth, swallowed a goodly portion. Now then! Fortitude and calm! He must neither strangle nor cough; he must show only polite gratification.

The liquid finally reached his stomach, where it subsided. Jaro slowly exhaled. He knew that a comment was expected of him. But first things first, as Hilyer would say. He raised his squat cup and in a single gulp drank what was left of the Old Particular. He blinked and put down the cup and tried to speak with decision: "I am not an experienced judge, but I would think this to be of superior quality. My instinct, at least, tells me as much."

"This instinct has served you well!" intoned Gaing. "You have discovered an important truth, and your candor is refreshing. One can learn much of a fellow by heeding the way he drinks his drop. Folk speak of what is closest to their hearts, and the variety is as endless as the Gaean race itself! I have heard grief and bereavement; also, songs of joy, sometimes in the same quarter-hour. Some men speak of their pedigree and the grandeur that is rightfully theirs; others confide secrets. Some talk of beautiful women, while others recall a kindly mother." Gaing raised the jug and looked inquiringly at Jaro. "Would you care for another half-gill? No? Perhaps you are right, since we have work to do. Tomorrow, incidentally, we will be giving the black Scarab yonder its final checkout." He referred to a sleek black spaceyacht, somewhat more compact than the *Pharsang*, but still an imposing vehicle.

Jaro could hardly find his voice. "Just you and me?"

"Correct! This job has now been assigned to us. It is time that you should start learning the checkout procedures."

Jaro returned to Merriehew in happy excitement. His new level of employment represented a large increase in status; he could now legitimately speak of himself as a spaceship mechanic, and presently he would learn to operate as well as repair a spaceship.

3

Three weeks later, at the end of his shift, Jaro walked along the line of dormant spaceyachts. As he approached the *Pharsang* Glitterway, he came upon Lyssel Bynnoc waiting restlessly beside the ship, while a pair of elderly gentlemen examined a map which they had spread out upon the starboard sponson. The older and more vigorous of the two dominated the discussion. He uttered terse stipulations, jabbed at the map with a stiff forefinger, while the other's comments went ignored.

Both gentlemen wore expensive garments and carried themselves with the assurance of high comporture. The eldest was tall, spare, with a long pale face, a mane of white hair and a pointed white goatee. His manner was crisp, and serene. The second gentleman was portly and sleek, with a powdered pink complexion and dog-brown eyes.

Lyssel leaned against the *Pharsang*'s port sponson, tapping her fingers against the glossy black surface. She noticed the approach of a personable young man; here was a possible relief from boredom. She arranged herself in a posture of lazy indifference; not until the young man drew near did she turn her head and fix her melting blue gaze upon him. To her surprise she recognized Jaro, whom she remembered from Langolen School. The acquaintance had been distant, since Lyssel always had more prestigious fish to fry: earnest strivers such as Hanafer Glackenshaw, Alger Oals, Kosh Diffenbocker and others of the same up-ledge ilk. Great things were predicted for such as these, and some had already been seconded into the Squared Circle Junior Auxiliary. Lyssel herself had been then and was now an energetic striver, with secret techniques of her own, which had gained her the black and silver clip of the important Jinkers. She liked prestige, but she enjoyed the functioning of her natural instincts even more, and was pleased to see Jaro, though she remembered little about him.

Jaro's reaction to Lyssel was more direct and similar to that of other healthy young males. He wanted to approach her, pay his respects and, after a minimum of polite preliminaries, carry her off to bed. Over the years, Lyssel had changed little. Fine dusty-golden hair flowed almost to her shoulders, the locks waving and swinging as she moved. Her eyes were round, innocent, and blue in a rather thin face, where a wide mouth continually jerked and altered to the butterfly flicker of her thoughts—smiling, pouting, pursing, twisting askew, sagging at the corners in comic remorse, or with teeth clenched over her lower lip, as if she were a child caught out in a naughty act. Her body was slight and flexible, and when she was excited it squirmed with the unruly energy of a small affectionate animal. Girls were wary of her and in her company felt like frumps. The boys, however, were fascinated and she was the topic of endless speculation. Was there fire behind the smoke? No one, so it seemed, had ever learned the truth, though many had given the problem their serious attention. She spoke with a gay lilt: "You're Jaro, aren't you?" Then she waited, as if expecting his sheepish grin of gladness at being noticed.

Jaro responded politely: "I'm Jaro. I've seen you at the Lyceum."

Lyssel nodded, thinking that Jaro seemed just a bit pompous, or perhaps even dull. "What are you doing around here?"

"No mystery; I'm working at the machine shop."

"Of course! I remember now! You're the brave boy who wants to become a spaceman!"

Jaro detected the tinkle of mockery, which Lyssel sometimes used to relieve boredom, much as a kitten sharpens its claws on the best furniture. He gave a disinterested shrug. The gibe had caused no reaction; Lyssel became nettled. She blew out her cheeks and wrinkled her nose to imply, in a sophisticated way, that she found Jaro rather tiresome. But Jaro had been looking over her head toward the *Pharsang*, and failed to notice. Lyssel scowled. Jaro was a nimp, hence dull and sober. Sober? She eyed him narrowly, and asked, "Why are you smiling?"

Jaro looked at her innocently. She went on: "It's not flattering to find you laughing at me."

Jaro, now grinning openly, said, "If the truth be known, I was admiring the view."

Lyssel's delicate jaw relaxed so that her mouth sagged open. Mystified, she asked, "What view?"

"The *Pharsang*, with you standing in front. It's like a page from an advertising brochure."

Lyssel's annoyance diminished. "So even a nimp can be gallant."

Jaro raised his eyebrows, started to speak, checked himself, then asked, "Who are your friends?"

Lyssel glanced toward the two elderly gentlemen. "They're persons of extremely high comporture: a Val Verde and a Kahulibah." She looked to see if Jaro were impressed, but discovered only mild curiosity. She indicated the plump gentleman: "That's my Uncle Forby Mildoon. The other, with the satanic goatee is Gilfong Rute. He owns the *Pharsang*, curse him!" Lyssel directed a disrespectful grimace against Rute's back. Noticing Jaro's startled expression, she explained, "He's absolutely exasperating, and irrational, to boot."

Jaro looked toward the gentleman in question. "He seems rational enough from here."

Lyssel could not believe her ears. "You can't be serious!"

"I'm just judging by the look of his backside," Jaro admitted.

"That's not the best way."

"Well then: what does he do from the front that is irrational?"

"He has owned the *Pharsang* for five years and has taken her up into space only once. Does that sound sane?"

"He might be troubled with space sickness, or vertigo. Why do you care?"

"I care very much and so does my Uncle Forby! Mr. Rute promised to sell him the *Pharsang* at a very low price, but now he backs and fills, and quotes first one price, then another, all absurdly high."

"It sounds as if he's not ready to sell."

Lyssel glowered toward Gilfong Rute. "If so, it's most inconsiderate of him."

"How so?"

"Because my Uncle Forby has promised to take me on a yearlong cruise as soon as he buys the *Pharsang*. But I'll be old and wrinkled before that day comes!"

"Don't fret," said Jaro. "As soon as I get my own spaceyacht, I'll take you out behind Wiggs' Wisp for a year or maybe two."

Lyssel haughtily raised her eyebrows. "You'd be required to bring my mother along as chaperone, and she might not want to go. She's a High Bustamonte and is intolerant of the lower ledges. If she knew you were a nimp, she'd call you 'schmeltzer' and put you off the ship."

"She'd put me off my own ship?"

"Yes, indeed, if she thought it correct."

Jaro had nothing to say in the face of this assertion. Lyssel leaned back against the ship and studied her fingernails. She was becoming bored with Jaro. He was nice looking in a sanitary sort of way, but he lacked the flair and hell-for-leather panache which made certain other young men more exciting company. Jaro, she thought unkindly, was limp and timid, just like any other nimp.

Lyssel looked over her shoulder, wondering how her uncle Forby was faring in his attempt to influence Gilfong Rute. Not well, to judge by his sagging jowls.

Jaro asked, "What are they discussing?"

"Oh—just business," said Lyssel airily. "Some sort of big construction development. If all goes well, and Mr. Rute invests, our problems are over. I'm supposed to help out by exerting my sweet blue-eyed innocence."

Forby Mildoon rolled up the map; the two men entered the ship, with Lyssel following. At the entry she looked back with an expression of unreadable import, then disappeared within. Jaro shrugged and went his way.

Eight

1

Three days later both Hilyer and Althea were promoted to full professorships, with substantial increments of stipend. Their status was also augmented, to such an extent that they were elected into the Altroverts: an unconventional non-strivers club of intelligentsia, non-conformists, nimps in high places and other free-thinkers, and even a few Lemurians.

The Faths pretended disinterest in their new status, but secretly they were delighted by the recognition, which they considered not only well deserved, but also long overdue. They even started to consider entertaining certain of their new associates at Merriehew House. "I haven't really used my lovely candelabra in ages," Althea sighed. "But also, Hilyer—please don't grumble—there's no denying that the old place needs to be smarted up both inside and out, and now we can afford it, there's no further reason to put it off. Then when we invite folk, such as Professor Chabath and Dame Intricx over for the evening, we won't be made to feel like vagabonds."

"I don't mind feeling like a vagabond," said Hilyer, who had a tendency toward frugality. "If anyone cares to fix that interpretation upon my conduct—well, then, let them have at it!"

Althea was not deceived by her husband's brave words. "Come now, Hilyer, I know that you enjoy dinner parties as much as I do, but you are just too stubborn to admit it."

Hilyer laughed. "Yes and no. If you want the truth, I'm afraid of spending a great deal of money to no good purpose."

"I don't understand what you mean!"

"You remember that rumor twenty years ago, about new suburbs and expansions from town? Well, I heard a whisper of the same sort of talk yesterday and I believe that, sooner or later, it's bound to happen."

"But not for a hundred years!" protested Althea. "Thanet has already expanded eastward, over the hills and into Vervil. Why should it suddenly explode in this direction?"

"You may be right," said Hilyer. "But if you're wrong, then it's to our interest to be out and away from the district before the congestion begins; and in this regard I had a casual offer for Merriehew house and grounds this morning."

"Indeed! Who from?"

"From the same person as before: a real estate type named

Forby Mildoon. He mentioned that he controlled several very nice homes in the Catterline district, and that if we could come up with ten thousand sols, along with what he called our old barn of a place, he'd let us have one of the houses. He pointed out that the houses were situated just over the hill from the Institute and hence very convenient."

Althea drew in her breath. "And what did you say to that?"

"I just laughed at him and told him his price was far too high. He said, very reasonably, that our place could hardly be sold at all in its present condition, but that he might come down perhaps a thousand sols, if we'd agree to certain conditions. I said that still was too high; and finally I badgered him down to sixty-five hundred sols and our property, but I stressed I could make no deal until I conferred with you and Jaro. He wanted to know what Jaro had to say about the case, and I told him that since Jaro expected ultimately to inherit Merriehew, and since he loved the place, his feelings must be respected. I told him that if he wanted to drop Merrihew from the deal, we might consider one of his houses at seventy-six hundred, or even eight thousand, as he had suggested."

Althea said scornfully, "I wouldn't want to live in one of those boxy little Catterline cottages under any circumstances; they're all built one on top the next in tiers! I could become angry at the wretched man for suggesting such a thing! It's truly an insult, and not so subtle as all that!"

On the following day Hilyer, in his office at the Institute, received a telephone call from Forby Mildoon. Mildoon spoke in jovial tones: "If you recall, we had a conversation as to your possible interest in a Catterline property. By the sheerest coincidence, an off-world client approached me this morning for exploration purposes. He intimated that he might be interested in a rustic property, somewhat out of town, which could be converted into a restaurant of a certain type. I thought at once of Merriehew. Now I don't want to encourage you with visions of wealth; he is operating on the cheap, and my commission would amount to little, but I have calculated that with your sixty-five hundred sols and Merriehew property, I could fit you into a lovely cottage in the splendid Catterline district, practically next door to the Institute."

Hilyer said crisply, "I'm afraid you must forget that proposition, Mr. Mildoon. In the first place, my son Jaro won't hear of it—"

Forby Mildoon's voice took on a peevish energy: "It seems to me that he should not be allowed to interfere with your comfort and convenience! After all, if I may say so, Merriehew is not a dignified residence for a pair of high-status academicians! It looks more like a resort for hoodlums and vagabonds."

"My wife is not interested in the Catterline district. She considers it common and vulgar, and asked if your own residence were in the Catterline."

"No, it is not," said Mildoon rather haughtily. "I live in Chermond Park Estates."

"I see. Well, it makes no great difference, since I think that we may safely consider the topic exhausted of all further interest. Good day to you!"

"Good day, sir," said Mildoon behind clenched teeth.

2

Toward the end of the Fall Term the Arcadian Mountebanks were hired to play at the Bumblebosters' Panics, a festival sponsored by the Isograms, a Squared Circle junior auxiliary. The Panics was a yearly occasion, celebrating the aggregate comporture of the Squared Circle Quadrants. For weeks volunteers and professionals had decorated the Surcy Pavilion to represent a street in the mythical town Poowaddle. False fronts simulated buildings of an unlikely architecture; balconies held lumpy pneumatic buffoons, caparisoned in the traditional Poowaddle costume: tall crooked hats with wide brims supporting burbling baluk birds and brass-footed squeakers; loose pantaloons, enormous shoes with up-curling toes. The merry Poowaddlers, who thronged the promenade, were expected to wear one or another version of the Poowaddle costume. Booths alongside the parade would serve free tankards of "Booble": a potion brewed from secret recipes but always more or less the same. Three orchestras, including the Arcadian Mountebanks, had been hired to play jigs and gallivants and it was said that if an Isogram failed to enjoy himself at the Bumblebosters' Panics, he was either dead or somewhere else.

At the time stipulated, the Arcadian Mountebanks took their places in a simulated grotto overlooking the central promenade. Thousands of minute purple and green lights twinkled above them, creating a soft illumination of indescribable color.

The Mountebanks played with their usual zeal, and at the end of their stint descended from the grotto in order to rest and take refreshment. Like the others, Jaro wore the costume of a Gitanque nomad: tight breeches of black velveteen, a grey-brown smock embroidered with rose-pink frogging, a loose cap of dark scarlet, with a long black tassel swinging over his left ear. Turning to survey the promenade, Jaro found himself face to face with a pair of revelers: Lyssel Bynnoc and a young man costumed as a Bumbleboster bravo.

Lyssel stopped short, stared. She wore an ankle-length skirt of soft white web, a black vest and a tiara of green agapanthus leaves, as might circle the brow of a woodland nymph. She cried out in hushed surprise: "Jaro! Is it truly Jaro the spaceman?"

Jaro admitted his identity. Odd! Lyssel, as usual, looked vivacious, fascinating, ready for whatever mischief might be afoot—in short, nothing extraordinary. Still, Jaro could not help but notice an odd discord. At their last meeting, she had not troubled to disguise the utter boredom she felt in his company. Why, then, the glad excitement she now displayed? Caprice? Perhaps.

Lyssel took stock of his costume, then looked up to the stage where Jaro had left his instrument. She asked in wonder, "Are you also a musician?"

"I get paid, if that proves anything."

"I see a suanola up there. Is that yours? Or do you play something silly, like the twittering toothpicks or the galloping spoons?"

"Just the suanola. The spoons are too much for me."

"Come, Jaro! You're far too modest, and it's not convincing!"

The Bumbleboster bravo took her arm. "This way, Lyssie. Our table is ready."

Lyssel worked to disengage herself. "Just a moment. I must think."

Her escort impatiently tried to lead her away. "Come along, Lyssie! Think at the table! There's nothing here to detain us!"

Lyssel pulled her arm from his grasp. "Kosh, don't be so masterful, and do stop that tugging! You'll pull my arm from the socket!"

"We'll lose our table," growled Kosh, with one antagonistic eye on Jaro.

Lyssel saw the chance for mischief. "Excuse me; I've been rude! Jaro, this is Kosh Diffenbocker. Kosh, this is Jaro Fath."

Kosh looked in puzzlement from Jaro to Lyssel, then spoke

impatiently: "Come along, Lyssie, enough of this foolishness! We'll lose our table if we don't hurry!"

Lyssel gave him a little shove. "Then hurry! Go! Make haste! Leap, bound and run! This is Bumblebosters' Panics; you can even play leap-frog along the way!"

"What shall I tell Hanafer?"

"Whatever you like; he's no concern of mine and he takes far too much for granted."

Kosh said uncertainly, "That's Hanafer for you. He knows what he wants and when he wants it."

"So I've noticed. For now, make sure of the table; I'll be along in a moment."

With poor grace Kosh Diffenbocker stalked away through the resplendent crowd. Lyssel turned back to Jaro, a smile trembling on her mouth. "Well then, Jaro, what do you think of our gorgeous Panics?"

"It's very grand. I like the decorations."

Lyssel laughed happily. "I worked on the committee. Look yonder! See that odd animal with the green hat and curled-over tail? I painted the entire tail, including the tuft! I was careful to select exactly the proper colors!"

"You did a splendid job. You were born to be an artist, rather than—" Jaro halted to look across the promenade. Lyssel demanded, "Rather than what?"

"Oh, let's say, a mysterious woman of a thousand intrigues."

"I want to be both!" declared Lyssel. "Why should I limit myself? Especially when I have important affairs to take up with you."

"Ha hm. What sort of affairs?"

Lyssel airily fluttered her fingers. "Oh, just affairs."

"I'm puzzled," said Jaro. "At the terminal you made it clear that I was not only a nimp but also a very dull dog. Now, suddenly, everything is different. It's fine Jaro, good Jaro, talented, delightful Jaro. Either you want something, or you have fallen in love with me and want to start up a whirlwind romance. So which is it?"

Lyssel shook her head in wonder. "I can't believe that you're so cynical! When we met at the terminal I was worried for my uncle, and perhaps I seemed a bit thoughtless. Today is different."

"Exactly so," said Jaro. "It's today I wonder about. Why, suddenly, are we on such good terms?"

Lyssel reached out her forefinger and touched the tip of Jaro's nose: an artful act which made her physical presence very real. Jaro decided that a love affair with Lyssel would be pleasant—if, perhaps, full of surprises. And also highly unlikely, in view of Lyssel's social strivings. He asked, "Is that an answer? If so, I don't understand it."

"You weren't meant to understand. That is how I conceal my secrets."

"Too bad," said Jaro. "I don't have time for mysteries, so I'll go back to being bad Jaro the spaceman."

Jaro felt the loom of a tall shape at his back. Looking about, he found a bulky young man in the flamboyant market-day costume of a Poowaddle dog barber. It was Hanafer Glackenshaw, his face congested with anger. He addressed Jaro: "What's all this? Why are you here? You're a nimp and this is the Bumblebosters' Panics—strictly Squared Circle! That makes you a damnable schmeltzer as well!"

Lyssel came forward. "Hanafer, don't be such an idiot! Can't you see he's one of the musicians?"

"So what? He should be out of sight, behind the partition! Not down here!"

"Hanafer, please be reasonable! Jaro is doing no harm!"

"I am utterly reasonable! Behind that partition he is a musician; out here, simpering like a halfwit, he's a schmeltzer."

Lyssel shook her head in vexation. "You are becoming hysterical! Come now; Kosh is holding our table." Over her shoulder she gave Jaro a quick glance, and led Hanafer away.

The episode had definitely annoyed Hanafer. He had never liked Jaro, whom he considered both smarmy and conceited. Secondly, to find a nimp like Jaro preening himself out in society, as if he had striven up the ledges, was deeply offensive.

On the way to the table Hanafer complained to Lyssel: "Why do you trouble to notice him? He's a schmeltzing moop!"

Lyssel spoke flippantly, "Be just, Hanafer! He's very intelligent, and he plays the suanola nicely. Also, he's handsome in a strange archaic way, don't you agree?"

"Certainly not!"

Lyssel enjoyed teasing Hanafer. "Don't you think you could be more lenient, just for once? I'd like to invite him to our table; he's actually an interesting person."

Hanafer grated, "He can be the third coming of four-toed Gezemyer, for all I care. He's not in the Circle, and that's what counts in my book."

"Hanafer, you really are extreme. I'm sorry that I must tell you this, but it's true. The Squared Circle is not everything in life."

"Ha hah! The Circle may not be everything, but it separates quality from schmeltzers, bounders and moops!"

"Surely, Hanafer, you're not referring to Jaro?"

"I am exactly and precisely referring to Jaro. I call him a cad, a gak and a peeker, and if he starts smelling around you, I'll be forced to teach him his piddles and squeaks." Hanafer alluded to the parental discipline inflicted upon an unruly child.

"Well, you might as well know! I'm inviting him to the Multiflor, where he'll be one of the strolling musicians, and I expect you to be courteous."

"We'll see. But if he starts schmeltzing, I'll quickly set him right."

3

Three days passed, during which Lyssel receded from the forefront of Jaro's mind. Then, late in the afternoon, as he left the Lyceum, she came up beside him. "Jaro! You were about to walk past without so much as noticing me!"

Jaro had made several staunch resolutions, but now, somewhat to his surprise, he heard himself say, "If I had seen you, I surely would have noticed." Resolutions were easier to make than to keep.

Today Lyssel wore a simple dark blue frock with a white collar. She asked, "Why do you look at me like that?"

"I'm trying to think."

"Oh? Thinking what?"

"Thinking that I should politely say, 'Hello, Lyssel; goodbye, Lyssel.' "

Lyssel came a step closer. She pointed toward the sky. "Look! The sun is shining! I'm not a female devil with four fangs. I want us to be friends!"

"Certainly. Whatever you like."

Lyssel looked quickly around the forecourt, then took Jaro's arm. "Come, let's go somewhere else. Everyone notices everything, and gossip travels on wings."

Without enthusiasm Jaro allowed himself to be led away. "We'll try the Old Den," Lyssel told him. "It's quiet this time of day and we can talk."

At the Old Den they found a table on the back terrace, in the shade of three ancient olive trees, whose branches had been twisted and interlaced to form an arbor. A waitress served them jugs of fruit punch. Jaro sat passively, watching the flux of Lyssel's expressions. Presently she became impatient and leaned forward. "I've been wanting to talk to you for ever so long."

"Now's your chance! I'm here and I'm listening."

Lyssel grimaced sadly. "I don't think that you take me seriously."

"Naturally not. What do you want to talk about?"

Lyssel pretended to pout. "You, mainly."

Jaro laughed. "I can't think why."

"Well, for instance: I've heard that there's a mystery about your early life, that the Faths are not your real parents."

"That's true enough. When I was six years old they rescued me from a gang of hoodlums and saved my life. This was on another world, during one of their expeditions. Afterwards they brought me back to Gallingale and adopted me. That is the story of my life."

"But there must be more than that!"

"True. It's all very complicated."

"You don't know your real father and mother?"

"No. Someday I hope to learn the facts."

Lyssel found the account fascinating. "You might well have been born into a family of high prestige, or whatever they call 'comporture' among the outer worlds."

"It's a possibility."

"And so that is why you want to become a spaceman?"

"Partly."

"What if you went off into space but never found what you were searching for?"

Jaro shrugged. "I wouldn't be the first."

Lyssel sipped at the fruit punch. "So—you might leave Gallingale and never come back."

Jaro looked off across the arbor as if trying to see the years to come. Finally he said, "I'll always come back to Merriehew, if only to visit my parents."

Lyssel chewed at her lip. "The Faths might prefer to live somewhere more convenient than raggle-taggle old Merriehew."

Jaro shook his head. "They'd never be happy anywhere else. We're agreed as to that."

"Still, you never know. They might change their minds."

"Not if I can help it. Last week some slick real estate type tried to sell them a box in the Catterline district. He was obviously a scoundrel and my father just laughed at him."

Lyssel winced. "Your father should not be so judgmental. The agent was probably acting in good faith."

"Anything is possible."

Lyssel reached out and squeezed his hand. "That's far more charitable. It's a trait I want you to practice, so that you'll be able to sympathize with me and help me with my own problems."

Jaro disengaged his hand. "I'll sympathize from a distance, where there's no chance of becoming involved."

Lyssel's mouth dropped piteously. "But I thought that you wanted us to become friends!"

Jaro grinned. "I might have used the word, but I probably meant something else."

Lyssel said cautiously: "There's nothing wrong with the word 'friends.' "

"Of course not. But 'friends' go to the same parties together, whereas we have to run down here to the Old Den just to talk."

Lyssel seemed uncertain. "That's no great matter! If you behave and help me with my plans we can still be friends—more or less," she added lamely.

"Let me explain," said Jaro. "You exert a strong force. This force swirls my creative juices back and forth until I want to seize you and squeeze you and carry you off to bed. Friendship comes later."

Lyssel said decidedly, "Nothing of that sort is feasible. If I were to be seized, squeezed and dragged off to bed, I would fear for my reputation. Next, I would reprimand the culprit, even if it were you."

"In that case—" Jaro made a fatalistic gesture "—there is little scope for a relationship."

"You give up very easily," said Lyssel crossly. "It is almost insulting! Especially when I was about to invite you to Multiflor! I mentioned it at the Panics, remember?"

"Not really."

"It's the Jinkers' Lawn Party, and I want you to be on hand. There will be flowers everywhere and you're certain to enjoy it."

"Me? I'm not a Jinker, or anything else. I couldn't get past the first dandelion. Further, if Hanafer saw me he'd raise a great outcry and call me schmeltzer."

"No matter! You'll be coming because I asked you specially,

and it's not all that formal. I'm on the committee and we want to make it the prettiest occasion of the season. There'll be showers of flowers, and big iron jugs brimming with deep purple Gradencia; and then, of course, instead of an orchestra we'll want you to be costumed as the resident satyr, and wander about playing pretty music on the suanola."

Jaro asked in a hushed voice, "You want me to wear a costume?"

"Don't fret, we have a proper costume in mind; it's wonderfully droll, with a tall crooked hat, green pantaloons, and a funny sheep's tail fastened at the back, where tails are usually attached." Lyssel giggled. "A string connects the tail to your knee, so that when you cavort the tail whisks about; it's truly comical!"

Jaro sat staring at Lyssel in bemusement. Lyssel happily continued. "As for me, I'll be a Blue Impling, with blue lace slippers. The costume is mostly me, but everything is a bit daring at the Multiflor: that, in fact, is true Jinker style. Along with the Gradencia we'll serve iced Titilanthus in authentic milk-glass urns; also a vat of a new recipe created just for the party; it's called Flurrish Zabamba. They gave Yasher Farkinbeck a taste and it made him very frisky, so I'm told. You'll enjoy yourself."

Jaro reached across the table and took her hands. "Lyssel, we are about to hear the jangling discord of two lawn parties in collision."

"I don't understand."

"I should say, two versions of the same party. Whichever you choose cancels the other."

"Oh dear, must we have histrionics?" Lyssel tried to disengage her hands. "You look so grim! Please let me go!" Jaro released her. "I'll tell you about the two parties. The first is a triumph. The weather is fine; the refreshments are memorable; the garden satyr has played well and amused everyone with his cavorting; Hanafer Glackenshaw is glad; Yasher Farkinbeck is frisky; Lyssel Bynnoc is radiant: her beauty has seduced every boy and antagonized every girl."

"Wonderful!" cried Lyssel in rapture. "Let's go no further, this is the Multiflor I want."

"But wait! Listen to the second version! At this Multiflor you and I arrive together. I am your escort and we are wearing similar costumes. You are carrying my suanola, which I may or may not play, depending upon my mood—perhaps after a taste or two of Flurrish Zabamba. We are together during the party, and at the proper time we leave and go off into the evening. It has been a pleasant party."

Jaro paused, but Lyssel could only stare at him slack-jawed.

Jaro said, "If we choose one party, the other disappears. For instance, if you chose the first party, at the end the satyr would take his pay and go off to his camp. It wouldn't be Jaro, of course."

"You can't be serious!"

"Certainly I'm serious."

"But the second party is utter nonsense! I could not participate in such a fiasco!"

Jaro rose to his feet. "In that case, nothing more need be said. I'm going home." He started for the door. A few seconds passed, then Lyssel came running after him. She seized his arm and pulled him to a halt. "I've never known anyone so irascible!"

"But you're insulting! You hypnotize me and vamp me, just so you can dress me up as a funny satyr, to play the suanola free of charge. You don't even like me."

Lyssel stepped closer. "You catch me up on things I didn't mean! I think it's you who just pretends the interest."

Jaro held out his arm. "Look! See how my hand shakes? I'm fighting my primitive impulses. They are real."

Lyssel grinned up at him and seemed to wriggle, as if by reflex. "So long as you obey my commands, I don't mind. In fact, I rather like it, since it makes me feel invincible."

"It makes me feel nervous and tired. The game is over and I'm going home." But Jaro hesitated. "I still wonder what you really want of me, and how far you'd go to get it."

Lyssel put her hands up to his shoulders. "I made a mistake, I admit it!" She moved even closer, so that Jaro could feel the touch of her breasts. He knew he should back away and leave the Old Den but his feet were reluctant to move. He said: "Tell me the truth."

Lyssel grimaced. "What truth? The main truth is that I want everything! But I don't know how to get it, or any of it. I'm confused." She fell silent, then spoke in a low voice, more to herself than to Jaro, "I don't dare! All my comporture would be lost if we were discovered." Jaro started to draw back. "I want no more intrigues, and I don't want to disgrace you. So then—"

From across the room came heavy voices; turning, Jaro saw Hanafer Glackenshaw with two of his friends: the hulking Almer Culp, along with the lean and rapacious Lonas Fanchetto.

Lyssel dropped her arms and stepped away from Jaro. Hanafer

cried out in brassy triumph: "They told me I'd find you here, along with old Mooper!"

"You are being extremely rude!" said Lyssel. "Please leave, and at once!"

"It's not rude to explain hard facts! This is a damnable moop, and he must be taught his place."

"You don't know what you're saying. Jaro is courteous and talented, and he is far more genteel than you are. Now hear me! I've invited him to Multiflor. He'll be a probationary Jinker, so please don't call him a schmeltzer."

"Of course he's a schmeltzer!" roared Hanafer. "He's a nimp, isn't he? How can he be even a probationary Jinker?"

"Because I'm on the committee, and I can nominate whomever I please!"

"But not a nimp! That's sheer farce, and proves he's schmeltzing!" He swung upon Jaro. "I'll give you some advice. Keep away from the Multiflor. We don't want bounders or gaks or schmeltzers at our parties. We strive and claw up the ledges and we don't want to look up to see some disgusting nimp grinning down at us! So then—you heard me; what do you have to say?"

Lyssel cried out: "Hanafer, stop trying to bully Jaro! You're only making a fool of yourself, and I certainly won't think kindly of you if you go on like this!"

Hanafer's face became distorted. "I'm not the fool; it's you who stands here, letting this bounder nuzzle you! Don't you realize that he's a schmeltzer and really repulsive?"

Lyssel said, "Hanafer, behave yourself. You are definitely not at your best!"

Hanafer ignored her and turned to glare at Jaro. "Well, nimp? We'd better have an understanding. Are you planning to strut and schmeltz at the Multiflor, or will you behave like the nice little nimp you damned well better be?"

Jaro spoke with an effort. The situation was embarrassing. He did not wish to attend Multiflor; he was not anxious to fight Hanafer, who was large, heavy and mean, and from whom he could expect a drubbing. Hanafer had public opinion on his side; none of the strivers liked schmeltzers, and Jaro's status as probationary Jinker was unconvincing. Still, Jaro found that he could not meekly submit to Hanafer and retain his self-respect. Against all logic and inclination and basic common sense he said, "I'll go where I like, and you'll have to put up with it."

Hanafer took a slow step forward. "And you plan to show yourself at the Multiflor?"

"My plans are none of your affair."

"Schmeltzing is everyone's affair."

Lyssel stepped forward. "He's coming because I invited him to be my escort! So now, behave yourself."

Hanafer stared at her in wonder. "I thought that I was to be your escort! You told me to be sure to wear my Scarlet Knave costume!"

"I changed my mind. I'm to be a Blue Impling and your costume would clash with mine."

Hanafer signaled his two friends. "Grab this bounder and throw him out! If I started, I don't know where I'd stop."

Lonas and Almer came forward: Lonas with massive shoulders hunched; Almer with a bony arm extended, long thin fingers like insect claws, clutching at the air, apparently in order to fascinate Jaro and expedite his withdrawal.

The proprietor appeared. "Stop; that's enough! I'll have no rowdy tussles in here! One move and I'll call the monitors!" He turned to Jaro. "As for you, young man, you had better leave now, while the going is good!"

Jaro shrugged and departed.

Lyssel swung upon Hanafer: "You are a boor! I am absolutely ashamed of you!"

"Not so!" Hanafer blustered. "You told me that I would be your escort at the Multiflor and that later we'd go out to the Seven Mile House for supper."

"I never agreed to that, and if I did it was only conditional."

"So now you want to go with the schmeltzer instead?"

Lyssel drew herself up. "When I want your advice, I'll ask for it. Until then, please mind your own business."

"Yes, of course. Just as you say." Hanafer turned and marched from the Old Den, followed by his friends.

4

Jaro finished his evening shift at the space terminal and started home. The inter-urban bus, discharged him where Katzvold Road entered the Nain Woods, with Merriehew still half a mile north. The night was warm and heavy, with the blue-green moon Mish drifting among high clouds.

The bus vanished toward town, leaving silence behind. Jaro set off to the north through the Woods, moving soft-footed along the road, as seemed appropriate on such a night as this one.

The moon drifted behind a cloud, the road disappeared into darkness, and Jaro slowed his pace, to avoid straying into the roadside thickets. Tonight for some odd reason, the road seemed unfamiliar, as if Jaro had missed the way and now wandered an unknown part of the woods. Foolishness, of course—still, something seemed amiss. Was that a sound? He stopped to listen. Silence. Dubiously he continued along the road. After a few yards he stopped again; no mistake this time! From high in the trees, came a soft doleful sound, stiffening the short hairs at the nape of Jaro's neck. He listened, but silence had returned to the woods.

Jaro went on slowly, feeling the way with his feet.

A moment passed. Again the quiet sound floated down from above. Jaro raised his head to listen; it must be the hooting of a night bird, though like none he had heard before.

Jaro stirred himself and proceeded, step after step. Clouds parted; the moon drifted out into open sky. Wan moonlight spread down through the foliage, to lay a pattern on the road. Again the sound: an eery clucking. Jaro stopped short, and searched the high foliage. A fluting voice cried out: "The Black Angels fly down from the back of the moon!"

Something stood in the moonlit road fifty feet ahead. It was seven feet tall, draped in a flowing black gown, with black wings lifting high from the shoulders. Under a black cowl eyes like disks of jet in a gaunt white face stared down at Jaro, holding him transfixed.

From right and left came four masked shapes in grotesque costumes: capes draped over abnormally wide shoulders, from which wings raised high, like those of the figure in the road. To his sick surprise, Jaro found that he had become a rag doll, helpless either to run or to fight.

Moving with ponderous deliberation, the four Angels set upon Jaro; they bore him to the ground and struck him with long flexible truncheons. Jaro held up his arm; down came the truncheon; a bone broke. Jaro toppled, and the blows continued. Old memories flooded into his mind: The glare of the hot sun on the Wyching Hills, the taste of roadside dust; the thud-thud of cudgels pounding his thin ribs. He groaned, more from pain than the agony of recollection.

On this night in Nain Woods the truncheons measured blows meant not to maim, but to punish. A deep voice spoke, its utterance grave and stately: "The Black Angels of Penitence once more do their duty! Let schmeltzers beware, now and forever!"

From the others came a rumble of antiphony: "It is always thus! Let the schmeltzers beware! It is thus, and thus, and thus!" The truncheons rose and fell in emphasis.

The deep voice spoke: "You have been adjudged a schmeltzer: now you must make amends. Say you are sorry!"

Jaro struggled feebly, but was thrust back down and kicked heavily in the ribs.

The voice intoned: "Declare your falsity! Say you are sorry and will keep to your place! Will you speak? Or do you need further correction? Aha, you will not speak! Well then, so be it, and it's all your own fault!"

Down came the truncheons. The Black Angels, affronted by Jaro's silence, worked with righteous zeal to correct the intransigence of their victim; they struck with heavier arms, their truncheons held high, until Jaro lay passive. Amazing! Even while Jaro's flesh cringed to the blows, deep inside his head sounded a gust of mocking laughter, as if somewhere, something took joy in the event, and Jaro felt even a deeper fear.

The Black Angels stood panting. One of the towering figures kicked Jaro heavily. "Speak now! Recite your apology!"

Another Angel muttered: "It is useless. He is stubborn as bangdong stink."

"Stubborn or dead."

The four bent over Jaro. "He has had a smart lesson, no more. It will moderate his vanity."

Jaro's senses drained away. He felt almost at peace. It was good, this receptivity! It functioned like a reservoir, into which emotion and purpose drained and were collected, so that none was wasted. His mind went dim, and he lay still.

The Black Angels performed their other work. They clipped away Jaro's hair and glued a ridiculous cock's-comb of white feathers to his scalp. They painted his face black and tucked a long bushy white plume into the waistband at the back of his trousers. They loaded him into the bed of a van and drove off toward Thanet.

An hour before midnight a group of students leaving a late lecture discovered Jaro in the forecourt of the Lyceum, where he had been lashed upright to the stanchion of a yardlight. A placard hung from his neck. It read:

I WAS A SCHMELTZER! I APOLOGIZE. THE BLACK ANGELS OF PENITENCE HAVE ORDAINED IT SO!

5

An ambulance conveyed Jaro to the hospital, where his hurts and broken bones were treated. He was concussed. Ribs, arms and clavicle had been broken. He was lucky, so it was said, to have escaped a fractured skull. It seemed that the Black Angels had conducted their punitive measures in a frenzy of excitement. The police made routine efforts to identify the Angels, but there was little popular indignation at the punishment of a schmeltzer. Such a creature was no better than a leech, and since the police could not control schmeltzing, then society was forced to protect itself. In general, the deed was considered a students' lark and a salutory example for everyone concerned.

Jaro remained in the hospital for two weeks. The Faths came daily to visit him, but found it hard to seem cheerful and optimistic. The police had been casually polite. They claimed that diligent inquiry had produced no clues.

One day, as if by afterthought, Hilyer asked Jaro if he could put names to any of the Black Angels.

Jaro seemed surprised. "Of course! There were four: Hanafer Glackenshaw, Kosh Diffenbocker, Almer Culp, Lonas Fanchetto."

"Then we will prosecute."

Jaro would not hear of it. "I could prove nothing. There were no witnesses. The Justiciary would never be allowed use of the Truth Machine. Even if they were found guilty, they would only be censured, and I would be warned to avoid future provocation. They emerge with dignity; I look feeble and foolish."

"But we cannot let this outrage pass! It would be shameful!"

"Yes; indeed it would."

Hilyer compressed his lips. "You are cold as a fish; you show no emotion! Aren't you angry?"

Jaro smiled. "I am angry, no fear as to that. When the time comes, the anger will be there and ready."

Hilyer grunted. "I don't think that I understand you."

"No matter."

Hilyer studied the pallid face. "Surely you don't intend to take the law into your own hands!"

Jaro gave a painful chuckle. "Certainly not at the moment."

The response failed to satisfy Hilyer, and he left the hospital in an unsettled mood.

Jaro was visited by a half dozen fellow students, with whom he had become more or less friendly. All expressed sympathy for both the beating and the humiliation of the feathered headpiece and the rear plume. They were surprised to discover Jaro's extraordinary sangfroid. "There's no humiliation, if a person does not feel humiliated," said Jaro. Basil Krom, who studied sociology, argued the point. "That is as may be. Here at Thanet humiliation is almost a thing in itself. Why? No mystery. The competitive social system makes them vulnerable to ridicule. At all costs they must maintain face. This is why your friends are baffled by your unconcern."

"First of all," said Jaro, "I have no reputation to destroy."

"And second?"

"Since I am indifferent to ridicule, there is no fun in it, and it will soon stop."

"And thirdly?"

"Thirdly is not yet projected."

Lyssel failed to include herself among the visitors, nor had Jaro expected her. Gaing Neitzbeck, however, showed himself as soon as visitors were permitted. At the sight of the battered face Jaro felt a surge of comfort and relief. He had not realized how much stress still weighed upon him.

Gaing, not a demonstrative man, still gave Jaro a pat on the shoulder, then seated himself. He said gruffly, "You might as well tell me the whole thing."

Jaro described the events of the dreadful evening. "I am not proud of myself. I heard a weird sound from the tree; I saw the effigy with the high wings and I became paralyzed. I stood numb, like a hypnotized chicken. Now I feel weak and ineffectual."

Gaing considered Jaro a moment. "Evidently you want to make changes in yourself."

"Yes," Jaro muttered. "I'll find some way to cure the weakness, or flaw—whatever it is."

"Such an episode is hard on the pride," Gaing agreed. "But don't suffer on that account. Pride is intellectual self-judgment. It's a mixture of hope and fantasy, and should be put aside. 'Assurance,' which is a measure of competence, is a more useful standard."

Jaro said hollowly, "That's a very fine remark, but lacking competence, I might as well look for my poor bedraggled pride, nurse it back into shape."

Gaing grinned amiably. "You have a few odd competences, but none will protect you from another good beating."

"True. But I hope to make changes. Perhaps you can advise me."

Gaing nodded. "I can indeed. The skills are like any other. They must be learned, then practiced, until they become second nature. However, you are in luck. The skills can be taught and there is a qualified instructor at hand. I refer to myself. At one time I thought to make a career with the IPCC, but events interfered. If you want to know the truth, they ejected me, on grounds which were almost trivial. They claimed that I was unconventional and obeyed orders only when it suited me."

"Preposterous," muttered Jaro.

"I also had occasion to contend with probably the most vicious race extant in the Gaean Reach, or—as in this case—Beyond. I learned and I survived. Today I am slow and lubberly compared to myself of twenty years ago, but my mind is still adroit and what I know you shall learn, if you are so motivated."

Jaro said in a voice thin and reedy by reason of emotion, "I am motivated, and I wish to learn so badly that I am sick in the stomach."

Gaing smiled. "I know your persistence. As soon as you are able to walk, we shall start. Meanwhile, read." He laid a parcel of books on the bedside table. "Start with the compendium."

Jaro delayed several days before informing the Faths of his plans. There seemed no gentle way of breaking the news. Jaro said, "I've decided to undertake lessons in self-defense. I hope that you'll approve."

Althea raised her eyebrows in pained surprise. "Have you really thought the situation through?"

"Of course."

"It's not the way of conciliation! It's the same thing as equipping yourself with an arsenal of weapons, and surely someone will be hurt! Is it worth putting yourself into this position?"

"Ha hah," said Jaro. "What of the position I'm in now?"

Hilyer, eyes narrowed thoughtfully, said, "I'm not sure I know what you mean by 'self-defense.' "

"It's simple enough. If I am attacked again, I want to be able to protect myself."

"That sounds reasonable, on the face of it. But aren't these tactics a form of bellicosity, and don't they seriously injure your opponent?"

"No more than necessary, or so I should hope."

Althea cried out, "That's a vain hope, when someone lies crippled on the ground."

Hilyer asked, "Where will you learn such skills?"

"I think you have met Mr. Gaing Neitzbeck, who works with me at the terminal?"

"I remember him well," said Hilyer with a sniff.

Althea said, "He doesn't seem a very cultured person."

Jaro laughed. "Don't let his appearance fool you. He's intelligent and well informed. More than that he is competent. At one time he served with the IPCC and can teach me whatever I need to know."

Hilyer was silent for a moment, then blurted, "Perhaps this is the wrong time to make careful ethical distinctions. You have been hurt. Make no mistake; I am as angry as you! But I want to take revenge through the designated channels of social accommodation. These are proper and permitted; in short, they are civilized. I don't want you to do violent deeds, as if you were a space vagabond or a pirate of the Beyond."

Jaro said stonily, "I was attacked. I could not respond. I lay helpless on the ground. I would be wrong to let it happen again."

Hilyer made a small gesture of defeat, and turned away.

NINE

1

Upon returning home from the hospital, Jaro continued to study the manuals which Gaing had brought him, and in due course undertook some of the exercises, gradually extending himself as his strength returned.

"At the start go slow and easy," Gaing told him. "Work no more than ten minutes on any one exercise; otherwise your nerves go slack. Confine yourself to about six routines every session. Try first for accuracy, then speed. Do not become bored and ease up. Each routine is the basis of a combination, and must be practiced until it becomes reflexive. There is a long pull ahead of you; don't lose heart."

"I'm not complaining," said Jaro. "In fact, I don't know how best to thank you."

"Don't bother."

"Still, I wonder why you spend so much time with me. I am grateful. Is there any explanation? If so, what?"

"The questions are reasonable," said Gaing. "I can't give you any single answer. At the moment I have nothing better to do. You badly need the training, and it would be a shame to waste good raw material. Then, self-interest is involved. I'd like to think that I am laying up credit for the future. Someday you might be able to return the favor. Also, in all the Gaean Reach I count only two friends. You are one of them."

"Who is the other?"

"You know him. His name is Tawn Maihac."

2

During the same week Jaro returned to school. His hair had not grown out evenly. He brushed it back as well as possible, but still could not subdue tufts or conceal pallid spots where the hair had been slow in growing back.

No matter, he told himself and went to his classes oblivious to the stares of the other students. In a day or two their attention would shift, and they would no longer notice him. In the meantime, he must accept the notoriety with detachment.

Jaro took his lunch in the cafeteria, then went out to sit on a bench at the side of the forecourt. Lyssel appeared and, after seeming not to notice him, changed her mind and came to look him over. "Hm," she said. "They did a fine job on you."

"They were thorough," Jaro agreed.

Lyssel studied him carefully. "You seem quite debonair! It's baffling! Aren't you upset?"

"Such things happen. It's best to be philosophical."

"Don't you understand? They made an example of you." Lyssel's voice was light and amused. "They took all your pride and now you are shamed."*

---

*Inexact rendering of the word "tchabade": a hurting complex emotion, encompassing all the following: drained of mana; emasculated; forced to submit, as if to perverted sexual acts; demoralized; rendered negligible; defeated and left behind; stripped of all comporture. In short, a vicious, debilitating emotion.

Jaro shrugged. "I hadn't noticed."

Lyssel was aggrieved. "It affects me as well. My plans are now a muddle." She turned him a crafty sidelong look. "Unless you are still willing to help me, as you promised."

Jaro looked at her in disbelief. "What are you saying? I made no promises. You must be thinking of someone else."

Lyssel said angrily: "You told me that you were fascinated and hypnotized! You showed me how your hands shook with emotion. That was you, Jaro Fath, so don't deny it."

Jaro nodded sadly. "I remember something of the sort. But the past is gone and done with."

Lyssel's face had become frozen, so that she no longer looked pretty. "Then you won't help me?"

"Probably not, even if I knew what you wanted."

Lyssel appraised Jaro as if she had never seen him before. Then her mouth became contorted and words seemed to erupt from her throat. "You are unique, Jaro Fath! You strut around school smirking and bland, as if you were nursing coy little secrets. You are like a whipped dog, smiling and cringing and curling its lip to beg for tolerance."

Jaro grimaced and sat erect on the bench. He said, "I expect that someday I'll find all this amusing." Lyssel seemed not to hear. Her voice rose in pitch. "You gain no sympathy, showing yourself like this; in fact, no one can understand why you're here! You'd be wise to pick up your books and leave."

"That would be sheer folly! My next class starts in ten minutes; I wouldn't be here otherwise."

Lyssel said scornfully, "You don't care who sees you? You don't care what anyone thinks?"

"Something like that."

Hanafer Glackenshaw came out on the forecourt. He stood a moment in a majestic posture, shoulders thrown back, legs apart, arms clasped behind his back, tight golden curls glinting in the sunlight. He turned his head slowly, first to the right then to the left, allowing everyone a view of his noble profile. He saw Lyssel and Jaro and his brow clouded. He crossed the forecourt, his stride slow and portentous. Halting, he stared down at Jaro. "I see you are back and busy as a bee."

Jaro said nothing. After a meaningful glance toward Lyssel, Hanafer said, "Rumor has it that you'd been warned against grazing in forbidden pastures, where you hadn't been invited."

"Rumor is correct," said Jaro. "That's what happened."

Hanafer jerked his head toward Lyssel. "Yet here you are, back again, snooping and sniffing around places where nimps aren't welcome. Do you get my meaning?"

Lyssel spoke. "Hanafer, please don't be unpleasant. Jaro means nothing wrong."

"Bah!" said Hanafer. "He means nothing whatever. He smiles meekly; he licks his lips; he is not even annoyed. If he values my good opinion, he'll do his socializing with the other nimps."

Lyssel spoke with disgust. "Hanafer, you are really offensive!"

"Pah! What difference does it make? He doesn't care."

"Wrong," said Jaro. "I am annoyed, but I don't want to waste it just now. There's no hurry."

"You talk foolishness, and you're probably mad. Well, that's quite all right; be as mad as you like, just as long as you don't come schmeltzing, because it won't be tolerated."

A bell sounded. Hanafer took Lyssel's arm, but she jerked away and ran off across the forecourt, with Hanafer marching glumly behind.

Jaro watched them go, then picked up his books and went off to his own class.

3

Two months later the term ended. During the winter recess Hilyer and Althea went off on a short expedition to the Baneek Isles of the world Lakhme Verde, in order to record and document the so-called "Tymanghese" orchestras, which produced a music of tinkling waterbells, sound-spangles, quavering gongs controlled by a flexible reverberatory rhythm: a music which some compared to the surge and retreat of silver surf, others to "daydreams in the mind of Pasiphae the goddess of music." On Lakhme Verde each village supported one or more orchestras, and almost everyone either crafted or played one of the exquisitely flexible instruments.

The music had long been intractable to the analysis of musicologists, and the Faths were determined to apply certain new theories upon the gorgeous textures of a sound which not even the musicians of the isles claimed to understand completely.

Jaro, meanwhile, worked to the limit of his energies, training himself in the techniques demonstrated to him by Gaing. He was impatient and constantly demanded new routines, new moves, new tactics. Gaing refused to yield until Jaro had perfected every phase of the old material. "You are advancing fast enough. I don't want you to burn yourself out."

"No chance of that," said Jaro. "I feel that this is what I was made for; I can't get enough of it; I won't stop until I learn it all."

"You won't do that, for sure," said Gaing. "Some of the systems are thousands of years old, and everyone thinks he has quicker and better moves than the old masters. I used to think that myself. I was probably wrong."

"So—how far have I come?"

"You've done well. So far we've been keeping to relatively basic material—no acrobatics, no exotic combinations."

"When do we start those?"

"When you develop the musculature and the body. By the time I'm done with you—or even before—your assurance index should be quite high. Meanwhile, we shall proceed methodically. After all, there is no hurry."

"I'm not so sure," said Jaro. "This will be my last term at the Lyceum. After that, I don't know what will happen. The Faths won't tell me where they found me until I graduate from the Institute."

Gaing asked, "Don't they keep journals which describe their expeditions?"

"I think so, but they've put them away, out of my reach. They say they'll tell me everything once I get my degree, but I don't care to wait so long."

Gaing shrugged his heavy shoulders. "Let's get back to the drill. That's definite and real."

The spring term at the Lyceum began. Jaro's academic record was such that he was placed in a special classification, and allowed wide latitude in the scheduling and conduct of his courses. Jaro chose to study at home, reporting to his instructors weekly via the telescreen. He was thereby freed to concentrate upon the ever more taxing exercises prescribed by Gaing. He began to notice changes in his body. His shoulders and chest deepened; his flanks, thighs, and haunches became hard as leather; his forearms, wrists and hands seemed belted over with sinew and the bones themselves had become dense and heavy. He had started to learn complicated combinations and exotic exercises, which could seriously injure an opponent unless controlled. Gaing insisted on speed, accuracy and balance above all else; as always, Jaro was not allowed to proceed into new routines until the old material had become as automatic as walking.

One day Gaing told Jaro: "You are now well into the third level of proficiency, which is solid achievement. Other levels are still ahead, and the field branches out into a hundred specialities, which are not relevant at the moment. I refer to horrifying sounds, illusions, powders and mists, photic adjuncts, miniature weapons, and the like; there is no end to the field. At the moment, it's best that you continue with the fundamentals. You still have far to go, although you need no longer consider yourself a tyro. Increase your index of assurance, if you like."

Jaro only grinned and continued his exercises.

On the same day Hilyer brought home an item of news which he had gleaned at the Office of Land Registry. As he sat down to his afternoon tea, he imparted the information to Althea and Jaro.

"You'll recall that the old Yellowbird Ranch to our south at one time belonged to Clois Hutsenreiter?"

"Of course," said Althea.

"Just so. A few years ago he sold the property to a syndicate, the Fidol Combine—for rather a low price, as I remember. Today, I happened to be in the land office, and out of curiosity I looked up Fidol in the registry. I found that most of Fidol is owned by Gilfong Rute, who is an eccentric millionaire and a Val Verde. Twenty percent of Fidol is held by Forby Mildoon, a real estate developer, or something of the sort. This is the same Forby Mildoon who tried to sell us the Catterline House. It all gave me pause to wonder. I asked a few questions and learned that Rute is a flamboyant type, with a penchant for imaginative investments, both on Gallingale and off-world."

Althea asked, "Why should he want the Yellowbird land? It's just wild country, much like our own, only not as pretty."

"There are always rumors, but they never come to much. I've heard talk of a luxury development on the property, where only Sempiternals would be allowed. Rute wants to be a Sempiternal, but none of the three clubs will take him. He's too unconventional for the Clam Muffins, and too domineering for the Tattermen. The Quantorsi have applications across three generations. Apparently he hopes to snoozle his way into the Sempiternals by means of the exclusive development."

"That sounds strange to me," said Althea. "How could he become a Sempiternal if none of the three will accept him?"

Hilyer shrugged. "Osmosis, or something of the sort. In short, I don't have a clue, and it's probably all a mare's nest."

Jaro said suddenly: "Forby Mildoon? He is Lyssel Bynnoc's uncle. Rute has a beautiful yacht at the spaceport which he never uses; Lyssel told me that Forby Mildoon wants to buy it, but Rute quotes him all manner of fancy prices."

"Evidently he doesn't really want to sell," said Hilyer.

Jaro went off to his schoolwork, while Hilyer and Althea looked in their reference works to learn something of the world Ushant, where during the summer break they would attend a Grand Conclave of Aesthetic Philosophers. Over dinner they asked Jaro if he cared to accompany them. "Ushant is a fascinating world in itself," declared Althea. "The folk are said to support a philosophy which elevates awareness to its maximum sensitivity. The tactics of consciousness in themselves becomes a creative art."

Hilyer added: "Don't forget, that if you study for a degree in aesthetic philosophy as we advise, the Conclave should be of great help to you."

"If nothing else, you'll make valuable contacts," said Althea.

Hilyer nodded sage agreement. "We'll be mingling intimately with authorities in many fields: anthropologists of all kinds, aesthetic analysts, cultural philosophers, savants of comparative art and parallel development, symbologists such as ourselves, and even Dean Hutsenreiter will be on hand. It should be an inspiring occasion."

"I'll think about it," said Jaro. "At the moment I'm so busy I can focus only on schoolwork and my exercises."

"Hmf," said Hilyer. "How long do you intend to keep up these exercises?"

Althea said with a sniff: "Until he can maim some poor innocent person with a single touch of the finger."

Jaro laughed. "I can do that now. Who do you want maimed?"

"Please be serious," said Hilyer. "Certainly there must be a term in view."

"I agree," said Jaro. "But at the moment I'm just halfway into the subject, and the more I learn the more I want to know."

Hilyer used his most sardonic voice. "I hope you'll have some of that remarkable zest left for your work at the Institute."

4

The fall semester ended. There was a two week break, then Jaro entered his final semester at the Lyceum.

Time passed swiftly. The most important social event of the year, the Dombrillion, a grand ball for the graduating class, would take place a week before commencement. The Dombrillion, an official school function, disregarded social difference, so that in theory everyone, from the lowliest nimp to the strivers clambering the high ledges might mingle in good fellowship; in practice, each club made plans for its own tables and ordained a special costume for its members.

The romantic overtones of the occasion, began to color Jaro's imagination. He could not avoid wistful pangs at the thought of the parties and festivities from which he was excluded. It was by his own choice, he told himself. If he truly so desired, he could attend the Grand Masque, without difficulty. For an escort, the girls of the Outsiders Club were ready to hand, and afforded a wide latitude of choice. These girls were a heterogeneous lot and included nimps, off-worlders, provincials, dropouts from halfway up the strivings, a miscellaneity, which included misfits, anarchists, religious zealots and semi-sociopaths. Many of these girls were quite charming; others were capable of unpredictable conduct. Some moped, wept, cursed or danced with great bounding leaps. Some made obscene gestures, and wore their hair in varnished horns tipped with incandescent bulbs. One girl had arrived at a formal ball wearing only the coils of a two-headed snake. Another, having taken excessive drink, had sung roaring sea chanties with the orchestra, though the orchestra at the time had been playing a sedate passicaglia. Still others were irrepressible madcaps. In the end Jaro thought it best to seek an escort elsewhere, should he, in fact, decide to attend the Dombrillion.

The idea pulled him in different directions, and he felt a sour amusement for his own inconsistencies. No matter how brief the time, he wanted to share the pleasures of high comporture, while avoiding the hardships of clambering, toehold by vertiginous toehold, up the ledges. It was, he thought, an unreasonable and faintly discreditable yearning, though he could not ignore its existence. Practically, he should reconcile himself to staying at home, at the risk of denying himself a romantic memory. Jaro continued to feel troubled, no matter which direction he leaned.

A week before Dombrillion the graduating class gathered at

a traditional afternoon assembly, for the purpose of socializing, photographing each other, signing yearbooks, making plans for the summer, and generally engaging in sad-sweet reminiscences for events of an era already lost.

Attendance was compulsory. Jaro dressed neatly, ordered his black mat of hair, and appeared at the assembly. The forecourt had been gaily decorated for the occasion with streamers, bunting, free-flight torpedo balloons, and the blazons of thirty clubs. To right and left long tables offered tarts, pastries, sparkling wine and fruit punch.

Jaro signed the register, surveyed the forecourt, then went off to the side and sat on a bench. He would remain for a period, then he would leave as unobtrusively as he had come.

Such were Jaro's plans, subject to the changes dictated by events. As he watched the coming and going of his classmates, he became mildly puzzled. None were exactly as he remembered them. A transforming influence had been at work: age. He had not seen them for a year. No doubt they would observe changes in him as well, should they give him more than a cursory glance. But no one seemed to notice him, where he sat brooding and alone. Could the disgrace of his humiliation still cling to him? One way or the other, it made no difference. Jaro allowed a faint smile to twist his lips, though not a cheerful smile.

He sat back and watched the students moving about the forecourt. He saw neither Kosh, nor Almer, nor Lonas, nor Hanafer. Lyssel came into view. She had been lost among a group of girls gathered across the court. They moved and swirled apart and she appeared, light-footed, almost dancing with mirth and excitement. She wore a charming dark green frock with a short pleated skirt and green knee-length stockings. Jaro could not control a twinge of emotion. It was neither lust nor yearning to possess—at least, not altogether—but, rather, a sad disquiet. Lyssel represented youth and life and frivolity, and all those phases of existence which for one reason or another had been denied him. With all her flaws she was immensely appealing.

Jaro watched her. She had not seen him, and clearly her mind was anywhere but on Jaro Fath, the odd nimp who wanted to be known as Jaro the spaceman. In Lyssel's case there had been few changes. She was still gay, flamboyant, radiant with that verve which made men young and old want to hold her tight and immerse themselves in her magic.

Lyssel thought of something important: food and drink! She

detached herself from her friends and ran to the buffet, to make a selection from among the delicacies on display.

Jaro jumped to his feet and sauntered across the forecourt. When Lyssel reached for a brochette, her elbow struck an object which she saw to be a human arm. Looking over her shoulder, she became instantly still. Then, with graceful deliberation she put the brochette on her plate and spoke to the empty air: "I believe that I am in the presence of the reclusive Jaro Fath."

A voice responded: "I'm Jaro, right enough, but I'm not reclusive."

Lyssel looked around. "So it is Jaro, for a fact! And you are reclusive indeed! I haven't seen you for months!"

Jaro laughed. "It's you whom I haven't seen for months. Are you reclusive?"

"Of course not!" Lyssel selected a pickled tree crab from a platter of assorted sea fruit. "I have been striving and studying and tumbling around the Cycle of Seasons, as convention dictates. Meanwhile, you have shrouded yourself in mystery."

"My life has been anything but mysterious," said Jaro. "I've been doing all my classwork at home and working all my spare time at the terminal."

"Really? Then you haven't disappeared because of that Black Angel affair?"

"Not directly."

"What do you mean by that?"

"It's too complicated to explain."

Lyssel shrugged. She loaded her plate and took a goblet of wine; Jaro did the same and the two went to sit on a nearby bench.

Lyssel turned to look at Jaro, and never had her wide blue eyes seemed more innocent. "Isn't it a shame how everyone likes to think the worst of someone else?"

Jaro agreed. "It is a shame."

"They say that after you were taught your piddles and squeaks you were too embarrassed to appear in public, and that's why you've been hiding all this time."

"Wrong," said Jaro. "Still, they can say it again, for all I care."

Lyssel compressed her lips against a grin. "But, surely, the beating must have caused you some concern?"

"Well, yes," Jaro admitted. "It's hard to stay civil, when things aren't going just right."

Lyssel nodded wisely. "I wonder why you showed yourself today?"

"It's compulsory. Also, I wanted to pick up my yearbook."

"How so? You belong to none of the clubs and that is what the yearbook is all about; it reminds us of our striving."

Jaro shrugged. "Someday, when I am wandering among the outer constellations, I'll look through the yearbook and wonder how far these hopeful faces have striven up the ledges."

Lyssel grimaced. "What an eery thought! You make me feel all squirmish."

"Sorry."

Lyssel became vexed. "You are the most extraordinary person I know! I look in your face and I find only a mask of mysteries!"

Jaro raised his eyebrows. "The same could be said of you, with all your secrets."

Lyssel decided to treat the remark with hauteur. "I don't know what you are talking about."

"Then listen! I will ask a simple question, which you cannot misunderstand. Will you answer?"

"Maybe. What is the question?"

"You wanted me to do something for you. What was it?"

Lyssel laughed. "It was something trivial, and now I remember what you wanted me to do in return."

"Oh! Something trivial as well?"

Lyssel showed him one of her most eccentric grimaces. "You wanted to seduce me and make me your clandestine lover. Is that trivial?"

Jaro smilingly shook his head. "And you agreed?"

"As I recall, we never came to any decision."

"So—what was it you wanted of me?"

Lyssel shrugged. "It was long ago."

"And the need no longer exists?"

Lyssel pursed her lips. "I didn't say that. You might still be able to help me."

"Under the same conditions as before?"

Lyssel, still in her frivolous mode, said, "Nothing has changed. I couldn't tell you anything or do anything unless I were sure of you, which I'm not."

Jaro held out his hand. "Notice! The fingers no longer shake!"

Lyssel gave him her empty plate. "Get me another goblet of wine, if you please. While you're gone, I'll try to think."

Jaro took the plates to the buffet and returned with two fresh goblets of wine. "So: what have you decided?"

"I'm still thinking." Lyssel took the wine and then, as if by impulse, leaned toward Jaro and kissed his cheek. "Thank you. You are sympathetic; I've decided that I like you." Jaro carefully concealed his surprise. What swift new idea had come over Lyssel, so that suddenly she seemed soft and warm and intimate? In what direction was she now trying to lead him?

"All else aside, I'm still surprised to see you here," said Lyssel.

"The occasion isn't that dramatic," said Jaro.

"Are you planning to attend Dombrillion?"

"Probably not. What of you? Are you going with Hanafer?"

"No, and I've made this clear to him. He is furious, especially since I'll probably go with Purley Walkenfuss, whom he considers his great rival, and who is already a Tin Chicken."

On daring inspiration Jaro suggested, "Perhaps you'd consider going with me."

Lyssel laughed incredulously. "Do you want to cause Hanafer a heart attack? He still hates you; it's an obsession. If he found us together at the Dombrillion, I don't know what he'd do."

"Then you won't go with me?"

Lyssel sat sipping wine, and looking off across the forecourt. Jaro waited, wondering as to the thousand small pieces she was fitting together to form a decision. Slowly she turned her head and appraised Jaro. "I can't go with you to Dombrillion. There would be a great scandal which I can't afford, just when I'm trying to slide up into the Human Ingrates." Her voice trailed off. She jumped to her feet, and turned to face Jaro, who had also risen. "Something has occurred to me. It may well be for the best. Tonight my cousin Dorsen plays at a recital. I'm obliged to be on hand. You can escort me, if you like. You'll be able to meet some of my family, including my Uncle Forby. You'll like him; he's Kahulibah and of no small consequence. After the recital, I think my grandmother is planning a supper in honor of Dorsen."

"I don't like the sound of this very much," said Jaro.

Lyssel tilted her head and smiled her most winsome smile. "Jaro! I can't go with you to Dombrillion, but you can escort me to the recital, which will be ever so much nicer." She touched his shoulder and leaned toward him. "You'll see! I'll make it so!"

"How?"

Lyssel spoke in a soft voice. "Really, Jaro! Need you ask?"

"Hm. What time shall I pick you up, and where do you live?"

Lyssel hesitated. "We must be careful not to offend my grandmother; she's a woman of very exact principles. I'll tell her you're a musician and we'll meet at the conservatory; it's at the back of Pingaree Park, beside the Vax Memorial."

Jaro decided that the time had come to gauge the force and direction of Lyssel's intentions. He hesitated, calculating how best to proceed. Lyssel misunderstood the quality of his hesitation. She spoke in a tumble of half-muffled words. "I should mention that the recital is an Institute function. No one can call you a nimp, or a schmeltzer; still, you will be occupying my social level, and meeting my admirable family, all of whom are persons of both gentility and comporture. I hope that you are pleased with the prospect."

Jaro's jaw dropped, then he laughed. "You have it exactly wrong. I'd prefer if you left both your family and your comporture at home. I want to take you out to Mountain Lake Lodge where we could eat fried fish, drink Blue Ruin and spend as much time in bed as possible."

"Jaro!" cried Lyssel. "This is absolute fantasy! I'm committed to the recital!"

"No problem," said Jaro. "After the recital we will make our excuses and go off by ourselves. Do you agree?"

Lyssel grimaced. "My Uncle Forby might very specially want you to join us for the supper."

Jaro shook his head. "That's not sensible! I don't know your Uncle Forby. Now tell me; I must know! Is it yes or no?"

Lyssel sighed, threw back her head so that her tawny locks fell back over her shoulders, and gave him a look of mournful reproach. "Do you so urgently need to involve us in intimacy that you are willing to ignore the risks of scandal?"

Jaro paused to reflect, then said: "Not unless you too are willing."

Lyssel was taken aback. She chewed her lip. "I hardly know what to say."

"The risks can be minimized, almost to nothing," said Jaro. "There are worse ways of spending an evening, as I suppose you realize."

"That is not a flattering line to take, Jaro. Can't you express yourself in more glamorous terms?"

"I can recite some cold facts."

"Oh? So what are these facts?"

"I want none of your family, none of your Uncle Forby, none of your cousin's music, nor your grandmother's supper. It's you whom I want."

"Jaro, you are absolutely primordial, like one of our brutish ancestors who lived in a cave. What if I say no?"

"Then I say no to the recital, since I don't want to meet your relatives."

Lyssel sighed. "Well, let me think. I suppose I can avoid the supper, on one pretext or another."

Jaro now understood that she earnestly and anxiously wanted him to meet Forby Mildoon, for reasons obscure. This was an interesting idea and he wondered at its import. Would she allow him to make love to her in order to fulfill this purpose? She might or might not be chaste, or semi-chaste, but she was definitely a teaser and he need waste no qualms on her behalf; Lyssel would do what was most entertaining for Lyssel. All in all, it was an amusing game. "So what is it to be? Yes? No?"

Lyssel nodded, but Jaro suspected that already Lyssel was formulating hedges and qualifications in case of need.

Through the portal came Hanafer with a group of his friends. Lyssel saw them and smiled sadly. "There's a Daffy-Down-Dilly party tonight. Hanafer wanted me to attend. I refused, by reason of the recital. If he discovered that you had been my escort and that we had gone off afterward, he would be upset. But don't worry; he won't find out—at least, not from me."

Jaro looked across the forecourt. "There he is now. Tell him as much as you like."

Lyssel looked at him, startled. "You surely don't want me to tell him!"

"I don't mind. I might tell him myself."

Hanafer went to the registration table, then rejoined his friends. After a moment of badinage he moved off toward the buffet. Noticing Lyssel and Jaro, he stopped short. They stood in more intimate proximity than he thought either tasteful or appropriate. Hanafer's golden eyebrows rose; his jaw thrust forward and he cried out: "Hoy there, schmeltzer! You don't seem able to learn! You are grazing in the upper pastures again! Don't you see the sign? It reads: 'Gaks, moops, leps and schmeltzers: Keep out!' So, cut your stick and hop off on the double, like the good little strankenpus you are. Quick now! Cut stick!"

Jaro said to Lyssel, "Hanafer at last has become intolerable."

Lyssel uttered a nervous laugh. "Hanafer merely wants his own way. You had better go. Call me at home later."

Jaro shook his head. "Althea Fath has explained how to deal

with these situations. I must assure Hanafer that I mean no harm and explain the destructive force of anger. Hanafer will see his mistake and apologize."

"Try if you like," said Lyssel. "Here he comes."

Hanafer stalked across the forecourt. He halted, spared Jaro a single sidelong glance, then took Lyssel's arm. "Lyssie, let's get away from here; I can't stand the smell of schmeltzing. I think I've made this clear."

Lyssel pulled her arm free. "Please, Hanafer! I get very tired of being yanked this way and that."

"Sorry! But let's settle down to a glass of wine and make our plans for Dombrillion."

"Don't waste your time," said Jaro. "I'm taking Lyssel to Dombrillion."

Hanafer's face sagged in incomprehension. Jaro went on: "We also have plans tonight."

"And what is happening tonight?" Hanafer spoke slowly in a nasal voice of maximum menace.

"It's a recital at the conservatory, Hanafer, and beyond your mental capacity. Afterwards we'll probably drive out somewhere for a midnight supper."

Lyssel gave a choked laugh. "Wonderful! But don't tease poor Hanafer; he's quite angry enough."

"Then you're going with this ballygagger to the recital?"

"Truly, Hanafer, it's none of your affair. I wish that for once you'd behave yourself."

Hanafer clenched his fingers once, twice, then stalked away. Lyssel looked after him. She said softly, pensively: "You've done something quite rash."

"Oh? What?"

"You've started something that can't be stopped."

Hanafer had rejoined his comrades; the four stood muttering, occasionally glancing toward Jaro.

Lyssel shuddered. "They are like beasts, and they don't mean you well. Aren't you afraid?"

"Not at the moment. Where shall I meet you tonight? What should I wear?"

Lyssel dubiously gave instructions. "Suddenly I'm not so sure that this is a good idea. My mother is extremely genteel and not likely to be difficult. But my grandmother is imperious to such a degree that I've seen her despise a stately old Lemurian simply because he took a cream tart from the tray instead of anchovy toast. As for your clothes, you will be safe in black with simple Belminster trousers. Wear nothing either green or spotted with orange. Be neat and polite, and remember that you are a musician."

Jaro compressed his lips. "I feel as if I'll be walking a tightrope."

Lyssel came toward him. "No, Jaro! Tonight, tonight! I am excited! But all must go nicely, and you must get along well with Uncle Forby."

"Very well," said Jaro. "Tonight I shall demonstrate every aspect of high etiquette. I will eat anchovy toast and forego my new green cravat! For conversation, I'll describe the suanola and maybe Tawn Maihac's froghorn."

Lyssel said hurriedly, "Just be nice to Uncle Forby; he could be a valuable friend."

"I'll do my best. Goodbye for now. Is Hanafer watching us?"

"He's been doing nothing else."

Jaro put his arms around Lyssel and kissed her. She stiffened at first, then melted against him.

Jaro said: "I've been wanting to do that for years."

Lyssel grinned up at him. "It would have been nicer if it were not done to spite Hanafer."

"Hanafer hasn't even noticed," said Jaro. He started to kiss her a second time, but she held him away. "Hanafer has noticed everything—and so has everyone else." Lyssel stepped back and out of Jaro's grasp. "One kiss can be explained away as a friendly farewell; a bit maudlin of course, but no cause for excitement. Two kisses mean that the kissers enjoy it. Three kisses indicate scandal."

"Was Hanafer counting?"

"Very carefully, but now he is strolling away. Hm. Odd. Hanafer is better known for his brusque comments." She glanced at Jaro sidelong. "I'm afraid that you have hurt poor Hanafer's feelings."

"Hanafer must learn stoicism," said Jaro.

Lyssel looked away. She said softly, "Sometimes you frighten me."

5

When Jaro telephoned during the early afternoon, Lyssel's response was slow and hesitant, as if she were coping with a series of unforeseen difficulties.

"Everyone is in a lather," she told Jaro gloomily. "Uncle Forby can't be found; apparently he's at an important conference, and no one knows when he'll be available. My grandmother is in a state of fulmination, which means that we all walk around on tip-toe." Lyssel went on to explain that Jaro's function as an escort would be more or less nominal, in view of the special circumstances.

"By 'special circumstances,' do you mean your grandmother?"

"I'm afraid so. My Aunt Dulcie had planned the party, but nothing suited my grandmother, and now she has come raging in like a wild bull and is changing the arrangements. Still, the recital shall occur and I will have carried out my part in the bargain with you."

Jaro was puzzled. "What bargain is this? And how, with such facility, have you carried it out?"

"Please, Jaro! Don't be tiresome. You wanted to be my escort, and I have arranged it. Now listen carefully. The plan is more or less as before. Dame Vinzie—that's my grandmother—wants to celebrate the birthday of my Aunt Zelda tonight, along with everything else. The party will convene for sundowners at Primaeo, Dame Vinzie's mansion on Larningdale Slope, then proceed to the Conservatory at the back of Pingaree Park. After the recital, the party will return to Primeo for an intimate family supper."

Jaro asked: "And where do I fit into the scheme?"

"Things aren't going as smoothly as I had hoped, especially with Uncle Forby missing. But you can meet us in the lobby of the Conservatory. I'll introduce you as a musician, and you will no doubt be invited to join the group, and share Dame Vinzie's box. You may even be allowed to sit beside me, depending upon whether Dame Vinzie perceives you as a nimp and a milksop, or as a bona fide student of exotic music." Lyssel went on to explain that Jaro must conduct himself with impeccable gentility, since the other members of the party would be observing his every move. Lyssel would quietly explain his lack of comporture by citing his connection with the Professors Hilyer and Althea Fath, who must be considered authorities of transworld prestige. Lyssel might also mention Jaro's ambition to explore the music of lost tribes on remote worlds. "In any case," said Lyssel, rather tartly, "You must be modest and discreet and not try to expound any of your private theories. You might thereby ease past the suspicions of Dame Vinzie, though there is no chance whatever that you will be asked to join the supper party."

As for her mother, Dame Ida Bynnoc, Lyssel advised Jaro to contradict none of her remarks, on pain of being labeled a "brash young nincompoop." Jaro thought that Lyssel sounded cool and distant, as if she now regretted the occasion and feared for the outcome. He wondered if he should bring up Lyssel's undertaking to slip away with him after the recital. He decided to say nothing. The whole idea, in any event, had never been more than a bubble of dream gas, that neither he nor Lyssel had truly expected to be realized. Lyssel was probably adept in the making of such gauzy promises which she found exciting but which she never intended to validate.

Jaro sighed and shrugged. If Lyssel chose to retreat from a personal relationship, it was probably all for the best. Lyssel was pretty, but her mind-processes were not at all in concord with his own. It was notable, he thought, that when she called from home, the irresponsible exuberance of youth, along with the hints of sexual abandon were absent, leaving a residual personality which seemed cautious and calculating. He remembered his time at Langolen School. Lyssel had been pretty and teasing and provocative; she had changed little save to acquire a certain intensity of flavor. Even then, she had not seemed as fascinating as Skirlet Hutsenreiter, and whenever Skirlet appeared, Lyssel seemed to become pinched and wan. Strange! Jaro thought back across the years. Dear gallant little Skirlet! What had become of her? She had departed Thanet and nothing more had been heard from her.

The afternoon passed.

Lyssel called Jaro with last minute instructions. She sounded more taut and distracted than ever, and was still concerned for her uncle. "He called us, and it's all very annoying as Grandmother likes to have affairs exactly in order."

"He has probably met some friends at his club," said Jaro.

"He had some important business, but it was supposed to be only a formality, and tonight we would celebrate. Well, no matter. You're still coming, I take it?" Lyssel sounded less than enthusiastic, as if she hoped Jaro would find reasons to beg off.

"I'll definitely be on hand," Jaro assured her.

There was a moment's silence; then she said, "Very well, though I may not be able to give you much personal attention. In fact, if Uncle Forby isn't on hand to ease the way"—she broke off. Then she said, "It may be a bit more difficult, since both my mother and my grandmother are very keen on social distinction."

"Quite all right," said Jaro. "I have other reasons for wanting to be on hand."

Lyssel asked suspiciously, "What reasons are these?"

"Perhaps I'll tell you sometime."

"Hmf. Well then, please be prompt, as I can't wait for you a single instant."

"I'll be there."

6

Jaro dressed with care, avoiding any extravagances which might be considered foppery. He drove the family runabout into Thanet but, lacking membership in the Pro Art Association, he was required to park in a public area at the back of the Institute and walk through Pingaree Park to the Conservatory.

In due course Lyssel's party entered the lobby. Jaro stepped forward and was introduced, the party barely breaking stride for the conventional interchanges. Still, all went well enough, thought Jaro. There were no suspicious challenges, nor haughty glares; indeed the redoubtable Dame Vinzie barely noticed him. Dame Ida, Lyssel's mother, swept him with a glance which was penetrating though not hostile. The rest of the group was indifferent. Forby Mildoon was conspicuous by his absence. Perhaps on this account, Dame Vinzie, Dame Ida and Lyssel seemed tense, brooding and grim. Jaro saw that if he wished a congenial evening, his demeanor must be both suave and self-effacing, and he allowed himself a sheepish smile for his own duplicity.

The group entered the Conservatory, Jaro and Lyssel bringing up the rear. They went directly to the box; there was a moment or two of bustle and confusion with Dame Vinzie's hoarse voice booming across the auditorium. Unobtrusively Jaro found a seat beside Lyssel, at the side of the box, where no one seemed to notice him. Lyssel's manner was distant. Jaro sat quietly, observing the company and wondering what had occurred to alter

Lyssel's mood so notably. Her face was pale and drawn; but as usual she looked demure and dainty wearing a dark blue gown, decorated with a few chaste stripes of white and pink. Around her forehead she wore a band of dark red and blue embroidery, with a moonstone cabochon at the forehead.

The company settled themselves, while Dame Vinzie took stock of her environment and made no secret of her opinions. Presently a decorous conversation came into being, and even Jaro was allowed to utter a sentence or two. He conducted himself with such propriety that even Dame Ida, sitting keen eyed on the other side of Lyssel, could find nothing to criticize. Dame Ida was a seasoned matron, rather short, with a stylish bosom, a lily-cream skin and pink curls. She was so immaculately groomed as to seem glossy, as if she had stepped from the pages of a fashion magazine. Here, thought Jaro, was Lyssel in years to come, when youth had drifted away.

Dame Ida, like everyone else, deferred to Dame Vinzie, an extremely tall and ugly woman with a heavy torso, lank arms and legs and great bony hips. A ruff of iron-gray hair surrounded her scalp and rust-colored blotches mottled her heavy face. Her features were large, coarse and vulgar: eyebrows beetled over deep glaring eye-sockets; folds of leathery skin draped down her cheeks and overhung her jaw; her nose plunged and hooked to cover her upper lip. In spite of all this, Dame Vinzie projected such vitality and bravura, that her ugliness became a positive quality, and commanded fascinated attention. Her voice, loud and harsh, was like a prodrome of her person; her most private and confidential remarks could be heard across the chamber, though obviously she cared not a fig. Surrounded by her kin, she seemed an elemental matriarch, reeking with mana. Jaro thought that she gave off a taint like that emitted by the hanging carcass of an enormous gaunt beast. Jaro looked from Dame Vinzie, past Dame Ida to Lyssel. Three generations, three individuals in a line! Staring closely, he could trace a similarity, grotesque though the idea might be. Never again, he thought, would he be stimulated by Lyssel's charms.

Lyssel, noticing his attention, whispered: "There! Now you've met my family; aren't they splendid? My mother is like a darling doll, so precious and beautiful, and everyone says that Dame Vinzie is absolutely magnificent."

Jaro changed the subject. "Where is your uncle?"

Lyssel's momentary animation vanished and her face became more pinched than ever. "Today he suffered a setback and in consequence he is ill."

"What happened to him?"

Lyssel clamped her lips. "He was deceived by that terrible Gilfong Rute, and it has cost us all dearly."

"All of you?"

Lyssel's cheeks sucked in; she thrust her face forward so that her nose seemed to prod at the air; for an instant Jaro saw a wispy indefinite sketch composed in pale pastels of Dame Vinzie. The glimpse flickered away as rapidly as it had come. Jaro caught his breath, and sat still and nerveless. He could not take Lyssel now if she had been offered to him nude in a tub of whipped cream. "We all share Uncle Forby's distress," said Lyssel, and turned quickly away.

Dame Vinzie noticed Jaro for the first time. She gave him a five-second scrutiny, then dismissed him just as a fisherman tosses a trash fish back into the water.

Jaro looked down at his program, which read:

> "Tonight: the Tala-Lala Strike-offs perform a group of inspired musical illusions after the mode of the five New Aeon Heralds, followed by a recapitulation to create a blindingly expressive unity."

Reading further, Jaro learned that the program, despite the exquisite accuracy of its patterns, might not be instantly accessible to the unprepared listener.

The quintette filed out upon the stage, settled themselves and tuned their instruments. Whenever Jaro had attended a recital of live music, he found that this was often the time he enjoyed the most: the random sounds, still sweet, altering to become ever sweeter and more meaningful as they approached concord, meanwhile building up a most exciting and pleasant tension.

The music began. Jaro soon conceded defeat. The "illusions" surpassed his understanding in all directions at once. At intermission Dame Vinzie stated that only the masterful technique of her granddaughter Dorsen made the Katzenjammer tolerable. Owing to the fine acoustics of the chamber, the remark was carried to every ear in the house.

Jaro reserved his own opinions, though he cautiously agreed with Dame Ida that the music seemed a bit dense. Dorsen brought a fellow musician to the box, a somber young tamurett player, who tried to explain the music to Dame Ida. "You are hearing material of a special sort. Admittedly no one will leave the hall whistling one of our melodies. The notes are intended to function not as entities in themselves, but as boundaries, or limits, defining the empty silences between. In the juxtaposition of these so-called 'empty silences' and the tension of their interaction, the true beauty of the music is to be found."

Dame Ida said that, while the music no doubt had merit—otherwise, surely, no one would be playing it—she still found it beyond her comprehension. Jaro felt safe in stating that he shared her feelings, but no one paid attention. Dame Vinzie wondered loudly why the musicians simply did not put away their instruments and allow the audience to enjoy the silence in its purest form.

The music began again and the audience listened dutifully. At the end of the recital, Dame Vinzie marched from the box, followed by the rest of her company, with Jaro bringing up the rear. In the lobby Dame Vinzie paused to speak with acquaintances. Jaro and Lyssel went out to wait on the front terrace. Lyssel said, "The music was quite grand, don't you think? I hope you enjoyed it. It has really been a great evening for you, or so I should think. You met my mother, who is a Kahulibah, and you were also introduced to Dame Vinzie, which is truly an honor. She is a Sasselton Tiger, and greatly admired. You should feel quite grateful to me."

"Grateful for what?" demanded Jaro in sudden outrage. "You made me listen to that music—worse, in company with that old harridan. When I sat down to the left of your mother, she carefully picked up her purse and moved it to her right side. Do you think you have done me a favor? I think you have played me a ghastly joke!"

Lyssel threw up her arms and stamped her feet in a fury of her own. "Then why did you come?"

"I had my reasons."

"Oh? What reasons?"

"They do not include our original plans for this evening. I can assure you of this, since I never believed you in the first place. I know you too well for what you are."

Lyssel darted glances right and left. "Hush! You are acting like a vulgarian, and everyone is looking at you."

From the lobby came Dame Vinzie. She swept past Jaro as if

he had not existed. Dame Ida gave him a curt nod; then she too hurried away. Lyssel cried: "Everything is topsy-turvy and I don't know what to do. Good night!"

Lyssel ran off after the others. The group entered the stately old conveyance which awaited them beside the terrace. They swept grandly down the drive and disappeared through the gloom of Pingaree Park, and Jaro was left alone on the steps. He waited a few moments while the audience filed out and departed. Behind him the lights of the Conservatory began to go out. Only the eternal flame in a bronze lantern remained to illuminate the terrace.

Jaro hunched his shoulders against the tendrils of mist swirling down from Mount Vax and through the trees of Pingaree Park. He descended the steps and set off toward where he had left the runabout. The path into the park wound between ancient yews, cedars, madrone and many indigenous species. Above him foliage blotted out the stars; a faint illumination seeped through the trees from scattered lights in the parking area.

Jaro walked fifty yards without haste. He stopped to listen. Nothing, save the sigh of the wind in the trees.

Jaro proceeded another few steps, then stopped again. He hissed through his teeth with impatience. Had he been forced to sit through the "Strike-offs" and the proximity of Dame Vinzie and Dame Ida for nothing? At last he heard what he had expected: the soft thud of hurrying feet.

Jaro smiled a soft pensive smile and removed his jacket, which he carried under his arm. He listened again. The steps sounded more loudly, and Jaro could see the swing of tall black wings and the flap of black robes. He placed his jacket neatly on the loam to the side of the road, then turned and waited.

7

In the morning there was news of a most curious and dramatic event. It seemed that four youths about to be graduated from the Lyceum had gone out on some sort of prank, for they wore the ritual garments of the Black Angels of Penitence. But their light-hearted escapade had come to a disastrous end. At midnight a late pedestrian in Pingaree Park had come upon the seriously incapacitated bodies of the four bravos.

The victims were all prominent students at the Lyceum, of good comporture and excellent social prestige. Their names were:

Hanafer Glackenshaw, Kosh Diffenbocker, Almer Culp and Lonas Fanchetto. All had been set upon by a gang of thugs and beaten without mercy. None escaped grievous injury: broken bones, crushed knees and elbows, multiple fractures, bruises and contusions. Further, the group had been carrying a quantity of depilatory compound, for purposes known only to themselves. This substance had been smeared over their own heads, with the result that all were now stone bald, and would remain so for several months to come.

Police Inspector Gandeth had not yet been able to take a statement from the victims. His remarks to the press emphasized his personal outrage: "It appears that the four youths were out on a lark when they encountered a band of hooligans, who indulged themselves in acts of unconscionable savagery. This sort of conduct is intolerable! Be assured that we will bring the perpetrators to justice, without fear or favor.

"As soon as possible, I will interview the victims and ascertain facts; at this moment they are still under sedation and it seems that all will be kept in the hospital for at least three weeks.

"The youths were scheduled to be graduated from the Lyceum next week; their participation in this ceremony, of course, is now impossible."

Two days later came news that Hanafer Glackenshaw had revived sufficiently to speak, but it appeared that he had been so demoralized by the episode that he was unable to give a coherent account of the attack. The same proved to be the case with all the victims, until the police began to suspect a conspiracy of silence and threw up their hands in disgust. The four were Black Angels of Penitence and evidently had been involved with illicit mischief of their own; so there the matter rested.

TEN

1

In the morning, as the Faths sat over breakfast, the telescreen brought news of the atrocities committed upon the Black Angels, frolicking by night in Pingaree Park. It was a deed of unmitigated ferocity, declared the announcer. Each of the Black Angels would be hospitalized for weeks.

Both Hilyer and Althea were appalled by the news. Hilyer declared, "I don't know which should be deplored the most: the Black Angels or the thugs who beat them so viciously."

"Both groups are wicked," said Althea. "They live by violence! Pain is their watchword!" She looked across the table to where Jaro sat meekly eating his breakfast. "Isn't this sort of thing enough to dissuade you from those ugly exercises?"

"Not at all," said Jaro. "The exercises are protection. They increase my stamina. If attacked, I shall run away at full speed, and none of the thugs will be able to catch me."

Althea looked at him doubtfully. Hilyer said, "He is making a joke. A poor joke, I might add."

"I hope you'll never need such an advantage, joke or no joke," said Althea with feeling.

Hilyer changed the subject. "I heard a most interesting rumor yesterday. Do you want to hear it?"

"Of course," said Althea. "Is it scandalous?"

"It's strange and sad. You remember a few years back when the old Yellowbird Ranch was sold?"

"Yes, of course. Dean Hutsenreiter owned it at the time and was probably swindled."

"The agent was Forby Mildoon. He placed the property with Fidol Combine. Gilfong Rute held eighty percent of the stock, and Forby Mildoon, was allowed the remaining twenty percent. Yesterday Fidol announced that it had sold its Yellowbird properties to Lumilar Vistas, a corporation wholly owned by Rute. The price was established by the land assessor, and was valued as wasteland, so that Mildoon's twenty percent came to very little. It was a secret deal; Mildoon learned of the sale yesterday afternoon, to his outrage. He went to Rute's club and threatened a law suit, which troubled Rute not at all. Mildoon lost his temper. He pulled Rute's beard and struck him over the head with a folded newspaper. Rute turned away with a smile of easy dignity, while Mildoon was ejected from the premises. He now faces censure from the Inter-club Committee, and there the matter rests."

"Aha," muttered Jaro. "The mystery of the missing Forby Mildoon has been solved."

"Missing from where?"

"From the recital at the conservatory last night."

Hilyer smiled. "Forby Mildoon was in no mood for music last night."

Jaro thought that still another mystery might have been illuminated. Lyssel had been urgent and persuasive when she had invited him to the recital. At the recital her personality had altered; she had been stiff and cold. What had caused the change? There was still no definite answer, but events were starting to drift into identifiable shapes.

Hilyer asked Jaro's plans for the day.

"It's 'Clean-out Time' at the Lyceum. We're supposed to empty our lockers, turn in laboratory equipment, visit our classrooms and the like. What of you two?"

"Nothing of consequence. Just the usual end of term routines."

Althea told Hilyer: "Don't forget! We're to pick up our accreditations for the Conclave! Otherwise, we won't be allowed into Dimplewater!"

"Right!" said Hilyer. "We'd best arrive at the office early; there's quite a contingent from Thanet—including Dean Hutsenreiter himself. He's reading a very profound paper: 'The Extensional Dimensions of Philosophy, as illustrated by the William Schulz Linguistic Tensors.' "

"Hm," said Althea. "It sounds a bit tortuous."

"So it is. I hope he's more organized on his paper than he is on his financial affairs. According to rumor he's in a quagmire."

"But how can that be?" Althea demanded. "He's renowned for his intellect!"

"Perhaps a bit too much intellect," suggested Hilyer. "Schulz's tensors operate in seventeen dimensions, where both Schulz and Dean Hutsenreiter are quite at home. Finance operates along a single y-axis: buy low, sell high. Dean Hutsenreiter transacts business across too many dimensions and bank officials can't grasp his Non-Zero Mathematics."

Althea clicked her tongue. "Hilyer, you can be devastating when you choose."

Hilyer smiled thinly and turned to Jaro. "You knew his daughter, did you not?"

"Skirlet? Yes. She's been off-world, at a private school; I don't know where."

"I knew once but I've forgotten," said Althea. "I remember that it's on an island. The students sleep in tents and classes are conducted on the beach. I'm told it's very expensive, even though the students are fed bananas and fried fish from the lagoon which they catch themselves."

"It must have been a strain on the girl," said Hilyer. "Here she's a Clam Muffin; there she's just another girl floundering around after some fish."

"Perhaps that's why her father sent her away," suggested Althea. "To bring her feet back to earth."

Jaro protested at once. "Skirlet isn't like that! She's not at all vain! The fact is, she doesn't care who thinks what about her!"

"Isn't that a rather lofty attitude?" suggested Althea mildly.

"Yes—for good reason."

"You are surprisingly vehement," suggested Hilyer drily.

Jaro grinned. "She's extremely pretty. I've always wanted to know her better, but then, she's a Clam Muffin, and it's difficult."

Althea said vaguely, "Clam Muffins do all sorts of odd things. It's part of their reason-for-being."

Hilyer smiled sardonically. "I suspect she's home because her off-world expenses became too much for Dean Hutsenreiter to handle."

Jaro looked up in surprise. "Skirlet is back at Thanet?"

Hilyer nodded. "I saw her yesterday in the Dean's office."

"That's interesting news. How did she look?"

Hilyer shrugged. "I didn't notice much change. She still uses that careless damn-your-eyes pose that in anyone else would be called 'insolence.' She's still something of a tomboy, to judge by her clothes and her figure. Still, it's easy to see that she's grown up a bit. I thought she looked tired, to tell you the truth, and perhaps depressed. She did not recognize me, of course."

Althea said brightly, "I expect that she's come to complete her education at the Institute." She turned to Jaro. "You'll be seeing her next term in your classes; won't that be nice?"

"Not if she snubs me and acts insolent," said Jaro, grinning at his father.

"It's a pity you can't come with us to Ushant," said Hilyer. "Unfortunately it would interfere with your first term at the Institute."

Althea said soothingly, "There will be other occasions, and as always your education must come first."

Jaro had glumly accepted the prospect of four more years as a scholar, when every instinct urged him to search out the secrets of his beginnings, but he no longer quarreled with Hilyer and Althea. Sometimes he wondered if ever he would know the truth. These occasions of doubt always stimulated a surge of obstinacy from somewhere deep in his mind, and resolution returned.

After breakfast Jaro took himself to Gaing's office at the space terminal.

Gaing had learned of the previous night's event in Pingaree

Park, and he gave Jaro a brief dispassionate inspection. "There seems to have been a bit of a flare-up last night near the conservatory."

Jaro grinned. "The Black Angels were involved, or so I'm told. They'll be flying low for a time."

Gaing nodded. "So what's the schedule for summer?"

"Just the routine. The Faths will be gone and I'll be alone. I intend to repair the roof and give the place a coat of paint; then there will be a week or so of formalities before I can enter the Institute. Meanwhile, I'd like to continue my lessons, and work as many hours as possible at the shop."

"That can be arranged," said Gaing. "I'll be glad for your help; the work has started to pile up. Next week we have a shakedown scheduled for the big red Mark Nineteen Space-eater. Unless the owner is aboard, you can take her out and bring her in."

"Great! Thank you very much!"

Gaing nodded. "Now let's work out some kind of schedule."

2

Halfway through the morning Jaro arrived at the Lyceum and busied himself with the duties required of departing students. For some it was a melancholy experience. Clean-out Day and commencement marked a transition: behind was youth, with its normal quota of games, irresponsibility, small love affairs, and a mock-serious striving up the ledges, which were of great symbolic significance and the best of training for the future.

Jaro went about the familiar halls, gathering up belongings, bidding farewell to his instructors, a few of whom he had liked. At noon he went to the cafeteria, and took his lunch of a sandwich, salad and fruit tart to a table. As he started to eat, Lyssel entered the room, wearing a fetching white skirt and a dark blue pullover. She was alone and seemed, so Jaro thought, rather peaked, and subdued, as if she were not feeling well. She noticed Jaro only when he came up behind her and took her tray. She turned in surprise. "This way," said Jaro. "Over here to my table."

Lyssel's face tightened, and she stood stiffly silent, staring at her tray. "Come!" said Jaro. "We're holding up the line."

Scowling, Lyssel marched behind him to the table and ungraciously seated herself.

Jaro pretended not to notice. "I was pleased to meet your family. They are not at all as I expected."

"Oh?" Lyssel could not with decorum refuse to answer; also she was curious. "Where were they different from your expectations?"

"They all seem persons of decision, with energetic personalities."

Lyssel responded with a curt nod. She spoke grudgingly, "You're quite right; they are very important persons, and of excellent comporture as well. My mother has just received a bid from Ambrosiana. She could slide into the Kahulibahs any time she liked."

"Interesting," said Jaro. "How did you enjoy the recital?"

Lyssel said gloomily, "I couldn't understand it, nor could any other sane person. Dorsen is as bewildered as anyone else, but she is forced to play as the director indicates. She's now practicing a work by Jeremy Cavaterra, which she says is nicer."

Jaro asked cautiously, "I hope that everyone thought well of me?"

"Does it matter?" asked Lyssel. "Dame Vinzie thought you were an usher, and could not understand why you sat in the box. My mother did not care for you very much; she said that you were a pussyfooter and a schmeltzer. She said the way you were sitting, so stiff and uneasy, gave her to think that you had just wet your pants."

"Whisht!" said Jaro. "If I ever meet her again, I won't know what to say."

Lyssel made no response. Jaro sighed. "Luckily, my internal equilibrium, or pride—whatever it's called—doesn't need compliments for survival."

Lyssel remained silent. Moody and sullen, she nibbled at her lunch, then pushed it aside. She eyed Jaro stonily. "How odd to hear you speak of pride and self-respect! When Hanafer calls you a moop, you merely simper and show him your pretty eyelashes." She turned away. "I must be going. You, of course, have your various secrets to attend to. Also, you must not neglect to pay off your gang."

"Gang? What gang?"

"Come, Jaro, don't be vapid! I mean the gang you hired to thrash Hanafer and the others last night."

"There was no gang. I was alone. Hanafer jumped me from

the bushes with his Black Angels. Do you want to hear the whole story?"

Lyssel gave a slight nod. Jaro proceeded. "I went to the conservatory last night. Why do you think I went?"

Lyssel said coldly, "It's surely clear! Everyone knows it! You went to schmeltz with me and my high-status family."

Jaro smiled. "You could not be more wrong! I went to lure Hanafer and his Angels. I made sure he knew what was happening, and he took the bait. Hanafer and his group came to Pingaree Park, where they hoped to teach me penitence. I was waiting for them. I was alone."

Lyssel's eyes were round with incredulity. "It can't be true! Hanafer said there were seven or eight big burly types, probably Kolaks. You are not telling the truth, and I can't abide liars!" She rose to her feet.

"Wait! When will you go again to visit Hanafer?"

"Late this afternoon."

"Tell him that you want the truth. Tell him that if they continue their lies, I will wait until they are out of the hospital; then some pleasant evening I will find them. I will be alone. I will do worse than before, so that they will come out from the hospital hopping and crawling, like broken mannequins. Will you tell them that?"

Lyssel shivered, turned and walked away, shoulders drooping. Jaro watched her go, wondering why he felt sorry for her.

On the occasion of commencement, Jaro encountered Lyssel. He asked: "Did you consult Hanafer?"

Lyssel nodded. "I gave him your message."

Jaro waited.

Lyssel looked off across the hall. "He said that there was no gang, only you. He said that you were a devil, that he would avoid you as best he could for the rest of his life." She started to move away, then looked back over her shoulder. "And I will do the same."

3

Hilyer went off to his office at the Institute, only to discover he had forgotten a sheaf of documents which he would need at a committee meeting. He telephoned home; Althea found the documents and sent Jaro to deliver them. Returning to the telephone, she notified Hilyer that the problem had been solved and that Jaro was on his way.

Hilyer expressed his relief, then said, "We've just had another offer for Merriehew."

"Indeed! Was it that odious Mildoon character again? I wouldn't deal with him if he offered me Queen Kaha's jewels in a gold warming dish."

"It wasn't Mildoon. This man was dignified and handsome, like a retired justiciant. He gave his name as 'Pomfrey Yikes,' from a company called Beneficial Properties."

"So: what did you tell Mr. Yikes?"

"I said we were on the verge of departing for Ushant, and could not even talk to him until our return. He said that he would approach us later. I asked the identity of his client; he said he was not at liberty to say. I told him not to call back until he was ready to divulge this information; that, in effect, we would deal only with principals. He said that he would take advice, and there the matter rested."

"Strange how these offers continue to surface," mused Althea. "It's almost as if someone knows something we don't."

Hilyer gave a cynical chuckle. "That's taken for granted."

"It's a real mystery!" said Althea. "There is no intrinsic value to the ramshackle old place except to the three of us. It's quiet and peaceful; we can hear the wind in the trees and at night the troubadour bats."

"There'll be changes if anyone starts a development along Katzvold Road."

"That's all just talk," said Althea. "It's been going on for years and nothing has come of it."

"Possibly true," said Hilyer. "It's also true that Merriehew is falling apart. The roof leaks; we need new windows in the kitchen, the timber should be treated with Constor. It all means money, time and effort, and what do we have in the end? A cranky old farmhouse with floors out of level and every wall askew. Sooner or later, Jaro will be going off on his own, and we'll be left to rattle around in an untidy old barn."

Althea spoke in surprise, "I've never heard you say such things before!"

"I suppose I'm in a bad mood."

"Personally, I'm fond of the old place. I don't want to sell, and I'm sure that Jaro feels the same."

"Very well," said Hilyer. "Just as long as you don't insist that I paint the place from a ladder."

They spoke a few moments longer, then Hilyer said, "Jaro has arrived with my documents. Goodbye for now."

4

Jaro, upon leaving Hilyer's office, returned to the corridor. A few yards ahead double doors led into Dean Hutsenreiter's glossy suite of administrative offices. As Jaro approached, the doors slid open and a slender dark-haired girl stepped out. She wore a jacket and short skirt of pale blue twill; her figure was taut and erect; she held her head high, eyebrows arched, mouth compressed. Noticing Jaro, she stopped short and waited for him to approach.

Jaro thought that she had changed very little. A tousle of short dark locks still clasped her face, with small indication of purposeful planning; she still carried herself with the swaggering bravura that was part of her fabulous legend. She might have been an inch or two taller and her figure was no longer that of a hungry waif. She appeared more serene, less fractious than the Skirlet Jaro remembered, so that he was not surprised when she greeted him with civility. "You are Jaro Fath."

"Of course I'm Jaro Fath! Who did you take me for?"

Skirlet smiled a humorless smile. "No one in particular. I just wanted to start off on the proper footing."

Jaro looked at her incredulously, and her smile slowly faded. He said, "I heard you were home and I was wondering when I would see you."

Skirlet looked over her shoulder toward her father's offices. "This is not the best place to talk. Come."

The two descended to the street and crossed to an open-air cafe beside the broad Flammarion Prospect. They seated themselves at a table under a green and blue parasol and presently were served iced fruit juice.

For a time an awkward constraint held them silent. Jaro finally asked a polite question, "Are you planning to enroll at the Institute?"

Skirlet laughed: a strange bitter laugh, as if the question were hopelessly naive. "No."

Jaro raised his eyebrows. The response had been incisively

final. He tried again. "What have you been doing since last you were home?"

Skirlet looked at him stonily. Jaro became uncertain. He said, "On second thought, it's not important. Don't feel obliged to answer."

Skirlet spoke with dignity: "Excuse me. I was trying to arrange my thoughts. What happened was, in a sense, simple. I was sent off-world, to the Aeolian Academy at Glist, on Axelbarren. I was graduated with honors. I met a number of people; I had some interesting adventures, and now I am home."

"It sounds pleasant enough," said Jaro. "Is this what you are trying to tell me?"

"Not altogether."

Jaro waited while Skirlet brooded upon her experiences. She said at last, without emphasis: "There were good times and times not so good. I learned a great deal. Still, I don't want to go back—now or ever." Then, after a pause: "What of you? I see that you have not yet run off into space."

"No. Not yet. But nothing has changed."

"You still feel compelled to trace down your past?"

Jaro nodded. "As soon as possible—which means after I take a degree at the Institute. The Faths insist and I have no choice."

Skirlet studied him dispassionately. "And you are not angry with the Faths?"

Jaro stirred in his chair. "No."

"Hmf. Still, you'd skite off into space this instant, if you were able."

"Probably. I'm not sure. There's much to be done before I go."

"Hmm. What are you studying at the Institute?"

"Engineering, dynamics, space science. Also, Gaean history and musicology, to appease the Faths."

Skirlet asked, "Do you think I have changed since you saw me last?"

Jaro reflected. "I don't know what you want to hear. But it seems to me that you are still Skirlet Hutsenreiter, though even more so. I've always thought you—I can't find the proper word—pretty? Beautiful? Perturbing? Charming? Amazing? Nothing quite fits."

"What about 'enthralling'?"

"Yes, that's close."

Skirlet nodded thoughtfully, as if Jaro had corroborated one of her own deeply felt convictions. "The years go past. I used to think of them as slow tragic heartbeats." She turned her head, looked down the Prospect. "I remember a handsome boy from long ago. He was very clean and neat; he had long eyelashes and a face full of romantic dreams. One afternoon, on an impulse, I kissed him. Do you remember?"

"I remember. My head was in the clouds. I'll become that boy again, if you'll kiss me some more."

"You couldn't change back, Jaro. Even worse, I could never, ever be that girl again. When I think of it, I want to weep."

Jaro reached out and took one of her hands. "Perhaps we haven't changed quite as much as you think."

Skirlet shook her head. "What has happened to me is beyond your knowing. In fact, it's probably beyond your imagining."

"Tell me about it."

Skirlet spoke with sudden resolution. "Very well; if you are interested. But there is something you must do. The girl who left four years ago was Skirlet. She has become someone else called 'Skirl' and that is what you must call me now."

"Just as you say."

"I'll tell you more or less what happened. It can only be an outline, with most of the details omitted—otherwise I'd be talking for a month. It will be hard to abbreviate, since what I leave out will be as strange and intricate as the rest."

"I'm listening."

Skirl slouched back into the chair. "A hundred things, a thousand things have happened. It's hard to put them into order." She deliberated. "After I left Langolen School, my father said he was closing Sassoon Ayry, and I must go to live with my mother on Marmone. I explained that her palace was an erotic jungle; he said: 'Pish-tush!'; that I should be able to cope with it, with whatever degree of involvement suited me best. I told him the question was moot, since I refused to go there. I reminded him that he had promised to send me to the Aeolian Academy, which was rated highly by experts. The staff not only provided an education, but exerted themselves to make the school congenial. The countryside was beautiful, with a sea to the north, forests and moors to the south and the city Glist nearby.

"In any case my heart was set on Aeolian Academy, but my father said that it was too expensive, and that he needed all his money to finance his trip to Old Earth. The money for this trip he had 'borrowed' from one of my trust funds—which meant, of course, that I would never see the money again. I told him that unless he sent me to Aeolián I would appeal to the Clam Muffin Committee for redress, and they would surely clap him into what is called 'corrective jurisdiction,' which would severely limit his options. I had a few hundred sols left in another trust fund; he took this money and said: 'Very well; you want to attend the extremely expensive Aeolian Academy, and so you shall!' He showed me his peculiar grin which makes him look like an old fox eating garbage, and I knew that something might be awry. Nonetheless, he told me to pack, that I was enrolled at Aeolian Academy, and the next day I was on my way." Skirl paused. "Now I must cover more time and many more events. I'll try to hint at them, but for the most part you must use your imagination—which is a pity, since the reality was so wild and rich. I won't even try to describe Axelbarren itself.

"I arrived at Glist, and was delivered to the Aeolian Academy. I fell in love with the place instantly. The euphoria lasted until I found that I was not enrolled as a Clam Muffin with private quarters and a formal cuisine. Instead, I was assigned to what was called 'Scratch-arse Dormitory,' a kind of economy class barracks where disadvantaged students were accepted. I took my meals at a long table in Roaring Gut Refectory, and bathed in a communal shower. Further, I was required to work twelve hours a week to help defray my expenses. I explained to the Superintendent that there was some mistake; that I was Skirl Hutsenreiter, a Clam Muffin, and would require accommodations commensurate with my status." Skirl smiled at the recollection. "The Superintendent laughed, as did everyone else in the room. I told them quite smartly that their conduct was boorish, and if they did not correct their attitudes, I would see that they were reprimanded. 'By whom?' they asked. 'By me,' I told them, 'if no one of the proper authority were on hand.' They lost patience with me and declared, rather curtly, 'We are that authority!' They told me to read, digest and obey all school regulations, or risk expulsion. But as I turned to go, the Superintendent told me that I could work my stint as a tutorial assistant. I agreed, and presently was introduced to my ward, a girl about my own age, from a very wealthy family. Her name was Tombas Sunder; she was not in any way backward or deficient. Her problem seemed to be absentmindedness and a disinclination for the drudgery involved in schoolwork. She was rather slight, languid and graceful, romantically pale, with long dark hair, large dark eyes. We became friends at once and she insisted that I share her private rooms, which were more than adequate for the two of us. I met Myrl Sunder, her father: a legal consultant, so he described himself. He was not a large man, but deft and strong, with patrician features and soft gray hair in notable contrast with his dark sun-beaten skin. His wife had been killed five years before in an accident, and he never referred to her, nor did Tombas.

"His conduct was civil and correct. I told them something of myself and my background, I mentioned that I was a Clam Muffin, and tried to explain the Sempiternals and their relationship with the striving under-clubs, but I fear that I only confused them, so I spoke no more of my status.

"Myrl Sunder adored his dreamy absent-minded daughter. He was pleased to find that we worked well together. The material itself gave her no trouble, but she would start day-dreaming unless I kept her attention fixed upon the topic at hand. We never quarreled; she was docile and affectionate, and she also had a mind teeming with wonderful and strange ideas. When I listened to her I was often fascinated, often a bit taken aback by the macabre elements which decorated her fantasies. She prattled cheerfully of her erotic experiments, which were more playful than profound, and I responded with anecdotes of Piri-piri. All the while I wondered how anyone could have thought her deficient. We talked hours into the night, and always I heard something surprising or unconventional. Sometimes her ideas were so wild and mysterious that I wondered if they might not have reached her from a higher psychic plane.

"Tombas liked to brood about questions to which there were no answers: What came before the beginning? Would the universe persist if all living things were dead? What was the difference between Something and Nothing? Then she would ponder the meaning of death. Perhaps, so she suggested, life was no more than a dress rehearsal for what happened afterwards. It was a subject to which she returned far too often, and finally I insisted upon more cheerful topics for our conversations.

"So went the second term. It was a pleasant situation for me. I had luxurious lodgings and all the money I needed. My father never communicated with me. Tombas was more or less as before, though we no longer talked at such intimate lengths. She had other friends: a sculptor, teaching assistants in the Philosophy Department, a musician. Her social life seemed ordinary enough. The second term ended. We removed for the summer to their beach house on Cloud Island. Here many strange things occurred but I can't digress. Though there is one thing I should mention. Tombas spent much time alone on the beach, watching the surf roll in. Then, for a time, she occupied herself building sandcastles, using a slurry mixed from sand, water and the juice of sea-pink bulbs which hardened into a light crusty foam. She formed this material into domes, spires, cloisters, arcades, courts, balconies. She used an architecture expressing fantasy and magic in a style quite strange to me. Tombas always seemed to become restless when I went with her to the beach, so for the most part I let her go alone. One day I went down to find her doing nothing very much and she seemed disposed to talk. The castle was finished, she said; she would build no more. I told her it was beautiful and asked where she had seen such an architecture. She just shrugged and said it came from a place twelve universes away from our own. She pointed to a window. 'Look through there.' I looked through the window and could not believe my eyes. The chamber was furnished with beautiful rugs, chairs, tables; in a large bed a girl lay sleeping.

"Tombas spoke. 'Her name is Earne; she is about our own age, and this is her palace. She has notified her two best paladins that they must come to her and that she will receive whomever arrives first. From the west comes Shing, built of jet and silver. From the east comes Shang, built of copper and green moidras. They will meet in front of the palace and fight to the death. The survivor will go to her bed and take her in love. Which shall it be? One, should he win, will give her a life of delight and loving care; the other would visit upon her a set of horrifying degradations.'

"I thought that it was rather a doleful story, and bent to look once again through the window. I saw only sand; nothing else.

"Dusk was falling and a cold wind was blowing in from the sea. Tombas turned away; in silence we returned to the house.

"Thereafter, Tombas lost interest in the beach. The wind and the spray worked on the castle; it crumbled and became a heap of sand. Whenever I passed I wondered what had happened to Earne. Who had claimed her: Shing or Shang? But I never raised the question with Tombas.

"The summer passed, third term began. Things were much as before. Late one evening we were sitting together in the dark. We were drinking a soft Blue-flower wine, and we were both in an unusual mood. Quite casually Tombas said that she thought she would die quite soon, and that she loved me and wanted me to accept all her possessions and use them as my own.

"I told her that the idea was preposterous, and that she would do nothing of the sort; further, that she should not allow herself to think such dismal thoughts.

"Tombas only tilted her head to the side in her own particular way, smiling. She told me she had been shown expansion beyond limits, in a revelation. Now she knew so much, and her head was so crammed with facts, that she could only process a small segment of her knowledge during any given interval.

"I said that it sounded interesting, but why must it include her death?

" 'It was inevitable,' said Tombas. She went on to explain that the five senses had constructed a cardboard facade to deceive the mind. With enlightenment had come a tragic vision of reality. She had glimpsed the terrible truth behind the facade. There was no recourse; submission was the optimum response, in that it put an end to struggle. Submission offered surcease from agonies of hope and love and wonder.

"So—there was the answer: total abnegation, and a quick yielding to death, if only to put an end to hope.

"I said that it was sheer hysteria which caused her to say such things. How, for instance, could she know that death was at hand? She told me that she could see her body as a three-dimensional armature, washed with films of color: pink, yellow, blue, cerise—these colors flowed over the armature and—according to her preception—signified various phases of normality. But now a rust-colored shape had appeared and indicated the onset of mortefaction.

"I had heard enough. I jumped to my feet and turned on all the lights. I told her that such talk was obscene and disgusting.

"Tombas only laughed her gentle laugh, and said that truth could not be altered by invective. Why recoil from sweet beautiful death in such a passion of righteousness?

"I asked after the source of these ideas, and who had been talking to her? I asked if she were having a love affair, perhaps with the same person who was guiding her thoughts? Tombas became vague, and said that such questions led into blind alleys; that only truth was important, not personalities.

"There the matter rested." Skirl paused, then: "Once again, there is too much to tell. These are the high points. I reported to Myrl Sunder. He became furious. I told him all I knew and all I suspected. He altered before my eyes, to a man focused upon a single objective. He intended to find and deal with the person or persons who had suborned his daughter's mind and possibly her body. Suddenly, I saw that he was a very dangerous man. I learned that by profession Myrl Sunder was an effectuator who masked himself as a legal consultant. Together, he told me, we would learn what was going on. As a start, he arranged medical examinations for both myself and Tombas. We were pronounced sound, though Tombas showed symptoms of some odd and ambiguous mental disorder for which they could recommend no treatment.

"Tombas resented the attention. She felt that I had betrayed her trust, even though I had been subjected to the same examination. She saw through the game, and became rather cool.

"I conferred again with Myrl Sunder. He pointed out that I was optimally situated to discover who had such influence over Tombas, and he commissioned me to do so. Very discreetly, I started to collect information. The trail was not hard to follow. It led to a certain Ben Lan Dantin and two others. They were instructors in the School of Religious Philosophy. Tombas had taken a course in Religious Derivations from Dantin and they had engaged in long after-class discussions, and evening meetings as well.

"Myrl Sunder called on Dantin after I told him what I had learned. Both the romance and the instruction came to an instant halt. Dantin made some lame excuse to Tombas. She seemed puzzled but not greatly disturbed. I thought it was very odd, and my opinion of Dantin was not enhanced. He was a curious sort: slim, graceful, quite young but intellectually precocious, with a grave pale face in an aureole of dark curls. His eyes were large, luminous, dark hazel; his mouth was so tender and his smile so sweet that many of the girls wanted to kiss him where he stood. This group did not include me. To look at him turned my stomach. I thought him over-ripe, decadent and depraved, if in an interesting way.

"Tombas knew nothing about my involvement and it wasn't long before we resumed our old relationship. One day she told me, quite casually, that she had decided to die at the end of the following day.

"I was shocked. I argued for an hour, but she said only that it was for the best. I pointed out that she would be leaving behind her father and myself to grieve. Tombas said that there was an easy solution: all of us could die together. I told her that we wanted to live, but she only laughed and said that we were being foolishly stubborn. I left her to herself and informed Myrl Sunder of her plan.

"The day passed and the night. On the next day Myrl Sunder took us to lunch at Cloud Country, a restaurant floating high in the sky just under the drift of cumulus clouds. It is a beautiful place, unique in the Gaean Reach, and an inducement for the saddest and most defeated person to stay alive. We sat at a table beside a low balustrade, overlooking the city Glist and the surrounding territory. Tombas showed no great appetite and seemed very pensive, but Myrl Sunder managed to introduce a powerful sedative into her food. By the time we had returned to the surface she was drowsy and by middle afternoon she was sound asleep in her own bed at home.

"The afternoon waned and the sun fell toward the horizon. At sunset Tombas stopped breathing and was dead."

Skirl hesitated, then said, "I don't want to go through all the details but, touching just the high points, this is what happened next. I have already mentioned that Myrl Sunder was an effectuator, and a person of very strong character. I went to live in his house, where I disposed of Tombas' belongings: a very melancholy task. I sorted through her letters and her diary and discovered names. I continued my classes at the academy and after several frightening adventures I learned what there was to be known. It was heartbreaking information. Tombas had been induced to die for several reasons. The most mysterious was a sort of refined necrophilia, elaborately codified so as to produce an erotic mental sensation. Dantin was the leader. He had invented the precepts of the cult as an exercise in a peculiar sort of psychic sexual perversion. The two disciples were Flewen and Raud, all equally twisted. Tombas was their fourth victim, and had brought them all a weird joy impossible to describe in ordinary language.

"Sunder was pleased when I told him of my discovery. He made his plans with care, since the three were wary. He captured them with my help and conveyed them to the summer home overlooking the shore where Tombas had built her magic palace.

"Obeying Sunder's instructions, I took myself into the kitchen and set about preparing our dinner. Sunder led the three down to the beach and I went on with my work.

"In an hour Sunder returned, smiling. As we sat over soup, I asked what had happened. He explained without diffidence. The tide was now at low ebb. He had buried them in the sand up to their necks, facing out to sea, and left them to watch the incoming tide. But they would derive small pleasure from their own deaths and might not even drown, as the sand crabs would find them at once.

"As we ate, we spoke of the future. He told me candidly that he had become accustomed to me, and that I had come to represent the daughter he had seen vanish into the murk of her own imagining. He wanted me to live in his house; meanwhile, I could continue at Aeolian Academy. Or, should I be so inclined, I could become his assistant, and he would train me in the techniques of an effectuator, and this is what happened. I took extra courses at Aeolian Academy, and they gave me an early certificate. I helped Sunder in his work, and—far more importantly—I took the place of poor dead Tombas, who had killed herself by some means that was still beyond our understanding.

"Sunder taught me as much about effectuating as I could assimilate. He emphasized that in the main, the work consisted of gathering information and fitting it together, though at times it could be dangerous. He put regular sums into my bank account until it reached five thousand sols, which he said should cover most contingencies, if he were not around to deal with them himself.

"Four months ago Sunder was sent on a mission to the world Morbihan, in the back region of Aquila, where he was killed by bandits.

"His younger brother Nessel inherited the house and told me that I must leave, the sooner the better. He confiscated my bank account claiming that five thousand sols was far too much. He allowed me a thousand sols, which he said must suffice.

"I departed the Sunder house with very little more than my clothes. I discovered that I was homesick, and so here I am: once more a Clam Muffin but otherwise destitute, since my father as usual is surviving by miracles of juggling invisible bank accounts. In a week he'll be off to Dimplewater on Ushant, to a conclave of xenologists, or something of the sort. How he proposes to finance the junket I can't begin to guess."

"So, you'll have Sassoon Ayry to yourself while he's gone?"

Skirl laughed. "It's the same as before. He wants to close the house, to save maintenance costs."

"So what will you do?"

"I intend to become an effectuator." Skirl spoke defiantly, as if she expected either amusement or a challenge.

Jaro formed his reply with care. "Do you mean, right away, or sometime in the future?"

"Right away. Don't look so blank. I worked with Myrl Sunder. I learned a great deal."

"The work is dangerous."

"I know. Still, Sunder was killed not because he was an effectuator, but because he was mistaken for a rich tourist."

Jaro frowned up into the green and blue parasol. "Before you can even get started, you'll need to know Gaean law, police procedure, forensic science, criminal psychology, the arts of disguise, the use of weapons and technical equipment. Most of all, you'll need capital for working expenses."

"I understand all this." Skirl rose to her feet. "I am going to the library. I want to find how to qualify for an effectuator's license. I have probationary papers issued at Glist, and they may be valid here."

The two left the café, and paused in the street. Jaro said tentatively: "When the Faths leave for Ushant, I'll be alone at Merriehew. If you like, you can move in with me. There is plenty of room, and you can have as much privacy as you wish."

Skirl seemed to ponder. Jaro went on. "When the rain comes down during the evening and the wind blows through the trees, it's very pleasant to sit before the fireplace, dining late and listening to the storm."

Skirl pursed her lips and looked aside. She said at last, "I can't think of any reason to do so."

"Nor I, really."

"Then why did you ask?"

"It was an act of daring folly."

Skirl shrugged. "If I get bored—or cold, or wet, or hungry—I might look in."

5

The Faths would travel to Ushant aboard the great passenger packet *Francil Ambar*. Having made many such excursions, they both were packed and organized the day before their departure, and so were able to spend a quiet evening with Jaro.

Hilyer spoke of the Great Conclave at Dimplewater. "To be honest, up to a month ago, I knew very little regarding Ushant—

only that it was a soft, kind world, hospitable to tourists, with a highly civilized population. The tourist brochures use the words 'delectable' and 'paradise-in-being.' Last week I went to the library and discovered a great deal more." Hilyer settled back in his chair and told Jaro what he had learned.

"Ushant has been located and explored since five thousand years ago, and from the first has been considered a world congenial to human settlement, with magnificent flora and an almost total absence of noxious fauna. Where the River Leis joined the River Ling, the combined waters had flooded a vast plain of hummocks, dips and hillocks, to create a region of innumerable small islands. The original settlers built their airy palaces upon these islands, in gardens of bargeoaks, nenuphars, sparkle-tufts, cedars, deodars and flowering dendrons. In time the area became fabulous Dimplewater, City of the Thousand Bridges.

"From the beginning, the folk who came to live on Ushant were a special sort: 'well-educated, strongly individualistic, with an aversion for the swarms and clots of humanity which had once pressed in on them—pulsing, breathing, smelling of humid flesh, raucous with noise, vile as their own swarms of pet animals,' as Ian Warblen, one of the early settlers, put it.

"Today the folk are intensely sophisticated and sensitive to all the aesthetic nuances. They collect beautiful objects and make them part of their living experience. Still, their most distinctive trait is an extreme autonomy, which prompts them to live alone.

"This privacy is modified, from time to time. They belong to yacht clubs and enjoy regattas on the central lagoon; they constantly attend seminars upon arcane subjects; they take their children out into the backlands on camping trips. Occasionally they will participate, either as hosts or guests, at intimate dinner parties, where no more than five persons are present. These will usually be folk who share a mutual interest, the more esoteric the better. At such events the cuisine is superb and the etiquette ritually exact. Off-worlders are seldom invited; when this is the case, their solecisms give rise to wry comments.

"Love affairs are both intense and highly romantic though of short duration. Children are nurtured in crêches with little parental attention.

"As individuals, the folk of Dimplewater are polite, though the off-worlder often finds them a bit cool. Their most distinctive trait is not at all obvious. This is the fact that each lives psychologically alone, as if he himself were an island.

"Very odd," said Jaro. "It seems something of an affectation."

Hilyer shrugged. "It is more serious than mere social panache. Everyone is rich; everyone is proud; no one feels a need for social support, so each person lives his life and celebrates his tamsour alone."

" 'Tamsour'?" Jaro was again puzzled. "What is 'tamsour'?"

Hilyer leaned back in his chair, looked toward the ceiling and spoke in the ponderous voice he reserved for important topics. "If I could answer that question, I'd rank as the foremost xenologist of the Gaean Reach. It is an idea which baffles off-worlders, tourists and sociologists alike. Still, I can describe 'tamsour' and some of its effects. It seems to mean the totality of one's life, condensed into a single drop of essence, a single profound symbol, a single moment of total enlightenment. But these are words and tamsour can't be put into words."

"It sounds like a spasm of hysterical revelation," said Jaro.

"To a certain extent. But the tamsour has extraordinary power, so that society at large acts like a mass of radioactive material. At random intervals one of its components becomes unaccountably over-stressed and explodes in a great gout of energy. This person always provides a dramatic peroration; it is expected of him and he seldom disappoints. Tamsour is the theme; and the substance is usually personal aggrandizement, sometimes a bit of self-pity, but never apologies for past misdeeds, real or imaginary."

Hilyer took up a cartridge from the table. "I have here the record of one such peroration." Hilyer dropped the cartridge into his sound reproducer. "You will hear a man speaking to an attentive audience. The man is abnormally excited; he is over-stressed and beyond reason. Presently he self-destructs, as dramatically and poetically as possible. The episode arouses wide critical interest and is discussed in murmurs of knowledgeable analysis."

"Odd."

"Ha!" said Hilyer. "You haven't heard the worst of it. Sometimes the death-seeker gathers quantities of beautiful goods: rugs, porcelains, rare wood filigrees, bibelots, ancient curious. Often he heartlessly confiscates such precious objects from his friends and neighbors, taking care to seize their most treasured possessions. He heaps these priceless objects around a central pylon and sets them ablaze, dancing a jig on a high platform, singing out his own requiem. Listen: this is the declamation."

Hilyer touched a button on his instrument. A sonorous voice cried out: "Here I stand, the darling of time, the king of light, the soul of love, the blissful, precious and beloved core of all being! I am the pre-eminent one, who was destined for great things! I knew it; everyone knew it; it was self-evident. Now, where is the golden promise? I cry out against injustice; it is rampant in the cosmos and at last it has tricked me, so that I see no choice except to end the entire sorry mess. But if I die not in victory, at least I stand resplendent in the glory of my tamsour! If the cosmos thinks to play this tragic joke upon me, the cosmos shall suffer more than I, since I go out in a suffusion of beauty! This smoke I breathe, it is like incense; I am intoxicated with the beauty of my going! Let the cosmos beware! The future is blank, but I shall glory in my sunset colors of death! I will be famed for my great tamsour! Now behold: I soar from my place on high; I fly in utter brave and parabolic elegance to the end of all!"

The voice ended. Another voice said without emphasis: "The gentleman Varvis Malapan has just plunged a hundred feet to his death, and so has consummated his tamsour. He is no more. The cosmos he ruled has disappeared, and is less than a void. It is gone, beyond memory."

Hilyer retrieved the sound cartridge. "An occasion like this is uncommon. Perhaps one person in a hundred feels strongly enough about his tamsour to so dedicate his being."

"I find it a bit eery," said Jaro.

6

Jaro accompanied the Faths to the space terminal and saw them aboard the majestic *Francil Ambar*, then waited while the ports slid shut and warning lights shone from the start-off pods. The great shape rose into the air. Jaro, standing by the rail of the observation terrace, watched until the ship was lost to sight behind high clouds. For another five minutes he stood by the rail, gazing aimlessly across the field, into the sky and over the forest beyond; then turned and went to the machine shop.

"The Faths are gone," he told Gaing. "I feel useless and dull.

Perhaps I'm more dependent upon them than I like to think."

Gaing poured him a cup of tea. "So what's on your schedule?"

Jaro sipped the tea and seemed to derive energy from the bitter brew. "The usual: work, workouts with Bernal. I'm just starting to get the hang of what he calls the 'low trapezoid.' "

"Learn well! The trick may save your life some day."

Jaro flexed his arms. "I feel better already. Have you had your lunch?"

"Not yet."

"Then let's step over to Sad Henry's; it's my turn to buy."

Over lunch Jaro told Gaing of Skirl and her problems. Gaing was impressed. "She sounds like a girl with spirit."

"Worse than that; she's a Clam Muffin."

"You have Merriehew to yourself; why not invite her in to keep house for you?"

"The thought has occurred to me," Jaro admitted. "It's an impractical daydream at best. At worst, I'd be doing all the cooking and the washing-up as well."

Gaing nodded soberly, but made no comment. Jaro went on. "I'm not sure how it would work out. She might distract me from what I really want to do, which is to find out where the Faths first came upon me."

"That should not be too hard."

"Hah! The Faths have carefully muddled their records: they know I'll be searching, and I've looked everywhere I could think of already. One day I found a note from Hilyer: 'Jaro, please don't make a mess of the papers in this drawer. Sometimes you are not too neat.' "

"What did you do?"

"I started to write below the message: 'There would be less mess if I knew where to look.' But I decided that this was undignified, so I put the note back the way it was."

"This reminds me," said Gaing. "I have some news for you. Do you remember Tawn Maihac?"

"Of course! He left without saying goodbye; I was afraid that something bad had happened to him."

Gaing, intending a winsome smile, showed Jaro a twisted leer. "You were more right than wrong."

"What happened to him?"

"I'll let him tell you himself. He'll be back in Thanet before long."

7

The Faths were gone. Jaro was alone at Merriehew. The house seemed full of whispers, and Jaro's footsteps rang hollow through the empty rooms. At night when he lay in his bed, he sometimes thought to hear echoes of Hilyer's stately periods, or a whisper of Althea's gurgling laugh, but more often the mutters and grumbles and twitters came, so it seemed, from the house itself.

Jaro telephoned Sassoon Ayry. He heard only a recorded message to the effect that the house was closed for an indefinite period, but that important inquiries might be directed to the secretary of the Clam Muffin Committee. Jaro placed such a call and asked for Skirl's address. As he had expected, the information was coldly denied him. Jaro gave his name and asked that Skirl Hutsenreiter be notified that he had called. The voice said that his request would be duly processed, which Jaro took to mean a quick trip to the wastebasket. However, halfway through the evening Skirl reached him at Merriehew. Her voice was chilly and she came directly to the point: why had he called?

Jaro explained that he wanted to make sure that all was well with her, and he hoped that she had found accommodations to her taste.

Skirl said that at the moment conditions were satisfactory; in fact she was occupying her old quarters at Sassoon Ayry.

Jaro expressed surprise. He thought the house had been closed.

Correct, said Skirl. She had entered by a secret route and planned to maintain a covert residence until her father returned. There were disadvantages; for instance, she dared not use the telephone, nor otherwise advertise her presence for fear of alerting the guard who patrolled the grounds, nor could she gracefully receive visitors.

Jaro asked what she had learned at the library. Nothing encouraging, said Skirl. In her opinion, the requirements for an effectuator's license—even a beginner's permit—were far too rigid. She was not nearly old enough; she had not taken a degree in criminal law, nor yet had she trained with the IPCC. The "General Instructions" also noted that a substantial working capital was of the greatest importance. She had also been discouraged by the statement: "A competent effectuator must be able to mix unobtrusively into any and every social milieu, from the most squalid back-country brothels to the salons of beautiful and cultured artists. Danger frequently is rife."

Jaro tried to lift her spirits. "There are bound to be challenges, but you are well equipped to cope with them."

"In a back-country brothel?" snapped Skirl. "I am a Clam Muffin, after all!"

Jaro said thoughtfully: "You must select your cases with care."

"Sometimes that is not possible," said Skirl. She continued to read from the "General Instructions":

> " 'The skillful effectuator is a special sort of person. He combines high intellectual capacity, a protean social presence, ruthless executive skills. He is clever, creative, expert in the use of weapons. He must be immune to pain and adaptable to any cuisine, no matter how bizarre it may seem initially. MOST IMPORTANT! He must have at his disposal a working fund which—' "

Skirl threw the "General Instructions" aside. "In effect they deny me my learner's permit, which would serve me as well as a license. I still have the certificate Myrl Sunder gave me; it will suffice."

"What about the financial reserves and a legal degree? If you studied a term or two at the Institute, you'd have better qualifications."

"Yes, so it might be, but the prospect does not appeal to me."

Skirl broke the connection before Jaro could suggest a picnic in the country or a visit to Blue Mountain Lodge, or some other such outing. Jaro leaned back in his chair, and sat drinking beer from Hilyer's favorite mug, which Althea never allowed him to use, on grounds of lèse majesté. He considered his own plans for the summer. They could be divided into three categories. First, he would work at the space terminal as many hours as convenient. Second, he would continue his training in the ever more complicated study of hand-to-hand combat. Thirdly, he would take advantage of the Faths' absence to search for records which would help him discover his origins.

ELEVEN

1

The Faths arrived at the Ushant spaceport early in the day. Entry formalities were minimal and by mid-morning they were on their way to Dimplewater, twenty miles north, aboard a train of open-sided observation cars which took them at a leisurely pace through the flamboyant jungle known as the Gages of Lyrhidion. Clusters of pink, black and orange feather-ferns shuddered in the breeze, emitting puffs of sweet-scented spores which, when collected and compressed, yielded a confection much enjoyed by local folk. At intervals maddercap spines rose two-hundred feet, to stand stiff and rigid as poles. Each spine terminated in a ten-foot knob, from which spurted a corona of orange flames, regular as flower petals. The flames burned perpetually, and by night, from an altitude, the Gages of Lyrhidion seemed a field of flameflowers.

For much of the distance, the train followed the course of a slow river, in and out of the shade of green weeping willows and lantern jasmines. Wooded islands appeared at intervals, each with a rustic cottage, its porch overlooking the water.

Arriving in Dimplewater, the Faths went to their hotel and were shown into quarters of more than adequate comfort. Wide windows opened on a typical scene: a bridge of carved age-darkened wood, the waterway below, a strip of ebony trees with salmon-pink heart-shaped leaves; then beyond, at a distance of two hundred yards, the rotunda of the Hotel Tia-Taio, the venue of the conclave; and a marvel of architecture in its own right. The hemisphere of the rotunda, blocks of colored glass six inches thick fused into an integral shell, rose two hundred feet above ground level. Sunlight, refracting through the glass, illuminated the interior with a coruscation of color. By night, light of a similar quality issued from a massive globe suspended on an iron chain. Construction of this globe was simple but elegant. To a matrix of iron web, faceted jewels had been fixed: rubies, emeralds, sapphires, topazes, jacynths, a dozen others. Light from an internal source, passing through the jewels, illuminated the chamber with colored light richer and deeper than the light from the daytime rotunda.

The Faths presently left their hotel, crossed the bridge and walked under the ebony trees to the rotunda adjoining the Hotel Tia-Taio. In the lobby they chanced upon Laurz Mur, the chairman of the arrangements committee. Laurz Mur was quietly handsome, if somewhat stately and impersonal. Althea found him both fascinating and amusing; Hilyer was not at all amused, and considered Mur little more than an elegant dilettante.

Mur invited them to lunch, where he exerted himself to be a pleasant companion, so that even Hilyer's suspicions were lulled.

Mur was much interested in the Faths' special field: artistic symbolism, with an emphasis upon musical forms.

"I myself take a rather more perceptive view of the subject than does the ordinary amateur; indeed, I confess to a few trifles of original research, and a document or two relevant to my conclusions. No, no!" he demurred as Althea asked to look over his papers. "First I must put them into their final form."

Mur refused to speak further of his work. He addressed Hilyer, "Have you seen the schedule?"

"Not yet."

Mur produced a pair of pamphlets which he gave to Hilyer and Althea. "You will find that you are to take the podium tomorrow morning. I hope that this is convenient?"

"Very much so! I'll be happy to give my talk, then relax for the rest of the conclave."

"As I recall," mused Laurz Mur, "there's another speaker from Thanet scheduled for tomorrow afternoon."

Althea glanced at her copy of the schedule. "That will be Dean Hutsenreiter. His paper deals with the permutations of language and is said to be very profound."

Mur consulted his notes. "I'll miss him, since I have a meeting I must attend." He gave his head a sad shake. "But then—I will never undertake such a task again."

Althea inquired, "I've been looking down the list, and I don't see any local names save your own. Are there no scholars on Ushant?"

"Not many. For one reason or another our most notable savants go off-world to study, where they take their honors and seldom return. Again, we are not particularly apt at abstract research. We have many outstanding musicians, but few musicologists."

"Interesting," said Hilyer. "May I ask a personal question?"

Laurz Mur smiled politely. "Of course."

"You are wearing on the epaulet of your jacket a set of small devices, which look like recording equipment. What is their purpose?"

Laurz Mur's smile became a trifle thin. "The explanation is rather complex; with me, the devices are no more than a habit, since I do not take their purpose seriously."

"And as for that purpose?"

Laurz Mur shrugged. "Folk since time immemorial have kept journals and diaries for themselves. These devices assist in that purpose. They record the events of one's life, and for a fact become an excellent reference should someone forget an important fact or an appointment."

"How do you deal with such a volume of information?"

"We set aside a few moments of each day to organize the material. What is important, we save. The rest we discard. It is an obsessive habit, but for some reason we cannot break it. Now you must excuse me. I have enjoyed our meeting and will certainly cherish it among my mementos."

The Faths looked after his retreating back. "Amazing folk," said Hilyer. "Do you know what I think?"

"Probably," said Althea. "Tell me anyway."

"These folk live in near-ideal circumstances; still, they are morose. Why? Because the wheel of time is grinding away at their lives, and they have no place to go. They collect pretty trinkets and write in their diaries. Every day it's the same. The moments of their lives fleet past, along with their hopes for a glorious tamsour. I may or may not be using the word correctly."

"Hmf," sniffed Althea. "No one cares whether I have a nice tamsour or not."

"You won't get much sympathy on Ushant. They are worried about themselves only."

"You may be right."

"Laurz Mur wasted very little time with us. He finished his lunch, then took off like a flushed grouse," noted Hilyer.

"We did not exhilarate him," said Althea. "Hilyer, tell me the truth: do I exhilarate you?"

"No," said Hilyer. "But you're comfortable."

2

On the following day Laurz Mur called the conclave of xenologists to order. Standing on the speaker's podium, he swept the audience with an appraising eye. Five hundred xenologists came under his purview: every sort of philosopher, explorer, biologist, anthropologist, historian, cultural psychologist, linguist, analytical aesthetician, philologer, dendrologist, lexicographer, cartologist, and a dozen other more recondite professions. Some were scheduled speakers; others would listen and engage in the important work of intellectual cross-fertilization. Still others had brought papers they intended to read, if the opportunity offered, or even if not: somehow, by hook or by crook, the precious paper with its carefully honed phrases and engaging new ideas must be heard!

Laurz Mur completed his survey and, apparently satisfied, raised a satinwood baton and with a graceful gesture struck a small bronze gong. The audience quieted. Laurz Mur spoke. "Ladies and gentlemen! Needless to say, it is an honor of the highest degree to address so many famous savants. It shall be a notable passage in my mementos! But there is no time to indulge in mutual benedictions. We run on a strictly regulated schedule and will adjourn this morning's session promptly at noon. Without further ado, I introduce to you the first speaker: the distinguished Sir Wilfred Voskovy."

Sir Wilfred stepped forward, a sturdy gentleman with a high brush of coarse black hair and rather surly features. His flamboyant garments offered a host of sartorial decorative niceties distinctly at odds with his melancholy countenance. In a burst of insight, Althea told Hilyer that Sir Wilfred had been forced to wear the overly striking garments at the behest of his wife, which also explained his dour expression.

Sir Wilfred's message was also cheerless. The societies of the Gaean Reach are now so complex, disparate, and scattered so far, deep, and wide that we can no longer think in terms of comprehensive scholarship, sublime though that notion might have seemed to our forebears. To express my thesis more broadly, the volume of knowledge has grown ten times faster than our ability to classify, much less understand it.

This is a bleak prospect for the future, as well everyone in this august audience recognizes. The basic purport is that our careers are demonstrably exercises in futility, and the conscientious among us will henceforth accept our salaries with a pang of guilt. The time has come for us to alter our perspectives and to become realists, rather than academic fossils, dreaming of a past age of innocence.

"So—what now? Is all lost? Not necessarily. Our field of expertise, as redefined, becomes simply taxonomic. No longer will we collate, analyze, synthesize, and search for felicitous correspondences. Our cherished and delightful laws of social dynamics must be relegated to the same box as the theory of phlogiston. Now we are realists! Even so, we will be hard-put even to keep abreast of new information, much less analyze it. Why delude ourselves?"

A florid man in the front row jumped to his feet. In a sneering pugnacious voice he called out a reply to what Sir Wilfred had intended as a purely rhetorical question. "Obviously, to keep our jobs!"

Sir Wilfred turned a haughty glance down at the man and continued.

"There are at least two routes past the seeming impasse. First, we can arbitrarily nominate a number of settled worlds—let us say, thirty or forty, or even fifty—and declare these worlds the only suitable arena for serious study. In so doing, we ignore all other human activity, no matter how astounding. What if these new inklings are tragic, or sensational? Or rife with human drama? We care nothing; we elbow the unwelcome information to the side! After all, we are the authorities, so we tell our students, and we know best. The so-called 'control group' of worlds, with their readily accessible cultures, will provide a manageable range of data, and each of us may vote for the inclusion of his favorite world. By this means, we maintain the dignity and repute of the profession. Our studies are as profound as we like and we are all eminently comfortable. Meanwhile, our students learn the rudiments of cultural anthropology, which they can apply as they see fit. If mavericks or mad geniuses among our group choose to study other societies, let them do so; it is all one to us. We simply laugh them to the side, and as we control the grants, tenures and salaries, they will quickly come to heel."

"Preposterous!" called the florid man in the front row. "What an imbecilic notion!"

As before, Sir Wilfred paid the gentleman no heed. "The second concept is more complicated. We assemble a gigantic information bank—a data-processing apparatus of unprecedented scope. Our task then alters; we merely collect information and feed it into this mechanism without piddling or doodling with the details, as if we knew what we were doing. The machine accepts the information in a raw state, unclassified, undigested, unanalyzed. That is all there is to it. The machine has been programmed to collate and rationalize. Our lives have become tranquil. As we sit chatting in our clubs, drinking beverages of choice, a subject might arise in which we take a casual interest, or perhaps we wish to settle a bet. In the bad old times—by that, I mean now—we would be forced to exert ourselves. By the new system, we merely reach out a hand, touch a button, and the relevant information is provided on the instant. We are no longer paltry underpaid low-status academics; we have started to live the good life. We no longer distinguish ourselves by our former constricted field; now we are Doctors of Erudition! It is, I am assured, a glorious prospect.

"Now then: a final word. Certain smug boffins whose names I will not mention, though I can see their hangdog grins from where I stand, would boom and huffaw to their tenure committees as slavishly as ever. But, aha! Here is the great joke! We are the committee!"

"Bah!" sneered the florid gentleman in the front row. "If your idiotic scheme were in force, what else would we be good for?"

"You can sell your corpse for pet food," said Sir Wilfred. "Also, that of your wife should she predecease you, and she need never learn of your intentions. Guard her well and cherish her; she is like money in the bank."

Laurz Mur said, "Thank you, Sir Wilfred, for your provocative concepts; I am sure that they will linger with us. Next is the eminent Professor Sonotra Soukhail, a Grand Tantricist of the Antimates, and a Ninth Degree Putra. She will offer us excerpts from her paper on the mountain villages of Ladaque-Royale. I believe that she has something interesting to tell us regarding the human kites and the wind wizards of the Pittispasian Cliffs, which as we all know limit the Central Massif of the Second Continent, where it abuts on the Groaning Ocean."

The florid man rose ponderously to his feet. "You are evidently referring to the planet Ladaque-Royale, Sagittarius FFC 32-DE-2930?"

Laurz Mur said, "I do not have immediate access to the Final Functional Catalog, but I suspect that you have supplied the proper nomenclature, for which we owe you our gratitude."

"And Professor Soukhail is a Putra?"

"Exactly so; to the Ninth Degree."

"In that case I am more than gratified. We may listen to this lady with confidence."

Laurz Mur nodded politely. "Now then, here is Professor Soukhail. Madame, you may proceed with your address."

The Putra, a squat broad-faced woman with a shock of stiff auburn hair, spoke to the man in the front row. "You are correct in your designation, sir. Are you familiar with Ladaque-Royale?"

"I have studied the White Wizards in depth! In fact, I can perform the Floncing River Miracle, and I have gained access to the Tantric of the Pellucid Way."

"Aha!" said Sonotra Soukhail. "I see that I cannot take liberties with the truth! But no matter; I will bridle my imagination and make do with a recitation of fact."

Sonotra Soukhail need not have concerned herself; her unadorned facts were fascinating and she embellished them with photographs of her swooping gliding subjects, and she declared the abilities of the white wizards to be explained only in terms of thought transference. She looked down to the florid man in the front row. "Am I right in this belief, sir?"

"You are correct, in every respect," said the man solemnly. "I would endorse your remarks even were I not your husband."

Laurz Mur stepped to the podium. "There will be a few moments delay while Professor Soukhail removes her exhibits."

For a period Hilyer and Althea sat in silence. Then Althea whispered to Hilyer: "When she spoke of thought-transference and such things, I could not help but think of Jaro and his early troubles—which I hope are at an end."

Hilyer considered the matter. "She takes the subject rather far afield. The 'Tantrickers' seem almost abnormal in their attributes, and the 'White magicians' are remarkable, to say the least. But I don't connect any of this with Jaro."

Althea said dubiously, "Jaro's experiences have certainly been unusual. There might be connections which we haven't noticed."

"Nonsense!" said Hilyer gruffly. "Jaro has never communed with these streams of trans-temporal rays, nor does he do the seven Devoirs of Daily Duty."

Althea was not totally convinced. "Jaro is certainly a special case. He knows it as well as we do, and it must gnaw at his mind. No wonder he wants to learn about his origins."

"And so he shall, in due course, but his education comes first, and I am afraid that he is not cooperating to the fullest."

"However so?" cried Althea. "I feel that he has really been quite amiable."

"Amiable, perhaps; cooperative, partly. For instance, he is dropping courses in 'Non-semantic Poetry' and 'Symbology of Color' in order to find more time for his work at the spaceport."

Althea thought to change the subject. "Look yonder, just past the man in the blue cape. It's Dean Hutsenreiter in a most unsuitable hat!"

Hilyer turned to look. He exclaimed: "Never bother the hat! Who is the unsuitable woman?"

Althea studied Dean Hutsenreiter's escort, who stood a foot

taller than Hutsenreiter himself. Her legs and arms were long and limber; her buttocks were sleek; her bosom was splendid, and her face was a mask of marmoreal disdain for the stares which were focused upon her. She wore a striking skin-tight gown of purple and green, along with a tall conical cloth-of-gold turban. "Could that be his wife, the Princess of the Dawn, from Marmone?"

"I don't think so," said Althea, "but I can't be sure. Whoever she is, how can he afford her? I thought he was in deep financial trouble."

"It's a mystery to me. At any rate, I don't think she's a Clam Muffin."

Laurz Mur appeared on the platform once again. "Time presses and we are running just an iota late. Without further ado I will introduce our next speaker: a scholar of impeccable credentials, the Honorable Kyril Hape."

Up to the podium stepped a tall man with a beak of a nose, fierce black eyes, a shock of white hair. Laurz Mur spoke further, describing Hape as a man whom he himself had revered almost since childhood; he was a linguist preeminent in the field, originally from Old Earth, now resident at the site of certain intriguing ruins, whose location he was not yet ready to reveal.

Mur relinquished the podium to Hape who described his efforts to translate the inscriptions on a set of eighty-five iridium alloy sheets, discovered in a shallow cave near his camp. His recital was essentially a tale of incessant efforts to wring meaning from the incomprehensible markings. He told of the various artifices, techniques and tests he had used over the years—all to the same effect. As he finished, he glanced toward Laurz Mur. "I suppose that by local standards I have earned for myself a very lowly and rather sordid tamsour." He spoke with a grim smile. "I am sure that I am using the word incorrectly, but no matter. I have devoted many years to these inscriptions, and I have nothing whatever to show for my work: not even a pension from my university. They discharged me from their faculty over ten years ago. Still, I will scratch by, one way or another. It may even surprise you to learn that I have several new approaches I am desperately anxious to apply to the cursed inscriptions, and I can hardly wait to return to my office. I do not truly know whether I have been cheated by the cosmos or not.

"I might point out that, over yonder, as smug as ever and no doubt as erroneous as ever in his theories, sits Clois Hutsenreiter. I worked with him once and even the laborers called him 'Careless Clois,' and every night they would take away his money at some gambling game. Since then he has mended his fortunes, and has become Dean at an institute of higher learning. How did 'Careless Clois' achieve this office? By assiduous proctosculation, so I am told. Also, he married a deluded heiress without informing her of a previous—"

Dean Hutsenreiter jumped to his feet and called: "Where is the monitor of ceremonies? How long will he tolerate this insane rhodomontade? We hear the warblings of a madman; can we find no surcease? Monitor, do your duty, if you please! Exclude this demon of verbal turpitude!"

Laurz Mur stepped forward and with great sangfroid urged Kyril Hape to step down from the podium, or at least modify the tenor of his address. Hape protested that he wished to recount several other anecdotes of possible interest to the audience. He cried out: "This afternoon you will hear 'Careless Clois' as he attempts to refute my remarks. Be warned! You will hear sophistry and innuendo!"

Laurz Mur gave a meaningful signal.

Kyril Hake said, "I see that time is of the essence and I must terminate my remarks. I can only suggest that you hold tight to your purses when Clois is near, and lend him no money. Alas! My lifetime has come and gone! Unless in my last golden years I decipher the plaques, my career will lack distinction. I will mention in passing that I suspect Clois Hutsenreiter of fabricating these selfsame plaques and hiding them where he knew I would find them. Is he innocent or guilty of this crime? Look at his face now; you will see that he is smiling very broadly. It is not the limpid smile of innocence.

"That, ladies and gentlemen, concludes my remarks."

Kyril Hake bowed to Laurz Mur and stepped down from the platform, to the accompaniment of applause from the audience.

Hilyer muttered to Althea: "A most unconventional address!"

Althea nodded. "Unconventional or not, Dean Hutsenreiter showed little enthusiasm."

Laurz Mur spoke. "Next you will hear the remarks of Professor Hilyer Fath, from Thanet Institute, at Thanet on Gallingale. His topic, so I understand, is 'Aspects of Aesthetic Symbology.' "

Hilyer marched to the speaker's platform. Ordinarily, he was comfortable with such occasions; today, Dean Hutsenreiter sat in the audience. Hilyer squared his shoulders. There was no help for it. To avoid being distracted from the substance of his remarks; Hilyer must keep his eyes averted from the Dean whose eyes glowered from beneath the brim of his eccentric scarlet hat.

"My subject is vast," said Hilyer. "However, it is coherent and universally consistent. I for one would reject the constraints Sir Wilfred Voskovy would impose in the name of manageability. After all, where is the harm in superabundance? If you are invited to a banquet, you denounce not too much fine food, but its absence. Let us continue to celebrate the delectable crime of gluttony, with no thought for the hollow-eyed vegetarian who glares at us so enviously. Is it not plain then? Sir Wilfred must search for a new credo. 'Abundance,' 'Plethora,' 'Diversity'—these are the sign-posts pointing the way to a fine 'tamsour,' to use, or perhaps misuse, one of the peculiar local concepts. So much having been said, I take up my principal theme.

"Time is short and my scope is limitless; I will tell you only a few descriptive anecdotes. They will be both brief and to the point, since my subject, to be well and truly comprehended, requires an emotive perception of the symbols under consideration. I emphasize that every separate symbology requires an enormous and extremely subtle study. I am sadly amused by persons who pretend to chic or avant-garde status by feigning enjoyment of the music of a culture different from their own. By so doing they instantly brand themselves as poseurs.

"Still, it is possible to perceive the symbols without understanding their emotive force. There is, in fact, an intellectual satisfaction in simply recognizing the patterns. Often, I even think that I enjoy the music, though surely it is for the wrong reasons. Musical symbology must be imbibed with the mother's milk and the mother's voice and the sounds of the native homestead.

"My field is therefore doubly complex, since any study of a music must entail analysis of the society from which the symbology has sprung. The analyst will find fascinating correspondences which link the musical symbology with other aspects of the matrix. For instance—" Hilyer mentioned several societies, described their somatypes and typical costumes and played representative segments of each society's music. "You must listen closely. For each society I play first festive music, then music of circumstance, then funeral music. You will note interesting differences and interesting correspondences."

So went Hilyer's presentation. He finished with the statement: "Aesthetic symbology, naturally, is not confined to music, though it is perhaps most accessible for study. Other systems are more complex and more ambiguous. The concepts may also be contradictory. I warn my students that if they hope to impose absolutes upon aesthetic symbology, he or she had better turn to a more malleable study."

Hilyer returned to his seat. Althea assured him that his remarks had nicely engaged the interest of the audience, and that even Dean Hutsenreiter had muttered what appeared to be grudging praise to his companion. "And now, if you are of a mind, I think I'd just as soon adjourn for a time."

" 'Adjourn'? You mean, 'leave the hall'?" Hilyer was surprised. "Whatever for? The session still has an hour to run."

Althea grimaced. "So it does, but I have already heard too much of urgencies and moods and transferences. Perhaps I too am a borderline 'sensitive,' or whatever such folk are called."

Hilyer looked dubiously to right and left. "You go if you like. I'd feel conspicuous if I went now."

Althea subsided into her seat. "I'll wait. But let's leave as soon as possible."

Hilyer agreed and Althea reluctantly composed herself.

Laurz Mur introduced Dame Julia Neep, who discussed a topic which she called "Sick Societies." Before embarking upon her topic she also took time to refute Sir Wilfred for his proposals. "Like Hilyer Fath, I deplore this sort of dreary pessimism. If we took Sir Wilfred seriously, we would terminate the conclave at this very instant and all go home, resign our places of honor and spend the rest of our lives in vegetarianism and apathy. I, for one, refuse to do so. Now then, some of you may be thinking that my topic 'Sick Societies' is no less grim and portentous than that of Sir Wilfred's topic. Already my presentation has been called: 'Dame Neep's Brief Introduction to Eschatology.' This, of course, is a canard. For every 'sick society,' dozens are healthy, where anything and everything may and probably does happen. Still, this is no reason for us to throw our hands in the air, cry havoc, and pull the coverlets over our heads." She frowned down at the florid man in the first row, who had jumped to his feet. "Well, sir?"

"You are addressing a literate audience. If your scholarship is as muddled as your metaphors, we are in for a painful morning." He bowed curtly and resumed his seat.

Dame Neep examined him for a moment, then said, "My topic is 'Sick Societies' and you will serve very nicely as a case study. Do you care to step up on the podium and submit to my examination?"

"Certainly not!" said the man stiffly. "Not unless first you step down here and submit to my own examination."

Dame Neep proceeded with her topic, describing the characteristics of a sick society: its symptoms, maturity, decline and ultimate decay. "The superficial indications are by no means consistent. For instance, a static society need not be sick, if it is challenged by its environment. A society with disparities in privileges or wealth may be healthy if upward mobility is possible. The same society is sick if there is no such mobility, while rewards and perquisites are given to drones and parasites. Isolated societies may well become strange and queer, but not necessarily sick; their risk is great, however, since they receive no corrective criticism; they are not aware of what might be a morbid degeneracy. Isolated societies are almost inevitably doomed to decay. Sacerdotal, religious or priest-dominated societies are like organisms with a cancer."

Dame Neep briefly developed her concepts, took some questions from the audience, then left the podium.

Laurz Mur stepped forward, now wearing a conical hat of black velvet which accentuated the elegant pallor of his face.

"I wish to thank Dame Neep for her cogent remarks. I see that the time is verging toward that hour which we had stipulated for recess. We shall try to meet this schedule." A prim little smile appeared upon his face. "On Ushant we cite the dictum: 'All events must obey their imperatives.' So then—while the time is brief, only about six minutes, it will suffice for my own short presentation, which I was too modest to include upon the official calendar.

"The truth is, that in my own personal style, I too am a sociologist of a stature, so I believe, equivalent to your own. I make this assertion without embarrassment. 'Ah!' you cry out in wonder, and you whisper back and forth: 'In which field does Sir Laurz so quietly excel?' " Laurz Mur gave his head a sad shake. "It is a complex story, too detailed for the time available to us. Suffice it to say that my papers, embodying truly novel concepts, have never been published, and the propositions which should have gained universal currency, have gone unheard, wasted, like so much trash. I have toiled like the fabulous Heracles against this shame; I have submitted my papers to every organ of intellectual broadcast I could discover. Unanimously they refused to cope with the novelty of my ideas. That is the gist of the story, and though saddened, I will not complain. Instead, I have organized this conclave, where I can take a moment or so to express my views.

"This gathering includes the top skim of social anthropologists and savants of related sciences from across the Gaean Reach. Indeed, there is not one of you who has not published on Old Earth, and this of course is the touchstone of achievement. I congratulate you all, and, so saying, I request a brief period of your attention—now only three minutes until recess—to a truncated exposition of my views. And why should you not? You are here by my invitation and through the intricacy of my arrangements. When foundation funding was inadequate, I made up the shortfall from my private purse. So, as you see, I have committed a great deal of myself to the success of this conclave.

"But time is short, and I must make haste if I am so much as to adumbrate the scope of my thinking. I deal with the mystery of life, personality and individual destiny: concepts which are embodied in the idea of 'tamsour.'

"My thesis is that I have generated a cosmos by my own striving: a cosmos which draws its élan from my own life energy and uses my noble impulses to augment its own characteristics. This cosmos, so I might have hoped, considering my natural attributes, should have been amiable and supportive, but as you have heard the opposite was the case and I met malice at every turn. Is it not strange and wonderful, that this cosmos of my own creation should in its arrogance draw itself up before me, mocking and sarcastic, to become my implacable tormentor?" Laurz Mur leaned forward, face stern. "For a time I felt that we were evenly matched, but now the cosmos gains strength, and would reduce me to a paltry squeaking sub-thing, had I not found a means to blast the cosmos and its most precious darlings." Laurz Mur glanced at a clock and took up his satinwood mallet. "Ladies and gentlemen, the hour verges upon the time of recess, and the most glorious, most dramatic tamsour ever conceived. I have outwitted the cosmos! I batter it, I destroy its precious things, I smash its ornaments; I knock it awry; I annihilate it! The time is—now!" He struck the gong with his mallet.

The central chandelier grew suddenly luminescent. For the fraction of a second, those who were looking up saw it separate into flying shards of colored glass with an eye-searing glare behind, which instantaneously expanded to fill the rotunda and explode the colored glass of the great hemisphere into splinters, and so ended the conclave at Dimplewater on the world Ushant, in a tamsour which would excite murmurs of awe for centuries to come.

TWELVE

1

The big old house echoed to the sounds of emptiness. Jaro realized, with sorrow and guilt, that he had taken Hilyer and Althea for granted, as if they would be with him forever. But now they were gone, exploded into luminous dust, along with all their kindness and humor, and he could not bring them back.

Jaro sorrowfully put sentimentality aside and set about the dreary process of reorganizing his life. He arranged for the removal of all the Faths' personal possessions; otherwise, everywhere he looked he would be reminded of their cheerful presence. Out the door went shoes, clothes, lotions and cosmetics, oddments of this and that, as well as much of the heavy old furniture which the frugal Hilyer had refused to jettison. Althea's candelabra? They represented so much of Althea, her joy and enthusiasm, that Jaro could not bring himself to include them in his house-cleaning. Some he stored in a pair of cabinets; others he arranged along a high shelf, where they imparted color and vitality to an otherwise drab room.

During the first two days after receiving the news from Ushant, Jaro made several attempts to reach Skirl, both by way of the Clam Muffin Committee and at Sassoon Ayry. On the third day a cool voice, responding to his call to Sassoon Ayry, notified him that the bank had seized all of Clois Hutsenreiter's assets, closed the house to tenancy. The former occupants of the house were no longer in residence. Jaro asked, "Where, then, is Skirl Hutsenreiter?"

The cool voice replied: "The bank cannot supply this sort of information. Such questions should be placed with an appropriate agency."

2

The next morning Jaro was visited by a gentleman of obvious comporture, wearing a Kahulibah emblem. He was suave of demeanor, sleek of torso, impeccably groomed and barbered, with sparse dark hair, plump cheeks, large dog-brown eyes. With each movement he exuded a waft of forest-fern essence.

The gentleman introduced himself. "I am Forby Mildoon, an acquaintance of your late father. What a dreadful tragedy! I happened to be passing along Katzvold Road, so I thought to drop in and express my condolences."

"Thank you," said Jaro. Forby Mildoon stepped forward and Jaro perforce had to move aside. Mr. Mildoon marched into the house. Jaro looked after him with raised eyebrows, then shrugged and followed Mr. Mildoon into the sitting room.

"Please be seated," said Jaro formally. Mildoon made an all-inclusive assessment of the room; then, after considering his limited choice, settled gingerly upon the couch. "I see that you have been hard at work," said Mildoon. "Very sensible; it's the best way to ease your emotion. I trust that things are going passably well?"

"Well enough."

Mildoon made a gesture of sympathy and once again looked around the room, showing no more approval than before. "I hope you are not alone. You should be with your friends, or at your club."

Jaro said stonily, "I have work to do."

Mildoon smiled and nodded his endorsement of Jaro's activities. "It appears that before long you'll be moving into more suitable accommodations?"

"I'll stay here. Why should I move?"

"Hm ha. It's rather a desolate old barn for you to be rattling around in; don't you think?"

Jaro made no reply. Mildoon gave a small self-conscious cough and shuffled his feet. "Oh me, oh my! How the time dashes past, with worlds of work confronting me! I must be on my way." He started to rise, then paused, as if at the advent of a sudden thought. "Perhaps I should not bring the matter up at this time, but I'll do so anyway, out of respect for your late father. Over the last few months he's shown some interest in selling the property. I had to tell him that the market was rather limp, but only yesterday I got wind of what might turn out to be an advantageous situation. Do you wish to hear the details?"

"I don't think I'm interested. I plan to do some remodeling, then I might rent."

Mildoon gave his head a dubious shake. "Remodeling is a risky business and you may well end up pouring money down a rathole. I've seen many such projects come to grief."

Jaro, now half-amused, said, "It might be cheaper and end up safer to do nothing whatever."

Mildoon blew out his plump cheeks. "If you can tolerate such a dreary life out here in the rain and wind! It's a virtual wilderness!"

"I'm used to it; in fact, I like it."

"Still, you'd be better off selling, in my opinion, and at once, while the market is still showing signs of life. In fact, I'll go out on a limb and bend the Association's scalebook of values to its limit and make you an offer myself."

"That's nice of you," said Jaro. "What sort of offer did you have in mind?"

"Oh—probably as much as fifteen thousand, though you'd have to act quickly before the bottom falls out of the market."

Odd how eager Forby Mildoon's eyes had become, thought Jaro.

"For just the house? And I keep the acreage?"

Mildoon's face expressed shock and injured dignity. "Of course not! I'm quoting for house and acreage together."

Jaro laughed. "There's five hundred acres of beautiful forest and meadow out there!"

Mildoon made an incredulous sound. "Five hundred acres of stone and muck is closer to the truth! It's a breeding ground for stimps and leeches: sheer sodden wasteland."

"The price is far too low," said Jaro. "Not nearly enough for my purposes."

Mildoon's glossy bonhomie began to wear thin and his voice sharpened. "Just what, then, is your figure?"

"Oh—I don't know. I haven't given the matter any thought. I'd probably want something closer to thirty-five or forty thousand, or more."

"What!" Mildoon was scandalized. "I can't raise that kind of money! We must be realistic; these are the stern facts of life. If I gave you as much as twenty, or even nineteen thousand, my family would lock me away in a padded cell!"

"Your family is a ferocious tribe," said Jaro. "As I recall, you are related to Dame Vinzie Bynnoc."

"Well—yes. She is truly a grand old lady, and an inspiration to everyone! But back to Merriehew—"

"All taken with all, I am not yet ready to sell."

Mildoon ruminated, rubbing his chin. "Let me see. I suppose I could noodle a bit here and doodle a bit there and take this rundown old place, and the acreage, off your hands for seventeen or eighteen thousand. Call it kindly benevolence, if you like."

"Rundown or not, the house is where I can live, until I decide what to do with myself. In the meantime, the market may improve, or someone may make me a better offer."

Mildoon became instantly alert. "Have you had other offers?"

"Not yet."

Mildoon squinted thoughtfully up at the ceiling. "Needless to say, my time is worth money, and I can't chase acorns up and down Katzvold Road. If you'll close the deal now, I'll go as high as twenty thousand. The price is good for about five minutes, then it drops again."

Jaro looked him over curiously. "I gather that you are buying for your own interests?"

"Only as a wild speculation, which I don't know how to justify."

Jaro laughed. "Don't worry an instant about your recklessness. I don't plan to sell."

Mildoon inquired plaintively, "Why are you asking so unreasonable a sum?"

"I want to finance some extensive space travel."

Mildoon pulled at his chin. "I will pay five thousand sols for a three-year option. This may be your wisest move! If you like, I'll write out the document here and now and place five thousand sols in your hand! Doesn't that sound like an attractive deal?"

Jaro smilingly shook his head. "It's worse than ever. Why do you want the property so badly? Because of Lumilar Vistas?"

Forby Mildoon blinked rapidly. "Where did you hear of Lumilar Vistas?"

"Simple enough. Clois Hutsenreiter sold Yellowbird Ranch to Fidol Combine, which sold out to Lumilar Vistas, to your great disadvantage, so I am told."

" 'Told'? By whom?"

"By my father. He saw a notice to this effect in the newspaper."

"Stuff and nonsense! Sheer bullypup!"

Jaro shrugged. "Maybe yes, maybe no. I don't care one way or the other."

Forby Mildoon jumped to his feet and with minimal civility departed Merriehew.

3

Halfway through the afternoon Jaro received a telephone call from Skirl Hutsenreiter. He asked, "Where are you? I've been trying to call you for days."

"I've been staying at the Clam Muffin Club." Her voice, thought Jaro, seemed flat and dispirited.

"You should have called before! I've been worried about you!"

Skirl's voice remained cool and impersonal. "I've been busy with a hundred details. The house is sequestered, of course. The bankers locked me out, which is why I'm at the club."

"For how long?"

"A week or so, I suppose. Everyone is being nice to me, since now I'm officially a homeless orphan. I don't know how long the mood will last."

"What about money?"

"I've been trying to find some—which reminds me of why I called you. My father's lawyer is Flaude Reveless. He showed me a clause in the Yellowbird sales contract between my father and Fidol Combine. Father was conceded a small percentage of any further sale of the property, if it occurred during the next five years subsequent to the sale. Fidol sold to Lumilar Vistas and activated the clause, which Mr Reveless noticed; otherwise the clause would have been ignored and, indeed, Lumilar pretended that the clause was invalid because my father was dead. I said that I wasn't dead and I wanted to collect the money before the bank found out about it, so Mr. Reveless and I went to the Lumilar offices to straighten things out. While Mr. Reveless explained matters to Gilfong Rute, I wandered around the Lumilar offices, and finally looked into the architect's studio. On the walls hung drawings and sketches of Mr. Rute's latest scheme: a very large and very luxurious development to be known as Levyan Zarda. There would be a magnificent club, with facilities of every kind, as well as about fifty private secluded manor houses. The rest of the property was designated 'Outdoor Sport,' 'Swimming' and

'Wilderness.' As I studied the charts I became aware of a most surprising situation: Levyan Zarda was situated on a block of properties which I recognized to be Yellowbird Ranch, Merriehew and the lands north of Merriehew to the river."

"This is remarkable news," said Jaro. "It explains a great deal."

"Yes," said Skirl. "I thought that you would be interested. In any event the architect discovered me in his office and became fearfully cross. He said that the drawings were confidential and that if Mr. Rute discovered me snooping about his private affairs, where he had already spent half a million sols, he would take definite steps to ensure my discretion. It sounded menacing. I told him not to worry, that I had seen nothing of interest, and I went into the outer offices to wait.

"After a few minutes Mr. Reveless appeared. He told me that Gilfong Rute had grumbled a bit, but in the end had issued a warrant for the amount due. The next step was to place the money without delay into another bank, secure from the loan officers at my father's bank, which we did. As a consequence, I have salvaged about twelve hundred sols from the estate. There is another four hundred sols in a small trust fund my father forgot to loot, and Mr. Reveless says that this is also at my disposal. The bank is going to allow me my clothes and a few personal possessions. What next? I don't know, except that I'll be starting my career as an effectuator, whether I'm licensed or not. What about you?"

"I'll be going back to work at the terminal; in fact, I'm seeing Gaing Neitzbeck tonight at the Blue Moon Inn."

"I thought that the Faths left you well off."

"So they did. I have a monthly income of five hundred sols from the investments, but I can't touch the principal until I am forty years old. I still can't finance space travel, even if I knew where to go. That could be your first job as an effectuator: discover where the Faths found me."

"I'll think about it. It shouldn't be too hard."

"So you say. I've been looking high and low. When can I see you?"

"I don't know. Don't telephone me at the Clam Muffins; they won't take your call."

"Just as you like," said Jaro coldly. "In any event, thanks for the information regarding Lumilar and Levyan Zarda."

"Yes; I hope you will find it useful. Now I must go." The line went dead. Jaro turned away, frowning and dissatisfied. The call had provided him much to think about; otherwise, it had not been gratifying. Skirl seemed more remote than ever. What was he to make of the entrancing, if perverse, little creature?

4

As dusk settled into evening, Jaro met Gaing at the Blue Moon Inn, a combination saloon and restaurant at the edge of the woods, halfway between Thanet and the space terminal. The Blue Moon was the closest approach to a true spaceman's saloon as might be found in the rather prim purlieus of Thanet. The patrons for a fact included genuine spacemen from the terminal, attracted by the cosmopolitan cuisine and the easy atmosphere. Also on hand were stylish young couples of middle status, hoping to discover intrigue, hints of exotic vice, the heady flavor of illicit adventure.

Jaro and Gaing found a table in the shadows, where they were served tankards of beer and platters of pepper steak. Tonight Gaing was even more taciturn than usual, as if he were preoccupied with private concerns. Jaro was puzzled. Gaing's temperament was seldom other than impassive.

While they devoured their dinner Jaro told Gaing of Forby Mildoon's visit to Merriehew House. "When he made his first offer, he was casual and seemed to care little whether I accepted or not. Gradually he became nervous, and finally he cried out in sheer misery that he lacked the money to meet my price; then he wanted an option. I began to wonder about his urgency. Then I thought of Gilfong Rute, and wondered no longer. I even felt sorry for Lyssel Bynnoc who took me to meet her uncle Forby Mildoon at the Conservatory. Poor Lyssel! Forby Mildoon never arrived; it was the day Rute had dumped him from Lumilar Vistas and the Levyan Zarda project. This morning he thought to steal a march on Gilfong Rute—but failed."

"Tragic," said Gaing. "Very sad."

"This afternoon it all came clear. Skirl discovered that Gilfong Rute needs to spread his project across Merriehew. His plans are extremely secret. Mildoon would like nothing better than to whipsaw Gilfong Rute into a large settlement."

"Sweet revenge, indeed!" said Gaing. "Now you need only wait until Rute appears with an offer, and you can name your own price."

"The same thought has occurred to me."

Gaing pushed away the empty platter and called for more beer. Jaro watched him carefully, wondering what might be gnawing at his mind.

Gaing turned half the contents of the tankard down his throat, then scowled off across the room. Jaro silently waited. Gaing swung back to stare fixedly at Jaro, who began to feel a quiver of uneasy guilt. He searched his mind, but could recall no recent mistakes.

Gaing spoke. "I have something to tell you; I don't know where to start."

Jaro became more alarmed than ever. "Is it my work? Have I done something wrong?"

"No, nothing like that." Gaing tilted his tankard again and set it down with a thump. He growled: "It's something you know nothing about."

"That's a relief, or so I suppose. Tell me what it is."

"Very well." Gaing signaled for more beer, which arrived immediately. Gaing drank and set down the tankard. "You'll remember that Tawn Maihac brought you to the machine shop."

"I remember, of course."

"He introduced you to Trio Hartung and to me. You became my apprentice."

"I remember that too. How could I forget?"

"The arrangement was not accidental. Maihac and I are old shipmates. We found that you had been brought here by the Faths. We expected that the man who killed your mother might come here to kill you. His name is Asrubal. We waited and watched, but Asrubal did not come, and you are still alive. We consider this a success."

"Yes; it is nice," said Jaro. "I like being alive. Why should Asrubal want to kill me?"

"Asrubal would not kill you outright. First he would question you with great care. He wants to find some documents and he thinks you know where they are hidden."

"Ridiculous! I know nothing of the sort. I don't remember anything."

"Asrubal probably realizes this, which is why you have led a placid life."

"It doesn't seem placid to me. But why should you and Maihac worry so strenuously about keeping me alive."

"No mystery! I worry because I do not want to train another apprentice. Maihac worries because he is your father."

"My father!" Jaro, after an instant, was not as astounded as he felt he should be. "Why didn't he tell me himself?"

"Because of the Faths. You were part of the family and everyone was happy; the truth would have brought the Faths much distress and grief. Now they are gone, and there is no reason why you should not learn the truth."

"So why did Maihac leave Gallingale?"

"Many reasons. I'll let him tell you himself; he'll be back very shortly."

"And when he comes back to Thanet—what happens next?"

Gaing shrugged. "I suspect he has plans of a sort, but what they are I have no idea." He rose to his feet. "Now I'm going home, because I do not want to talk anymore."

5

By noon of the next day Jaro had finished his house-cleaning. Out the door had gone threadbare old rugs, sagging furniture, a great deal of accumulated detritus from attic and cellar. Finally, little of the Faths' remained to haunt the house save for Althea's candlesticks, which Jaro knew he could never discard.

Jaro sat down to decide what to do next. He was interrupted by a call from the Faths' lawyer, Walter Imbald. After making polite inquiries as to how Jaro was coping with his new position in life, Imbald said, "I have on hand a letter and a parcel which Hilyer and Althea Fath intended that I should deliver to you, under certain circumstances. Do you care to call at my office?"

"I'll be there at once," said Jaro.

Imbald maintained a modest office halfway along the Flammarion Prospect. A female clerk of uncertain age and severe disposition announced Jaro to Imbald, then took him into the inner office. Imbald rose politely, and Jaro saw a middle-aged gentleman, slight of physique, keen of feature and sharp of eye. Strands of mouse-brown hair had been marshalled sternly back across his scalp. His emblem denoted membership in the obscure and dull Titulary's Club, while a small black and green button indicated association with the more lively Brummagems. His comporture therefore would be limited, not at all fashionable but sedate, solid and consequential: a ledge or two short of the Squared Circles, much less the Lemurians or the Val Verde. Imbald greeted Jaro without effusiveness, and indicated a chair. "Please be seated." He resumed his own place. "As a matter of fact, I've been waiting for you to call."

"Sorry," said Jaro. "I've been busy sorting myself out. Everything has come at me in a rush."

Imbald nodded briskly. "As you must know, the Faths bequeathed everything to you, without qualification. Their assets are conservatively invested, providing you a very handsome income. The principal, I might add, cannot be adjusted or tampered with until you are forty years old, and presumably at an age of discretion. This stipulation was inserted at my earnest importunity. In any case, the Faths contrived to make you a very fortunate young man."

Jaro said stiffly, "I am properly grateful, though I would much prefer to have them back."

"They were fine people," said Imbald, without any fire of conviction. "What, may I ask, are your plans for the house and property?"

"I'm in no hurry to make up my mind."

Imbald pursed his lips judiciously. "Just so. If you have any questions, don't hesitate to call on me. But now to our principal business. About three months ago the Faths put a letter and a parcel into my custody. I will give you the letter now."

Imbald opened a drawer of his desk and brought out a long brown envelope which he handed to Jaro. "I do not know the contents of this letter. I assume that it pertains to the parcel which was also put into my care."

Jaro read the letter.

"Dear Jaro: This is written as a hedge against a set of highly unlikely circumstances: which is to say, the sudden death of both of us. If you read this letter—the Fates forfend!—it means that these unlikely and sorrowful circumstances have cataclysmically come to pass, and we therefore mourn (along with you, so we hope) the passing of our lives. We are now talking to you from beyond the vale! A strange thought, as I sit here writing this! But, as you know, we try to be both logical and providential. It is foolish to leave anything to chance, when this element can be eliminated. So—if you read this, the event we all deplore has occurred, and we are dead! Nor, on a less awful scale, will you have finished your curriculum at the Institute. We recognize that you are susceptible to impulses which might propel you out upon a wild crusade in search of your origins, before you take your degree. We believe this to be inadvisable, and hope to make a rational sequence of events easier and hence preferable to you.

"Be assured! We sympathize with your anguish, and we are reluctant to be the agents of your frustration, but we are convinced that it is in your best interests that you gain that education which will establish for you a solid and respected place in society. It is an excellent thing to have earned a degree at the Institute!

"So, to this end, we have placed the information which is yours by right in a trust account, which will be opened to you the day after you are graduated from the Institute with representative honors.

"Naturally we hope that you will never read this letter. On the day following your matriculation you will be mystified by the little ceremony we make of its burning.

"Your loving foster parents, Hilyer and Althea Fath."

Jaro looked at the lawyer. "I do not intend to continue at the Institute."

"Then you will never receive the parcel placed in the trust account."

"Is there no way to bypass these provisions? Neither Hilyer nor Althea Fath fully understood the urgency which presses on me."

The lawyer inspected Jaro curiously. "If I may ask a personal question, why not obey the wishes of your foster parents? They seem reasonable enough, and there are many worse fates than a career at the Institute."

"I have a friend with a great deal of experience," said Jaro. "He explained that the Institute is like a fancy aviary for tame birds. No one flies very far afield. The biggest bird sits on the highest perch. Everyone below must keep a wary eye cocked upward."

Walter Imbald rose to his feet. "I am happy to have met you. If and when you are graduated from the Institute, please call on me again."

Jaro took his leave and returned to Merriehew. The visit to Walter Imbald had been disheartening. Imbald, while perfectly correct in his conduct, had projected a mood of cold disapproval and even something close to dislike, as if Jaro, in defying the wishes of the Faths, had thereby revealed himself to be an ingrate and a vagabond.

Jaro sat brooding, his mind flitting from one set of ideas to another. He noticed, with a twinge of regret, that already his feelings toward the Faths were altering, and becoming abstract; in fact, he could not avoid a low-key resentment for their attempts to coerce him into a structured style of life, where he could never be comfortable.

Perhaps they had loved him not so much for himself but as the ideal exemplar of all their philosophical ideas, and if Jaro failed to conform to this ideal image, then he must more or less subtly be punished. Still, he would not allow peevishness to distort his thinking.

What of Merriehew? Gilfong Rute had confidently situated his wonderful Levyan Zarda across the Merriehew acreage; the act seemed more than a little arrogant in its assumptions. Perhaps Rute foresaw no difficulties in dealing with an inexperienced young student. Perhaps a few thousand sols more or less, to be paid out to this student, was a negligible item in the full tally of Rute's putative expenses. Perhaps there would be attempts to awe him, or employ agents of intimidation. In any event, there was no point in considering renovating, or even so much as a new coat of paint, until the issues had been clarified. And what of the most disturbing development of all, which was Tawn Maihac?

Jaro telephoned Gaing at the space terminal. "Jaro here."

"Yes, Jaro?"

"Have you had any news of Maihac?"

"Nothing more than what you already know."

Jaro spoke again of Gilfong Rute and his need for Merriehew and its acreage for the Levyan Zarda development. "Rute seems very confident he can take up Merriehew whenever he finds it convenient."

Gaing thought for a moment, then asked, "Do you have a will?"

"No."

"I suggest that you make a will, now if not sooner. If you were to die tonight, Maihac would inherit, but Rute does not know this. He probably thinks that you would die intestate and that there would be no near relative, whereupon he would find means to acquire the property. So make a will at once, and let everyone know that a will exists. This is cheap insurance."

In a subdued tone Jaro asked, "Do you really believe that Rute would have me killed to get hold of Merriehew?"

"Of course. Such things happen."

Jaro wasted no time placing a call to Walter Imbald.

"Walter Imbald here."

"This is Jaro Fath."

"Ah, Jaro. What is the problem?"

"No problem, except that I want to make a will at once, this very afternoon."

"That is possible. Is it a complicated will?"

"No, quite simple." Jaro described the terms of the will. "If you will draw up the document, I'll come to your office and sign it immediately."

Imbald showed no surprise. "The will can be ready in twenty minutes."

"I'll be there."

Jaro took himself to Imbald's office and signed the document which Imbald had ready for him. Imbald at last permitted some of his curiosity to show. "These legatees: Tawn Maihac, Gaing Neitzbeck—who are they? I know the identity of Skirl Hutsenreiter, of course."

"Maihac is my father; Gaing Neitzbeck is a friend, as is Skirl."

"And why the haste?"

"Gaing Neitzbeck advised it, when he found that Gilfong Rute might want to acquire Merriehew for a big development."

"Ah yes! I understand his thinking. I agree. The will is a good idea."

6

Jaro drove the Fath's old runabout back along Katzvold Road, arriving at Merriehew House just as the sun sank behind the low hills to the west. He entered the house and stood for a moment in the hall. He felt restless and irresolute. Too many things had happened, or were about to happen or might happen; there was imminence in the air, and Jaro felt uneasy. He decided that he was hungry and went into the kitchen. He consulted the larder, wondering what to feed himself. Soup might be nice, along with bread and cheese, and a salad. He brought a carton from the pantry, then halted, listening. The sound of light footsteps running across the porch. A moment later the chime sounded. Jaro went to the door and opened it, to find Lyssel Bynnoc smiling up at him. Jaro stared, non-plussed; of all the persons he knew, here was the one he least expected.

Lyssel spoke, with a gay lilt: "May I come in, Sir Orphan?"

Jaro hesitated, looking her up and down. He stepped aside, and Lyssel, turning him a saucy side-glance, moved past him into the house. She was using her most beguiling mannerisms, which suggested to Jaro that she had some practical purpose in view.

Jaro thoughtfully closed the door and turned to look after her. Today she wore dusky-white pantaloons, tight at the hips, loose at the ankles and a pink blouse. Her hair was gathered into a tuft, tied with a pink ribbon.

Jaro asked formally: "To what do I owe the pleasure of this visit?"

Lyssel gave her hand a jaunty wave. "Oh—a little bit of this and a little bit of that. Also a dollop of curiosity, to see how you are managing your very own, very private, life." Jaro studied her, as if she were a strange being from a far world. Lyssel protested, laughingly: "Jaro! Why do you look at me like that? Am I so startling? Or am I too plain for your taste?"

Jaro shook his head in bemusement. "Really, Lyssel! What do you expect? The last time I saw you was months ago. You gave me the leper treatment and were extremely supercilious. So now you come frolicking into my house, blithe as a tumble-bug, and I can only guess at your intentions."

Lyssel grimaced, pursing her lips, wrinkling her nose. "Jaro! I'm surprised at you!"

"Oh? How so?"

"I've always considered you debonair, but now you glower at me and keep me standing in the cold hall. Wouldn't it be nicer if you escorted me into the parlor, where I see a fire in the fireplace?"

"Oh, very well. Come along." Jaro allowed Lyssel to precede him, and she at once went to warm herself at the fire.

"It's a bit bleak in here," said Jaro. "I've removed most of the old furniture. I'll bring in some new pieces, if I stay on."

"So—you've decided to live here? Or will you sell?"

"Nothing is certain yet."

"My advice would be to sell—probably to my Uncle Forby. He'd give you far and away the best price."

"He's made me an offer already."

"And what did you tell him?"

"I told him no."

Lyssel looked for a moment into the fire, then turned to face him. She put her hand on his shoulder. "I'm puzzled, Jaro."

"About what?"

"You've changed! Something harsh and grim has come over you. Whatever happened to the Jaro who was so sweet and wistful, and who always seemed to be thinking dreamy romantic thoughts? I found that Jaro most sympathetic."

"And that is what you came to tell me?"

"Of course not!" Lyssel gave her head an indignant toss, which sent her tuft of golden curls flying. "May I make a personal comment?"

"As you like."

"You have become far too sardonic. Why are you laughing?"

"It was just a stray thought—not too funny, really."

Lyssel relaxed, her suspicions lulled. "Whatever the case, I'm glad I came." She looked around the room. "Poor Jaro! You must be lonely. But then, you were always something of a solitary person. Even just a bit unusual."

"Perhaps so."

"I think that you should sell this dreary old bat-trap for what you can get, and move into a smart little apartment near the Institute."

Jaro shook his head. "This place isn't so bad—and it's free."

"It lacks panache."

"Forby Mildoon doesn't seem to mind. He's desperate to buy, with or without panache. In any case, I won't be starting at the Institute."

Lyssel came a step closer. She looked up, her blue eyes searching his face, seeking trust and hope. "At one time I thought you were attracted to me, remember?"

"Of course I remember. I still am."

"You told me that you wanted to gather me up and carry me off to bed."

"I remember that, too. It seemed a good idea at the time."

Lyssel feigned dismay. "Have I changed so much for the worse?"

"No, but now I'm afraid of Dame Vinzie."

"Pooh! She's just a funny old pussy-cat. Right now she's probably in the kitchen playing Snap with the cook."

Jaro turned away to place another log on the fire. Lyssel watched him intently, then went to sit on the couch. She patted the space beside her. "Sit, Jaro. Be nice to me."

Jaro obeyed. Lyssel leaned against him. "Kiss me, Jaro. You want to, don't you?"

Jaro obligingly kissed her, and Lyssel, sighing, pressed even closer, and Jaro was hard-put to maintain the chilly-minded detachment which, so he had resolved, must guide his conduct.

Lyssel looked up into his face with a melting blue gaze. "You'll do as I ask, won't you?"

"I'm not sure."

"Jaro! Don't be difficult! Kiss me again."

Jaro kissed her, then asked: "What would you like me to do next?"

Lyssel sighed. "I don't know. I've never felt like this before. You could do anything you wanted with me."

"That's a good idea. I'll do it; in fact, we'll do it together." Jaro started to unbutton her blouse. She looked down and watched him. One button—two buttons—three buttons! One of her breasts appeared through the opening. Jaro bent to kiss it, then started on the other buttons. Lyssel restrained him. "First, Jaro, I want you to agree to help me; then you can do what you like."

"Help you how?"

Lyssel looked into the fire. In a soft musing voice she said, "Today a wonderful scheme came to my mind, and it's something I want more than anything else there is: more than being taken up into the Quantorsi, more than a grand house on Lesmond Hill. But I need you to help. It would also be to your benefit, since it would bring you a very handsome price for Merriehew."

"That sounds too good to be true."

"But it's quite real and within reach! All we need is cooperation between us."

"In what way?"

Lyssel looked mysteriously right and left, as if she feared eavesdroppers. "I'll tell you a great secret. It involves Gilfong Rute and a company called Lumilar Vistas. They plan a large, very lavish, very expensive, development. It is called Levyan Zarda. Rute might want to use a part of Merriehew, but it would need expert dealing to extract top price from him, and for this job Forby Mildoon is very well equipped. Part of the deal—in fact, this would be Uncle Forby's commission—would include Rute's spaceyacht, which he never uses. It is a splendid ship, a Fortunato Glitterway, and it's like new. If Uncle Forby is able to secure the *Pharsang*, he will take me on a long cruise: down through the Pandora Chromatics, and the Polymarks and perhaps even down to Xanthenoros. Wouldn't that be wonderful?"

"Very wonderful. How do I fit into these plans? Am I invited on the cruise?"

Lyssel thought for a moment. The idea, so it seemed, had not previously entered her mind. As he watched, Jaro's erotic fervor began to diminish. Lyssel made a small gesture, as if to dismiss a triviality. "I can't speak for Uncle Forby, and of course it will be his yacht. But that's a long way off." She nuzzled him. "Must we talk of such things now? You need only assure me of your faith."

"Yes, but these side issues are important. For instance, would your mother and grandmother be joining the cruise?"

Lyssel frowned. "Really, Jaro! You ask the most extraordinary questions! They might very well join the cruise."

"Would they approve of you and me sharing a cabin?"

Lyssel blew a vexed little puff of air from between her compressed lips. "The situation would be most awkward! I don't know how it could be arranged, unless you shipped aboard as crew, and perhaps we could meet secretly, though Uncle Forby might not approve. No matter what else, you'll surely get a generous price for Merriehew—probably more than the place is worth."

"Let's discuss that another time. Right now we have better things to do." He unfastened the fourth and fifth buttons.

"No, Jaro!" cried Lyssel, pulling her blouse together. "We must be definite before we go another inch."

"I don't understand your plans; they are too complicated. For now, let's put them aside."

"The plan is simple." From her pocket she brought a folded paper, a coin and a stylus. "You don't need to think at all. Just take this sol, and sign your name to the paper. Everything will be nicely arranged and we can relax."

"What am I signing?"

"Nothing of consequence. Just what we have been discussing. No need to fret; just sign."

Jaro turned her a quizzical side-glance and read the document:

> I, Jaro Fath, in consideration of one sol, grant to Lyssel Bynnoc or her agent a five-year option to buy the property known as Merriehew, including its house and acreage, at a price to be negotiated, but which in no case shall be less than sixteen thousand sols, but may be as much as four

thousand sols more, depending upon market conditions.
I append my signature.

Jaro, with eyebrows raised, turned Lyssel another side-glance, then carefully placed the paper on the fire, where it flared up and burned to a crisp. Lyssel pressed her hands to her mouth and gave a cry of consternation. Jaro said, "That's out of the way! Let's get on with our buttons."

Lyssel jerked away. "You don't care an ounce for me! You only want to do things to my body." With trembling fingers she buttoned her blouse.

"I thought that's what you had in mind when you came here," said Jaro with unconvincing innocence.

Tears rolled from Lyssel's eyes. "Why do you thwart me and hurt me so terribly?"

"Sorry," said Jaro, grinning. "That isn't what I had in mind."

Lyssel glared at him, face pinched, eyes glittering. Before she could express herself further, the telephone across the room chimed. Jaro frowned toward the instrument. Who could it be? Jaro called out: "Speak!"

The face of a middle-aged gentleman, apparently of a mild and affable nature, appeared on the screen. "Mr. Jaro Fath, if you please?" The voice was cultured and rich.

"Jaro Fath here."

"Mr. Fath, I am Abel Silking, of Lumilar Vistas."

Jaro heard Lyssel gasp in agitation. "Jaro!" she cried in a husky half-whisper. "Do not speak with this man; it will ruin us!"

Abel Silking had been speaking. "I happen to be on Katzvold Road near Merriehew. I wonder if I might drop by for a few minutes, to discuss a matter of mutual interest?"

"Now?"

"If it is convenient for you."

"No, no!" cried Lyssel in a furious undertone. "Don't let him come here! He will spoil all our plans!"

Jaro hesitated, recalling Lyssel's unbuttoned blouse and the unfinished business it represented. But much of his ardor had receded. Lyssel started to whimper: "Jaro! Think! Only think what it means! Think of us together!"

"You make too many conditions."

"No conditions! Take me! Then you'll do what is needful from sheer joy." Jaro winced. How cheaply they held him; how easily they thought to seduce him! It was humiliating. The last flicker of desire vanished.

Silking's voice had been coming from the screen: "Mr. Fath? Are you there?"

"I'm here," said Jaro. Lyssel sensed his purpose. She had been defeated. Her dreams were exploded; her glorious hopes in a twinkling had become nothing more than dismal memories, dry as dust. Jaro heard her run across the room, out the front door, along the porch and away. He turned back to the telephone. "Mr. Silking? You can come if you like. I don't think you'll gain anything, since I'm not ready to make any commitments—but I'll listen to you at least."

"I will be there shortly." The screen went blank.

Five minutes later the door chime sounded. Jaro admitted Abel Silking, and conducted him into the sitting room. Once again he apologized for the spartan ambience of his household. Silking made an absentminded gesture, to signify his lack of interest in the condition of Jaro's house. He wore a fine pearl-grey suit, almost a match for his glossy gray hair. His face lacked notable characteristics, being smooth, urbane, with a waxen skin, a small pale mouth under a gray wisp of mustache. Below the quizzical arch of his eyebrows his eyes were mild and attentive.

"Mr. Fath, first let me offer the sincere condolences of myself and of Lumilar Vistas."

"Thank you," said Jaro. While formidable, Silking seemed less shifty than Forby Mildoon.

"Nevertheless life goes on, and we must continue to swim with the flow of events which, for better or worse, cannot be avoided."

"Here, you must speak for yourself," said Jaro. "I'm in no hurry to jump into this current, or flow—whatever you call it. Splash about to your heart's content, but don't involve me."

Abel Silking smiled a prim smile. He glanced around the room. "I deduce that you are planning either to renovate, or rent or sell."

"My plans are very loose."

"I understand that you are starting classes at the Institute?"

"I think not."

"And what will you do with your property?"

"I'll live here for a time. Perhaps I'll rent the house and travel."

Silking nodded. "Lumilar Vistas might be interested in making you a very fair offer."

"Don't bother. My price is quite high. You might even call it 'unfair.' "

"How high? How unfair?"

"I don't know, and as I hinted, I'm not ready even to think about it. I'll tell you this much. I've had other offers, from persons desperate to buy. The property is evidently valuable."

"I am authorized to make you the very handsome offer of thirty thousand sols."

Jaro said soberly, "I'll discuss your offer with the legatees under my will. They are naturally interested in any transactions involving Merriehew."

Silking raised his eyebrows. "I'm surprised that you have a will! Who, may I ask, are your legatees?"

Jaro laughed. "Their identity is of no relevance at the moment—only the fact of their existence. Goodnight, Mr. Silking."

Abel Silking went to the door, where he paused. "Please do not enter into any other negotiations before notifying us, since we regard ourselves as the party of primary interest."

Jaro said politely, "If and when I decide to sell, I will certainly sell to my best advantage."

Abel Silking showed Jaro a faint smile. "You must take into account the importance of Lumilar Vistas, and the almost frightening amount of persuasion we can bring to bear. Goodnight, Mr. Fath."

"Goodnight, Mr. Silking."

The door closed. Jaro heard the measured tread diminish along the porch. Through the window he saw Silking step into a luxurious black vehicle. It slid down the drive, turned into the road and was gone.

Jaro went out upon the porch. The area was dark and quiet, save for the rustle of the wind in the trees. He stood motionless, the skin of his back tingling, listening for the murmur of ghosts among the wind noises.

The night was cold. Jaro shivered and went inside the house.

The fire in the fireplace had burned low. Jaro stirred it up and added a pair of logs. He went to the kitchen, prepared and consumed his delayed supper of soup, bread, cheese and salad, then returned to sit before the fire. He thought of Lyssel, who would be seething with hatred and grief. What an odd mercurial creature was Lyssel! She had come to Merriehew prepared for any eventuality, except defeat. The program must have been plotted with the connivance of both her mother and Forby Mildoon.

Their scheme could not fail. It was simple, forthright, cogent. Lyssel would tease and befuddle the hapless young nimp until he steamed with lust and eagerly signed the option: process complete.

Lyssel, despite all the legends she had generated over the years, was sexually cool: perhaps even frigid. She would approach the project with many reservations. As Jaro sat staring into the fire he seemed to hear the conversation of the three plotters as they devised their strategy:

LYSSEL (peevishly): It's all so intimate and sweaty. I'm not sure I'm up to it, if he insists.

MILDOON: Get the option, by hook or by crook!

DAME IDA: Do what is necessary. A bit of fornication in a good cause is quite acceptable.

LYSSEL (pouting): I would feel so foolish! What if he still resists me?

DAME IDA (scornfully): It's been done many times before. I assure you of this.

MILDOON (emphatically): Think *Pharsang!* One way or another, get the job done!

DAME IDA: You have the equipment; use it to advantage. It doesn't improve with age.

In that style, thought Jaro, the three plotters must have programmed the events of the evening. Lyssel would no doubt explain her failure upon the sudden appearance of Abel Silking.

The program had been long in the planning. Jaro thought back to the Bumbleboster's Panics, when Lyssel had come upon him in the uniform of the Arcadian Mountebanks. Even then, she had identified him as an avenue of infiltration into the Fath household, where he might persuade Hilyer and Althea to sell Merriehew to Forby Mildoon. The ploy had failed, and the Angels of Penitence had broken Jaro's bones. But Lyssel had persevered, striving ever more valiantly, and on this evening allowing Jaro to unbutton five buttons and kiss her breasts.

Lyssel would not be back. The game was over. Never again would she tempt Jaro with her nuzzlings and squirmings. Everything considered, it had been an interesting episode, and Jaro had learned a good deal, though not enough. Into his mind drifted the face of Skirl Hutsenreiter. His pulses quickened. What if Skirl had come to Merriehew, offering herself if Jaro would only sign a simple little paper? What then? Would he have signed? Jaro grimaced, fascinated by the idea.

He jumped to his feet, stirred up the fire. Of course not; the idea was absurd. Never in a million years would Skirl use herself in such a manner.

Or would she, if the need were strong enough?

Jaro sat looking into the fire.

An hour went by. He decided it was time for bed. A noise? He cocked his head to listen. Footsteps on the porch? Who could be calling this time of night? Surely not Lyssel, back to make amends! Jaro ran to the door, turned on the porch lamp and looked out the window. It was not Lyssel, meek and shivering, who stood waiting for admittance.

Jaro opened the door. Tawn Maihac stood leaning against the porch railing. For a few seconds the two looked at each other, then Maihac asked, "May I come in?"

THIRTEEN

1

Jaro could think of nothing to say. He stepped back and Maihac entered the house. Jaro closed the door. Maihac turned and once again the two appraised each other. "I expect that you are angry with me," said Maihac. Jaro was not sure what he felt. He could not deny the thrust of Maihac's statement. Why had Maihac never identified himself? Why had he departed Thanet without so much as a farewell? He said at last, "I admit that my feelings were hurt, but I suppose that's of no great consequence. You knew what you were doing and you must have had good reason."

Maihac smiled: a fleeting smile which for an instant illuminated his entire face, revealing a range of sentiments which came and went too quickly for Jaro's total perception.

Maihac put his arm around Jaro's shoulders and hugged him. At last he stood back, now grinning. "I've been wanting to do that for a long time, but I didn't dare. You are right. There were good reasons for what I did. I think you'll agree when you know the entire story. Nevertheless, I apologize."

Jaro made himself laugh. "Say no more. What's important is that you're here now. Come; let's go in where it's warm."

Jaro led the way into the sitting room. Maihac went to stand by the fire. Jaro asked, "Are you hungry? Is there anything you'd like?"

Maihac shook his head. "I have only just arrived on Gallingale. Gaing told me something of your situation, and I thought I should let you know I was back."

"I agree, completely! Where are you staying?"

"I haven't settled anywhere yet."

"Then stay here! The house is empty; I'd be happy for your company."

"I accept with pleasure."

The two pulled up chairs to the fire. Jaro brought out a bottle of the choice Estresas Valley wine Hilyer had put aside for a special occasion. As Jaro filled the goblets he said, "I hope that you'll explain the mysteries which have been gnawing at me."

"Certainly, as soon as I relax a bit."

"Could you answer me just one question? Do you know where the Faths first found me?"

"No. The Faths would never tell me, and I am as anxious to find out as you are—perhaps more, since it is where Jamiel, your mother, was killed."

For an instant the familiar old image flickered in and out of Jaro's mind: the gaunt man in the black hat and black frock coat silhouetted against the evening sky. He said, "The Faths were secretive to the edge of obsession. They thought that I would go kiting off into space if I knew where to go. They were right, of course. The records are gone—wiped clean. I've searched everywhere, without success. It was mainly Hilyer's doing, I'm convinced. He was fanatic about such things."

"We'll look again," said Maihac. "I'm also fanatic when necessary. Something is bound to show up." He looked around the room. "I see you've moved out most of the furniture, although I recognize the candelabra."

"I couldn't let them go. There is too much of Althea in them."

"Are you planning to renovate?"

"I'm not sure. When you're in the mood, I'd be interested in your opinions."

"Pour me some more of Hilyer's good wine. As for my opinions, they may be worse than the problem. Still, I'll listen and let you know what surfaces."

"Do you mean now?"

"Why not? I'm comfortable."

Jaro refilled the goblets and told Maihac of Forby Mildoon's attempts to buy Merriehew, of Skirl's discovery that Levyan Zarda, as planned, included Merriehew's five hundred acres. He told of Lyssel and her desperate methods. "She was quite relentless, up to a point." Jaro thought back over the episode. "Poor Lyssel! She attempted an imaginary seduction, in which she needn't get her feet wet. It was all very strange. If I had signed, Forby Mildoon would have used the option to secure the *Pharsang* from Gilfong Rute. When Abel Silking called, Lyssel left in a panic." Jaro told of Silking's visit and his representations in favor of Lumilar Vistas. "In the end, he made some threats, which were none too subtle. It was an interesting evening."

Maihac rose to his feet.

"If you were to invite me and perhaps Gaing Neitzbeck to assist in your dealings with Lumilar Vistas, I think you could dismiss Mr. Silking's threats without any further concern."

"You are invited."

"Very well," said Maihac. "We'll take the matter under study. Now, where do I sleep?"

2

In the morning, over breakfast, Maihac told of the circumstances which had brought him to Gallingale.

"My original home was a big two-story house at the fashionable end of a village called Cray, in the backlands of the world Paghorn, in the Aries sector. My father and mother were genteel folk; in fact, they were, respectively, schoolmaster and school nurse at the local elementary school. They were natives of Phasis, also in Aries, where they came from upper-class families. I never understood what brought them to Cray, at the edge of Long Bog, which means next to nowhere. I was the youngest of five children. The first four were girls. Our house was the finest in town, except for Vaswald the saloon-keeper's mansion. My mother was determined to raise us as ladies and gentlemen, using a book called *Godfroy's Guide to Delicate Manners* for reference. At every meal we were faced with a full range of utensils. The local folk used only scoops and what they called 'nuppers' for cracking the shells of boiled bogworms. As I think back, they were really a loutish folk." Maihac laughed. "The villagers had invented a fine game. During the day girls and young women were safe enough, but at night the village bucks put on masks and skulked about the town looking for females who themselves had donned masks and come out in search of adventure. There was never any violence, I must say, and if a girl or a woman had a real need to be out, and wore no mask and carried a lamp and protested convincingly, she usually fared nothing worse than a pat on the rump and was sent on her way. No one suffered all that much. My sisters, needless to say, were not allowed to run the streets. When I was sixteen I was sent to Phasis to visit some relatives. I was offered a job as steward aboard a tramp freighter, which I accepted, and never returned to Paghorn. I don't know what has become of my family, for which I am ashamed. So began my career.

"Some years later I was mate on another rackety old freighter, the *Distilcord*, under captain Paddo Rark. On the world Delia's Vale we discharged cargo, but the shipping agent had nothing on hand for onward transport. Captain Paddo sent me and Gaing Neitzbeck, the engineer, out around the backcountry to roust up some cargo. When we returned, we found Captain Paddo and the steward murdered and a gang of robbers looting the ship. Gaing and I killed the robbers, buried Captain Paddo and the steward; then we loaded the cargo we had scratched up and departed Delia's Vale. Gaing and I were the only crew. Paddo Rark had been alone in the world; and now Gaing and I were also de facto owners of the *Distilcord*.

"At the first opportunity we supplied ourselves with appropriate papers, registered the *Distilcord* in our own names and started carrying cargoes of opportunity.

"We did well enough and enjoyed ourselves immensely; it was a good life for two energetic young vagabonds. Then one day we put down on the world Nilo-May, single planet to the sun Yellow Rose, and landed at the chief spaceport Loorie. And this is where our troubles began."

The telephone chimed.

Jaro went to respond and after a moment returned. He spoke with embarrassment: "I must meet someone in Thanet at once. I'll be back inside the hour. Can the story wait this long?"

"No problem. I'll unpack my gear."

3

Jaro drove the old runabout into town—along Flammarion Prospect, past the Institute, into Vilia Road, up Lesmond Way to Sassoon Ayry. In the street stood Skirl, beside two small pieces of luggage. She wore a dark blue jacket and a short dark blue skirt; she stood erect, face taut and serious. Jaro pulled up beside her. They looked at each other, neither showing any expression. Jaro jumped to the ground, loaded Skirl's luggage into the runabout. "Is this all? You won't have much of a wardrobe."

"That's all the guards let me take. They said that they had strict orders from the bank to let me take only the barest essentials."

"Odd."

Skirl gave a careless shrug. "I had to leave behind some things I rather liked, but it makes no great difference. The bankers were angry because I would not pay off my father's debts, using the flimsy excuse that I had no money."

Jaro shook his head in wonder. He opened the door. Skirl climbed aboard and they were off, down Lesmond Way.

Skirl said, "I decided to move from the club before my welcome expired. Since you are living alone in Merriehew, neglected and motherless, I decided to apply for the post of housekeeper."

"You are hired," said Jaro. "You can sleep either with me, or you can have the main bedroom with a private bath, whichever appeals to you."

"That is a bad joke," said Skirl severely. "I will want as much privacy as possible."

"Just as you like. Your duties won't amount to much. At the moment there is another guest. We'll share whatever work needs to be done."

"Who is the guest?"

"He is a spaceman named Tawn Maihac." Jaro paused, then added, "He is my father."

Skirl turned him a skeptical side-glance. "Is this another of your fantasies?"

"Of course not!"

"That is startling news."

"Absolutely. When I found out, I was startled to the extreme."

"How did you find out?"

"Gaing Neitzbeck told me."

"Very interesting. What is he like?"

"It's rather hard to describe him. He's competent and versatile. Have you ever heard of a 'froghorn'? No? It doesn't matter. Maihac is quiet and not at all dramatic, but he is hard to ignore."

"You seem to admire him."

"I do, very much."

"Does Mr. Maihac belong to any important clubs? Is he a grandee of some sort?"

"Not that I know of."

"A pity."

"I suppose so. It's too bad he's not wealthy."

"But he's not?"

"No. I'm probably better off than he is."

"I suppose you are certain that the facts are correct?"

Jaro considered. "I don't think I'm the target of a swindling scheme. At least, he hasn't tried to borrow money yet."

"Has he explained the six missing years of your life?"

"There are gaps in his knowledge. He doesn't know where the Faths found me. That's something I'll have to search out for myself."

"Hmm. And when will you start searching?"

"I've already looked through all the records and journals I can find. I've come up blank. Still, sooner or later something is bound to show up."

"Then what?"

"It's a question of money. I have an income, but it's not enough to take me off-world."

Skirl said with determination: "As an effectuator, I plan to earn a great deal of money. I might need assistance. If you chose to work with me, you might find the decision profitable."

"That's a long-range project."

"Perhaps. Perhaps not."

"We would be partners; is that your idea?"

Skirl uttered a cool laugh. "Definitely not. If you come under my command, you will be assigned cases too vulgar or too sordid to interest the Executive Director, which is to say, me."

"That is straightforward, certainly. I'll give the offer some thought."

They arrived at Merriehew. Jaro unloaded Skirl's luggage and Maihac came out to help. Jaro made introductions, then he carried Skirl's luggage to the room designated for her use.

Jaro told Skirl: "Maihac is in the middle of a most interesting account, and I want to hear the rest of it. Perhaps you'd care to join us."

"Of course," said Skirl. "I'll make some tea first, if I may?"

The three sat in the old parlor, teapot and nutcakes on a low table. Jaro told Skirl, "You have missed something of Maihac's early life. He was born near a village called Cray, hard by the

Long Bog, on a world at the back of Aries. At the age of sixteen he became a spaceman. A few years later he and Gaing Neitzbeck came into possession of a tramp freighter named the *Distilcord.* In due course they brought a cargo to the world Nilo-May, in orbit around the star Yellow Rose, at the edge of the Reach. This, according to Maihac, is where his troubles began. Am I right?"

"Quite right," said Maihac. "Except that Yellow Rose marks not only the edge of the Reach, but also the fringes of the galaxy, with blank space close beyond."

4

Maihac took up his tale. "Before arriving at Nilo-May, Gaing and I had enjoyed a pleasant life, drifting among the stars without a schedule, wherever the chances of a cargo took us. At every port we found odd new colors, strange smells, new combinations of sounds, surprising flora and fauna as well as human-folk with unfamiliar habits. We learned the techniques of dealing with merchants who knew tricks so ingenious that it was a pleasure to be cheated. We heard dialects so broad that we could barely understand them. Vigilance was always a good idea, for the sake of both profit and survival. The most flagrant dangers more often than not we brought on ourselves, by gambling at games we never quite understood, or showing too much interest in the innkeeper's daughter.

"At Port Hedwig on the world Trasnoy we arrived with a cargo of small power-tools, only to find that the consignee had gone bankrupt. Freight charges, storage fees, port tax, imposts, bribes and duties would have totaled more than the value of the goods themselves, so that unloading the cargo was not feasible and the *Distilcord* was permitted only four hours to be off-planet. We departed Trasnoy on an outward slant into a region as remote as any we had ever visited."

Maihac paused while Skirl refilled his teacup. Jaro asked if he preferred other refreshment: more of the Estresas Valley wine, or perhaps a taste of sour-mash rye whiskey, which Hilyer often described as "Nectar of the Gods"?

Maihac, stating that the day was a bit too young, declined both wine and spirits, as did Skirl. Maihac continued with his narrative.

The *Distilcord* swung around the star Yellow Rose, approached the world Nilo-May and landed at Loorie, the principal and only spaceport. Loorie was little more than a village, shaded under enormous trees, with a long main street terminating at the ramshackle spaceport.

Landing formalities were nominal, after which Maihac and Gaing were at liberty to dispose of their cargo as best they could.

In response to Maihac's question, the clerk in the terminal office informed them that two freight brokerage-houses were active in Loorie, the Lorquin Shipping agency and the Primrose consolidators, both with offices along the main street. The clerk was dubious about their prospects. "Lorquin and Primrose are both what I would call 'special-purpose' firms, each with its established clientele. Still—who knows? It does no harm to try. In fact, yonder stands Aubert Yamb, from Lorquin; he has come to check over the weekly mainfests. Go speak to Yamb; he can tell you more than I can."

Maihac and Gaing, turning, observed a plump moon-faced man, somewhat past his first youth, with taffy-colored hair hanging down past his cheeks. He stood by a bulletin board, making notes from the documents on display.

The two approached and introduced themselves. "We understand that you are an official at Lorquin Shipping Agency?"

"That is true, to a limited extent," said Yamb. "In actual fact, a single official rules the roost; the rest of us bow to her command."

"Still, you may be able to advise us. Our ship is the *Distilcord;* we carry a cargo of valuable tools which we want to sell. Lorquin Agency can do very well for itself if it acts quickly and makes us a fair offer. We hope to avoid protracted negotiations."

"Hmm." Yamb pursed his pink lips. "I'm afraid that you do not understand the trade practices in vogue at Lorquin Shipping. Conceivably Dame Waldop might take your goods on consignment, if you paid storage charges and accepted the scope of her commission. She might even buy outright, if the price were right, and you might as well forget the word 'fair.' "

"This is not encouraging," said Maihac. "What of the Primrose Consolidators?"

"Again, they might take a few items on consignment. Primrose is essentially the hub of a cooperative, which consolidates, imports and exports for ranchers and small concerns. By some miracle it survives from year to year, and so must serve a need. The executive directors are my Aunt Estebel Pidy and my cousin

Twillie. I know their business well and I can assure you that while from sheer foolishness they might buy your cargo, they are not so foolish as to pay for it."

"And there are no other freight brokers in Loorie?"

"None. Lorquin at times will buy such stuff as this, then take it elsewhere for sale. But expect no gratifying price: Dame Waldop's penury is notorious."

"Where is 'elsewhere'?"

Yamb made an ambiguous gesture. "Oh—here, there; parts more remote."

"Where would that be? We are already at the end of nowhere."

Yamb screwed up his face, torn between a desire to correct Maihac's assertion and the restraints of proprietary discretion. He said at last, "I shall say no more at the moment, and I hope that you will not reveal that I have hinted of markets elsewhere; Dame Waldop is quick to curb loose tongues."

"You need fear nothing; we are discreet."

Yamb rubbed his chin thoughtfully. "In fact, do not even recognize me in public, since I must guard my bona fides. Are we agreed?"

"Agreed. Tell us more about Dame Waldop, so that we will know best how to deal with her."

"She is a great wowser of a woman; her stature and sheer presence are both impressive; she beetles over everyone with an important bodice, while her buttocks are like steel pontoons. She is starkly austere, and—dare I say it!—a bit of a martinet. Do not quote me on any of this."

"So then, it seems that we are forced to deal with this imposing woman?"

"You have no choice, unless the director himself is on hand. His name is Asrubal, and he is as inflexible as Dame Waldop, and even more sinister."

"We can only do our best," said Maihac. "Unless we deal with the Primrose Consolidators."

"That would be pointless, since they are not allowed to transact business on Fader." Yamb stopped short and glanced guiltily over his shoulder. "I am far too free with my tongue."

"Forget all I have told you."

"It is not even a memory."

Yamb sighed. "I am relieved. Excuse me now; I must go."

5

According to the authoritative *Handbook of the Planets*, Nilo-May had been located originally by the legendary Wilbur Wailey.*

The star Yellow Rose, along with Nilo-May, wandered across an empty gulf near the edge of the galaxy, in a region almost forgotten by the rest of the Reach.

To the east of Loorie rose the Hoo-Woo Hills; to the west, across ten miles of morass, lay the Bay of Bismold; to south and north were farms and other agricultural enterprises. Except for the district surrounding Loorie and a few outback stations, the world was uninhabited by Gaeans, and in fact was a savage wilderness.

An equatorial desert girdled the planet, with channels connecting a pair of shallow oceans to north and south. Odd oily rivers originated in the desert uplands and flowed through forests of punkwood trees and gigantic sprawling dendrons of many colors. Beyond spread swamps punctuated by floats of cottonpuff and stalks of blackrod supporting persimmon-colored pads, where large lizard-like beings danced and gyrated, leaping from pad to

---

*Wilbur Wailey, after a stint as locator, began to conduct enterprises of a questionable sort. His supreme achievement, by his own assessment, was his "Empire of Song and Glory." On a world so far Beyond and so lost among the galactic wisps and starstreams that five thousand years later, it still had not been rediscovered.

To this world, which Wailey named Safronilla, he brought bevy after bevy of handsome young women, whom he recruited by a variety of tactics. To some he paid generous bonuses; others he kidnapped, from convents, colleges, holiday camps, beauty pageants, spiritual improvement groups, and the like. On one occasion he captured an all girl fife, bugle and drum corps, along with their instruments. A few months later he induced six hundred and fifteen prime Type-A virgins of the Pellucids aboard one of his ships, on the pretext of viewing his collection of tropical fish. Once all were aboard, and were looking here and there for the fish, the doors closed, and the ship flew off. On Safronilla the Pellucids disembarked but their indignation went for naught. One by one, methodically, assiduously Wilbur Wailey got each of them with child—not once, but several times. Fifteen years later he made the rounds again, this time inseminating his daughters with neither prejudice nor favoritism; as he did his grand-daughters in the sunset of his life.

When anthropologists gather for a gossip or an excursion into shop talk in the lounges of their clubs, sometimes late in the evening after several tots of Pusser's Regulation or Old Tanglefoot have been consumed, someone may make a reference to Wilbur Wailey and his career. After a few moments someone else will say: "They don't make men like Wilbur Wailey nowadays!" And for a time the group is quiet, while everyone thinks his or her own thoughts, and wonders how it goes now on far Safronilla.

pad. Often they built conical structures of fiber and mucilage thirty feet high. Through small round windows the lizards thrust their heads, looked to right and left, then jerked back into the darkness. Along the equator a curtain of perpetual rain hung from a high wall of black clouds, constantly fed by trade winds from south and north, sweeping together, colliding, rising high into the upper atmosphere, to curl over and flow back toward the poles. The Swamps along the fringes of the desert and beside the rivers seethed with life. Balls of tangled white worms, prancing web-footed andromorphs with green gills and eyes at the end of long jointed arms, starfish-like pentapods tip-toeing on limbs twenty feet long; creatures all maw and tail; wallowing hulks of cartilage with pink ribbed undersides.

At Loorie the population of seven thousand folk lived by a low-key philosophy, which renounced haste, tension, and strident ambition. Visitors often spoke enviously of the "unflappable sangfroid" which they had discovered at Loorie. Others, of a different temperament, used such terms as "apathetic" or "lazy," to describe the same conduct.

The structures of Loorie, when viewed as a group, created an effect which was unique, even quaint, though no individual structure by itself seemed remarkable. The architecture was uniform: walls of punkwood planks slabbed from dendrons, cemented with their own sap, supported nine-sided roofs, which in turn were surmounted by a selection of ironmongery, to the owner's taste: wind-vanes, ghost-chasers, spin-wheels, fortune-fonts, and the like. Commercial enterprises lined the main street: the Natural Bank, the Fragrant Hotel, Cudder's Market, Lorquin Shipping Agents, Tecmart, the Peurifoy Refreshment Parlor, Bon Ton Salon, an IPCC office of the Fifth Grade, staffed by a pair of local recruits, and further along the street, the Primrose Consolidators. Dendrons grew in the back-yards and open spaces, casting shade and exhaling a dry peppery odor.

Maihac and Gaing stopped by the Peurifoy Refreshment Parlor, seating themselves at the front, in the shade of black and green foliage. A small girl, wearing an ankle-length gown of brown muslin, looked from the dark interior, subjected the two to a slow inspection, then marched out to inquire their needs, and presently returned with pots of beer.

The local time was about noon, to judge by the altitude of Yellow Rose. It shone without dazzle, producing a serene light which played odd tricks with perspective. The streets were quiet.

The townsfolk moved sedately about their affairs, slippers gliding silently across the pavement. Some walked with heads bent, arms clasped behind their backs, as if engrossed in abstract calculation; others paused to rest on benches where they contemplated their plans for the day. They showed themselves as neither gregarious nor voluble. Persons passing on the street gave each other suspicious side-glances under hooded eyelids. When friends or business associates met and communication was necessary, they first looked right and left over their shoulders, then spoke in guarded undertones, as if imparting matters of secret import. On this basis, Loorie seemed a veritable hive of intrigue. A flight of three long-billed birds, pink with black crests rising along their necks, glided overhead. Their wings, narrow and of remarkable span from tip to tip, flapped almost negligently. As they flew, they issued a succession of discordant calls—the loudest sounds to be heard across Loorie.

From the Peurifoy garden, Maihac and Gaing could look across the street and through a large window into the front office of the Lorquin Shipping Agency. In the shaded gloom of the interior a large woman with broad shoulders and an extraordinary bust marched back and forth, waving her arms as if addressing someone who could not be seen. "That must be Dame Waldop," said Maihac.

"She is formidable, without a doubt!" said Gaing.

"She seems excited, or even in a state of outrage," said Maihac. "Perhaps she has caught Aubert Yamb out in a breach of company protocol, and he is now learning of his mistake." Maihac finished the beer. "Are you ready to make ourselves known?"

Gaing drained the heavy earthenware pot. "Now is as good a time as any."

The two crossed the street and entered the premises of the Lorquin Shipping Agency. In the center of the room Dame Waldop halted in mid-stride, swung about to face her visitors, head thrown back, magnificent bust thrust forward. Aubert Yamb crouched over a desk at the back of the room, making notes in a ledger. He glanced furtively at the two spacemen, then returned to his work. Dame Waldop raked her visitors with glinting eyes set beside a long thin nose. She asked, "Well then, gentlemen? What do you wish?"

Maihac explained the business which had brought them to the Lorquin Agency. Dame Waldop listened a moment, then cut him off with a quick hacking gesture.

"We have no need for such gimcracks. We are not hucksters here at Lorquin; we are brokers and shippers of important merchandise only."

From the shadows came Yamb's voice. "Dame Waldop, recollect, if you please! The director has mentioned a need for outbound cargoes."

"That is quite enough," snapped Dame Waldop. "Your advice is not to the point." She turned back to Maihac and Gaing. "Where are your samples?"

"We have brought only this." Gaing displayed a small device. "It is a hole-driver. You touch this sleeve to a hard surface, stone, wood, metal or synthesite, press this button and a hole of exact dimension and depth is driven into the material. Next, if you choose, you dip a stud into adhesive, tap it into the hole, the stud is permanently bonded; or it might be an eye-bolt or hook. With a special kit you can affix half of a door hinge permanently to a wall. It is simple, foolproof and efficient."

"What price do you expect for this shipment?"

"There are forty-five hundred items. They retail at about eight to ten sols apiece. Our price is fifteen thousand sols for the lot."

"Ha hah! Absurd!" She beckoned to Yamb: "Go with these men to their vessel and make a careful invoice of what is being offered, with all pertinent information."

"To prevent a waste of time," said Maihac, "what is likely to be your offer, assuming all to be in order?"

Dame Waldop shrugged. "I might go as high as two or three thousand sols. Out here, at the end of everything, and no other market near, that is a fair price."

"There is always Fader," Maihac suggested.

Dame Waldop reared her head even farther back than before. She rasped, "Who mentioned Fader to you?"

"There was talk at the spaceport."

"Such talk is sheer bosh! They should know that the Lorquin Agency serves as the sole commercial conduit to any other transport or shipping service, and I suggest that you avoid intrusion into a settled line of business."

"If three thousand sols is to be your top offer, we will waste no more of your time."

Maihac and Gaing departed Lorquin Shipping, and continued along the street to Primrose Consolidators. Pushing open a punkwood door, they stepped into a long narrow room, dim and shadowy, smelling sour-sweet of unfamiliar spice, aromatic woods and leathers, and the moldering dust of ages. To the left, behind a counter, a plump young woman worked sorting dry beans into appropriate basins. Her blond hair was tied into a bun; her face was heavy, with a lumpy nose and a small pink mouth.

Nearby on the counter a placard read:

Dame Estebel Pidy, Manager.

The young woman was out of sorts and ignored her visitors until Maihac asked, "Are you the manager?"

The woman looked up with a scowl and pointed to the placard. "Can't you read? Ebbie is manager. I am Twee Pidy, Superintendent of Research and Off-world Operations."

"Excuse me," said Maihac. "Where is the manager?"

Across the room, half-concealed in the shadows, sat an older woman, with wide cheekbones and graying hair hanging to each side of her face, like that of Aubert Yamb. She rose to her feet and came forward. "I am Estebel Pidy; I manage what needs to be managed, which is little enough."

Once again Maihac explained their business. As before, he evoked no positive reaction in his audience. Estebel Pidy lacked all interest in serious dealing. "We act for the local merchants, importing their needs and exporting whatever comes in from the back country. It is a small-scale business, barely enough to keep us afloat. We can't compete with Lorquin; they work off-world altogether, where the wealth can be had for the asking."

"Or taking," sniffed Twee Pidy. "That is, if Aubert can be believed."

"Then you should play the same game."

"That is not so easy," said Estebel Pidy. "The Lorquins own two ships, the *Liliom* and the *Audrey-Anthey;* they shuttle these ships back and forth to Fader, carrying cargo in both directions. We have not so much as a crank-leg flitter."

"I told Dame Waldop that we would take our goods to Fader, and she became perturbed. Why is that?"

Twee Pidy looked up from her work. "Need you ask? They want no interference with their trade! If you took your tools to Fader, you could sell them at your own price."

Dame Estebel said mildly: "The Roum are odd folk, to judge

by Asrubal of Urd. They are too proud to bargain; they pay the price with haughty disdain. This is what we hear from a very good source."

Twee said spitefully, "Now you know why Dame Waldop guards the Fader trade. No one else may taste the fruits of this golden tree: that is the Lorquin creed."

"How can they bar us from Fader? Do they control the spaceport?"

"There is a single spaceport, at a place called Flad. It is open, but what then? Two thousand miles of secret ways lead to Romarth, where the goods are sold. At Flad you are alone, in a wild waste, with no one to buy your goods. If you wander a hundred yards you may be captured by the Loklor and taken off to 'dance with the girls,' as they put it."

"So why not land the cargo directly at Romarth?"

"That is forbidden. Even the Lorquin Agency must secure a special warrant, should they need to bring a shipment directly to Romarth."

"So it is not impossible."

"It seems not, if you carry a special warrant, which is seldom issued. The Roum value their splendid privacy, and they fear that outsiders might supply the Loklor with weapons."

"Where does one apply for the warrant?"

"At Romarth; where else? But why trouble yourself?"

"There is no mystery," said Maihac. "It is the difference between Dame Waldop's two or three thousand sols, and the fifteen or twenty thousand we might collect from the open-handed Roum. For us Fader is only another port of call."

Estebel became impatient. "Our time is valuable. We can tell you no more."

Twee Pidy blurted resentfully, "Quite so, in all respects! If right were right, these two should pay consultation fees!"

Maihac smiled his most ingratiating smile. "One last question, which we dare not put to Dame Waldop."

"Oh, very well," sighed Estebel Pidy. "What is it this time?"

"After we leave Loorie, where do we look to find Fader?"

Estebel Pidy said, "When the sun has set, go outside, look into the sky. To one side is the bright galaxy; to the other is the black void, where one star hangs alone. That star is Night Lamp, with its planet Fader."

6

The *Distilcord*, leaving Yellow Rose astern, set a course away from the glimmer of the galaxy and out into the void. Far ahead glittered Night Lamp, a vagabond star which had broken free of galactic gravity to wander alone, without orbit or destination.

Time passed; Night Lamp grew bright and the *Distilcord* approached the world Fader. Maihac, searching *HANDBOOK TO THE PLANETS*, found no entry. Other reference works were also devoid of information. The ship's macroscope computed the diameter to be slightly less than Earth-standard, with an approximately equal gravity. A single continent occupied much of the southern* hemisphere, with an ocean covering the remainder of the planet. Mountains corrugated the southern edge of the continent, with a deep dark forest shrouding the central area and a vast steppe sprawled across north, east and west. Neither the city Romarth nor any other settlement was immediately evident. Maihac finally noticed an agglomeration of white structures in the forest, camouflaged by the trees which grew among the structures and lined the avenues. A radio beacon located the spaceport Flad, alone in the middle of the northern steppe. The macroscope showed a desolate spatter of wind-blown sheds and warehouses. Maihac dispatched a notification of arrival, but received no response. He tried again, with the same result. Without further ado he set the *Distilcord* down upon the landing field near the terminal office. To either side were warehouses, a dormitory for staff, a makeshift machine shop, miscellaneous sheds: all in various stages of dilapidation. The steppe spread away in all directions, marked only by a road leading off to the south.

The terminal building baked in the sunlight. No one came out to inspect the *Distilcord*.

Maihac and Gaing alighted, and noticed in the open doorway of the machine shop a large man with a tangle of black curls and a black beard, who watched incuriously as the two of them crossed the field to the terminal office. They pushed through a door of

*If an observer imagines himself standing at the equator of a planet, facing the direction of rotation, north is to his left and south to his right. The polarity of the north and south poles, in terms of magnetic flux, may or may not correspond to the rule cited above, which essentially establishes that the planet's sun shall rise in the east and set in the west.

molded sinter and entered a dingy lobby. The single occupant sat at a counter, relaxed, hands clasped before him, apparently in a state of profound reverie. He was middle-aged, thin, with a scholar's pallor, ascetic features and a fastidious droop to his mouth. He wore a crisp gray tunic with a blue medallion clipped to his shoulder. He was, thought Maihac, an odd sort to be minding the counter at this remote and dusty outpost.

The terminal manager, if such he were, became aware of Maihac and Gaing. His face changed; apparently he had been asleep with his eyes open. Rising to his feet, he looked through the window at the *Distilcord*. He turned back to the newcomers. "That is neither the *Liliom* nor the *Audrey-Anthey*; who are you?"

"The ship is the *Distilcord.*" Maihac supplied registration particulars, which the manager looked over without any real interest. He examined Maihac and Gaing again, more closely than before. "Then you are not from the Lorquin Agency?"

"No; we represent ourselves exclusively."

"So why do you come to Fader? It is a far voyage."

"We carry a cargo of small tools which we hope to sell at Romarth."

The manager asked dubiously, "Are these weapons, or can they be used as weapons?"

"Absolutely not; they are useful only in the construction business. We want to discharge our cargo at Romarth, which would be both efficient and convenient."

The manager showed a sour smile. "Those words have no currency at Romarth. The Roum do no work; hence no one cares much for either convenience or efficiency."

Gaing spoke impatiently: "If only for our own convenience, may we proceed to Romarth?"

The manager shook his head. "Not without a special warrant, lacking which, you would be placed under instant arrest, and lose both ship and cargo."

"In that case, please issue the proper warrant."

Again the manager shook his head. "It is not as easy as all that. My authority is nil, or even less, since I am here for purposes of penal cogitation—now, happily, at an end."

Maihac asked, "Who then has the authority?"

The manager pulled at his chin. "The only person with authority around here is Arsloe, at the machine shop."

"The man with the black beard?"

"Yes; a surly sort of fellow, and an off-worlder like yourselves.

He talks to Asrubal by radio when he wants something; even so, he can't do anything for you. The warrant is available only at Romarth itself."

Gaing asked gruffly: "How do we get the warrant if we're not allowed to go after it?"

"Aha!" the manager exclaimed. "You think to have posed a tricky paradox, but you are wrong. You travel to Romarth for the warrant, then return."

"Fair enough," said Gaing. "We will fly there in our flitter."

"No," said the manager. "Nothing is easy on Fader. Such an act is also illegal."

"Why is that?"

"Because the flitter might fall into the hands of the Loklor, and become a dangerous weapon. They are enough trouble already; we take pains to deny them weapons and other such equipment. If you wish to go to Romarth, you must use the regular transport, like anyone else. There is in fact a train departing Flad tomorrow morning." For the first time the manager showed a trace of animation. "I will be traveling aboard this train myself; my term of penitence is over and tomorrow I leave this dust hole and that sullen beast Arsloe behind—forever, or so I hope. I must take pains, of course, to avoid my previous faults."

"What did you do?" asked Gaing. "Did you—" and he coarsely suggested an act of sexual perversion committed upon the young daughter of the Chief Magistrate.

"No, nothing like that. What I did was worse. I gave voice to unpopular opinions."

7

Maihac and Gaing returned to the *Distilcord*, where they discussed their options. They could depart Fader and try to sell their cargo elsewhere, or they could make an effort to sell at Romarth. In the end they decided that Maihac should travel to Romarth aboard the train, while Gaing remained at Flad to guard the *Distilcord* and its cargo. It was an arrangement which pleased neither, but the manager had informed them that ships left unguarded were apt to be looted by bands of wandering Loklor.

The trip to Romarth required six or seven days: three days across the Tangtsang Steppe, three or four days through the Blandy Deep Forest. If the warrant were granted expeditiously,

Maihac would be back in two weeks. If the warrant were refused, Maihac would still return at best speed. Meanwhile he would keep in touch with Gaing by means of a portable radio.

The sun set among streaks of plum and carmine cirrus. Dusk fell over the world, giving way to black night. In the east a large dim moon the color of silver-gold alloy floated into the sky, followed by another of the same size and color. Far to the south, a night creature set up a wild wailing which presently died, leaving behind an oppressive silence. The moons drifted across the sky and settled into the west. Hours passed. In the east the sky showed a saffron blush and presently the sun rose. The train had been assembled: a massive tractor unit rolling on six large wheels, a passenger wagon, a service wagon and three goods wagons. Maihac climbed aboard; half an hour after sunrise the train departed Flad and trundled south across Tangtsang Steppe toward far Romarth.

Maihac found himself riding in the company of four other passengers, including the former terminal manager, whose name, so he learned, was Bariano of Ephrim House. The other three passengers were Roum of mature years, all of Urd House. Their demeanor was notably self-important, if not haughty. They used a chilly punctilio in their dealings with Bariano and, after a glance at Maihac and a few muttered words among themselves, they ignored his existence. While conversing among themselves they used a dialect incomprehensible to Maihac. When Bariano was included in the conversation, they spoke standard Gaean, using a stilted accent. Immediately upon boarding the train they commandeered a table at the rear of the car, where they spread out documents and entered upon earnest discussions. Bariano sat to the side, looking out over the steppe, and Maihac did the same. There was little to see. The landscape was bleak, relieved by low hills in the distance and an occasional lonely sentinel tree. Closer at hand were thickets of brittle thornbush, spinneys of dull yellow spindlegrass, patches of lichen, the color and texture of scab.

After a time Bariano became bored with his introspection and, rather grudgingly, allowed himself to converse with Maihac. He intimated that he held the other three passengers in low esteem. "They are no more than petty functionaries, intoxicated with their own importance, which is small. They come out to Flad at intervals to validate the Lorquin bookkeeping. Of course they never find even the most modest peccadillo, let alone any serious transgressions, since they are Urd, of the same house as Asrubal. Have you noticed their pink shoulder clips? That means their faction is Pink, while the faction of Ephrim House is Blue. Nowadays the factions are of little importance; in fact, it is a dying tradition. Still, it gives them no reason to love me. Also, I must admit that my time of penitence has marred my rashudo."

" 'Rashudo'?"

"A local word. It means 'reputation,' 'self-respect,' and much more. You will find that the Roum psyche is highly complex, beyond any you have ever known before."

During late afternoon the train was halted by a troop of six Loklor nomads. Bariano told Maihac: "They are collecting a toll. Do nothing; say nothing. Show no curiosity. They will not become fractious unless provoked."

Maihac, looking through the window, saw six grotesque creatures close to seven feet tall: so massive and so awful as to seem almost majestic. Their skins appeared to be a horny integument, mottled yellow and russet. Their foreheads slanted back, narrowing into crests barbed with short spikes. The lower half of the faces were pinched and thin, so that under the nose-beaks, the mouths were small and folded into pads of cartilage. They wore greasy leather aprons, black vests, and iron-shod sandals.

The driver of the train paid them six jugs of beer, which the Loklor slung over their shoulders, then filed past the passenger car. For a moment they leered through the windows at the passengers, then turned and loped away, across the waste. The tractor's six wheels thrust at the road and the train lurched off to the south. On the following day another Loklor band appeared and collected another toll of the strong brew known as "Nacnoc." Bariano and the three Urd officials became visibly tense. Bariano muttered to Maihac: "These are Strenke—the worst of all. If they come to look at you, sit like a stone or they may take you away, to 'dance with the girls' by the light of the two pale moons."

The Loklor, however, snatched their jugs and stood back, allowing the train to go its way with the five passengers sitting stiff as statues, eyes fixed on the floor.

After the train had rolled a quarter mile, the passengers relaxed. The Urd officials gave vent to a flurry of angry remarks. Bariano, with a gloomy smile, told Maihac, "There you find the reality of the Tangtsang steppe, and perhaps of all Fader. We no longer control our habitat, if ever we did."

"I have a suggestion," said Maihac. "You might or might not want to hear it."

Bariano's eyebrows lofted high. "Aha! It seems that we have overlooked some elemental concept! Fortunately, you have come to set things right!"

Maihac ignored the sarcasm. "A pair of armed guards with power-guns might solve the problem."

Bariano pulled thoughtfully at his chin. "The idea has a pleasing simplicity. We recruit several guards, arm them with imported power-guns. They ride the train and shoot a number of Loklor and deny them their Nacnoc. So far, so good! But what of the next run? The Loklor might gather on the Beresford Bluffs and roll boulders down the slopes, smashing the train and killing both guards and passengers. Then they confiscate the power-guns. At Romarth there is great anger and we send out a punitive expedition. The Loklor take to the forest and disappear. But they are not ones to forgive and forget! They surround Romarth, infiltrate the city by night, and take their revenge. Thereafter, we accept the inevitable and pay their toll. Your suggestion, despite its virtue of easy comprehension, is flawed."

"Perhaps so," said Maihac. "But I have another, which you might like to hear."

"Of course!"

"If you moved the spaceport to Romarth, you defeat all your problems at once."

Bariano nodded. "This scheme, like the first, is marked by its noble simplicity. Still, it has already occurred to us and has long been rejected, for a fundamental reason."

"What is the reason?"

"In three words: we want to insulate Romarth from the Gaean Reach. Our ancestors traveled as far as they could, out of the galaxy, across the void to the star Night Lamp. Isolation was the guiding principle then, at the dawn of our history, as it is now in the sad glory of our sunset."

Maihac ruminated for a time, then asked, "Is the mood at Romarth so generally melancholy?"

Bariano chuckled sourly. "Do I seem so dreary? Remember that I have just completed a term of punitive meditation at Flad, and I have become dour. But I am not the typical Roum cavalier,* who fends aside unpleasant ideas as if they were symptoms of leprosy. He builds his world and his perceptions in the context of

*cavalier: an inexact translation, still more accurate in its overtones than "young nobleman," "knight," "bravo," or any other such expression.

his rashudo. He fixes all his attention upon the instant, which of course is sensible. There is no need for panic; imminence does not hang in the air, and the tragic grandeur of Romarth exalts the spirit. Still, the facts are dismal. The population is declining; half of the wonderful palaces are empty, home to the horrid creatures we call 'white house-ghouls.' In two hundred years—perhaps more, perhaps less—all of the palaces will be empty and the Roum will be gone, except for a belated straggler wandering the lonely avenues, and the only sounds will be the padding of the house-ghouls as they prowl the moonlit halls of old Romarth."

"It is a cheerless prospect."

"True, but we dismiss such thoughts with cool bravado and focus upon the arts of living. We are anxious to wring the last drop of sentience from every instant of life. Do not think us hedonists or sybarites, even though toil and drudgery are absent from our lives. We devote ourselves to the joys of grace, beauty, and creativity, all of which are controlled by strict conventions, along with much else. My disposition has always been restless and skeptical, and these traits have not served me well. At a symposium, I declared that modern efforts to create beauty were trivial and repetitive; I stated that everything significant had been done a hundred times over. My opinions were held to be pernicious. I was sent to Flad that I might revise my thinking."

"And you made the adjustment?"

"Naturally. In the future I will keep my opinions to myself. The fabric of life at Romarth is delicate. Even my petty perturbations strain the social accord. If the spaceport were situated at Romarth, we would be exposed to a never-ending flux of novelty and contradiction; perhaps cruise ships would come and go, bringing hundreds of tourists to stroll our promenades, convert our old palaces into hotels, to sit at cafes around the beautiful Gamboye Plaza and Lallakillany Circus. The spaceport remains at Flad. We are spared the miseries of social infection."

"You might be losing more than you gain," said Maihac. "The Reach is diverse. Have you thought to go out from Fader and explore other worlds?"

Bariano found the idea amusing. "We all must deal with reckless impulses from time to time. Wanderlust is a basic urge. Still, there are practical reasons why we seldom travel. We are a fastidious folk. Proper food and lodging are priced beyond our means to pay. We are not interested in picturesque squalor. We cannot abide dirt or tainted food or foul accommodations. We don't care to ride public transport among crowds of ill-smelling natives. Since suitable facilities command excessive prices, we prefer to remain at home."

"I must disabuse you," said Maihac. "Your fears are exaggerated. I agree that when you travel, you must take the bad with the good; everyone knows this. But the good, or at least the decent, is far more common and not hard to find. You need only take local advice."

Bariano said somberly, "So it may be, but these practical problems are simply too large to be solved. We can count on very little off-world income, since our exports barely pay for our imports. The surplus in Gaean sols is limited. Even if we wanted to travel off-world, we lack the sols to take us past Loorie."

Maihac reflected. "Lorquin Agency negotiates both imports and exports?"

"True. There is usually a profit, which is deposited to our individual accounts at the Natural Bank at Loorie, where the accounts earn interest. Even so, they never amount to much; certainly not enough to take us away on a grand tour of the Gaean Reach."

"In spite of all this, does anyone ever take the risk and go traveling?"

"Seldom. I have known two gentlemen who chose to wander. They traveled to Loorie, withdrew their funds from the Natural Bank; they took passage to unknown worlds of the Reach, and never returned. There were no messages. It was as if they were lost in an ocean of ten trillion faceless souls. No one wishes to share their fate."

An hour later Maihac noted another group of Loklor, standing on the round swell of a sand dune, silhouetted against the sky. They watched stolidly as the train passed, apparently indifferent to the prospect of Nacnoc.

Bariano could not account for their seeming lassitude, except to remark that all Loklor were unpredictable. "These are Golks—probably as wicked and weird as the Strenke."

Maihac asked, "How can you distinguish one Loklor from another?"

"In the case of the Golks, it's simple enough. The Golk women weave a cloth from eel-grass. If you will notice, these bucks wear skirts of the stuff, rather than leather aprons."

Maihac saw that, for a fact, the massive haunches were wrapped in clay-colored kirtles, leaving the saffron russet chest bare. He watched until the Golks could no longer be seen, then turned back to Bariano. "Are they intelligent?"

"After a fashion. At times they seem quite cunning, and I must say that they have a ghastly sense of humor."

"Are they to be considered human?"

"To answer that question I would need to describe their origin. It's a complicated story, but I'll be brief."

"Speak on!" said Maihac. "I've nothing better to do."

"Very well. We go back about five thousand years. The first settlers included a group of idealistic biologists, who tried to create strains of specialized workers. Their best success was the Seishanee. Their most awful failure turned out to be the Loklor. That is the story in its most abbreviated form. In short, the Loklor are not so much a human variation as a human deviation. They approximate humanity much as a nightmare approximates a birthday party."

Shortly after noon the train approached a tall dark forest, which Bariano identified as the Blandy Deep, marking the limits of the Tangtsang Steppe. An hour later the train halted beside the Skein River, near a dock at which a massive barge lay at moorings. The barge was constructed of a dense glossy black wood, to standards of craftsmanship Maihac thought remarkably rich and exact. From a bluff bow the hull swelled to an almost voluptuous mid-section, then faired with the grace of a resolving chord to the full transom, which was broken by six mullioned windows. The forepeak, deckhouse and sterncastle, in the same manner, were conceived and crafted to standards of baroque elegance; at bow and stern, stanchions supported heavy lanterns formed of black iron and colored glass.

Passengers boarded the vessel and were taken to cabins in the deckhouse. Lines were cast off; the barge drifted away downstream. After a quarter mile, the Skein veered to enter the Blandy Deep, and henceforth the barge moved through the somber shadows of the forest.

Days and nights passed. The river ran smooth and easy, curving this way and that, under the spread of high foliage.

Silence was absolute, save for the purl of water under the hull. At night a pair of large moons cast a serene light through the foliage in a manner which Maihac found almost dreamlike in its effect. He said as much to Bariano, who responded with a condescending shrug. "I am surprised to find you so enthusiastic. It is, after all, a mere trick of nature."

Maihac looked at Bariano quizzically. "I am puzzled to find you so insensitive."

Bariano was never pleased when Maihac's opinions differed from his own. "To the contrary! It is you who lack aesthetic discrimination! But why should I be surprised? As an off-worlder you cannot be expected to share the Roum delicacy of perception."

"I am confused, certainly," said Maihac. "The leaps and bounds of your thinking have left me far behind, like a spotted hound chasing a coach through the dust."

Bariano smiled a cool smile. "If I am to correct you, I must speak without euphemism, but do not take offense!"

"Speak freely," said Maihac. "You might tell me something I don't know."

"Very well. It is simply that your aesthetic judgments are amorphous. It is naive to detect beauty where none has been specifically intended. The subject is large. Often you will notice an agreeable aspect of nature, effected by random or mathematical processes. It may be serene and congenial, but it is the work of chance and lacks the human afflatus. There is no pulse of positive creativity to infuse it with true beauty."

Maihac was taken aback by the uncompromising sweep of Bariano's analysis. He said cautiously, "You make very narrow distinctions."

"Of course! That is the nature of clear thinking."

Maihac pointed ahead to where the moonlight, filtering through the foliage, cast a filigree of silver light and black shade upon the dark water. "Don't you find that a pretty effect? Deserving, at least, of notice?"

"The scene is not without charm, but your mental processes are untidy. Surely you will notice that the scene lacks conceptual integrity. It is chaos; it is abstraction; it is nothing!"

"Still, it evokes a mood. Isn't this the function of beauty?"

Maihac pointed ahead to where the moonlight, filtering through the foliage, cast a filigree of silver light and black shade upon the dark water. "Don't you find that a pretty effect? Deserving, at least, of notice?"

"The scene is not without charm, but your mental processes are untidy. Surely you will notice that the scene lacks conceptual integrity. It is chaos; it is abstraction; it is nothing!"

"Still, it evokes a mood. Isn't this the function of beauty?"

"Just so," said Bariano with equanimity. "But let me cite you a parable, or, if you prefer, a paradox. Assume that you are lying in bed asleep. Your dreaming brings you into the company of an alluring woman who starts to make exciting suggestions. At this moment a large dirty pet animal clambers upon the bed, and sprawls its hairy bulk beside you with its tail draped over your forehead. You move restlessly in your sleep and in so doing press your face against one of its organs. In your dream it seems that the beautiful woman is kissing you with warm moist lips, causing a delightful sensation. You are thrilled and exalted! Then you wake up and discover the truth of the contact, and you are displeased. Now then: consider carefully! Should you enjoy the rapture of the dream? Or, after beating the animal, should you huddle cheerlessly in the dark brooding upon the event? Arguments can be developed in either direction. If you wish, I will apply some of these arguments to our previous discussion."

"No, thank you," said Maihac. "You have said enough. In the future, whenever I seem to be enjoying anything in my sleep, I will make sure of its reality."

"A wise precaution," murmured Bariano.

Maihac said no more, aware that he would only reinforce Bariano's theories in regard to denizens of the Gaean Reach.

Toward the middle of the third day, docks and rustic cottages began to appear along the riverside, then an occasional mansion surrounded by old gardens. Some of the structures were almost palatial; some were old, some were very old and some were in a state of decay. From time to time Maihac glimpsed folk in the gardens. They moved with easy languor, as if enjoying the quiet of the forest.

Bariano commented, "This is not the season for rustification, although many houses are occupied all year round. When there are children in the family, this is often the case. See there: children are playing on the lawn."

Maihac saw a pair of children running barefoot across the grass, dark hair flying. They wore knee-length smocks, one pale blue, the other gray-green. Maihac thought they seemed active and happy. Bariano said, "Out here they are safe, since houseghouls avoid the lonely forests." A pair of gardeners worked with shears to clip a hedge. They were of no great stature, slight of physique, but deft and quick with the gardening implements. They were sallow tan; dust-colored hair hung in a fringe around regular, if rather bland, features. "Who might they be?" asked Maihac.

"They are Seishanee. They do the work which needs to be

done, if the Roum are to maintain their way of life. They are indispensable to us. They cut the trees and saw the planks; they grow the grain and bake the bread; they repair the drains and mend the roofs. They are clean, docile and industrious. But they will not fight, and are useless against the Loklor or the night-folk, so the Roum cavaliers must unsheathe their swords and strike down the savages. Some say that it is too late. Every year the house-ghouls occupy another of the old palaces."

"Evidently you can't find an effective way to deal with these things."

"Correct," said Bariano. "They infest the crypts beneath the palaces, and apparently they have dug a mesh of connecting tunnels. They are always at the back of our minds, and no one likes to walk alone by night."

On the next morning the barge entered Romarth. The Skein curved past an ugly heavy-walled structure of brown brick, then slanted off to the northeast where the Blandy Deep trailed away to become, first, a savannah, then the Tangtsang Steppe.

The barge docked against the esplanade and the passengers alighted. Bariano pointed. "Yonder is the Colloquary, where the councils sit." He hesitated, then said, "I will take you to where you should place your petition. You will get a hearing easily enough, but do not expect a quick disposition of your case, since you will be jostling many fixed opinions."

8

Maihac paused in his account. "I don't want to bore you with too much detail—"

Skirl quickly said, "You are not boring me; not in the least!"

"Still, if I told you everything—all I learned about Romarth and the Roum, their customs, rashudo, philosophy and social interactions, along with a description of the palaces, the habits of eating and sleeping, the courtship rituals, the cultivated truculence of the cavaliers, the brooding dread of the house-ghouls—it would be a major undertaking, and this before I even started upon the most terrible adventure of all. Now then, Jaro: you may pour me a dollop of Hilyer's good wine, while I sit back for a moment or two."

Jaro poured out three goblets of the golden Estresas wine. Maihac leaned back in his chair and sorted out his thoughts. He said at last: "I'll try to give you a glimpse, at least, of Romarth, perhaps the most beautiful city ever conceived by the Gaean race. When I saw it, many of its great houses had been abandoned and its wonderful gardens left to decay. Decadence hung in the air like the odor of rotting fruit. Nevertheless, the Roum persisted in their reveries and played out their intricate ceremonies. Several times a day they changed their costumes, according to their roles of the hour.

"It is important to understand the nature of the original settlers. They were an intellectual elite, which included a contingent of genetic biologists. Gaean law had debarred them from pursuing what they considered their 'ultimate project'; on Fader no such restraints were applied.

"In the beginning the settlers made use of slave labor, but there were many disadvantages. The slaves became diseased or old; in any case they died, and they were expensive to replace. They were often obstreperous or sullen, or lazy; discipline was a nuisance, and ineffectual as well. In the end, the biologists selected several prime slaves, and used their genes to generate what they hoped to be a class of ideal workers. They produced strain after strain of experimental prototypes. Often their efforts bore unpredictable fruit: creatures with legs ten feet long, others so corpulent that they were comfortable only while floating in warm water. Another strain developed anti-social traits of intense virulence; they made glories of pain and intransigence. Screaming, clawing, tearing at everything, they broke through the walls and fled across the Tangtsang, where the strongest and most merciless survived to become the Loklor.

"Eventually the Seishanee were synthesized: a slender, graceful race of half-men with clay-colored skins and soft brown eyes. They were of limited intelligence, but docile, industrious and easy of temperament. A trivial displacement of a few atoms caused them to be epicene, only nominally male and female with rudimentary sexual apparatus. Hence, the Seishanee were generated from zygotes cultivated in the ugly brown brick structure known as the 'Foundance.' The third race of Romarth was something of a mystery. It was said, that the early geneticists had modified themselves, intending to produce a race of intellectual overmen, but the processes had gone wrong. Certain of the flawed 'overmen' had gnawed through their boxes and scuttled away to hide in the crypts of abandoned palaces. Seldom seen, the white 'house-ghouls,' as they became known, made excursions abroad under cover of darkness. In time they even penetrated the crypts of inhabited mansions, venturing slyly forth to commit horrid atrocities. Those who had seen them, and survived, found their tongues thickening when they attempted a description. Occasionally, the Roum cavaliers launched attacks, intending to destroy the creatures once and for all, only to find themselves fighting shadows, and many blundered into traps. Eventually they lost heart, and soon the situation was as before, or worse, when the house-ghouls took their revenge.

"The Roum were elegant folk, each believed himself the summation of all known excellences. Everyone spoke three languages: classic Roum, colloquial Roum of today, and Gaean. Every Roum was born into one of forty-two Houses, or septs, each with its unique style of conduct. Public policy was controlled by a council of grandees, sitting at the Colloquary."

Once again Maihac paused. "This is rather boring stuff—but the background is necessary to understanding what occurred."

Both Jaro and Skirl denied boredom. Maihac continued his tale. He took a few moments to describe the city itself; its avenues, its great houses, the general atmosphere of immense antiquity. He described the Roum, their elegant costumes and romantic, often passionate, personalities, especially among the swashbuckling young bravos.

Maihac immediately took himself to the Colloquary, where—following Bariano's advice—he sought out the Councillor Tronsic of Stam House, to whom he presented his petition. Tronsic, a stalwart gray-haired man of late middle age, proved far more cordial than Maihac had dared hope. Tronsic went so far as to offer Maihac lodging in his house, which Maihac was pleased to acccept.

At an appropriate moment Tronsic placed Maihac's petition before the Council. They received the document for consideration which—so Tronsic assured Maihac—was cause for limited optimism.

While Maihac waited he kept in touch with Gaing at Flad, by way of his portable radio. Maihac explained to Gaing that patience was in order, and that he hoped Gaing was not becoming bored. Gaing merely growled and said that he was catching up on his reading.

Maihac found himself the object of much curiosity. Tronsic told him that everyone wondered about life elsewhere in the

Gaean Reach, despite the belief that conditions were crude, unsanitary, and dangerous. Maihac replied that circumstances varied from place to place, and that if the Roum intended to travel, they must expect to take the bad with the good.

" 'Good'?" demanded a fashionable young cavalier named Serjei of Ramy House. "What can be found among these crude worlds to compare with Romarth?"

"Nothing. Romarth is unique. By all means, stay home if that is your preference."

Another of those who stood by said, "All very well; still, the fascination of exotic places is undeniable. Unfortunately, travel in tolerable style is overly expensive: rapaciously so, considering the sorry state of our incomes. After all, we do not care to go lumping along the road like ragamuffins."

Serjei said, "True! We don't dare risk running through our capital in some far place, so that we are forced to toil for sheer survival!"

His companion said, "Rashudo would be ridiculously compromised. We could never strike poses again!"

Maihac admitted that these fears were justified. "If someone wishes sumptuous lodgings and exquisite food, he must be able to pay, since no one offers such facilities free of charge."

Certain of the Roum were more venturesome than others. Among them was Jamiel, of Ramy House, a slender erect young woman of exceptional charm and intelligence. The many textures of her personality fascinated Maihac: most especially her unconventional thinking, her light-hearted sense of humor, which was unusual among the Roum, and her impatience with the strictures of rashudo. Maihac could not prevent himself from falling in love with Jamiel. He thought he detected a responsive emotion, and presently, taking his courage in hand, he proposed marriage. She agreed, with gratifying enthusiasm. The two were immediately joined by the traditional rites of Ramy House.

In response to Maihac's questions, Jamiel explained the complexities of the Roum financial system. Each House used an account at the Natural Bank of Loorie. The profits earned by Lorquin Shipping Agency were divided among the forty-two Houses, and deposited to the appropriate account.

Maihac thought the system rather slapdash and extremely susceptible to flexibility, if not corruption. He asked, "Who calculates this division of profits?"

"Asrubal of Urd," said Jamiel. "He is Director of the Lorquin

Agency. He issues a yearly report, which is inspected by three officials, and then the funds are distributed."

"And this is the only assurance that the funds have been divided fairly?"

Jamiel shrugged. "Who would complain? Rashudo insists upon disregard for such details; they are too paltry to engage the attention of a Roum gentleman."

"I can tell you this much," said Maihac. "The prices you pay Lorquin Agency for imported goods are two or three times the prices at Loorie, or anywhere else around the Reach."

Jamiel said that she long had held such suspicions, as had many of her acquaintances. She added, as a casual trifle of incidental information, that she had become pregnant.

Time passed. Maihac began to fear that his petition had been permanently pigeon-holed. Jamiel assured him otherwise. "When one deals with the Colloquary he must expect delay—especially should the factions become involved, as in the present case. The House of Urd is a member of the Plum-pink faction, and wants to discourage any infringement of the Lorquin Agency monopoly. The Blues would prefer changes in the system, perhaps a complete reorganization."

Maihac knew little of the factions, other than that their differences derived from ancient ideologies, of a subtlety beyond his grasp. Insofar as Maihac was concerned, it was clear that factional infighting must be resolved before he could expect a judgment on his petition.

Maihac continued to communicate regularly with Gaing, who grumbled ever more vehemently of the delay. Then, one day from Gaing came news of disaster. Loklor had burst into the supposedly safe landing area and had attacked the *Distilcord*. The cargo had been looted and the ship itself destroyed by three great explosions.

Maihac received the news while waiting in an anteroom at the Colloquary. Gaing revealed that he had seen Asrubal of Urd House at Flad immediately prior to the attack, and that Asrubal had been conferring with the Loklor. Asrubal had departed for Romarth aboard the agency flitter immediately before the attack and certainly was responsible. Gaing had taken into custody the manager of the Flad terminal, one Faurez of Urd House. Gaing had brought pressure to bear upon Faurez, who had finally told Gaing what he wanted to know. In the first place, it was intended that Gaing should have been killed, in order to avoid such a situation as now existed. Maihac listened, then broke into the chamber where the Panel of Councillors was in session. After some difficulty, he gained the attention of the councillors and described the destruction at Flad. He arranged his radio upon the long semicircular table and spoke into the mesh. "Are you still there?"

"I am here," came Gaing's voice, pitched in tones of outrage and menace. "For your information, I have never been more angry. Luckily for this scoundrel Faurez, I am a temperate man. He has saved his life by agreeing that the House of Urd takes full responsibility for these sorry events and shall pay all damages."

From one of the Plum-pink councillors came a cry of protest: "Hold hard! Hold hard! This man has received no official authorization to pay out so much as a pickled gallstone!"

"No matter," said the Chief Councillor. "Let us hear the evidence of this off-world gentleman."

Maihac spoke to Gaing: "Faurez is with you?"

"Yes; just as before."

"Be careful with him. He won't bounce."

"Not well. I have discovered this for myself."

"I am now in the council chambers. Councillors are ready to hear your report."

"Good." Once again Gaing told his tale, then said, "The manager of the terminal has agreed to tell you what he knows, Faurez, speak! Explain to the councillors what has happened."

From the radio came an emotion-choked voice: "I am Faurez of Urd; there is no point in equivocation, since this spaceman was a witness to the events and I will state the facts bluntly. Asrubal of Urd, arriving from Loorie, saw the *Distilcord.* He commanded the Loklor to destroy it and he ordered me to cooperate. After the *Distilcord* had been broken, he told the Loklor to kill Gaing Neitzbeck, then set off for Romarth in his flitter. Neitzbeck killed twenty Loklor with his handgun before they gave up the effort and departed. Neitzbeck took me by force and insisted that I report the true circumstances to the council. I do so without reluctance, since Asrubal performed a wicked act, and must accept the consequences."

The council put questions to Faurez, then at last indicated that they had heard enough.

Asrubal arrived somewhat later. He was instantly summoned to appear before the council. When at last he entered the chamber, he showed no guilt and in fact demonstrated indignation that he had been summoned at such an inconvenient hour. Instead of denying the accusation, he defended his actions with stony self-righteousness, claiming that Maihac and Gaing Neitzbeck had contravened traditional laws regulating commerce between Fader and the inner worlds.

"Nonsense!" declared Tronsic of Stam House. "There are no laws of commerce, only customs and usages. You have committed an unjustified depredation and must be punished with full severity!"

Asrubal roared in fury. "Do you dare speak of punishing a grandee of Urd? Rashudo is at stake!"

"Cease your fulminations!" the Chief Councillor ordered. "If you are called to account, your deeds alone will be judged, not your bluster."

The charges against Asrubal were formalized, and the process of prosecution put into motion. As might be expected, the case moved languidly along the tortuous processes of the Colloquary.

Meanwhile Jamiel's time came upon her, and she gave birth to twin boys: Jaro and Garlet.

Maihac wanted to bring Gaing to Romarth aboard the Urd flitter; the request was denied. Meanwhile the Loklor were gathering near Flad, intending to take revenge upon Gaing. A Lorquin freighter, the *Liliom*, was on the point of departing Flad; Gaing Neitzbeck had no choice but to return to Loorie.

The litigation, if nothing else, had wilted Asrubal's rashudo. This was a quality somewhat similar to "honor," but comprising more elements. "Rashudo" included flair, grace, impassive bravery, rituals of courtesy, exact to the flick of the little finger, and much else. After two years, Maihac was summoned to the Colloquary, where the councillors had finally arrived at a consensus. In the matter of the *Distilcord*, Asrubal was found at fault. He was censured and required to make compensation to Maihac for the *Distilcord* and its lost cargo. Asrubal listened to the judgment unmoved, his rashudo enforcing a stony indifference upon him.

Maihac addressed the panel. "Respected Councillors, what is the status of my original petition?"

"It is moot," said the Chief Councillor. "The *Distilcord* and its cargo are no longer extant."

"True. I ask therefore for a commercial charter, allowing me to carry cargo from off-world directly to Romarth, and also to act as agent for your exports." The exports, almost exclusively so Maihac had learned, were slabs of precious minerals, quarried and polished by the Seishanee: milk opal, silky green jade, a dense and heavy jet polished smooth as glass but completely absorptive of light, so that to look upon it was like gazing into a deep dark hole. There was also a pale green porphyry spangled with crystals of alexandrite; mottled blue and green malachite; water-clear volcanic glass streaming with red films of colloidal gold, often mingled with ribbons of cobalt blue. Such materials commanded high prices in the urban areas of the Reach, and Maihac suspected that the yield of these sales was not being properly paid over to the Roum. In short, the Roum were almost certainly the victims of a massive swindle. Maihac went on to say: "I guarantee you a far greater return than you are now afforded by the Lorquin Agency, which in my opinion is not dealing fairly with you."

Asrubal instantly jumped to his feet. "These remarks are irresponsible! This man is an odious agitator and a liar! The Lorquin Agency is well-tried and notably dependable. The off-world rascal must be called to account!"

The councillors sat in silence. The issue was uncomfortable. A certain Melgrave of Slayard House said ingenuously: "All of us occasionally make mistakes. Might not this be the right of it? The Lorquin Agency has simply made a mistake."

Ormond of Ramy said, "The Lorquin Agency may be careless, or it might be that someone is manipulating accounts and deceiving the naive director—or there may be another even less savory explanation."

" 'Explanation'?" demanded the Chief Councillor. "You have left me behind. Explanation of what?"

Maihac said, "The prices you pay for ordinary goods are double or triple the price for the same goods at Loorie. Transportation costs cannot in any way be responsible. I don't know how Lorquin markets your exports, but—if the pattern holds true—you are credited with only half of what is your proper due. In short, you are suffering either gross inefficiency or peculation on a grand scale. Only Asrubal of Urd is competent to provide you the facts."

A Plum-pink Councillor cried out in fury: "You are imputing peculation to a grandee of Romarth, namely, Asrubal of Urd House!"

Maihac asked, "And what if Asrubal were guilty of this peculation? What would be the result?"

"Impossible! His rashudo would forbid it, just as ours will never entertain so ignoble an idea!"

"Still, be kind enough to think the unthinkable. Suppose Asrubal were for a fact guilty of such a crime: how would he be punished?"

The Chief Councillor said, "If peccancy were proved, the person at fault would be expelled from Romarth."

The Plum-pink Councillor called out: "Are you truly accusing Asrubal of such a misdeed? Without proof, you are edging close to criminal slander!"

"I am suggesting a possibility. Asrubal need only produce his private ledgers to prove me wrong."

Asrubal uttered a sound of contempt. "I show my ledgers to no man; my rashudo is bond for my deeds."

Maihac told the council, "In that case, give me the commercial charter and I will supply proof that you are being cheated by Asrubal and his Lorquin Agency. In response, then you shall see who is the liar."

Asrubal rose to his full height and directed a clangorous diatribe against Maihac, whom he described as "a cunning off-world trickster, whom we would be wise to extirpate."

Asrubal was adjudged intemperate and aroused censure from the Chief Councillor, who also chided Maihac for overbroad accusations.

Maihac repeated: "Only give me the commercial charter, and I will prove that you are being cheated!"

"As to that, we shall see. First, let us adjudge our principal corpus."

"I wish to hear no more!" declared Asrubal. He turned and stalked from the chamber, ignoring both the traditional expressions of respect to the court, and all interest in the amount of the award. His contumacy surprised no one, nor did any of his peers become exercised. After eight thousand years of quarrels and accommodations, methods for dealing with almost any situation had been devised. Nonetheless, events continued to move slowly at Romarth. Another six months passed before Maihac was tendered a draught upon the Urd House account, at the Natural Bank of Loorie, to the sum of three hundred thousand sols. This was a payment of major proportions, especially to an off-worlder, and Maihac's popularity, never large, dwindled even further, especially among the Plum-pink faction.

A sense of crisis hung in the air. Maihac had been warned that he went in imminent danger of assassination, nor would his family be spared. By reason of marriage, Jamiel had renounced her ties to the House of Ramy, and no longer would House protection automatically shelter her, while the children were considered nameless out-worlders.

The time had come to leave Romarth. A Lorquin ship would be arriving at Flad, which would transport them back to Loorie, if they arrived at Flad within two days. A flitter would be needed; Tronsic of Stam House preempted the flitter reserved for the Councillors' use, and arranged a secret rendezvous with Maihac, since the Plum-pink faction would interfere if they learned of the plans.

Maihac and Jamiel gathered a few belongings, sedated the two children, and by secret ways went to the garden of the ruined Salsobar Palace, beside the river, just within the first shade of the forest.

The flitter awaited them, with a guard of three Blue cavaliers, who nervously urged them to haste. "The sun is over the horizon; there is no time to waste!"

Maihac and Jamiel loaded their possessions into the cargo bay and arranged the sleeping children on the backseat.

Across the garden something stirred in the shadows. Maihac stared, paralyzed by dread. He broke free and called to Jamiel: "Something is wrong; get aboard!"

Two shrouded figures emerged from the shadows. They wore long dark red gowns; their features were unnatural wads of bone and gristle. House-ghouls! thought Maihac. Jamiel cried out: "They are Madwomen in fear-masks! We have been betrayed!"

Maihac started to board the flitter. From a new direction came a clatter and a thud; half-a-dozen cavaliers disguised as ancient warriors converged upon the flitter. The warriors, wearing the grotesque masks of the traditional Assassinator, ran clumsily, pounding with knees high, bounding over marble benches, swords at the ready. At the back stood a gaunt man with a bony white face: Asrubal of Urd. He called out, "Do not kill! Take, but do not kill! He goes into the pits!"

The three Blue cavaliers made ready to defend the flitter.

Someone was trying to clamber into the backseat: one of the Madwomen. Jamiel struck at her with a stave, but was herself seized and flung to the ground. There was a tangle of writhing bodies. Cursing and kicking Jamiel tried to climb back aboard the flitter, but one of the women seized her and once again shoved her down. Jamiel pulled herself erect, swung the stave in a circle and drove the women back. Suddenly Jamiel was alone, and the two women were scuttling away with backs hunched over. Jamiel scrambled aboard, and Maihac took the flitter aloft. They won free with inches to spare. From Asrubal came a roar of fury. "They must not escape!"

Up rose the flitter: a hundred feet, two hundred feet. Below the Plum-pink warriors stood loosely, shoulders sagging in postures of defeat. The Blue cavaliers, meanwhile, retreated across the garden, their work done.

At three hundred feet Maihac hovered, with some idea of doing his enemies harm. Asrubal stood to the side, near the flow of the river, his pallid face stark against his black garments. Maihac stared down in wonder. Asrubal was playing a peculiar game: tossing a sprawling object high into the air, then catching it. He flung the thing higher than ever; it seemed to be a dummy, or a large doll. Asrubal made no effort to catch it, and it fell from a height to thud upon the stone flags. Asrubal picked up the bundle again, and threw it over the balustrade, into the river, where it sank out of sight.

From Jamiel came a low cry of unbearable horror; she clawed at Maihac's arm; he turned to look. Two forms lay on the back seat. One was a child; the other was a dummy.

Jamiel became hysterical and tried to jump from the flitter. Maihac restrained her. "Go back!" she screamed. "Oh, go back, go back! Help our baby!"

Maihac said drearily, "There is no help for him now. He's dead. If we go back they'll kill all of us."

"But we must do something!"

"I don't know what can be done."

"Garlet is gone!" cried Jamiel in a voice of heartbreak. "The Madwomen took him! I saw what they were doing but could not understand; who could be so evil? Garlet is gone!"

Maihac, stunned and incredulous, looked down at Asrubal, who stood apart, grim and majestic, legs apart, arms folded across his chest. Maihac studied him for ten seconds, then turned away. He took the flitter high and flew north across the Blandy Deep toward Flad.

Jamiel presently asked, "What will you do?"

"I don't know." Then, after a moment, "First of all, I must put you and Jaro on the ship to Loorie."

"And then?"

Maihac sighed. "I shall probably come with you. I can't bring the poor child back to life. Someday I will kill Asrubal—perhaps when I return to Romarth in my own ship."

Jamiel had nothing to say. Maihac took the draught for three hundred thousand sols from his pocket and tucked it into the pouch she wore at her waist. "You had better keep this with you for the moment. Remember, it is written to the interest of 'Bearer.' Anyone can apply for the cash. Remember also that it is valid forever and that while the money remains in the Urd account, it draws interest. When we take this money, we will be punishing Asrubal in a most hurtful way."

"That does not make me feel better."

"No. We shall do worse to Asrubal than take his money."

Jamiel said urgently, "I don't want you going back to Romarth—not now! You would be killed within the week!"

"I expect that you are right. But we are not helpless and we can still do Asrubal harm."

"In what way?"

"When we arrive at Loorie, this is what we will do."

Jamiel listened attentively. "Yes. It is a good idea, and it must be done." After a moment she turned, seized up the hateful dummy and threw it from the flitter. It whirled below them and disappeared into the forest.

During the middle afternoon they approached the space terminal at Flad. Maihac dropped the flitter upon the landing field, now occupied by the Lorquin space-freighter *Liliom*.

Maihac landed beside the freighter, set about unloading the luggage, while Jamiel, carrying Jaro, went aboard the ship in search of the purser.

From behind Maihac came the sound of heavy footsteps. He swung about, to look into the skewed yellow faces of four Loklor tribesmen. He was seized; his arms tied behind his back, and dragged away by a rope around his neck. In the doorway opening into the workshop Maihac saw a heavy black-bearded man watching, and his attitude of satisfaction could not be disguised. When he noticed Maihac's desperate gaze, he raised his hand in a casual salute and shouted, "Hoy, chum! Dance nicely with the girls! Maybe they'll let you pop it to them before they boil your head!" The rope jerked at Maihac and he heard no more.

9

The Loklor jogged off across the steppe, with Maihac running and stumbling behind. A mile from the terminal the Loklor came to their camp. They tied the end of Maihac's lead-rope to a wagon wheel. An hour passed, while the sun set among flaring orange and yellow clouds. Maihac cautiously tried to loosen the knot at his neck, without success. The Loklor were indolent and casual, but he was always under observation. Maihac studied his captors. They were all mature warriors of the "Third-fledge" category: massive, somewhat taller than Maihac, with prominent crests along their back-slanting scalps, hard nose-beaks and undershot chins. The males wore loose breeches; the women showed faces stained pasty-white and wore black skirts, dirty white vests and conical leather hats with ear-flaps slanting away from their heads.

Dusk fell over the steppe. A fire was built in an open place. One of the bucks came to look down at Maihac. "Now you will dance. Everyone new to the camp dances with the girls. They are fine dancers and you must be quick on your feet. After you dance we shall be done with you, since that is the extent of the instruction."

Maihac said, "I countermand that instruction! The new instruction is to remove this rope and take me back to the terminal."

The Loklor said dubiously, "This may be so, but first you must dance with the girls. When things are started, they cannot be altered. That is the way of water, earth and sky."

Maihac was dragged toward the fire, where six girls stood in a group, making restless movements: hopping, flexing arms, jerking heads back and forth, meanwhile appraising Maihac and making hoarse cooing sounds of excitement.

The rope was removed from Maihac's neck; at the same time an old woman began to draw groaning noises from an extremely tall narrow viol. She played a slow dismal tune, to which she chanted: "Fum dum dum! Dance tonight around the brave fire! Dance this old dance, under the sky of night! Old sand! Old fire! Nothing must change; it is always the dance of the girls!"

The viol scraped and groaned; the girls began to hop and kick ponderous legs, while circling the fire, and watching Maihac sidelong. Maihac was thrust reeling and stumbling toward the dancing girls. The nearest eagerly seized him and took him pirouetting around the fire; Maihac was aware of the rank odor of her body, and tried to pull back, but she passed him on to another in the circle. This one gave him a shove toward the fire. "Jump through the flames! Show us a fine bound! A sharp nip of my teeth will make you frisky! I shall nibble at your head, unless you show me a fine bound!" She thrust her face forward with teeth gleaming. "Jump!"

Maihac thought the flames too high and the fire too wide for jumping, and drew away, only to be seized by a third girl, who took him whirling light-foot around the fire, then gave him a quick twirl, and with a whinny of mirth tried to send him stumbling into the fire. Maihac had anticipated the move. Instead of resisting, he sagged; seized her free arm and sent her reeling backward, to flounder and fall across the fire, where she lay kicking like an overturned beetle. From onlookers came a clacking sound of approval, as if they applauded an act of splendid technique. The girls screeched in excitement and danced on, hopping and strutting even more energetically than before. Again Maihac was seized up and whirled away. He did not await the girl's convenience; during one of her strutting kicks, he grasped her leg and toppled her to the ground and kicked her head. He kicked again; cartilage crushed and she lay lax. Maihac took the knife from the sheath at her belt and dropping to his knees, waited until the next girl came to claim him. He lunged, slashed open her abdomen, then rolled to the side. The girl screamed in fury, and fell back, clutching at her entrails.

The music came to a sudden halt. The old woman called out, "The dance is at an end! Kill him with iron sticks!"

A warrior said, "Shut up, old woman! The orders were followed; he has danced with the girls and we have collected our iron. Now let him be buiskid, and we will bide our time; perhaps there will be new iron."

The girls pushed Maihac scornfully away from the fire. Maihac fended off their blows as best he could, grateful to be alive. One of the girls yelled, "You are buiskid, the lowest of the low! You must carry water and clean slops!" Maihac went to sit by the wagon wheel. No one took any further notice of him, save a pair of imps who squatted nearby, watching him intently. After a while Maihac crawled under the wagon and tried to sleep.

So began the most desperate period of Maihac's life. He learned that "buiskid" meant a sort of slavery. He was subjected to discomfort, pain and privation. He witnessed casual incidents of such horror that they became unreal; often he barely escaped personal participation in such events. For a time he lived minute to minute, until the minutes became days; then the days became months, during which his existence still seemed to teeter on a razor's edge. He wondered endlessly why he had been allowed to survive. None of his theories were convincing. In the end he decided that a mistake had occurred, or it might be that the Loklor preferred him as "buiskid" than as corpse. Finally he began to feel a glimmer of hope; perhaps, through luck, vigilance, rat-like cunning, and more luck, he might survive.

Maihac's role as "buiskid" included toil and casual abuse from anyone who felt in the mood. The acts lacked animus and were for the most part absent-minded. Loklor psychology, so he discovered, was remarkably simple. Emotional linkages were unknown; they made no friends and old rancors were quickly lost in the surge of new rages and punitive fits. This was a division of the Ginko tribe, which considered itself at least the equal of the awful Strenke. They knew neither love nor hate; they gave loyalty only to their tribe. They bred their women indiscriminately; the women then went to a special camp and gave birth to a litter of imps, and shortly afterward rejoined the tribe, leaving the imps in the care of Seishanee. The Loklor bucks were irascible and fought often, in encounters of measured intensity, ranging from scuffles to events resulting in severe damage or death. A rigorous Roum quarantine had denied them energy-guns; their weapons were basic: knives, iron-tipped pikes, short-handled axes with semi-circular blades. Maihac studied their techniques with care, looking for vulnerabilities which might, at need, be useful to him.

The Loklor skin was a horny integument which served as an armor, thin only down the back of the lower leg, under the chin and at the back of the neck. After some careful thought, Maihac unobtrusively fashioned himself a curious weapon: a pike four feet long, pointed at one end and at the other a thin curving blade, welded at right angles to the shaft, and looking something like a shallow hook, sharpened along its inner edge to the keenness of a razor. No one heeded his work save the two Loklor imps who had been detailed to guard him night and day, apparently to prevent him from slipping off across the steppe, though it was not clear why anyone should care. The answer, Maihac told himself, lay in the nature of the Loklor psyche. Once a process had been given momentum, it could not be altered until someone applied a contrary force, and the Loklor, if nothing else, were indolent. By now Maihac had become accustomed to their surveillance; wherever he went, no matter what his activities, he knew that somewhere near at hand the two imps would be crouched, button-black eyes fixed upon him.

An opportunity to test the weapon arose almost at once. A young buck, bested in an encounter with a stronger adversary, decided to perfect his techniques upon the person of someone useless, and so decided to kill the buiskid for practice.

Maihac noticed the purposeful approach of the young Loklor. He was well-formed, with a saffron yellow frontal carapace and nearly mature crest, which carried four two-inch, knob-headed prongs. He was taller than Maihac and more massive. He scooped up a handful of sand and tossed it at Maihac: the ritual notice of impending aggression. Maihac took up his new weapon. The Loklor halted. He uttered a screeching cry, performed a ritual pivot, tossed his axe into the air to demonstrate contempt, which was intended to discourage his opponent.

Maihac took a quick step forward, hooked the Loklor's neck with his weapon, and pulled his head forward; the falling axe struck the startled Loklor on his slanted forehead. Maihac jerked back the handle of his weapon with a slicing motion; the blade cut through the thin sheathing and halfway through the corded neck. The Loklor sagged to the ground, twitched and lay still. The onlookers made grumbling sounds of disappointment; the fight had lacked interest.

No one would notify Maihac that he had improved his status; he must make the move for himself, and whoever wished to object might do so. Maihac immediately abandoned his old tasks. Beyond a heavy-lidded glance or two, no one paid any heed. Girls took up the work he had abandoned and thereby improved the terms of his captivity to some small degree.

A week passed and Maihac, ever-vigilant, noticed a sinister circumstance. A group of warriors of "First-fledged" quality, was planning to involve him in one of their games: probably the gauntlet, ordinarily reserved for captives from enemy tribes. If the prisoner ran the gauntlet and survived, he was free to rejoin his tribe. Often the captive refused to cooperate and stood stoically motionless, while the warriors flayed him alive, stripping away the heavy skin, leaving behind a grisly yellow-orange caricature. The captive was now declared free and allowed to shamble off across the steppe toward his own tribe.

The preparations were ominous. Among those watching was Babuja, a "Second-fledge" veteran of massive proportions: seven feet tall, broad and deep in the chest, with short spraddled legs. The prongs of his crest stood stiff and menacing, two to three inches high; his horny chest-plates were scarred and carved, the color of dried blood. He had known much vicious combat, where his enormous strength had served him well. He had never achieved "First-fledge" rank by reason of a ponderous mentality, which sufficed well enough for "Second-fledge" combat. Babuja was complacent, inflexible and like most of the Loklor, disinclined to effort.

Maihac hesitated only an instant, since his options were not good. He scooped up a handful of sand and, sidling close, he flung it into Babuja's button-black eyes. Babuja, astounded, roared in fury and swung out his arm, to smite Maihac's chest and send him stumbling backward. Babuja looked about to see who had flung sand. Could it be that this trivial soft-skinned Roum had challenged him? Babuja's intellect grappled with the situation. There was no help for it; a challenge was a challenge. Meanwhile, the young bucks who had been preparing to run Maihac down a gauntlet, stood sullenly aside; Maihac had spoiled their game.

Babuja found his tongue. "Do you joke with me? It will be a painful joke. You will lose, and the girls will boil your head."

"What if I win?"

"You will not win."

"If I win, I take your 'Second-fledge' ranking."

"Just as you like." The concession was made indifferently, and in any event it meant little, since Loklor ignored inconvenient contracts.

The sun had set. The two moons floated low in the west over the silhouette of low hills along the horizon. To one side of the fire crouched the Loklor women, the dark red and dark blue of their pantaloons glowing in the firelight. The bucks stood apart, each stolid, alone with himself.

Babuja swaggered forward. "Come near, little fool. I will chop once; I will chop twice; then I will beat you with your own legs, until the girls come to take you to the kettle, for the boiling of your head."

Maihac sidled warily around the great hulk. Babuja watched him contemptuously, not bothering to raise his axe.

Maihac hoped to avoid the axe-strokes, any one of which would kill him, and to dart in and out of range. If his theories were flawed, his life, with its sentience, hopes and memories, had come to an end. He moved a foot closer, gauging Babuja's reach to the inch. Babuja must be persuaded to lunge out with the axe, when, for an instant, he might become open to counterattack. Maihac jerked a few inches closer. Too close! The axe flicked out. Maihac flinched to the side and the blade whistled close by his body.

He tried to slide around the towering figure but Babuja turned, swung the axe high and struck down again. Maihac was out of reach. Babuja grunted and glared. This was not the way to conduct a combat; a proper warrior fought to the din of clashing metal and the chunk of axe-blades driving into flesh. In the end the most durable warrior hacked his opponent to pieces—but this foolish Roum was averse to proper combat. Babuja tried a clever backhanded slash which had broken open many a torso in the past. Maihac fell flat; he thrust out his weapon and hooked Babuja behind the left ankle, then heaved back and the blade sliced Babuja's hamstring bone, leaving the foot dangling and useless. Down thudded the axe and the tip scored Maihac's shoulder. He rolled frantically away and pulled himself to his feet. Babuja tried to stride forward, but his leg buckled; he toppled and fell in a sprawling heap. Maihac seized the axe and struck down at the burly neck—again and again, until the head rolled loose.

Maihac moved away and stood leaning on the axe-handle while he caught his breath. He held out his hand. "Bring me beer." A woman scurried away and returned with a foaming pot. He made another signal, and the women came to tend his wounded shoulder. They washed the cut, stitched and sewed, and applied bandages. Maihac pointed to Babuja's head and gave orders. Without protest the women took the head aside; there they set diligently to work: first cutting out bones, brains and internal processes, then soaking the skin in oil, scraping away fat and fiber and in the end producing a headpiece consisting of crest with prongs, attached to an iron nose-beak. Maihac also took Babuja's necklace of knuckle bones and the ponderous axe. In due course the women brought Maihac the headpiece. Gingerly he fitted the folds of dark saffron leather to his own head, where they hung loosely, and assailed his nose with a sour stench. Nevertheless, Maihac thought to feel an infusion of Babuja's mana: a heady, almost awesome, sensation, which caused him to carry himself with a different posture and move more confidently to the food troughs, where before he had always waited for the scraps. When he strode about the camp, he sensed a shift of attitude toward himself; in some degree Maihac had been assimilated into the structure of the band. Still, whenever he chanced to look off to the side, there was one or the other of the watchful imps, assessing his every move.

Maihac made himself useful by repairing motor-wagons, and no longer felt in imminent danger of capricious attack, though he was still subjected to a great deal of physical buffeting by reason of a game the young Loklor played to work off excess energy. This was a wild unstructured catch-as-catch-can wrestling, into which Maihac was often drawn for lack of better adversaries. If he tried to avoid the sport he was mercilessly kicked back and forth, until in desperation he exerted himself, which usually won him further bruises and sprains. For the sake of survival he applied himself not to avoiding the conflict, but to excelling in it, and refining techniques which he had learned during his stint with the IPCC. He soon became able not only to protect himself from the worst of the pummeling, but to inflict such damage that he was no longer dragooned into playing the game. Nevertheless, to keep his own reflexes tuned, he occasionally joined the sport, reflecting that if he ever escaped from the Tangtsang Steppe and Fader, he would never again fear confrontation with any human adversary.

The Loklor band wandered far afield, back and forth across the continent. Maihac was not sure what might happen if he tried to go his own way. He suspected that he would be hunted down and killed, for no other reason than idle malice. Now it made no great difference, since he could not hope to survive a solitary journey to Flad.

Time passed: months, a year, two years. Maihac, driven by circumstances, assimilated many of the harsh attitudes of the Loklor; he became someone whom, as his former self, he would not have recognized.

The tribe wandered north, occasionally meeting other tribes. When this occurred, there might be formal salutes, and a ritual exchange of females. Occasionally challenges might be issued, and a champion from each tribe engaged in a duel by firelight. Once, to Maihac's surprise, the elders with saturnine humor pushed him forward to fight as the tribe's champion.

Maihac, far quicker and more agile than his opponent, managed to win the bout, though suffered a terrible wound in the process, which the women of the tribe matter-of-factly set to rights. He was neither congratulated nor given any recognition for his victory. He had won, the drama was over, the deed was done and had no bearing upon the future.

The tribe moved slowly to the southwest and came to a great river, which they dared not cross, since none could swim. They followed the river south, into a gloomy forest of tall conifers. After several days' travel, they came upon the abandoned white palaces of a ruined city. The Loklor long before had claimed one of the palaces as their own; now they found white house-ghouls stirring in the shadows. The infestation aroused the Loklor to a fury. They lit torches and set out to purge the palace of its inhabitants, and the house-ghouls melted away before them, uttering peevish outcries but offering no resistance.

They were gone, or so it seemed, leaving only a rank odor behind. Maihac went to examine the frescos in what had been a grand salon. He heard a soft sound; turning, he found a house-ghoul near at hand, pointing a long crooked arm toward him as if in woeful accusation. Maihac stood frozen. The house-ghoul, leering, reached out to grasp him; Maihac struck away the arm. The house-ghoul screamed and with a great flutter of its robes sprang upon Maihac, who was saved only by his reflexes. He rolled aside, and found himself engaged in the most terrible battle of his life, with the house-ghoul maintaining a constant screaming and imploring in a melodious voice. The creature at last became still, sprawled across Maihac, whose face had been torn open and scalp virtually ripped off. A number of Loklor had been watching; now they turned away. Maihac realized that they took him for dead.

10

The house was quiet. The Loklor were gone. Maihac knew the house-ghouls would be back. He crawled to the front of the palace, and looked up and down the river. He stared in wonder. The large building on the riverbank—could that be the Foundance? Was this city Romarth? He staggered along the river and presently met a group of cavaliers. They took him to the House of Ramy, where he was tended as best could be done.

Maihac found that his feat of surviving three years of captivity with the Loklor tribe had won him public acclaim and wide sympathy. He learned that there had been no news from Jamiel since her departure. The elders of Urd House had isolated themselves from Asrubal, currently absent from Romarth, and his group. They conceded that all were guilty of criminal attack upon Maihac, Jamiel and Jaro, and were jointly responsible for the murder of the infant Garlet. All would incur appropriate punishment. To Maihac the House of Urd offered apologies and an indemnity of five thousand sols. Maihac also wanted a document commanding assistance and cooperation from Urd representatives, at Loorie and elsewhere. The Urd Councillors initially resisted the request, finding it too broad and too vague. Maihac stated that he might need such authority to help him find Jamiel, who had flown to Loorie aboard a Lorquin Agency ship. The Urd Councillors, under public pressure, gave Maihac the document he wanted, as well as transportation to Flad on the Lorquin flitter and passage aboard the Lorquin freighter to Loorie. Maihac made the journey as soon as possible. Flying over the Tangtsang steppes he stared down at the familiar contours of the land, and tried to picture himself in the company of the Loklor. The images, of campfires, the food troughs, pain, fear and misery, were too real to be dismissed and too remote to seem truly real.

In due course Maihac arrived at Loorie. At the Lorquin Agency he showed his document to the imposing Dame Waldop. She scrutinized it at length, then said heavily, "What are your precise needs?"

"Three years ago a young woman arrived from Romarth with her two year-old son. Do you remember her?"

"Not well. As I recall, she seemed unhappy."

"Did you speak with her?"

"Only briefly. She asked the whereabouts of the Natural Bank. I gave her directions; she left with her child, and that is all I can tell you."

"Thank you. Now, secondly, where is Asrubal?"

Dame Waldop's voice took on a haughty edge. "As to that, I cannot say. He is not at Loorie, and I believe he has gone off-planet."

"And you have no clue as to his destination?"

"None. I am not his confidante."

"Excuse me a moment; perhaps your clerk knows."

"I doubt that very much!" declared Dame Waldop. "Let us not waste his time." Maihac turned to Aubert Yamb, who had been crouched over his desk pretending to hear nothing. Maihac glanced at the placard on his desk. "Your name, so I see, is Aubert Yamb."

"That is correct, sir."

"Do you know Asrubal of Urd House by sight?"

"Yes, sir. A stately and severe gentleman. When he says 'No' he does not blow a horn or ring a bell to emphasize his point."

"Where is Asrubal now?"

"He has gone off-world, to—"

Dame Waldop called out: "Yamb, do not utter inanities, in order to attract attention."

"Very good, Dame Waldop." Yamb bent his head over his ledger. He looked up again, and scratched the tip of his nose with his pen. "I will tell you, and you can properly tell the gentleman. Asrubal flew off to Ocknow on Flesselrig."

Dame Waldop clicked her tongue, and swung around in anger. "Yamb, you have far exceeded your function. I have long noticed this tendency in you and to this moment I have suffered under the threat of your indiscretions. You have interfered in matters unrelated to your task for the last time; in short, you are discharged, without references."

"This is sad news," said Yamb. "I tried only to be obliging."

"All very well, but if you wish to get on in the world, you must learn when to be helpful and when to avoid what I will call bumptious self-importance."

"Yes, now I understand. May I have my job back?"

"Absolutely not. Kindly work out the day as usual. Before you go, clean out the bins and lock up the telephones as always. Also, even if you must work late, make sure your books are current to the minute."

"Very good, madame. I will pay my wages from the petty cash."

"As you wish. Leave an itemized chit in the drawer."

Maihac had no further business with Dame Waldop, and departed the agency. In the shade of a blue-green dendron he paused to reflect the way his life had gone since last he had walked the main street of Loorie, and how everything had changed. He thought of himself as he once had been, and considered the man he had become. The thoughts were neither cheerful nor elevating and he put them aside. It was important that he maintain his emotions at an even tone, in order to enhance his efficiency. Three years with the Loklor, if nothing else, had taught him discipline. Often he had told himself that, if by some chance he survived his wandering across the Tangtsang Steppe, he would never feel gloom or misery again.

He looked to his left, where the street ended at the space terminal; then to his right, along an aisle of freakish dendrons, to where the road finally disappeared into a forest. Here, within the span of his gaze, was Loorie, home to two or three thousand secretive folk who muttered confidentially to each other when they met on the street, and walked with care so as not to produce the sound of footsteps. Crossing the street, Maihac entered the offices of the Natural Bank. He stood in a dim high-ceilinged lobby, with cashier's counters along one wall. Another wall was sheathed with narrow boards of porous golden punkwood. An empty desk, placed beside the wall, commanded a door which bore the legend:

HUBER THWAN
Manager

In the absence of a receptionist, Maihac opened the door and entered the office, which was another high-ceilinged chamber, with a handsome wainscoting of figured greenwood. Tall windows overlooked a garden; a heavy bottle-green carpet covered the floor. Behind an oversized desk sat Huber Thwan, who was short, stout, with a round pink face, a stub of a nose and a small pugnacious mustache. His rust-brown hair had been combed to form wings over his ears to right and left. His glossy dark brown suit seemed too splendid for the Loorie environment, as did his flowered cravat and his polished yellow shoes with two-inch heels and pointed toes. Maihac was greeted with a frown as if he had entered Thwan's office far too casually, and he failed to fit the mold of the bank's preferred customer; in fact, all taken with all, Maihac seemed a man with many undesirable characteristics. Thwan spoke severely: "In the future, you might prefer to be announced by my secretary. It is considered a more dignified procedure for us both."

"That is good to know," said Maihac. "I have just arrived from Romarth, and have not yet become civilized."

Thwan squinted sidelong at Maihac, his mustache bristling. "From Romarth, you say? Most interesting! So what, may I ask, are your needs?"

"They are simple enough. I want to examine the financial records of Urd House, and especially the accounts of Asrubal of Urd."

Thwan's jaw dropped. He stuttered a moment before he found words. "What an absurd notion! This is obviously impossible! Privacy of our clients is a sacred trust."

"So I expect. But—I carry a document authorizing my investigation. You have no choice in the matter."

Thwan became indignant. "This is most irregular! I cannot imagine how any such authorization could be valid!"

"See for yourself." Maihac tossed the document to Thwan's desk. Thwan jerked back, as if Maihac had tendered him a poisonous insect. He cautiously bent forward and looked over the document, grunting softly under his breath. He read and re-read the document, and finally leaned heavily back in his chair. "No more need be said. This document is definite. I will of course wish to make a copy for my files."

"As you like."

Thwan spoke now with false heartiness. "Well then—you wanted to look over the Urd account? That can be done as of this instant." A panel in the wainscoting slid back, to reveal a large screen. Thwan spoke a few words and information appeared on the screen.

Maihac studied the numbers for five minutes, putting occasional questions to Thwan, who responded with terse courtesy. Maihac presently said: "I see no record of a payment made to Jamiel Maihac, in the amount of three hundred thousand sols."

"No such payment was made. I clearly remember the circumstances. Several years ago a young woman presented this extraordinary draught. I informed her that I never carried so much cash on the premises; that it would have been both burdensome and unsafe. I told her that she had two options. I could submit the draught to the Natural Bank home office at Ocknow on Flesselrig, then wait for the next bonded shipment from Flesselrig, which might entail a delay of several months; or she herself could take the draught to Ocknow and apply to the Natural Bank, where Urd House also maintained an account—considerably larger, so I believe, than the balance entrusted to the local bank. I told her that she would find the latter course considerably more expeditious than waiting here for a shipment of cash. She accepted my advice, so I believe, and left the bank."

"Did she provide any hint as to her ultimate plans?"

"Nothing. I assume that she took passage to Ocknow by the first outbound packet."

"And she left no message?"

"None."

Maihac gave a disconsolate grimace. He looked once more at the screen. "Asrubal's account here is quite modest—about eight thousand sols."

Huber Thwan agreed that the amount indexed to Asrubal's credit was not exceptional.

"He maintains a separate account at Ocknow?"

Thwan blew out his mustache, to indicate his distaste for the question. He responded coldly: "I don't know the exact figures, but his Ocknow account is said to be quite substantial."

"One last question. Have you seen or communicated with Asrubal recently?"

"No, sir. I have not seen him for a considerable period—months, or even years. At the time he also was bound for Ocknow."

Maihac thanked Thwan and departed. Outside the bank, he paused to reflect upon what he had learned. It was not very much and none of it was heartening. He went to sit on a bench and watched the secretive folk of Loorie moving furtively about their affairs. The sun Yellow Rose sank into the afternoon sky and threw long shadows along the street. He saw Dame Waldop emerge from the offices of the Lorquin Shipping Agency and stride away, breasting the air with her bosom. The black-clad folk of Loorie lowered their heads and drifted to the side as she approached, then watched her with hooded eyes as she passed.

Maihac waited until she had disappeared from view, then crossed the street and looked through the window of the agency. He noticed Aubert Yamb sitting glumly at his desk. The door was locked; at Maihac's knock, Yamb reluctantly came to the door. He threw back the bolt, eased open the door to produce a gap six inches wide, through which he peered owlishly at Maihac. "The agency is closed for the day. If you return tomorrow, Dame Waldop will assist you with full attention."

Maihac pushed through the door and closed it behind him. "It's you I want to consult."

"I am no longer an employee," said Yamb. "I can conduct no official business."

"Quite all right. I want only information, for which I am willing to pay."

"Oh?" Yamb was interested. "How much?"

"Probably more than you expect." Maihac placed twenty sols upon the counter. "Let us start at the beginning. About three years ago I made certain plans with my wife. I told her that as soon as we arrived at Loorie, I intended to approach you in connection with some confidential work you would find financially rewarding. In essence, I wanted copies of documents which might later be used in a criminal prosecution. It so happened that I was delayed, so that Jamiel arrived at Loorie ahead of me. I am sure that she would have carried out our plans and made contact with you as soon as possible. Am I right?"

Yamb's face became a mask of sly cunning. He studied Maihac under lowered lids. "What was this young lady's name?"

"Jamiel Maihac. I am Tawn Maihac. How much did she pay you?"

"A thousand sols—and not a lead dinket too much, considering the risks."

"And you did the work exactly as she asked?"

Yamb looked anxiously over his shoulder toward the door. "Yes; I made copies of my ledgers over a period of five years. They detailed all business transacted during the period in question. She was pleased with the result."

"Good. You may now make similar copies for me. The pay will be the same."

Yamb's face fell. "Impossible. Even if I could, I would not dare, after the repercussions of the first case."

"How so?"

"Asrubal arrived from Fader a few days later. He was in a vicious mood. As soon as he entered the office he demanded my ledgers, and I assure you that my soul went numb. However, I feigned insouciance and politely produced the ledgers. At once he looked them over, muttering under his breath to Dame Waldop, who stood by nonplussed. Suddenly Asrubal bent down and smelled the pages. He looked up at Dame Waldop with an expression which chills me as I think of it now. He declared in a low rasping voice: 'These ledgers have been copied!'

"Dame Waldop cried out: 'Impossible! Who would do such a thing! Come; let us examine the machine. The meter will provide us the facts.'

"The two went into the back room and studied the meter, but I had no fear in this regard, since I had disconnected it during my unauthorized use. They emerged from the room with Dame Waldop leading, shoulders thrown back in vindication. 'As you see, the count is correct. Your nose, in this case at least, has misled you.'

"Asrubal turned to study me, with a disturbing intensity. 'Well, then, Yamb! Did you copy these ledgers?'

" 'Of course! Every week I copy them upon the computational machine! It is my duty, so that the information is instantly available to Your Honor! It is a simple matter. For instance, I call out "Export," then "Transactions," then utter the particulars of the transaction. It is a fine and satisfactory system.'

" 'I daresay. Did you copy the ledgers on the copying machine? Come; tell me at once! These documents are of cardinal importance!'

"I felt his gaze boring into my brain, but I have perfected a manner of guileless innocence which persuades the keenest inquisitor that I am a mooncalf, with nothing more weighty on my mind than a taste for well-buttered parsnips. I believe that I made this impression upon Asrubal, and left him baffled though still as dangerous as a coiled fire-snake. He questioned me for a time, but I only simpered and licked my lips in an unctuous manner which everyone finds disgusting. Asrubal finally turned away, throwing his arms into the air. For a time he continued to bedevil Dame Waldop, who denied all his imputations. In the end he deleted the information from the memory banks of the business machine, then he snatched up my ledgers and left the office. He was in a fury and his face was like sculptured bone."

"Did Jamiel indicate what her plans might be?"

"No. She went to the terminal and took outward passage. I was told that Asrubal made extensive inquiries, but I gather that he learned nothing definite."

Maihac produced a hundred sols. Yamb cocked his head to the side. "You bring forth that money with the careless ease of a wealthy grandee, to whom a thousand sols is little different from a hundred."

"Not exactly. Do you have something more to tell me?"

"Only the story of my life and the color of Dame Waldop's knickers, which I glimpsed one day when she slipped on a bit of fruit, which I had discarded, and fell flat on her fundament."

"You have nothing else?"

Yamb heaved a sigh. "Nothing whatever."

Maihac handed over the hundred sols. "You will need this while you prepare for a new career."

"No fear in that direction," said Yamb complacently. "I will assist my Aunt Estebel at Primrose Consolidators for a time, until Dame Waldop discovers that I have installed a number of mysterious shortcuts, so that I am indispensable. She will fume and curse, but in the end she will order me back to work. My response will be languid; this time she has gone too far and some of her allusions have been a bit close to the knuckle. I shall tell her so. Further, I will recommend a substantial raise in salary, a handsome new desk near the door, with a plaque identifying me as 'Superintendent of Finance' or some such title."

"You live an adventurous life," said Maihac. "Where is the IPCC office?"

Yamb opened the door and ushered Maihac out into the late afternoon. He pointed up the street. "Go to the second cross-lane. There, with the pedicure salon to one side and a great black bangle-blossom tree to the other, you will find the IPCC."

At the IPCC office Maihac identified himself to the young agent and inquired for messages. As he expected, the officer produced an envelope inscribed with his name.

The message read:

> Tawn Maihac: I have shipped out aboard the *Lustspranger* of the Demeter Line. A message addressed to the main office of the Demeter Line on Old Earth will reach me, and I will join you at the rendezvous you suggested.
>
> Gaing Neitzbeck

11

Maihac left Loorie aboard a packet of the Swannic Line, which took him to Calley's Junction on Virgo AXX-1 Thirteen, where he transferred to a tourist cruise ship, which took him to Ocknow on the world Flesselrig, the commercial and financial node serving much of the back sector. Maihac went directly to the main offices of the Natural Bank, where he was referred to one of the under-supervisors. This was Brin Dykich, who contrasted notably with Huber Thwan of Loorie. He was slim, personable, cooperative and wore no mustache. He took Maihac into his office, ordered in tea and asked how he could be of service.

"You will at first think my request irregular," said Maihac. "Perhaps even startling, but when you hear the background, I think you will see that all is in order."

"Please continue," said Dykich. "You have at least excited my interest."

"I am a former officer of the IPCC, retired in good standing. I am trying to lay a criminal by the heels. He is a thief, a swindler and a murderer; he is a Roum from the world Fader; his name is Asrubal of Urd House and he maintains an account in at least two branches of the Natural Bank—here and at Loorie."

"And you want information in regard to the account?" Dykich's tone was neutral. "Obviously, I cannot oblige you even though you have my sympathy. I have met Asrubal, and, quite candidly, I find him a nasty piece of work."

Maihac placed his documents on the desk. "This is my authority."

Dykich read the documents carefully, then looked up at Maihac. "This is a very powerful instrument. It gives you discretionary control over Urd House monies, even though they have been initialized into Asrubal's sub-account."

"That is my understanding."

Dykich pursed his lips dubiously and re-read the document. "Well, the instructions are clear. I presume that you wish to inspect the account?"

"Yes, if you please."

Dykich brought the relevant numbers to his screen. Maihac studied them for a moment. "Naturally, you are aware that there is a draught of three hundred thousand sols, issued against Asrubal's account, which still seems to be outstanding."

"I have noticed the reference."

"The draught was not funded at Loorie, and apparently it was not funded here."

Dykich looked over the screen. "True. We discharged no such draught. It is still extant and as good as cash."

"With accrued interest and dividends over three years, how much is it worth now?"

"Roughly four hundred thousand sols."

"I want to protect this money from any attempt by Asrubal to sequester it. How can this be done?"

Dykich reflected. "It is not a simple process, but it can be done. On the strength of this authorization, I can transfer an appropriate sum into a modified escrow, payable only upon presentation of the draught, which is made out to 'Bearer.' "

"Then please do so."

"Very well. I will calculate the exact amount, which should be close to four hundred thousand sols, and which, as you will notice, almost wipes out Asrubal's account."

"Asrubal will not be pleased. Make sure that neither he nor anyone else of Urd House can gain access to the account."

"I will place a stipulation to this effect." Dykich picked up the document and read it once more, with great care. He shrugged. "So be it. But I must make a certified copy of the document, which you will sign, for my own protection."

The copy was executed to Dykich's satisfaction. Maihac asked, "I take it that you have not seen Asrubal recently?"

"Not recently. Certainly not for months, perhaps longer. Now that I think of it, a message was left here about a year ago; the exact date being—" Dykich rummaged in his drawer and brought out a buff envelope. He studied the imprinted date. "It was left a year ago. Asrubal has not been here since then." Maihac reached out and took the envelope from Dykich's reluctant fingers. Before Dykich could protest, Maihac had opened the envelope and extracted the message. He read aloud:

"To Asrubal of Urd:

With the house where the woman died as my focus, I searched the area in concentric circles and finally came upon facts which I believe to be significant to a ninety percent surety. The only alternate hypothesis (ten percent probability) is that the boy died by drowning in the river. Far more likely, he was taken up by a pair of anthropologists named Hilyer and Althea Fath, and conveyed to their home in the city Thanet, on the world Gallingale. Public records make this opinion highly probable.

Terman of Urd."

Dykich stared at Maihac. "Are you well? You are pale as a ghost!"

"Jamiel is dead," muttered Maihac. "Asrubal has killed her."

12

"There's not much more to tell," said Maihac. "The message which Terman had left with Brin Dykich shocks me to this day when I think of it. I had hoped that Jamiel might have escaped Asrubal—but he had caught up with her. I can't bear to think what happened next. My life became focused upon two persons: Jaro and Asrubal. Even while I sat in Dykich's office, I wondered why Asrubal should be so anxious to track down Jaro. After long brooding, the answer came to me. It could only be that Jamiel had put the bank draught and the incriminating ledgers into a safe place, and died before Asrubal could wring the truth from her. The boy had escaped and might possibly know the hiding place.

The chance was remote but Asrubal could not neglect it; he could never feel secure until he had destroyed the ledgers and canceled the bank draught.

"Terman might or might not have communicated with Asrubal. I traveled to Thanet at once, and was much relieved to find that you were alive, well and in good hands. The Faths were raising you to the best of their abilities. Gaing joined me; he went to work in the terminal machine shop; I was hired as a security officer; between us we screened all incoming passengers. We gave special attention to ships arriving from the direction of Flesselrig and Nilo-May.

"Time passed; nothing happened; Asrubal never showed himself, nor did anyone else who might have been a Roum.

"I became edgy. Were my theories out of phase with the facts? I could not see where I could have gone wrong—unless Terman, after leaving his message with Dykich, had never again made contact with Asrubal, so that the information regarding the Faths had never been passed on. Perhaps Terman had died, or been killed, or had decided to settle permanently somewhere among the worlds of the Reach, rather than return to Fader. I communicated with Brin Dykich at Ocknow; he reported that no one had approached him in regard to the bank draught, nor had any further payments been made into Asrubal's account. I wondered what was going on. Finally I decided to try my luck with the Faths, and to become acquainted with my son. By this time I had learned of his truncated memory, which of course troubled me. Still, the memory might return and recall the circumstances surrounding the death of his mother, and what had happened to the ledgers and the bank draught.

"I went to a dealer in curios and bought several exotic musical instruments, including a froghorn, which I tried to play. It was very difficult and sounded the same whether I was playing good or bad. I registered at the Institute and undertook one or two of Althea's classes, where I casually mentioned my interest in exotic instruments. Althea instantly became interested in me, and nothing must do but what I come out to Merriehew to meet her family. We spoke of her adopted son and Althea could not restrain her pride for this boy who was turning out so nicely. I tried to find out where they had come upon this paragon, but Althea only stuttered and mumbled and changed the subject.

"I began to visit Merriehew regularly. In general, the evenings were successful, despite Hilyer's suspicions, which were automatic, even though I deferred to him and listened politely to all his opinions. I even brought over my froghorn and played for them. I pleased everyone but Hilyer, who was probably jealous of me, and also because I was a spaceman, and hence a vagabond. On several occasions I turned the conversation to your origins, but Hilyer and Althea were always evasive. Why, I could not understand at the time. It's no wonder that they considered me a bad influence—so much so that their invitations came to an end.

"Time was passing. I felt that I must do something positive, and soon. I left Gaing in charge and took passage to Nilo-May aboard a freighter. This was a mistake; the passage was cheap but it was slow. I finally arrived at Loorie where I discovered that changes had been made. Dame Waldop no longer ruled Lorquin Shipping. The new manager was a thin young woman, with eyes like flint pebbles and hair cropped short. Aubert Yamb had married his cousin Twee Pidy and was now employed at Primrose Consolidators. He was not too pleased to see me and he had little news to report. About two years before, Dame Waldop had departed Loorie for parts unknown. Yamb had seen nothing of Asrubal for an even longer period, and had no information as to his whereabouts. At the space terminal I searched the records and verified that Terman of Urd had taken passage from Loorie to Ocknow. I did the same; and for the next two years traced Terman as he moved from world to world in his search for Jaro. It was slow tedious work and very chancy; in the end the trail petered out and I was left with nothing to show for three years of effort. I decided to return to Thanet and try again to learn from the Faths where they had found you, even though I suspected that they would tell me nothing.

"Back on Gallingale, I found things worse than ever. The Faths were dead and Gaing had seen no sign of Terman or Asrubal or anyone else of interest. And that is about the whole of it."

FOURTEEN

1

After an hour of brooding, Skirl decided that the treatment accorded her by the bank had exceeded tolerable limits of disrespect. She telephoned the Clam Muffin Committee and described the offensive events. The bank, so she declared, in its contempt for herself and her status, was gnawing away the very foundations of civilized society.

The chairman of the committee asked her to compose herself for a brief period, while he set matters straight. Ten minutes later he called back to announce that the bank recognized its mistake, and now extended its apologies. The bank would be pleased if Skirl, at her convenience, would see fit to return to Sassoon Ayry, where she could secure all her belongings, at her leisure. The bank's personnel would be on hand to render all assistance.

Skirl thanked the chairman and said that, as always, it was a wonderful thing to be a Clam Muffin, to which the chairman agreed.

Jaro and Skirl at once drove to Sassoon Ayry, where they discovered a new spirit of cooperation. Skirl packed the most desirable elements of her wardrobe, then ranged the house gathering such objects as might be considered keepsakes, along with her father's collection of ancient Kolosti miniatures, and a fossil trilobite from Old Earth. Skirl and Jaro returned to Merriehew. Jaro carried the cases into the house and up to the bedroom now being used by Skirl. Jaro went off about his own affairs, while Skirl gratefully unpacked her clothes and changed into a dark green frock. For a moment she stood before a mirror, studying her reflection. She took up a brush and ordered the loose curls. She looked at herself again. Something was different; something had changed. Was it better, or worse? She could not be sure.

Thoughtfully, Skirl turned away from the mirror. She went downstairs to the sitting room. Jaro glanced at her, then looked again, more intently. "You look remarkably pretty! What have you done to yourself?"

"I changed my clothes and brushed my hair. Also, I'm no longer angry with the bankers."

"Something has made a difference in you," said Jaro. "What it is, I can't understand. Maybe it's because—" he hesitated. "But no matter."

Skirl looked at him suspiciously, then said, "I believe that you have problems which you are trying to solve."

"Correct. I want to find out where the Faths first came upon me."

"Ah yes. They never told you."

"Never, to the best of my recollection. Whenever I asked, they'd only laugh and say that it was a place far away and not important."

"What could be their motive?"

"Simple enough. They wanted me to take a degree at the Institute, and join the faculty. Above all, I must not become a spaceman and go careening off in search of my past."

"That seems a bit high-handed."

Jaro nodded. "Still, they wanted the best for me."

"I suppose you have searched their records?"

Jaro described the scope of his efforts. "I found nothing."

Skirl nodded sagely. "You need the services of a trained effectuator."

"Probably so. Have you any suggestions?"

"I might take on the case if the fee were adequate."

"The fee, sorry to say, is not adequate. In fact, it is nonexistent."

"No matter," said Skirl. "It's about what I expected. I'll take on the case in the name of good public relations. So relax! Your troubles are over."

"I hope so—but I doubt it. Hilyer did his work well. I have searched everywhere."

"You probably looked in all the wrong places, while the facts were climbing your leg."

"We shall see," said Jaro. "Where do you want to start?"

"First, I'll ask some questions."

"Ask away."

"Where did you search?"

"I studied their records. The journal for the year in question is missing. I looked through notes, invoices, receipts, authorizations, souvenirs, restaurant menus—still nothing. I cleaned out the attic. I discovered that no one has thrown away anything for a hundred years. I found horticultural records, Althea's schoolwork, broken chairs—but no accounts of off-world travel. I went through Hilyer's workshop inch by inch; I examined every book in the library. I searched all the likely places, then all the unlikely places. Still nothing. Not a breath, not a whisper. I checked through the journals all over again, looking for obscure references. Again—nothing."

"You may have overlooked a hint or a secret allusion."

"It's possible—but I think not."

"I'll start with the journals."

Jaro shrugged. "As you like. I'm afraid you'll find it pointless."

"There must be something left."

"Hilyer was a methodical genius. So far as I can tell, he overlooked nothing."

"I'll see what I can make of it."

Jaro left Skirl to her work. He found Maihac on the porch and began to speak of the various efforts to acquire Merriehew: Forby Mildoon, Lyssel and her unconventional methods, Abel Silking, and his threats.

"When I look back, I get angry," said Jaro. "They planned to befuddle the poor foolish nimp, so that he would sell his property for a song. Then, after they had turned him out upon Katzvold Road, they would whipsaw Gilfong Rute and squeeze him out of his Glitterway spaceyacht. Abel Silking's offer was better, but it included threats. I am not pleased with any of these people."

"I don't think Silking will try to carry out his threats, especially after we introduce him to Gaing Neitzbeck."

Feeling somewhat more cheerful, Jaro went to check on Skirl's progress. He found her disconsolately sorting through a file of miscellaneous papers which he had already examined several times. "What have you learned?"

"Nothing. Hilyer seems to have been cold-blooded and very determined to get the better of you."

"I don't want to remember Hilyer like that."

"Perhaps I'm not very charitable." She pointed to the shelf. "There is the journal for the year before you were found, and the journal for the year after. They are numbered '25' and '27.' Number '26,' the journal for the year in question is missing."

"It is probably part of the parcel Imbald is holding for me, should I come to my senses and register at the Institute."

Skirl turned away from the cabinet. "You're right. Hilyer was thorough. I've seen enough of his empty notebooks."

"There may be something at the Institute which Maihac missed. But enough for now. It's time to set out our first banquet. Gaing Neitzbeck will be on hand. Are you a good cook?"

"I don't think so."

"I'll cook, and you set the table, banquet-style. Althea's best tablecloths are in yonder cupboard; the crockery is in the kitchen cabinet."

"Very well," said Skirl. "What are you planning to cook?"

"Stew."

"That sounds nice. Perhaps someday you'll teach me how to cook."

"Certainly. Stew is easy. You put things into a pot, add water and boil. When everything is done, add salt, pepper and serve. It's an infallible recipe."

Skirl went to the cupboard. She selected a cheerful blue- and red-checked cloth, spread it over the table. She set out dishes to match and brought down one of Althea's candelabra, of a color and design she thought appropriate to the setting.

When Gaing arrived, the company took seats around the table. Dinner was served by candlelight: a salad of garden greens, stew, bread and olives, along with two bottles of Hilyer's Emilione Red dinner wine. Skirl dined with good appetite, but she had little to say and seemed preoccupied by private thoughts. They were evidently entertaining since Skirl had trouble repressing the grin which from time to time threatened to break through her mask of solemnity. Jaro watched her narrowly, wondering what might be the secret joke.

Maihac refilled goblets around the table and leaned back in his chair. "One field of inquiry remains: the faculty at the Institute."

Jaro said gloomily, "I've already asked. No one remembers what the Faths were doing twelve years ago."

"In that case we seem to have reached a dead end."

Skirl said carelessly, "It might be useful to consult the effectuator, whom you hired to solve the problem—at quite a low fee, I might add."

Jaro looked at her in sudden suspicion. "You have the answer? Is that why you've been grinning?"

"Perhaps."

"Tell us! Don't keep us in suspense!"

Skirl sipped from her goblet of wine before responding. Then: "The place is called 'Sronk,' on the world Camberwell."

"Really! And how did you find that out?"

"First deduction, then induction."

"Come now! Surely there is more to it than that?"

"Well, yes. When I took the candelabra down from the shelf, I noticed on the bottom a label, with a number and a name—in this case '21' and 'Dank Wallow, Mauberley.' After thinking a bit, I went to the cabinet and took out the journal numbered '21.' I found a reference to the world Mauberly and the village 'Dank Wallow' almost at once. I went back to the shelf and looked at the bottom of each candelabra until I found a label with the number '26.' The place cited was 'Sronk' and the world 'Camberwell.'So there you have it."

2

The communicator, when connected with the Institute library, produced information regarding the world Camberwell, including physical characteristics, several maps, a description of the indigenous flora and fauna, information regarding the peoples of Camberwell, the towns and their populations as well as a brief historical survey. The principal spaceport was beside the town Tanzig, ten miles south of the River Blass. Sronk was indicated about forty miles east of Tanzig, across the Wyching Hills.

"The next problem is how to get there," said Jaro. "That means money."

"Money and time, if you use commercial transport," said Maihac. "Camberwell is to the side of the main routes, which means the chance of bad connections at the junction ports."

"What is needed is a spaceship," said Jaro. "I can sell to Silking for at least thirty thousand sols, and probably somewhat more, depending upon Rute's anxiety. How much is a Locator 11-B?"

"Anything from five thousand sols for a ship with a hole in the hull and a fused energy box, up to twenty-five or thirty thousand sols for a ship in reasonable condition. But a Locator would be cramped, and perhaps we can do better," Maihac advised.

The telephone chimed. Jaro called: "Speak!" On the screen appeared the face of a silver-haired man of mature years, notably debonair, with regular features and a manner benign and bland. Jaro said: "Good evening, Mr. Silking."

Abel Silking smiled in modest self-deprecation. "Perhaps it is a bit late, but I wonder if you have reflected upon the offer I made you yesterday?"

"Yes," said Jaro. "So I have."

"And you have decided to accept, or so I hope?"

"Not quite. I have taken advice from Mr. Tawn Maihac, and he is now acting for me. You may speak to him, if you like."

Silking's mouth lost something of its genial curve, but his tone was as suave as ever. "Of course. The terms are the same for him as they are for you."

Maihac looked into the screen. "I am Tawn Maihac. Jaro has asked me to represent him in this matter. Your principal is Gilfong Rute?"

Silking responded cautiously: "More accurately, it would be Lumilar Vistas."

"I see. But since I can't deal with Lumilar Vistas, it will have to be Gilfong Rute himself. If he will appear at Merriehew tomorrow at noon, I will listen to his offer."

Silking's jaw dropped. "Mr. Maihac, you are issuing preposterous manifestos! I can't take you seriously!"

"No matter. Is Gilfong Rute at hand? If so, ask him if he cares to come here tomorrow at noon. It is the only way we will deal with him."

"Just a moment." The screen went silent. Three minutes passed. Silking reappeared on the screen, looking a trifle ruffled. "He says that he will be there at noon." Silking's mouth twitched in a small painful grin. "He made some other comments, which would be pointless to transmit. Mr. Rute, I should warn you, is not kind to folk who try to take advantage of his bonhomie."

"He needn't worry; there won't be much trifling here tomorrow."

3

On the next day, a few minutes short of noon, a large black luxury vehicle turned into the drive and halted near the house. Two men in blue and green uniforms jumped from the front seat, looked around to assure themselves that all was secure and opened the back compartment. Abel Silking alighted, followed by Gilfong Rute. Silking and Rute advanced upon the house; the uniformed men went to stand beside the vehicle.

Jaro opened the door for them to enter, then ushered the two into the dining room and made introductions. "This is Skirl Hutsenreiter, an effectuator. This is Gaing Neitzbeck, and you have spoken to Tawn Maihac. Please be seated."

"Thank you," said Silking. He and Gilfong Rute seated themselves on one side of the table.

Silking said smoothly, "Now then, the situation remains the same. You have heard the Lumilar Vistas offer; we have here—"

Jaro interrupted. "Mr. Silking, you may sit here as a witness, but please do not join the conversation. We will deal directly with Mr. Rute, and your remarks will only delay us. So please be silent or, if you prefer, you may go sit in the parlor and warm yourself by the fire."

"I will remain here," said Silking with a cold smile.

"As you like." Jaro turned to Rute. "You want Merriehew, and we are ready to sell. Tawn Maihac has prepared the papers we will need, and if you also are ready, there is nothing to detain us."

Rute asked impatiently, "What papers are these?"

"Just the ordinary certificates of transfer. There are two sets: one for us and one for you."

"Nonsense," declared Rute. "I have the proper forms at hand. Silking, bring them out. They are ready for signature."

"Throw them away," said Maihac. "Our papers are better."

"Never mind your papers," snapped Rute. "You were made an offer of thirty thousand sols. Do you accept or do you not?"

"Certainly we accept," said Maihac, "subject to certain conditions."

Rute was instantly suspicious. "What conditions?"

Maihac pushed two sheets of paper across the table. "Read the documents."

Rute picked up the papers and read. His eyebrows rose in amazement. "You can't be serious!"

"How could we be anything else? You own the *Pharsang* Glitterway?"

"Of course I own the *Pharsang*. Is there some question as to this? I had it built by the Rialco Spaceyards at Murtsey to top specifications."

"The point is not at issue. As you have noted, we wish to buy the *Pharsang*."

Rute rapped Maihac's documents contemptuously with the back of his hand. "That is sheer bullypup, and you are wasting my time. Let us get on with our business."

"The *Pharsang* is our business," said Maihac. "How much have you offered Jaro for Merriehew?"

"As you well know, the figure is thirty thousand sols. It is a generous offer and not negotiable; take it or leave it."

"We will take it, right enough, so long as the two offers are accepted in tandem."

"Come now, sir! Do not talk in riddles! There are no specifics to your offer; it is all a mare's nest."

"Listen then! Here are the specifics. We offer thirty thousand sols for the *Pharsang* Glitterway as part of a single negotiation."

Rute looked at Maihac in stupefaction. "You are mad! The *Pharsang* would fetch two hundred thousand sols or more any day of the week!"

"We are flexible," said Maihac. "If you want two hundred

thousand sols for the *Pharsang*, the price for Merriehew becomes the same. Specify any figure you like. We need only fill out the blanks on the documents, sign them and the transaction is complete—a matter of five minutes."

Rute jumped to his feet, face pink with rage. "This is a swindle, bald and outright. You barely make the effort to dissemble! You cannot do this to me; I am a man of high comporture, and I will not allow it!"

"Be reasonable," said Maihac. "You have already spent a great deal of money on your Lumilar Vistas project; I have heard as high as half a million sols. This is money thrown away unless you secure title to Merriehew."

Gilfong Rute, who had leaned forward with arm raised as if to pound the table, stopped short, fist in mid-air. "Where did you hear this figure? It is highly confidential!"

"So far as we are concerned, it will remain confidential. Now then: back to business. If you fail to take up Jaro's offer, he will convert the house into a rustic tavern which should do very well. He will subdivide the back acreage into low-cost residential units, along with an asylum for the criminally insane."

Rute only laughed. "You cannot flim-flam me so easily! On the other hand, I admit that I am not able to use the *Pharsang* as I had planned; still, you must come up with an extra hundred thousand sols."

"That is not possible," said Maihac. "We must make an even exchange, with the *Pharsang* in full operative condition, fully sound and provisioned, with fresh energy cans and new codes in all the synthesizers."

"This is extortion!" declared Gilfong Rute. "Do you think me a fat goose hanging on a tree, ready to be plucked?"

"Not at all. But we can't forget your attempts to swindle Jaro when you considered him a nimp and a witling."

"That is a mistake I will not repeat," grumbled Rute. "Well then, my time is valuable. Let us sign the documents and have an end to it. The Glitterway is yours."

Rute signed the documents with a graceless flourish, then stood back and spoke in hollow triumph: "I lost my spaceyacht, but with the money I will make from Lumilar Vistas, I can buy twenty more, should the mood come on me. You could have held me up for double what you demanded."

"No matter," said Jaro. "We are not avaricious."

4

Aboard the magnificent *Pharsang* Glitterway, Maihac could barely restrain his enthusiasm. "This is large enough to move passengers or freight," he told Jaro. "In short, you have a source of income about like that of a full professor."

"The Faths might not approve of the use to which I have put Merriehew," said Jaro. "In any case, I owe them all my gratitude."

Skirl asked, "So now, what are your plans?"

"First, a voyage to Camberwell, where I'll try to search out my six lost years. After that, I can't even speculate. But first things first. That means recruiting a crew."

"I volunteer," said Maihac. "You're the captain. Gaing should make an excellent chief engineer, if the prospective voyage suits him."

"It suits me very well," said Gaing. "I would be unhappy if you kept me off the ship. I have been grounded far too long."

"Gaing will be chief engineer and strategist. I will sign on as cook, roustabout, navigator, general dog's-body."

"We are still lacking a chief officer," said Jaro. "We'll want someone of exceptional abilities: resourceful, clever, kindly, with the soul of a vagabond. We'll want a person of high status—even a Clam Muffin if we could find one. We may or may not be able to recruit a qualified person."

Skirl asked hesitantly, "When are you taking applications?"

"Immediately."

"I wish to apply."

Jaro reached out, ruffled Skirl's short dark curls. She ducked away, smoothed her hair with both hands.

"You are hired," said Jaro.

"And my salary?"

"Not very much—about what you earn as an effectuator. If we put the *Pharsang* into commercial transport, we will share the profit."

"Gaing and I have had experience in this line of work," said Maihac. "It was a pleasant life—until we lost our ship on Fader. The episode taught us a lesson, and we will not make the same mistake again. Am I right on this, Gaing?"

"Those are my own feelings."

Jaro turned to Skirl. "Does this arrangement suit you?"

"I couldn't be more pleased."

5

Maihac and Gaing remained aboard the *Pharsang*; Jaro and Skirl returned to Merriehew. They dined on what remained in the larder and drank the last flagon of Hilyer's prized Estresas Valley wine, then went to stand by the fire. Outside a gentle rain began to fall. They spoke in soft voices, pausing often to reflect upon the extraordinary events, which in the end had brought them together. They stood close to one another. Jaro's arm was around Skirl's waist, and presently she reached out her own arm to hold him similarly. The conversation dwindled; each became increasingly conscious of the other's nearness. Jaro swung about, drew Skirl close and they kissed each other—again and again. Finally they paused to catch their breath. Jaro asked, "Do you remember the first time I kissed you?"

"Of course! It was after you nipped my ear."

"I think I loved you even then. It was a mysterious emotion, which puzzled me."

"And I must have loved you, too—although at the time I wasn't thinking clearly of such things. Still, I always noticed how handsome and clean you looked, as if you had been scrubbed thoroughly."

"What strange lives we are leading!"

"If we go off on the *Pharsang*, our lives will be stranger yet."

Jaro took her hand. "Something strange and wonderful is about to happen in the other room. I'm anxious to find out what."

Skirl held back. "Jaro, I feel very odd. I think that I'm frightened." Jaro bent his head and kissed her. She clung to him. "It isn't fright after all," said Skirl. "It's something I've never felt before; I think it's excitement."

Jaro took her hand again and they left the room. The firelight moved among the shadows and set glimmers of orange light moving among the shapes of Althea's candelabra. The room was silent save for the sound of the rain against the windows.

FIFTEEN

1

The *Pharsang* approached the world Camberwell, descended upon the city Tanzig and landed at the spaceport. The four members of the crew sealed the ship, passed through the terminal and stepped out into the cool air of Tanzig. Before them an avenue led into the disheveled old town with its cocked roofs and twisted clapboard siding. In the distance, dominating the city like three colossi, half-obscured by haze, stood the triple monument to the 'Delineator of Boons and Retributions'—one of the many sobriquets attached to the legendary magistrate.

Upon leaving the terminal, Jaro slowed his steps, aware of something stirring in his memory—a subconscious resonance, faint and fugitive, dying even as he tried to identify it. What could it be? The dank feel of the atmosphere? The hazy distances? The skyline of crooked roofs, angular and crotchety? The camphorous tang from the warped clapboards which sheathed all the structures of Tanzig? It was, for a fact, an odor hauntingly familiar.

Jaro noticed Skirl watching him. He liked to think of himself as stoic and impenetrable, but Skirl had become uncannily sensitive to the shift of his moods. Jaro sometimes felt that she knew more about him than he did himself. Skirl now asked, "What are you thinking?"

"Nothing in particular."

"There was something. Your face changed even while I was watching you."

Jaro showed a faint smile. "There is an old word: 'frisson.' I don't know if I'm using the word correctly, but I think that's what I was feeling."

"Really? I've never heard of it before. What does it feel like?"

"Something like a quick cold shiver at the back of your neck."

"Odd," Skirl mused. "I felt nothing like that."

"Of course not! Why should you?"

"Because sometimes I feel exactly what you are feeling. We probably have a telepathic link."

"I suppose it's possible."

The four rode an open-sided omnibus into the center of town, where an old woman gliding along the sidewalk on slip-boards directed them to the Bureau of Public Records. For two hours they searched musty files and handwritten directories, but discovered no mention of either Jamiel or her child.

They returned to the *Pharsang*. Gaing and Maihac unshipped the flitter; all climbed aboard. Taking to the air, the flitter flew off to the east, in the direction of Sronk. They passed across tracts of drab farmland, watermeadows grown over with thickets of tall cane, a village of small clapboard houses under crooked roofs. The Wyching Hills rose ahead: a tumble of tawny slopes, gullies, and smooth round ridges. Out to the horizon and beyond spread Wildenberry Steppe, with a few isolated farms occupying the strip between hills and steppe. A road led south to a small town: Sronk, according to the map.

The flitter crossed the hills, turned south, followed the road to Sronk and landed on a flat area to the side of the town square. The four passengers alighted and made a survey, discovering little of interest. In answer to Jaro's question, a passerby pointed out the Municipal Clinic, which unlike other structures of Sronk was built, not of warped clapboard under double- and triple-tiled roofs, but of rock-melt blocks with a flat roof of gray sinter. Jaro studied the building with interest, but nothing surfaced in his memory. On his previous visit, he probably had been more dead than alive.

Doctor Fexel was still in residence, and immediately recalled dealing with Jaro's battered body. "I remember thinking—idly, of course—that Jaro would make a splendid specimen for my anatomy classroom, since he demonstrated every trauma known to the textbooks."

Skirl patted Jaro's shoulder with a proprietary air. "He has survived rather nicely, don't you think?"

Fexel agreed enthusiastically. "It is a tribute both to modern medicine and to the skill of Doctor Solek and myself. Now that I think of it, Doctor Myrrle Wanish probably did the most to keep you in one piece, since you were determined to destroy yourself with spasms of utter hysteria. They were truly unbelievable—absolute paroxysms of fright and rage! Have you ever discovered the reason for such racking conduct?"

"No," said Jaro. "It remains a mystery."

"Most extraordinary! Let me see if I can raise Doctor Wanish. He'll be at his office in Tanzig, and I'm sure he'd like to speak with you. Fexel worked at his communicator. He spoke a few words, and Wanish's bearded face appeared on the screen. Fexel introduced Jaro, and Wanish instantly became interested. I recall your case distinctly. It was necessary to modify your memory; you were recalling something extremely traumatic and the reaction was killing you."

Jaro shuddered. "I'm almost afraid to learn what happened."

"You still know nothing of your early life?"

"Not very much. In fact, that is why we are here."

"Your memory shows no sign of seeping back?"

"Not really. At times I glimpse one or two images; they are

always the same. Sometimes I seem to hear my mother's voice, though I can't understand the words."

"It's possible that the broken matrices are trying to reform. Don't be surprised if a few recollections do come back."

"Can you do anything to facilitate this?"

Wanish reflected a moment then said, "I'm afraid not. Here's another point to consider. If your memory returned, you might not like what you discovered."

"Even so, I'd like to know the facts."

Doctor Wanish became brisk. "It has been a pleasure speaking with you. I wish you good luck in your ventures."

"Thank you."

The four returned to the flitter. Once aloft, they followed the road north, moving slowly at an altitude of two hundred feet, with Wildenberry Steppe to the right and the Wyching Hills to the left. Five miles along the road, Jaro became tense. This was where he had known fear and pain. The sensation became ever stronger, as if memory were clotting upon the broken matrices, making it vivid. Almost he could feel the heat of the sun on his bare skin, the gravel abrading his knees, the jubilant shouts of the shapes standing above him, their sticks beating down: thud! thud! thud!

Jaro pointed to a place on the road. "There. That is where it happened."

Maihac landed the flitter; they alighted blinking and squinting against the brightness of the day. Sunlight beat down upon their heads. To the west hills showed the color of dead jointgrass.

Jaro walked a few paces along the road, then halted. "It was here that the Faths found me. I can feel it! The air seems to vibrate."

"And how did you come to be here?"

Jaro pointed. "From over the hills. There was a river, a thicket of reeds, an old yellow house." Jaro thought back across the years. "Through the window we could see a man standing against the twilight. His eyes seemed to glint with four-pointed stars. I became frightened. My mother was frightened. There was confusion; something happened; she told me something. I can almost remember." Jaro squinted toward the hills. "She—I think that she must have put me into a boat." He stopped short. "No, that's not what happened. I went down to the boat by myself—alone. She was already dead. Still, I floated away in a boat. And the next thing I knew I was swimming through the dark. After that—nothing."

Skirl touched Jaro's arm. "Look."

A few hundred feet down the road stood a trio of squat young peasants, eyes small and black in moony faces. They gave no signal of greeting, and stared with impersonal curiosity. Skirl said softly: "These might have been the persons who beat you."

"They are about the right age," said Jaro tonelessly.

"Aren't you angry with them?"

"Very angry. But I don't think I'll do anything about it."

Maihac strolled down the road and spoke to the men. They responded with exaggerated deference, more mocking than real. Maihac returned. "They say they don't remember the episode. But they are lying—not out of fear, but for the sheer enjoyment of misleading an off-worlder. It's common enough."

"There's nothing to be learned here," said Jaro.

The flitter took to the air, and heading west once more crossed the Wyching Hills. A river flowing from the west reached the base of the hills, where it swung north to disappear at last into the haze. Five miles upstream a small town appeared near the river: Point Extase, according to the map, with a population of four thousand. Its structures, like those of Tanzig and Sronk, were built of warped clapboard, painted in any one of a hundred soft colors. Many of the houses were old and dilapidated; all had a rumpled look, and wore their roofs askew, like the hats of drunken old harridans.

The town was separated from the river by a strip of marshy wasteland, overgrown in part by dense stands of tall bamboo. The flitter slid around the outskirts of the town, with Jaro scanning the area below. "I don't see anything familiar yet," he told the others. "Let's get closer to the river."

The flitter swung away from the town and flew over the strip of wasteland beside the river. From the corner of his eye Jaro noticed an old yellow house. He pointed. "That is the place. I am sure of it!"

The flitter landed to the side of the house. The four stepped down to the ground. The house had long been abandoned; windows were broken; at the back of the porch a board had been nailed across the door. Old yellow paint flaked from the punkwood clapboard. At either side, weeds grew rank.

Jaro studied the house for a moment, then slowly approached. The others stood back, in unspoken accord that Jaro should explore the premises before others came on the scene and altered his perceptions.

Jaro, oblivious to everything but what was in his own mind,

stepped upon the porch, tugged at the board which had been nailed across the doorway and pulled it loose. He pushed at the door; creaking and groaning, it swung open, revealing a long narrow hall. Jaro entered, then turned aside into the front room. How small everything seemed! Odd! He stood looking about the dusty spaces and despite all his resolves, could not avoid a wave of melancholy: impossible not to grieve for what had once been dear and now was gone.

Something else inhabited the room—something heavy, baleful, inert. Jaro's pulse began to pound. He searched the shadows, but saw nothing to alarm him, and heard not so much as a whisper. He stood pondering, allowing one idea to lead into another. By degrees insight came to him. He could find nothing, because nothing was there. The pressure originated in his own brain, from vestigial memories scattered and left behind, after the therapy of Dr. Wanish. Jaro thought that if this were a hint of what lay latent in his mind, he would instantly stop brooding over the past.

The thought acted like a relief valve; the pressure, whatever its source, drained from the room. Jaro gave a wry, rather unnatural, chuckle; he was thinking wild thoughts, quite bereft of coherent logic. He began to mutter: "I am here, not by chance, nor by desire, nor by force. I am here because this is the way things must be. If I had not come by one route, I would have come by another. Now where did I get that idea? It is not altogether sensible. I am here—but why? Something is stirring."

Jaro stood like a somnambulist. Present time had become amorphous. He looked down a tunnel of time. He saw the yellow house; the door was open. He heard a voice, which he knew to be the voice of his mother. She stood before him; he could feel her nearness but he could not see her face. She was speaking to him. "Jaro, time is short; I have put all my loving strength into making myself known to you! I will print these words into your brain, by what is called hypnotic suggestion. You will never forget what I say, but it will come clear only when you return here, to this dreadful place. For me the end of time has come! I have commanded you to take the black box and hide it in your secret den. When you come back, go to recover the box. Then obey the instructions you will find inside. I place this charge upon you because your father is dead. His name was Tawn Maihac; be faithful."

Jaro heard his own voice, hoarse and faint as if coming from a great distance: "I will be faithful." He paused to listen. There was only silence, heavy and thick. He felt himself drifting, though where he could not decide, since all directions were the same. His vision blurred; he could no longer see the yellow house with the open door. The tunnel of time became a wisp and was gone.

Someone was calling his name. Jaro began to breathe again; how long had he stood in a daze? He turned his head, to find Skirl standing beside him, tugging at his arm and looking anxiously up into his face.

"Jaro! Why are you so strange? Are you ill, or faint? I've been calling you! You would not answer!"

Jaro drew another deep breath. "I'm not sure what came over me. I thought I heard my mother's voice."

Skirl looked nervously around the room. "Come; let's go outside. I don't like this place."

They returned into the open. Maihac asked: "What happened?"

Jaro tried to put his thoughts into order. "I don't really know—except that I thought I heard my mother's voice."

Maihac looked at him with eyebrows raised. After a pause he said, "How do you know it was your mother? What I mean is, did the voice identify itself?"

"Yes," said Jaro. "The voice identified itself. It mentioned hypnotic suggestion, so we need not look for a ghost."

"So what was the message? I assume it was comprehensible."

"I understood everything. She told me that you were dead, and that there was something I must do."

"And what was that?"

Jaro stood thinking. After a moment he set off around the house, pausing every three or four steps to survey the surroundings. Suddenly he became assured, and ran to a tumble of stones, perhaps once a kennel or a small shed, now overgrown with red lichen and black puffwort. Jaro dropped to his knees and pulled stones to one side. Presently he opened a dark hole, which he enlarged by moving aside more stones. He reached into the hole and groped, but without success. He removed more stones, then, dropping flat, he crawled into the opening, twisted on his side, and felt along an overhead ledge. Triumph! He backed out of the hole, holding a flat black box.

Jaro pulled himself to his feet and looked around him, into the faces of his companions. "I've found it, where she told me to put it!"

"Open the box," said Skirl. "I can't control my curiosity."

Maihac looked warily around the area. "Let's leave this place first. Just possibly Asrubal might have left someone on guard."

The four climbed into the flitter, and returned to Tanzig spaceport. Back aboard the *Pharsang*, with the flitter stowed in its bay, Jaro opened the box. He withdrew a buff envelope folded from heavy parchment, to which another, smaller, envelope had been clipped. Jaro put the first envelope aside and raised the flap of the second envelope, removed a sheet of paper, and for the second time in his life read a letter from someone who had loved him and now was dead.

The letter had clearly been scribbled in haste and in an extremity of emotion. Jaro read aloud:

> " 'I wonder who will be reading this, and how far in the future? I hope, Jaro, that it will be you. If I succeed in bringing you back, you will know that I could have done nothing else; so if you resent the coercion that I placed into your mind, please forgive me!
>
> " 'Now I am desperate. I have waited too long; I have seen Asrubal. He will soon find us, and then life will be gone and we will be dead! It is not a nice thought. We will know not even nothing, and fear not even the unimaginable! Jaro, what a queer fact, and it makes me shiver to think of it. If I survive, you will never read this letter. Since you are reading it you will know that events went badly, at least for me. But I expect nothing else, and I grieve only that I must place this burden on you, if you indeed survive.
>
> " 'Asrubal, or Urd House, is the feared one! He will have killed me, and he has killed Tawn Maihac, your father. I know this is so, since three years have passed, and he has not come to find us.
>
> " 'These are your instructions; follow them if you are able. The other envelope contains, first, a draught upon the Natural Bank at Ocknow, which, with accrued interest, will make up to a very large sum. Secure this money by placing it in a new account of your own. Secondly, make six copies of the documents in the large envelope. Place one of these copies in the bank vault; take the other copies to Loorie on the world Nilo-May, by the star Yellow Rose. Place one of the copies into the vault of the local

Natural Bank. Mail one copy to the Justiciar at Romarth on the world Fader, by the star Night Lamp. These documents will destroy Asrubal if and when they are received by the Justiciar. They must not fall into the hands of anyone from the House of Urd.

" 'Next, proceed to Romarth. This is dangerous and must be done carefully. At Loorie, locate Aubert Yamb, most likely to be found at the Primrose Consolidators. Identify yourself, induce him to charter a small spaceship and travel to Fader. Land near Romarth. This is illegal but you can protect yourself by stating that you are a special envoy to the Justiciar. As soon as possible, make yourself known to my father, Ardrian of Ramy, at his palace Carleone.

" 'When you meet the Justiciar, give him another of the copies and describe how you came by them. Assert that they demonstrate the criminal peculations of Asrubal of Urd. Assert that Asrubal has killed me, your brother Garlet, Tawn Maihac and also has tried to kill you. The duty I lay upon you is now fulfilled. You can do no more at Romarth, which, despite its beauty, is also most dangerous. Return to Loorie, and thence to Ocknow. Secure your money and thereafter pursue a happy life.

" 'Note: do not deal with Lorquin shipping; you will be killed and your body will be thrown into space. Lorquin is an agency of Urd House: which is to say, Asrubal.

" 'Fader is an old, old world; it is mostly wild and very dangerous. It is where your father met his death. At Loorie ask Yamb about conditions on Fader. Remember, Asrubal will kill you with pleasure.

" 'As I watch you I am heartsick, for now we will part. I love this brave little morsel of life named Jaro; I look across the room and see you as you are now, so earnest and handsome; you are wondering why I write so sadly, and when you read this letter you will know. My poor little Jaro. Once you had a twin brother, but Asrubal killed him, too.

" 'I have finished the letter. Now I will put a hypnotic force on your mind, to bring you back to this desperate place. You may not know why you are coming, but come you must.

" 'I can write no more. My love goes with you always;

even when I am gone, it will persist, and perhaps you will feel it. If you listen, it might even give you counsel. I have often wondered about such things, and perhaps soon I will know. You will notice that I am contradicting the dreary remarks I inscribed above. That is called 'hope'! As for now, I can do no more.

" 'Your mother, Jamiel.' "

After a time Skirl said softly: "Poor brave woman! So she was killed!"

Jaro found that tears were welling down his cheeks. Maihac said gruffly, "It is a melancholy letter."

Jaro opened the heavy brown envelope and withdrew the contents. There was a sheaf of what appeared to be commercial accounts and a bank draught upon the Natural Bank to the sum of three hundred thousand sols, payable to bearer, along with accruement of interest. Gaing examined the draught. "Sixteen years and more, at compound interest, the account will have doubled, or tripled, by this time, depending upon interest."

"The money belongs to you and my father," said Jaro. "It was intended as compensation for the *Distilcord;* it is not mine."

"The money is nice to have," said Gaing. "There is enough for us all."

Skirl asked: "And these other papers? They seem to be invoices or bills of lading, or something similar."

Jaro studied them. "They mean nothing to me. Still, my mother wanted them taken to Romarth, and I will do my best to oblige her."

"That is how it must be," said Maihac. "It is also dangerous, but not so dangerous as it might be if Gaing and I were not part of the company."

Jaro returned the papers into the envelope. "So far as I can see, there is nothing to keep us on Camberwell. I have even learned the facts of my missing six years."

Maihac rose to his feet. "I have an errand I must see to; it won't take me long." He left the ship.

Almost two hours passed. Maihac returned, looking grim and cheerless. He dropped into a chair and accepted a cup of tea. "I had not expected to find Jamiel alive, but now it's official. At the Registry of Vital Records I learned that thirteen years ago a woman known as Jamu May, residing at 7 Riverfront Way in

Point Extase, had been found dead in the river, the victim of unspecified foul play. Her son, age five or six years, was missing and presumed drowned." Maihac sprawled back in the chair. "I thought that perhaps by some miracle Jamiel might have escaped. But now there is no more hope. In some horrid way she had been done to death. We will visit Romarth and deliver the documents Jamiel won at such great cost. We shall go prepared, and Asrubal of Urd will not be happy to see us. He will know that we have come for revenge. I only hope that he is alive."

2

At Ocknow Maihac and Jaro visited the Natural Bank. Skirl remained aboard the *Pharsang*, while Gaing went to look for a shipyard capable of making the alterations to the *Pharsang* now considered necessary.

At the bank, Maihac and Jaro found that Brin Dykich now held the position of managing director. He made no difficulty about cashing the draught. As Gaing had predicted, the principal, compounding at six and three quarters percent, had far more than doubled itself. Six hundred thousand sols was redeposited in a new account; the balance was packed into a canvas bag.

Maihac told Dykich of how affairs had gone at Point Extase. Dykich reported that about five years previously Asrubal had come to his office, to demand that the draught, now seven years stale, should be voided. Dykich had refused, citing his instructions from the Council at Romarth. Asrubal had voiced bitter complaints; when Dykich remained adamant, Asrubal had stormed from his office in a cold fury.

Maihac and Jaro returned to the *Pharsang* with the canvas bag, now packed with cash. Gaing had found a reputable spaceyard and had arranged for alterations to be made upon the *Pharsang*.

Three weeks later armament of several types from heavy to light had been installed aboard the *Pharsang*. Additionally, power guns and target detection equipment had been fitted to the flitter, so that it functioned as a light version of an IPCC patrol craft.

Maihac took Skirl aside and explained the dangers which might beset the *Pharsang* and its crew on the world Fader. With great delicacy, Maihac suggested to Skirl that several options were open to her, any of which she might adopt without the slightest prejudice to herself or to the respect in which she was held. While the *Pharsang* and its crew pursued a dangerous program on Fader, Skirl could wait at Ocknow or even at Loorie, if she chose, until the *Pharsang* returned. On the other hand, Maihac was quick to add, should she wish to participate in the venture and share the attendant risks, everyone would take pleasure in her company.

Skirl responded in a stiff voice. She pointed out that, as a Clam Muffin, she feared nothing, and naturally her choice was the last option. She could not pretend to be pleased with Maihac for dangling the undignified alternatives before her. She declared that Maihac had tacitly called into question not only her courage and her adventurous spirit, but also her loyalty to Jaro and her honor.

Maihac protested with great fervor that Skirl had misunderstood his motives. He questioned neither her courage, nor her gallantry, nor her readiness to share Jaro's destiny, and certainly not her honor, which would have been unthinkable. He insisted that he had broached the topic only in the interests of orderly procedure. He wanted to make sure that Skirl knew everything there was to be known about the expedition, so that he need never feel guilty that he had allowed her a false sense of security. Maihac told her: "It is simply a matter of clearing my conscience, in case you are torn limb from limb by the Loklor. I would mourn you, of course, but I would be in a sense gratified to know that you had gone to your fate without any persuasion from me."

"You are conscientious," said Skirl. "Still, I am trusting you, along with Gaing and Jaro, to make sure that my person is protected at all times."

"I will do my best," said Maihac. "Jaro would never forgive me if I did less."

"Does Jaro know that you are talking to me like this?"

"Definitely not! Jaro is perhaps just a bit vain. He would never suspect that you might prefer wealth, comfort and safety to dying some unspeakable death in his company."

Both Skirl and Maihac laughed and parted friends, and the subject never arose again.

The *Pharsang* departed Ocknow and set off toward Yellow Rose Star. "The first objective is Asrubal," said Maihac. "If we find him at Loorie and deal with him there, so much the better. If not, then it's on to Fader and the city Romarth."

3

The *Pharsang* slanted out toward the fringes of the galaxy, the star Yellow Rose shining ever brighter. In due course the *Pharsang* dropped down upon Nilo-May, and landed at the Loorie spaceport. After the usual precautions against transitional shock, the four debarked, complied with routine formalities and were given the freedom of the town. They found themselves at the head of a long tree-shaded avenue.

The four surveyed the town, taking note of the cramped and eccentric architecture, the lassitude which pervaded the air, the surreptitious habits of the townsfolk, the tall dendrons which overhung the street: all in all, a placid, almost bucolic, scene.

Maihac led the way to the Peurifoy Refreshment Parlor, across the street from the Lorquin Shipping Agency. They seated themselves in the open air, under the shade of black and green foliage, and were silently served pots of beer. Across the street wide windows displayed the interior of the Lorquin Agency. Behind the counter stood a small thin-faced old man with a puff of white hair. Dame Waldop was nowhere to be seen.

"At Primrose Consolidators, just a couple doors away, we can look for news of Aubert Yamb," said Maihac. "When last I passed through Loorie, he had been discharged from the Lorquin Agency, and in my opinion is lucky to be alive."

When the four had finished their beer they walked down the street to Primrose Consolidators. Jaro went to make inquiries. He pushed open the door, stepped into a dim interior which was heavy with the scent of herbs and resinous woods. A counter ran down the length of one wall. Behind the counter sat Dame Estebel Pidy, or so a plaque on the counter informed Jaro. A long black gown hung loose about her bony frame; her skin was parchment pale; her mop of black hair was cut short at ear level with a brutal lack of finesse. She inspected Jaro with black eyes. "Yes sir; what are your needs?"

"I have some business with Mr. Aubert Yamb. Where may I find him?"

Dame Pidy answered peevishly: "He is in poor health; he will not care to discuss his affairs with creditors."

"No fear; I want none of his money."

"Lucky for you," sniffed Dame Pidy. "He has none, and you may be sure that his wife will tell you the same."

"I expect nothing else," said Jaro. "Where does he live?"

"Go three blocks north; turn down Titwillow Lane. His house is 'Angel's Song,' second on the right, under a canker tree."

The four, following directions, found "Angel's Song" deep in the shade of a sprawling black dendron which trailed heart-shaped blue pods.

They approached the front entrance, and were met by a slatternly woman with lank hair and a round suspicious face. She spoke sharply: "You have come to the wrong place; our quota is under dispute, and in any case it has long been over-subscribed."

"That is not our concern," said Maihac. "We have business with Aubert Yamb. May we come in?"

The woman refused to move. "Yamb is not well; he needs his rest."

"Nevertheless, we must see him," said Maihac. "Are you not the former Twee Pidy?"

"Yes, and I remain the same. What of it?"

"A few years ago I hired Yamb to do some important semi-official work; I met you at the time, as perhaps you will recall."

Twee Pidy tilted her head and scrutinized Maihac through narrowed eyes. "I recall you, well enough. It was a long time ago, and here you are again. What do you want now of poor Yamb?"

"We will tell him when we see him."

Twee flapped her arms against her hips. "Well, if you must, you must." Twee stood back from the door, to admit the visitors. She took them down a hall, meanwhile speaking over her shoulder: "He has been taking jinjiver tea to help his ague, but it only seems to make his eyes water; he has become very languid, and can no longer exert himself at toil of any description."

They were shown into Yamb's bedroom. Yamb lay flat on his back, staring toward the ceiling through red-rimmed eyes. The room was dark and heavy with frowst.

Maihac introduced the group. Yamb peered from face to face. He spoke querulously: "I am far from well, so what do you want?"

"Nothing much," said Maihac. "Consider this a social call. I have not seen you for twelve years."

" 'Twelve years'?" Yamb raised his head to stare in moony puzzlement. "Now I remember! You are the man who was lost on Fader and thought dead! Your name is—let me think—Tawn Maihac."

"Correct. Asrubal sold me to the Loklor but I escaped. So what do you know of Asrubal?"

Yamb slumped back upon his bed. "You are speaking of a basilisk; do not mention his name, even though he is now back on Fader. Twelve years ago I did rash deeds; by a quirk of fate I escaped detection. When I think of what might have happened, chills chase along my body like scurrying mice with cold feet. Ah! What days those were, to be sure!" Yamb spoke on, in a dreary monotone. "Twelve years ago—it seems an aeon! Dame Waldop ruled the office with her mighty bosom and fearful haunches. But even Dame Waldop could not resist Asrubal's fury, and was sent away in disgrace. I fared better, and came into my own at last. At the first opportunity I called myself 'Managing Director' and sat at the counter where old Pounter stands today. My moment in the sun was short. I tried to open up the Fader trade to Primrose, so that we could sell goods directly to Romarth bypassing the Lorquin Agency, but Asrubal turned ugly. To make a long story short, I was beaten, threatened and discharged from my post. So passed my proudest moment: the culmination of my career, so to speak." Yamb gave a soft groan. "It is truly the stuff of tragedy; do you not agree?"

Twee was becoming ever more restive. She called out: "You are tiring poor Yamb and taking up my valuable time! Already we have exceeded the reasonable demands of hospitality—unless, of course, you are planning compensation?"

"Nonsense," declared Maihac. "We are doing you a favor talking over old times. If anything, you should be preparing a feast of celebration."

Yamb uttered a choked guffaw. "At least you have brought me a gasp or two of amusement, which is all too rare in my life." Yamb gave a hacking cough. "Ah, my poor throat—dry as rusk! Woman, have we no tipsic to drink? Is not life to be lived as a glorious adventure, with tipsic to be shared among friends? Or must we whimper and tiptoe around all the good things, proud only of our frugal austerity? We cannot drink tipsic once we are dead! Bring out the bottle, woman! Pour with a loose wrist and an eager hand! This is a great day!"

Twee, tight-lipped, poured out tots of a yellow-green liquor, which tasted of aromatic pollen and left a tingle on the tongue.

Yamb smacked his lips. "That is the real stuff! I find that four tots of this spirit excites what I will call the 'romantic genius by which a gentleman converts dull ideas of the moment into paradisiacal illusions.' The episodes are sweet because they are so fragile. A jar, a jolt and dismal reality returns, nor will four more tots of tipsic repair the misfortune."

Twee interposed a bored admonition: "Come, come, Yamb; these folk are not all agog to hear your dithyrambs. If you have something to say, speak to the point, like a man of good sense!"

Yamb gave a hollow groan and fell back on his pillow.

"No doubt, my dear, but what you are right! Still, in a world better than this one, I would be served both ramp and pot-cheese with my gruel and show a fine leg as I danced."

"You are a complete visionary," muttered Twee. "Why are you not happy with what you have? There are many dead people who would gladly change places with you."

Yamb seemed to muse. "For a fact, it gives one to wonder as to the pros and cons."

Twee grumbled. "Put the idea out of your mind; it's hard enough taking care of you in your present condition."

Maihac rose to his feet. "A last question: Do you expect Asrubal back at Loorie soon?"

Yamb said fretfully: "I know nothing of his plans. At the moment he resides on Fader; no doubt, when he sees fit, he will return."

SIXTEEN

1

The *Pharsang* departed Loorie Spaceport and set off on a course which took it out and away, toward the brink of nothingness. Yellow Rose slid past off the port beam, dwindled to a saffron spark, and vanished. Fringe stars appeared, moved astern, and presently no longer could be seen. Far ahead the luminous smudges of other galaxies showed against the black.

Time passed. The *Pharsang* drifted outward through open space. A far point of light indicated a lonely lost star: Night Lamp.

Aboard the *Pharsang* the tranquil routines began to alter, as Night Lamp became the focus of attention. In due course Night Lamp took on rotundity, and revealed itself to be a yellow-white dwarf of middle size with an entourage of four planets. The first two were small lumps of seared crags and molten lava. The fourth and most remote was a dismal waste of black basalt and frozen gases. Third in the sequence was Fader, a world of wind, water, forest and steppe accompanied by a pair of moderately large moons.

The *Pharsang* approached and the horizons of Fader expanded below. The physiography was simple. On one side of the world a single continent sprawled across the north temperate zone; the rest of the world, except for polar icecaps, was submerged under a single all-inclusive ocean.

The *Pharsang* circled the planet and descended into the atmosphere. It dropped through a high scurf of alto-cirrus and finally drifted across the landscape at an altitude of five miles. Maihac studied the terrain, using a map to orient himself. With rueful fascination he watched the tawny landscape slide below. "We are over the Tangtsang Steppe," he told the others. "I see places I had hoped never to see again. Look over yonder!" He pointed. "See that huddle of sheds? That is Flad, the spaceport. Gaing, what do you make out?"

Gaing, turned the macroscope upon Flad. "There is a ship on the field—the *Liliom*, I believe."

"What are they up to?"

"The after bay is open. They've just started to discharge cargo."

"Hm," said Maihac. "I hope Asrubal is not planning a trip off-world. I would not like to lose him now."

"No one works too hard at Flad," said Gaing. "The ship should be in port another two or three days, maybe longer."

"That ought to be time enough, or so I hope," said Maihac. "Still, we'll take precautions."

"We can always put a hole in the *Liliom's* forward sponson," Gaing suggested. "That will keep the mechanics busy a week or two."

"It may come to that—if Asrubal is mysteriously missing from Romarth. Most likely it won't be necessary."

The *Pharsang* turned aside, and followed the road which led from Flad across the steppe to the barge terminus on the Skein River, then continued to the southeast across Blandy Deep Forest.

Toward the end of the afternoon Romarth appeared below. The *Pharsang* hovered invisibly at an altitude of three miles. Maihac identified what he remembered of the city's landmarks. "The irregular area with the six fountains, where the boulevards converge is the Gamboye Plaza. The two colonnaded buildings just over the bridge are the Justiciary and the chambers of law. The structure to the side is the Colloquary, where the councillors sit.

That squat brown building with the three green glass domes is the Foundance—one of the oldest structures of Romarth. It is a mysterious place where the Seishanee are brought into being and raised in a crêche until they are transferred to training camps along the river. It is considered poor taste to talk about the Foundance."

"How so?" asked Jaro. "What goes on at the Foundance?"

"I don't know. Jamiel was like everyone else; she never discussed the place."

"Peculiar."

Maihac grinned in sardonic recollection. "Among so much that was peculiar, I barely gave it a thought. By this time I was anxious to leave Romarth."

Skirl looked down through the observation window. "It's a city out of fairyland. What else is down there?"

"Hundreds of palaces. Some are in use; others have been abandoned to time and the white house-ghouls. The city reeks with history. Notice the wide boulevard beside the river; that's the Esplanade, where the cavaliers and their ladies go for their promenades. To the side are small cafés; everyone has his favorite, where he stops to take refreshment and watch his friends stroll by. An hour before sunset they all return home, to change into formal clothes for the evening's social occasions."

Skirl asked in wonder: "And no one works?"

"Only the Seishanee."

Skirl compressed her lips in disapproval. "It seems a vapid way of life. Have they no ambition? Perhaps they strive to join their best clubs?"

"Nothing like that. They are concerned only for 'rashudo.' "

"And what is that?"

Maihac reflected. "Only a Roum could explain. I think that if you mixed vanity, truculence, egotism, reckless disdain for danger, obsession with honor and reputation, the result might be close to 'rashudo.' The Roum observe an elegant etiquette, which you will constantly be violating. But no matter; it can't be helped. From the Roum point of view, we are barely civilized. It is useless to become irritated; it only serves to amuse them."

Skirl gave a sour laugh. "I can control myself. But already I don't think I like this beautiful city."

"Nor do I. When our business is done I hope to leave with great speed and never return."

2

Night Lamp set in a flare of melancholy colors. Dusk fell over the landscape. One of the moons climbed the sky followed by the other, where they glowed soft and silken like pearls in milk.

After some thought, Maihac seated himself at the saloon table and composed a short letter, using the stiff characters of Roum calligraphy:

> To Ardrian of Ramy at his palace Carleone:
>
> Sir:
>
> I regret that I must cause you distress, but it cannot be helped. I am Tawn Maihac; almost twenty years ago I took your daughter Jamiel in marriage. Six years later she was murdered, at Point Extase on the world Camberwell.
>
> The murderer is known to me. He is a Roum of Romarth. I have learned his identity only recently but I am here now to avenge this deed, by one means or another. With me is Jaro, who is Jamiel's surviving son. We wish to speak with you at once, privately, at which time we will deliver certain documents of importance. You will find us waiting near your front entrance.
>
> Tawn Maihac

Jaro and Maihac changed into garments similar to the informal costume of the Roum cavalier. They equipped themselves with appropriate gear, then climbed aboard the flitter, and descended upon Romarth. They landed in the garden of the palace Carleone, where Jamiel had once lived, then sent the flitter aloft by remote control, to hover inconspicuously three hundred feet above the garden.

Maihac went to the front door while Jaro waited in the shadows for a moment, then wandered across the terrace to a marble balustrade. The garden, in the light of the two moons, spread away to a wall of tall trees. As Jaro stood by the balustrade, an eery dreamlike mood came over him: a feeling from his childhood, when he had sometimes glimpsed this garden in half-waking moments. Then it had affected him with a wistful melancholy, suffused with sad-sweet overtones, like the fragrance of heliotrope.

Jaro stood leaning on the balustrade, collecting his thoughts. The mystery of the lost garden was now resolved. Another mystery remained: the woeful groans, which had persisted until the FWG Associates' Dr. Fiori had choked them off. Jaro listened, wondering if echoes of the voice might still reverberate at the back of his brain. He heard only the whisper of wind in the foliage.

Maihac's voice broke into his musing. He turned away from the garden and crossed the terrace. At the door Maihac stood with a gray-haired man of spare physique, with a square face and resolute features. His posture was stiff and his manner formal, as if Maihac were someone he was not happy to see.

Maihac spoke to Jaro: "This is your grandfather, Ardrian of Ramy House."

Jaro bowed politely. "I am happy to meet you, sir."

Ardrian returned a curt nod. "Yes; it is an occasion, to be sure." He turned back to Maihac. "Your appearance here is not a welcome surprise; it stirs memories far better left quiet."

"That is beside the point," said Maihac. "My message must have informed you of our purposes."

Ardrian made a skeptical sound. "The message, to say the least, was hyperbolic."

Maihac grinned. "I know the man who murdered your daughter and your grandchild Garlet. I thought it proper to notify you before approaching the Justiciar. If you prefer, we will disturb you no longer."

Ardrian said gruffly, "You are welcome at my house. Please enter, and I will listen to you with full attention." He stood back. Maihac and Jaro entered an octagonal atrium. Jaro looked about the room in awe. This was magnificence transcending anything of his experience. A high vaulted ceiling was supported by eight attenuated caryatids, which separated the circumference of the room into eight bays. Two of the bays, to right and left, opened into corridors. Another bay embraced the front door; the bay opposite opened into a parlor. The four remaining bays were paneled and painted in moth-wing colors to represent archaic landscapes. Jaro thought that the scenes so depicted had been inspired by folklore, or even memories of Old Earth.

Ardrian ushered his guests into the parlor, which Jaro found as impressive in proportion, richness of material, delicacy of color and detail, as the atrium and far more comfortable on a human scale. At the far end of the room four Seishanee arranged flowers in a large blue ewer, evidently creating a centerpiece for the table. They darted sly sidelong glances at Jaro, and Maihac, their half-smiles suggesting—what? Jaro could not decide. Secret mischief? Serenity? Innocent happiness? As they worked, they murmured together; Jaro wondered what they were saying. They were fascinating to look at, he thought: clean, deft, their features small and regular, their pale hair cut short in a fringe around their heads. To the side stood another Seishanee, wearing splendid green and gray livery. Jaro thought that he must be a Seishanee of advanced years, so different was he from the others. His torso was plump, his legs thin and bird-like, his head heavy, with a high dome of a forehead, a long thin nose hooking over a small heavy mouth and a nubbin of a chin. His manner, unlike that of the other Seishanee, was sedate and a trifle pompous.

Jaro seated himself beside Maihac. Ardrian asked, "May I offer you refreshment?"

"Not just yet," said Maihac. "We have a great deal to tell you. So that we need not repeat ourselves, I suggest that you call the Justiciar and ask him to come here, privately and alone, as soon as possible."

Ardrian smiled grimly. "For a fact, I am taken aback. You appear out of the night in a state of tremulous excitement and insist that I share your emergency. The logic of this evades me."

Maihac said patiently, "The reason for haste is not only logical; it is practical. If the murderer learns that I am here he might try to escape."

"Remote and unlikely," declared Ardrian. "First of all, who is this purported murderer?"

"You know him well. His name is Asrubal of Urd."

Ardrian raised his eyebrows high. "I know Asrubal of Urd; he is a grandee of high place. Your charge is serious."

"Of course."

Ardrian reflected a moment, then said heavily, "It is not for me to judge." He took a telephone disk from the sideboard. "I will do as you wish." He spoke into the disk, listened, spoke again, then put the disk aside. "Justiciar Morlock will arrive shortly. He lives close at hand; we will not have long to wait."

For a time there was silence, broken by the hushed voices of the Seishanee. Ardrian studied his visitors without cordiality, then said, "You have brought me bad news, but I am not surprised. When you took Jamiel off-world, I knew that she would come to a tragic end."

Maihac responded flatly, "You were her father; you loved her as much as I did and you have a right to bitter feelings—but they should be focused not upon me but upon her murderer. He was not an off-worlder; he was a Roum of Romarth."

After a moment Ardrian asked, "Do you intend to describe the circumstances of her death?"

"Certainly. She was killed while I was a captive of the Lok-lor. It has taken me thirteen years to discover where she had been killed and who had killed her. The only witness was Jaro. Unfortunately—or perhaps fortunately—his memory is incomplete." Maihac placed a parcel wrapped in brown paper on the table. "This is the parcel to which I referred. There is a letter inside, addressed to Jaro and written just before Jamiel died. When you read it, you will agree that justice must be done."

Ardrian's face became fractionally less severe. He seemed to give a small internal shrug and, rising to his feet, he went to the sideboard, where, after deliberation, he brought out a number of bottles, flasks and earthenware pots. He called over his shoulder to the portly Seishanee in the green and gray livery. "Fancho! Bring us a few trifles of this and that, if you please."

With stately tread, Fancho left the room. "That is my new major-domo," Ardrian told his guests. "You would not remember him. He is quite efficient, though a bit pompous. I often wonder what goes on in his mind." He returned to his bottles and with intense concentration poured fluids into a green glass carafe.

Pausing in his work, he inquired of Maihac, "Do you recall the art of mixing from your previous visit?"

"I'm afraid not," said Maihac. "Still, I remember that you were considered a master of the craft."

Ardrian showed a faint smile and continued with his mixing. "It is a minor art, to be sure, but one with a surprising range. The potion must accord with the mood of the company, which is sometimes a delicate judgment. But one does what one can." He finished his mixing and returned to his seat. Fancho, the grichkin major-domo wheeled up a service cart laden with oddments of pastry, skewers of toasted meat, pickled fish, crusts in pots of white sauce and pots of black sauce, honey-bulbs and the like. Fancho placed the cart where it was convenient to everyone, then went to the sideboard, poured liquid from the green glass carafe into goblets and served them with a flourish to Maihac, Jaro and Ardrian. "Well done, Fancho," said Ardrian. "Every day you become more expert."

"It is always a pleasure when I can do my work well." Fancho pridefully marched to the far end of the room.

Jaro looked after him with interest. "Is that what happens to Seishanee when they grow old?"

Ardrian seemed amused by the question. "Definitely not. Fancho is a grichkin—a special sort of Seishanee, and very useful too, I'm bound to say."

"I see." Jaro tasted the potion. He found it tart, and tingling, with a dozen fascinating flavors lingering on the palate. Maihac tasted and said, "Apparently you have forgotten nothing."

"Thank you," said Ardrian. "Perhaps I have lost a bit of directional energy, 'verve' if you like, but I may have gained in the shadings and afterthoughts."

Jaro sipped carefully, trying to discover the subtleties which evidently were accessible to the connoisseur. In the end, he gave up the attempt.

Morlock of Sadaj House arrived: a slender man of late middle age, with classically keen features, a scholar's forehead, narrow eyes and an uncompromising mouth. He wore a casual tunic, patterned in green and black diaper and black trousers. Ardrian introduced him to Maihac and Jaro, then poured out and served a goblet of his intricate mixture. Morlock sipped, gave a thoughtful grimace and said, "I make it to be your Toe-clencher Number Two."

"Just so," said Ardrian. "But we must not waste time exchanging compliments. Maihac is in a fury of impatience lest his murderer give him the slip. Am I right, Maihac?"

"Quite right," said Maihac.

Ardrian went on. "Maihac and Jaro have just now arrived and I believe that his spaceship hovers nearby. He tells me that my daughter Jamiel was murdered by Asrubal of Urd, and that he wants to see justice done."

"That is a fair statement," said Maihac. "The facts are unpleasant. When Jamiel and I and our two sons attempted to board the flitter taking us to Flad sixteen years ago, Asrubal and his henchmen ambushed us. We eventually managed to fight free to the flitter. Unaware that Garlet had been snatched from the flitter at the last moment, we took off. As we rose into the air we saw Asrubal with Garlet. He tossed the baby high and let him fall to the rocks below. We could do nothing.

"Asrubal then arranged that the Loklor should meet us at Flad, where they were to slaughter us. Jamiel and Jaro escaped to the spaceship; I was taken and dragged out on the steppe, and forced to dance with their girls. I managed somehow to survive, which seemed to amuse them. They held me captive for three years. During this time Asrubal tracked Jamiel to Point Extase on the world Camberwell. He wanted to recover the material in the parcel which I have just now delivered to Ardrian. Asrubal murdered Jamiel but failed to recover the parcel. Jaro escaped a second time."

Morlock said, "That is not a trivial accusation. How do you explain his crime? In short, what was his motive?"

"Asrubal is a thief. He has been robbing the folk of Romarth for many years. The proof is in this parcel. Asrubal murdered Jamiel to obtain these documents. Read them, but first read the letter Jamiel wrote a few minutes before her death."

Maihac opened the parcel, withdrew the letter, which he put into Ardrian's hands. "This is not pleasant reading."

Ardrian read stony-faced, then passed the letter on to Morlock, who also read. "You are right," said Morlock. "It is not a pleasant letter."

Maihac emptied the parcel of its remaining contents. "At my instruction, Jamiel secured these documents from Aubert Yamb, at the time a clerk for the Lorquin Agency.

"There are five ledgers here. They are, in effect, Yamb's workbooks in which he recorded Lorquin Agency's daily transactions. Notice that Yamb provides prices of all items bought or sold, both imports and exports. You will notice also that the mark-up on imports and commissions charged on exports, is never less than a hundred percent, and is in all cases imposed upon the folk of Romarth, and represents the profit which Asrubal has extracted from Lorquin Agency. In the course of time, it amounts to an extremely large sum. All the while the Roum are either too innocent, too trusting, too careless, or simply too stupid to protest. This is the reason Asrubal, twenty years ago, when I first arrived on Fader, opposed my application for a commercial charter. It is the reason he became my mortal enemy. It is the reason for Jamiel's death."

Morlock studied the ledgers, then passed them on to Ardrian. The two Roum read in silence, while Maihac and Jaro looked on, refreshing themselves with Adrian's Toe-clencher Number Two.

At last Morlock returned the ledgers to Maihac, who slid them back into the buff envelope. Morlock looked at Ardrian. "What is your opinion?"

"We have been victimized."

"I am of the same mind," said Morlock. "Asrubal is a sly thief. He has swindled us, mercilessly. According to Maihac, he is also a murderer—though his guilt may be hard to prove."

"Not necessarily," said Maihac. "When he destroyed my son Garlet, there were six witnesses. They were masked as Assassinators, but no doubt they can be identified."

"Even so, all may claim that they saw nothing."

"No matter," said Maihac. "If Asrubal slides away from justice, I will see that he does not slide very far."

Morlock frowned. "That is extravagant language and it puts me in an uncomfortable position. At Romarth, justice flows from ancient tradition. The advice of an off-worlder carries little weight."

"Let us be realistic," said Maihac. "When the off-worlder's wife and son were killed and he was taken to dance with the Loklor girls, and when the off-worlder returns in a powerful warship and descends to Romarth to inform the Justiciar of many other crimes: all this being the case, I feel that the off-worlder's opinions should be carefully heeded."

"True," said Morlock. "Especially in view of the powerful warship."

"We are reasonable men," said Maihac. "I need only say that if Roum justice is too feeble to cope with these crimes, I shall be disappointed."

"You are not alone," Ardrian told him gruffly. "Do not cry out before you are hurt; it embarrasses us all."

"Sorry," said Maihac.

Morlock smiled faintly. "I think that we understand each other." He picked up the telephone disk, called the Warden of Public Services and issued orders.

3

A platoon of regulators assembled at the north corner of the Gamboye Plaza. Here they were joined by the Justiciar Morlock and Ardrian of Ramy. The company marched north along one of the residential boulevards, and presently arrived at Asrubal's palace Varcial. Maihac and Jaro drifted overhead in the flitter. They observed the regulators deploy around the structure, blocking all routes of escape. The Justiciar, Ardrian of Ramy, the Warden and four officers approached the main entrance and made their presence known. After a pause, Asrubal himself came to the door.

Watching from the flitter, through the macroscope, Jaro looked into Asrubal's face, for the first time since he had seen it staring through the window of the old yellow house at Point Extase. He remembered a face, hard and white as if it had been molded from bone. Looking down, Jaro saw the same face on the man in the doorway. He sat limp as a succession of horrid images swept through his mind. He drew a deep breath. The images receded; his mind was empty.

Maihac looked at him. "What is wrong?"

"Only memories. Now they are gone."

Justiciar Morlock addressed Asrubal. "I have just received information which implicates you in certain crimes. I am obliged to place you in the custody of the regulators. From this instant you are a prisoner under official arrest."

Asrubal uttered a majestic baritone roar. "What nonsense is this? I am a respected grandee of Urd House; I cannot imagine the reason for such persecution!"

Morlock smiled. "Think hard! I am sure you will remember a detail or two of your misdeeds."

"My rashudo is superb! Do you intend to drag me off to Crillinx Jail?"

"Not to Crillinx Jail," said the Justiciar. "It has housed no one for three years and is uninhabitable. You are to be sequestered in your own apartments, which will be made secure and guarded. You may receive no visitors, including friends, family or kinfolk from the House of Urd, excepting only your advocate before the law, whom you may name tomorrow. Now we must submit you to a personal search, and we will inspect and secure your apartments as well."

Several times Asrubal had tried to complain, only to be silenced by the Warden. At last he was allowed to speak. He demanded angrily: "Of what am I accused?"

Justiciar Morlock responded: "You are charged with murder, peculation and fraud."

Asrubal stamped his foot in fury. "No man may impugn my rashudo; only I can make such a judgment!"

"Wrong!" declared Ardrian. "Rashudo is an interplay between yourself and your peers and collapses when contempt displaces approbation."

"Then answer me this: who is my accuser?"

"There are several such persons, including Tawn Maihac, an off-world gentleman; his son Jaro, Ardrian of Ramy and myself, the Justiciar. That is more than sufficient. You are now in the custody of the Warden and the regulators. You will be tried before a special court as soon as possible."

SEVENTEEN

1

Jaro and Maihac returned to Ardrian's palace Carleone, where they were presently joined by the Justiciar Morlock, in company with three high-ranking councillors. Ardrian took his visitors to a conference room paneled in pale green wood and hung with portraits of past Ramy patroons. The company took seats around an oval table, where they were immediately served refreshments by Seishanee footmen under the stately supervision of Fancho the major-domo.

Maihac and Jaro were seated at one end of the table and thereafter ignored by everyone, except Ardrian who tried to include them in the general conversation without success.

After ten minutes of small talk, Morlock made a casual announcement: "The company may be interested to learn that tonight I have placed Asrubal of Urd under house arrest, pending formal trial."

The news provoked a set of startled exclamations. "What are you saying?" "Most extraordinary!" "Are you disporting yourself with a joke, or a farce?"

"I am quite serious," said Morlock. "He is accused of several crimes, including fraud, theft, peculation and murder."

The councillors protested vehemently. "You are clearly the victim of a hoax!" stormed Ferodic of Urd, a tall thin-faced gentleman, with deep eye-sockets and a cadaverous pallor. "Asrubal is my kinsman!"

Crevan of Namary House, protested: "Surely, Morlock! You are acting with intemperate haste!"

Morlock said, "Gentlemen, if you are of a mind, I will explain the scope of the case."

"Please do so! We are on tenterhooks!"

In an unhurried monotone Morlock described his reasons for taking Asrubal into custody. The councillors listened with skepticism.

Esmor of Slayford complained: "At the very least, you have

over-reacted. Could not this little affair have been settled quietly?"

Ardrian stiffened. "You are alluding to the murder of my daughter as a simple 'little affair'?"

"Oh no! Of course not!"

Ferodic waved one of his bony hands. "But we must be logical. The charges have not been substantiated. The whole case may well be a phantasmagorium."

Morlock asked, "You believe, then, that these two off-world gentlemen are malicious lunatics?"

Ferodic glanced toward Maihac and Jaro. "I cannot judge their veracity on such short acquaintance. However, it must be noted that they are off-worlders."

Crevan said peevishly, "As for the Lorquin affair, I cannot understand so grand a foofaraw over a few misplaced sols."

Maihac offered a polite correction: "Asrubal probably stole more than half a million sols—not a trivial sum."

"The accusations have been made and must be investigated," said Morlock. "Tomorrow morning I will ask the councillors to place an indictment against Asrubal. Adjudicators will sit tomorrow afternoon."

"So soon?" cried Ferodic. "This would seem an excess of zeal!"

Morlock said stonily: "I have no taste for this sort of thing. I want to see the end of it as soon as possible."

Ferodic rose to his feet. "I must think about this situation and I will now take my leave."

The other councillors joined him. Ardrian conducted them to the front entrance.

Maihac and Jaro also prepared to depart. Morlock and Ardrian watched as Jaro brought down the flitter. Ardrian asked, "You will be back in the morning?"

"Whenever you say."

"In the morning, then."

2

On the following day Maihac and Jaro once again dropped down to Romarth, along with Skirl. Gaing remained aboard the *Pharsang*, connected by radio with Maihac. At mid-morning Ardrian took the three to the Colloquary, where the full company of councillors had assembled. In their costumes of ancient tradition, they made an impressive spectacle.

So began a process which for the most part the off-worlders found puzzling. After Justiciar Morlock's brief statement to the effect that Asrubal's name had been mentioned in connection with certain serious crimes over a time-frame of several years, and it was probably best that the adjudicators should clarify the case, Ferodic of Urd asked, "And who placed this information?"

"The gentlemen seated yonder."

"Are they not off-worlders, from the far off Gaean Reach?"

"That is so."

"Hmf. Their evidence might well be corrupted by ignorance or superstition."

"Unlikely."

Ferodic continued to grumble, but Morlock seated himself and thereafter took only a passive interest in the proceedings. The councillors exchanged remarks, sometimes irrelevant, sometimes cryptic. From time to time a question might be addressed to Morlock, who responded succinctly. At one point a councillor leaned forward and requested of Skirl that she recount the events of her life. Skirl responded willingly enough. She described Sassoon Ayry at Thanet, and her mother's palace Piri-piri on Marmone. She identified herself as a Clam Muffin, which along with the Quantorsi and the Tattermen, comprised that rarefied group known as the "Sempiternals," where status ceased to be a meaningful word. She found it difficult to relate conditions at Romarth with those of Thanet, since the civilized system of status, ledges of attainment and club membership was unknown at Romarth. Skirl ventured a guess that the state of high rashudo might approximate membership in one of the Squared Circles, or perhaps the Sick Chickens. Living conditions at Thanet were infinitely varied. Most people were employed at the work which interested them the most. Citizens occasionally owned spaceyachts, which cruised the worlds of the Reach in comfort; indeed, she and her companions had traveled to Fader aboard such a spaceyacht, which now hovered three miles above Romarth.

The councillors listened without comment, and finally told Skirl that they had heard enough. Jaro was then asked for a similar account of himself. He described the course of his own life, and stated that he had only recently learned the facts of his parentage. As he spoke the councillors appeared to lose interest. They muttered to each other, consulted notebooks and shifted in their seats. Jaro stopped talking in mid-sentence and went back to his chair. No one seemed to notice. He told Maihac: "It is your turn next."

"I think that they have heard enough," said Maihac. "They are now dealing with the problem of lunch."

"I don't understand this system," Jaro growled.

"That is beside the point. They follow the patterns of tradition, and we must follow behind them."

"But they have asked nothing about Asrubal!"

"They know all they need to know, which is that Morlock has asked that Asrubal be committed to the Adjudicators. At noon they will return this finding and troop off to lunch. That is the way things are done."

"I see."

At noon the councillors rose. The chief councillor intoned, "Asrubal, of Urd House, being accused of heinous offense, is remanded to the judgment of the adjudicators, who will certify who must suffer the penalties: the accused or the accusers."

Jaro turned to Maihac. "What do they mean by that?"

"In our case it is probably hollow talk. By traditional Roum justice, if charges were brought and the accused was found guiltless, then the penalties were inflicted upon the accusers, to teach them not to bear false witness. But it won't happen to us—not with Gaing watching from the *Pharsang*."

"Still, the idea is rather unsettling."

"Yes," said Maihac. "At Romarth this is true of many things."

Ardrian joined the three off-worlders. "That is all for the moment. The adjudicators will sit later today. Meanwhile, I will be pleased if you will join me for lunch. In fact, in the interests both of your convenience and the hospitality which is owed to you, I invite you to take up residence at Carleone."

"Thank you," said Maihac. "I think that I can answer for the others. We will be happy to accept the invitation."

"Very well," said Ardrian. "So it shall be."

3

The five adjudicators met during the afternoon—not at the Colloquary but in the grand hall of Asrubal's palace Varcial, in order that Asrubal should be provided convenient access to the proceedings. The adjudicators sat at the back of a long table, upon which Seishanee had arranged bottles, jugs, trays of pastries, salt fish, candied bird livers and the like, to fortify the law-givers against the rigors of their work. They were men of disparate physiognomy: tall, short, lean, plump, but all displayed the attitudes of high rashudo. The chief adjudicator, known as the Magister, was the oldest of the group, and presented the most distinctive appearance. He sat hunched forward, sharp elbows splayed to either side. A few strands of white hair lay across his scalp; his long ears, drooping eyelids and long thin nose gave him the look of a tired owl. He gazed about the chamber; satisfied that all was in order, he struck a gong and called out: "The Panel of Adjudicators is now in session. Absolute propriety must be observed. Let the prisoner appear!"

A pair of regulators brought out Asrubal and seated him in a massive chair beside the wall.

The Magister again spoke. "This is a court of high justice. Balance and equity prevail. In these precincts neither birth, house, faction or rashudo are recognized. Adjudication is exact. Often we arrive at a verdict before evidence is presented. Emotional demonstrations will not be tolerated. We will now begin. Justiciar Morlock, lay your case before the panel."

Morlock, using a flat voice, described the crimes of which Asrubal was accused. Asrubal listened without change of expression, staring at Morlock with round black eyes.

Morlock completed his preliminary statement and Jaro was called to testify. Morlock, the adjudicators and Barwang, Asrubal's counsel, all put questions, many bearing upon the case at hand, others whose relevance seemed far afield. The Magister enforced no discipline, so that Jaro often was asked two or three questions at once. He marvelled at the informality of the proceedings, even though the adjudicators themselves were sedate and dignified. Perhaps in their vanity they thought to ordain justice with only a fraction of their attention: if such were the case, it was the most consummate arrogance of all. As Jaro told what he knew, they made comments to each other and occasionally interrupted to ask new questions. Jaro carefully restrained his impatience and answered every question in full detail. At times the adjudicators looked to Asrubal as if inviting comment; Asrubal in response sometimes showed a thin smile; occasionally he burst out in sudden wild interjections: "Nonsense, all nonsense, do you hear?" And, "Stuff and bumbleyap!" And, "He is a liar and a scorpion; throw him out!"

Asrubal was represented by his kinsman, Barwang of Urd, a florid gentleman of middle age, fluent of tongue, with large dog-brown eyes, flowing locks of brown hair, a silken mustache, a small paunch which, along with rather large hips, he tried to hide under a loose cape of green and black velvet. He carried himself with a swaggering nonchalance which Jaro found annoying. Barwang wandered restlessly about the hall, occasionally pausing to listen, sometimes leaning over Asrubal to impart a confidential insight, sometimes leaving the hall, to return, listen a moment, then cry out, "Your Dignities! Asrubal and I both have had enough of this sorry farrago! It is an imposition upon my kinsman! Call off this persecution and let us have no more of it."

The adjudicators heard him with grave attention. At last one of them said, "Barwang's remarks have reminded me that it is time to adjourn. The Grandees of Urd have demanded a quick end to the trial, and after all we must not keep Asrubal locked up longer than necessary. We shall meet again one week from today."

The three off-worlders returned to the palace Carleone, where they were shown to their separate apartments. They bathed and were dressed in elegant evening garments by Seishanee servants.

The three gathered in the small parlor and were presently joined by Ardrian, who exercised his artistry in the creation of refreshing tonics. For an hour the group discussed the events of the day. Jaro said that the processes of Roum justice left him baffled.

Ardrian explained: "It is really quite simple. The Panel of Adjudicators sit relaxed. They observe, absorb and assimilate. A melange of information enters their minds, where it is sorted out on a subconscious level until all falls into place and a sure verdict is found."

Skirl asked, "Why did they recess court for a week?"

"Sometimes the adjudicators are a bit capricious. Perhaps they were tired or bored, or perhaps they like to think of themselves as manifestations of natural forces, moving at a relentless rhythm. In any event, you will have a week of free time to explore the beauties of Romarth and its exciting society. Remember, it is dangerous to venture into abandoned palaces alone, since the white house-ghouls are unpredictable and often will spring out upon you without warning. Even with an escort, you are not entirely safe." He rose to his feet. "Now we will go into the dining room. Tonight you will meet some of my friends and kinsmen. They will not know how properly to comport themselves. Deal with them patiently and if they behave in a style which seems peculiar, show no surprise."

"I will be cautious," said Jaro. "I can't speak for Skirl, of course. She is a Clam Muffin, and doesn't associate with everyone. Perhaps you should warn your kinsmen."

Ardrian looked at Skirl doubtfully. "She appears quite serene at this moment. In fact, she does not fit the usual concept of an off-worlder."

"Nevertheless, she is real and very much alive."

"Extremely alive," said Skirl.

The evening passed without untoward incident. The Roum seemed curious as to how life was lived among the outer worlds.

"Everywhere it is different," said Maihac. "The IPCC maintains a uniformity of basic law, so that a traveler will never be flogged for blowing his nose in public. Still, there is enough variety to make travel interesting."

"A pity it is so expensive," said a young woman.

Jaro said, "If Asrubal of Urd were not such a thief, you might have enough money to travel in style."

Broy, a cavalier of the House of Carraw, said stiffly, "Your remarks are tantamount to slander. Asrubal is a grandee of high rashudo. It is not fitting that an off-worlder should use such language!"

"Sorry," said Jaro. "I did not intend to offend you."

There was silence around the table. At last Broy gave a stiff nod. "I am not offended; that is another impertinence! I merely indicate to you the need for keeping a respectful tongue in your head."

"I shall do my best," said Jaro meekly. He noticed that both Maihac and Ardrian were smiling quietly. Skirl looked from Jaro to Broy in scorn and disbelief, but managed to hold her tongue. The occasion proceeded, but no longer as informally as before.

Later Ardrian told Jaro and Skirl, "You behaved correctly, exactly as I wished. Broy of Carraw is a sultry young popinjay. He also has connections among the Urd clan, and thought to strike a grandiose posture at your expense. You need not be concerned; it means nothing."

"I was not concerned," said Jaro. "I was more amused than otherwise. He is no threat to me."

"Don't be too sure! He has an uncertain temper and he is an expert swordsman."

"I'll do my best not to provoke him."

On the following day Jaro and Skirl were taken to view the abandoned palace Somar, seat of the long-extinct Soumarjian Sept. They were escorted by a pair of Ramy cavaliers and two others of Immir House. In awe Jaro and Skirl moved through the silence of the dim halls. In a library Skirl paused to examine the books which crowded the shelves. They were ponderous and thick, with covers of carved board and pages alternating text and hand-wrought illumination.

Roblay of Immir, who seemed to take a special interest in Skirl, stayed with her while the others went on into the grand salon. He explained the books. "At one time everyone kept a personal record in books of this sort. Each of these books tells the story of someone's life. The books are more than diaries; they are works of artful beauty, mingled with passages of poetry and intimate revelation, which the chronicler could note without embarrassment, since only after death might anyone look in his book. Picture pages were created in loving detail, using the most delightful harmonies of color, sometimes striking, sometimes subdued and misty. The costumes of course are archaic, but if you read the text, the folk in the pictures come to life, and march through the pages in their glories and defeats. The drawing, as you can see, is fluid and flexible, and matches the personality of the chronicler. Sometimes the pictures are innocent, as if seen through the eyes of a child; sometimes they are quietly passionate. It is often said that the books express the chronicler's wish to live forever. The folk believed, perhaps seriously, that they imparted the essence of themselves into their books, and that the books by some means would clasp time and make it a static thing, so that the person who created the book would forever be alive, half dreaming his way back and forth through the pages he had created so lovingly." Roblay grimaced. "I must say that we treat the books with reverence, when sometimes we visit one or another of the old palaces."

"And how old are the books?"

"The fashion came into vogue about three thousand years ago and continued for a thousand years or more. Suddenly, the fashion died out, and now no one would think of dedicating so much toil to a book."

"It is better than dedicating your life to nothing."

"Yes," said Roblay thoughtfully. "I am sure you are right." He took the book from Skirl and idly turned through the pages, pausing from time to time to study one of the exquisite decorations. "They were folk much like ourselves, of course, but it is amusing to see the quaint old costumes and try to feel the flow of their lives. They were a happier folk, or so it seems. Today there is weariness abroad. Romarth is decaying and can never be what it once was." He put the book back on the shelf. "I seldom look at these books. They put me in a dreary mood and afterward I gloom for days on end."

"Too bad," said Skirl. "If I were you, I would go out and explore the real worlds of the Reach, and perhaps find a congenial occupation."

Roblay smiled wistfully. "That means I might be forced to labor incessantly for food and shelter."

"It might turn out like that."

"At Romarth I neither toil nor labor. I live in a palace and dine very nicely. The contrast is hard to ignore."

Skirl laughed. "You live a sheltered life, like an oyster secure in its shell."

Roblay raised his eyebrows. "You would not say so if you knew me better! I have fought four duels and twice I have gone out to hunt house-ghouls. I am a captain of the Dragoons, but enough of me! Let us talk of you. For instance, and a very important question: Are you bonded to anyone?"

Skirl looked at him sidelong. "I am not sure that I understand you,"—though she did very well. Roblay was gallant and charming, and there was no harm in a bit of flirtation. In essence, so she explained to herself, she was studying the sociology of the Roum cavaliers.

"What I mean is this." For an instant Roblay touched her shoulder. "Are you free to make decisions, without accountability?"

"Of course! I direct my own affairs."

Roblay smiled. "You are an off-worlder; still you exercise a most curious appeal which I hardly know how to describe."

"I am exotic," said Skirl. "I reek with the tantalizing mystery of the unknown." The two smiled at each other. Roblay started to respond, but stopped short and jerked his head around to stare at the bookcases. Skirl thought to hear a furtive sound. She looked over her shoulder and around the room, at the same time drawing the hand-gun which Maihac insisted that she carry. There was nothing to be seen. In a husky half-whisper she asked, "What was that?"

Roblay, still staring this way and that, said, "Sometimes there are secret passages behind the walls—perhaps here as well, although Somar is supposed to be a safe house. Nothing is ever certain, of course. The house-ghouls like to spy; then, if the mood is on them, they reach out for someone who has not noticed them. They are unnerving beasts. Come; let us join the others."

On the following day Jaro and Maihac were summoned to the Colloquary to consult with Morlock and a pair of councillors, which, according to Ardrian, meant that the adjudicators were taking the charges against Asrubal seriously. Skirl, at loose ends, went out to wander the boulevards of Romarth. She finally came to rest at a cafe on the edge of Gamboye Plaza. Here she was joined by Roblay of Immir. "I saw you sitting alone," he told her. "I decided to join you and continue our conversation, which was interrupted by a creak in the woodwork."

"It was more than a creak," said Skirl. "It was a house-ghoul, deciding whether we'd be good to eat."

Roblay gave an uncomfortable chuckle. "So it might have been—though I don't like to think of it. We have always felt secure in Somar, since it is well into the near neighborhood."

"Why don't you exterminate the creatures once and for all? If this were Gallingale, there would be no house-ghouls in our basements."

"We have set out on these expeditions a hundred times. When we venture into the crypts, we become vulnerable and they play awful tricks upon us, so that we become too sickened to proceed."

"Something else which puzzles me is the Foundance. Tell me: how does it function?"

Roblay gave an uncomfortable grimace. "It is something no one wishes to talk about; in fact, it is off the edge of polite conversation, and in very poor taste to so much as notice the place."

"I don't mind a bit of vulgarity. Can we visit it and see for ourselves what goes on?"

Roblay seemed surprised. He looked toward the green-domed structure beside the river. "I have never thought to do so. I suppose there is nothing to stop us; the entrance ramp gives directly upon the Esplanade, for convenience."

"What sort of convenience? Tell me. You have hinted of what you know and I am curious."

"Very well. To start, I should say that one of every two hundred Seishanee is a sport; as he grows, he becomes something other than the usual Seishanee, and is known as a grichkin. He is ugly and squat, with a bald head, pointed on top, a long nose hanging over a little mouth and a trifle of chin. Most important of all, he is intelligent enough to think, to execute complex orders and to supervise the ordinary Seishanee. Every household employs grichkins as major-domos. The grichkins, so I believe, control the processes in the Foundance without interference from the Roum, who want nothing to do with the place. The grichkins take care of all the unpleasant household details. When a Seishanee servant reaches a certain age, he becomes careless and slothful; his skin turns yellow and his hair falls out; meanwhile, he becomes fat as a grape. In the early hours, when none of the Roum are abroad, the grichkins take the used Seishanee to the Foundance and slide him into the corpse bin, where he is processed and mixed into the slurry. When a Roum dies, we pretend that he is transported to a wonderful city among the clouds. This is the fable we tell our children when they ask what has happened to a relative who is suddenly gone. The truth is that the grichkins carry the corpse to the Foundance and slide him into the bin, and he joins the slurry." Roblay laughed without humor. "So now you know as much as I do. If you wanted to inspect the processes at close hand, no one would stop you and the way is open, but you would not like what you saw."

"Would I also be mixed into the slurry?"

"I think not. You would be ignored. The grichkins are mild and respectful, like the other Seishanee. Do you still want to visit the Foundance? I am told that the smell is not at all nice."

Skirl looked toward the heavy structure beside the Skein. "I may want to go another time—but not now."

"That is sound thinking, especially since I have plans which you will find far more interesting." Roblay took off his hat and put it aside. "Do you care to listen?"

Skirl was amused. "I have nothing better to do."

"Good! I will therefore assume that you are in a receptive mood."

"At the very least, I am listening."

Roblay nodded gravely, as if Skirl had uttered an aphorism of great profundity. "I will approach the matter indirectly. You are aware that the Roum way of life is different from all others."

"Yes," said Skirl. "I have noticed."

"What you cannot know is that our aesthetic perceptions are extremely sensitive. It is expected of us from birth; we grow into these capacities, so that we use every part of our mind in full flexibility. Some of us are telepaths; others command as many as nine distinct sensory perceptions, so that our consciousness is enhanced to a corresponding degree. I myself have attained a relatively high level of sensitivity, and I would like to share some of these insights with you."

Skirl smilingly shook her head. "Don't bother. You would be using words I would not understand."

"Ah, but the demonstration takes us far beyond talking! Naturally, you must be responsive and eager for exploration. What do you say to that?"

"I say that I want the program explained in greater detail."

"Of course! Come; we will go to my apartment."

"And then what?"

Roblay charged his voice with enthusiasm. "Our goal is to modulate the instants of existence as an impresario controls the musicians of his orchestra. Now then: do you believe me?"

"Of course! What happens first? Please explain, step by step."

Now a trifle sulky, Roblay said, "As we enter the apartment, each of us lights a ceremonial candle and each inhales the scent arising from the other's flame. This is a ritual of great antiquity and it symbolizes conjunction of the spirit at a certain level, which I will not define, since it takes us into the realm of mysticism. For the purposes of actuality, we carry the candles into my gray and lilac chamber and place them on the sideboard, to either side of my sacramental tourmaline, which is three feet high and a thing of great beauty. As we contemplate the shift of shades and lights, my servants disrobe us, so deftly that you never feel their hands. Next we are sprayed head to toe with a crust. For you the color shall be pistachio green; I will appear in a different tint and a different flavor. Next, we call for our masks."

Skirl was mildly puzzled. "Masks? Don't we know each other?"

"The masks are essential. They muffle the stirring of old doxologies. When the mask conceals your face, you will feel an airy floating sensation. Our outer selves are gone; we have become symbols.

"The servants will now arrange you on a table, where I chart a grid of half-inch squares upon your body, conforming to every curve and channel, all the nooks and swellings. Using the grid and a pulsing wand, I discover the sensitive zones of your personal surface. These are printed in color upon a large chart, which you will take away with you. It makes a splendid wall decoration, which your friends will admire.

"Now we delicately decrust each other, which is always amusing, and perhaps attempt a few erotic techniques, some orthodox, some novel, as the mood happens to overtake us. When fatigue arrives, the servants lift us upon membranes, carry us to a pool and lower us gently into warm water. As we float the water is activated, producing surges of turbulent bubbles. The effect is unusual, like felt music. The crust is now dissolved. The masks are removed and we are once more ourselves.

"The servants lift us from this languid pool on the membranes and carry us to another pool, where they place us on a slide. Down the slide we hurtle, into a pool of water colder than the coldest ice. There we float, enjoying the tingling of each dermal nerve. Finally, when we have exhausted the pleasures of the water, the servants remove us to a dais, where they stroke us with soft towels and dress us in costumes of white linen.

"It is now time to dine. By the light of the ceremonial candles the repast is served, and when the candles gutter and die, the occasion is at an end." Roblay rose to his feet. "So—what do you think?"

Skirl considered a moment. "It sounds very inventive, also just a bit strenuous."

"Not really," said Roblay. "Once you are masked, you become quite relaxed." He reached out to take her arm. "Come! Immir Palace is close at hand."

Skirl shook her head. "It's nice of you to ask, but even with the mask I don't think I would like someone charting my zones. Still, you've helped me understand some of the Roum traditions, and now I think I know why the Roum birth rate is so low." Skirl stood up, and backed away from Roblay's attempt to clasp her. "Please excuse me; now I must return to Carleone."

EIGHTEEN

1

Two days later Ardrian announced that a formal banquet was in prospect at Ramy Palace, residence of Kasselbrock, Patriarch of the Ramy Sept. Kasselbrock's invitation had included not only Ardrian and his kin, but also his three off-world guests.

"You may or may not enjoy the evening," Ardrian told them. "There will be ceremonies which you will not understand and formal conduct is a necessity. If you choose to participate, the servants will dress you in proper costumes, and I will ask my nephew Alonso to instruct you, at least to some small degree, in the elements of formal etiquette. Everything considered, I think you will profit by the experience, and you will be forgiven any small gaffes."

"It sounds delightful," said Skirl. "I am not concerned for my manners; my father, a Clam Muffin like myself, was something of a martinet. At an early age I learned gentility in all its phases. What is good enough for Sassoon Ayry is good enough for Ramy Palace."

Ardrian smiled grimly. "I see that my concern lacks basis, at least in your case. Tawn Maihac has learned from his previous experience, but Jaro is an unknown quantity."

"I will watch Skirl closely," said Jaro. "She will advise me if my conduct verges into the coarse and brutal. Still, I suspect that both Skirl and I will profit from any refinements your nephew sees fit to suggest."

Ardrian nodded. "So it shall be."

During the morning Jaro and Skirl wandered down the Esplanade, past the Gamboye Plaza. Ahead of them the brown Foundance huddled over the water, showing a high row of small windows and three flat domes of green glass. Jaro and Skirl approached. They halted, to gaze in something like awe at the ugly bulk of the structure. From the Esplanade a ramp led to a squat archway opening through the heavy walls. Within a wide hall could be glimpsed a partition, half glass, half concrete, at the left-hand side. For a time the two stood looking at the building. Jaro pointed to the ramp. "The way is open; do you want to look inside?"

Skirl hesitated. "I think not. I might see something I don't care to see. Also, I'm told that it smells bad."

"I'm not all that curious," said Jaro. "All across the Gaean Reach are things I don't care to know. This may well be first on the list."

Skirl said, "After some research you could write a book entitled: 'Things I Wish I Didn't Know,' or perhaps, 'Sights I Wish I Had Never Seen.' "

"Hmf." Jaro reflected. "I'd rather write a book called 'Things I like about Skirlet Hutsenreiter.' "

Skirl took hold of his arm. "How can I ever be vexed with you when you say nice things like that?"

Jaro grinned down at her. "I thought you regarded me as perfect."

"Close—but not quite."

"So where am I deficient?"

"You don't always obey me. And you want to wander around the Reach forever."

"And you don't?"

"Believe it or not; I'm sometimes homesick for Thanet."

Jaro laughed. "Sometimes I am too, when I think of Merriehew, but not seriously."

"Would you ever want to live there again?"

Jaro considered. "I don't think so. I'd be very restless."

"I could get you into the Clam Muffins," said Skirl thoughtfully.

"That would be nice. But both Sassoon Ayry and Merriehew are gone. Meanwhile, we have the *Pharsang* for a home, and there's the whole Reach to explore."

"True," said Skirl. And musingly: "Worlds without number."

Jaro turned her a glance of puzzled speculation, but made no comment. The two returned along the Esplanade, across Gamboye Plaza and back to Carleone Palace.

The time was mid-afternoon. Jaro and Skirl retired to their apartments, and with the help of Seishanee servants prepared for the banquet.

Ardrian escorted the three off-worlders to the Ramy Palace early, and for an hour ushered them through the magnificent halls and chambers, which were alive with light, color and the stir of human presence, where the corresponding places at abandoned Somar, no less magnificent, were drab and dull. Seishanee moved quietly through the shadows: slight supple creatures with pale skins and taffy-blond hair fringing their foreheads. A pair of pages stood flanking the base of the grand staircase. They appeared to be female, wore the uniforms of ancient guardsmen, and stood stiff and rigid, their hair caught up into peaks above their heads like candle flames. Each gripped the haft of a slender lance fifteen feet tall. They stood without so much as the twitch of an eyelid while the group passed in front of them.

Jaro noticed a low arch at the back of the stairs. It opened upon a flight of stone steps descending into the dark. In response to his question, Ardrian said, "There are crypts below all the palaces. They are used for storage and the aging of wine. Below are more sinister places as well: dungeons, if you like, now for the most part blocked off against the house-ghouls. They date back to what we call the Bad Times, when for a hundred years the houses made sly secret war upon enemy houses. It was a terrible era, of hate and revenge, of gruesome plots and awful deeds, of murder in the gardens, of kidnap and imprisonment forever in one of the deep dungeons. Some of the septs were destroyed to the last man, and only the abandoned palaces remain. Do not bring the subject into your conversation; it is considered bad form. In fact, I suggest that you volunteer no opinions, unless so required. If questions are put to you, answer as briefly and mildly as possible. I think that you will understand the logic behind this program."

The three off-worlders were introduced to their host, who seated them at the foot of the oblong table. Sixteen other guests took their places and Seishanee footmen served the first courses.

The banquet proceeded. Jaro and Skirl modeled their conduct upon that of other guests and apparently committed no egregious blunders. As Ardrian had recommended, they spoke little, drank sparingly and held both arms and elbows demurely close to their bodies. They found the cuisine palatable, if flavored with unfamiliar condiments. The company comprised gentlemen and ladies, of obvious respectability and rashudo. Skirl and Jaro encountered impersonal courtesy, but little cordiality. Halfway through the banquet, a plum-cheeked gentleman with a ruff of white hair and a small white goatee, having consumed considerable wine, addressed Skirl in a rather waggish manner, "You are enjoying the banquet?"

"Yes, of course!"

"Good! Enjoy yourself while you have the opportunity. A banquet such as this must be unique to your experience."

"To some extent," said Skirl. "The palace is magnificent. My own home, Sassoon Ayry, is not nearly so grand, but not by the choice of my father, who lost all our money through foolish speculation. Grandeur like that of Ramy Palace is impossible without money, since workers must be paid high wages and slavery is illegal everywhere across the Gaean Reach."

"Aha!" said the gentleman. "You miss the point! The Seishanee are not slaves; they are, simply, Seishanee. Our way is much the better way."

Skirl agreed that the gentleman undoubtedly knew best. She ate a crystallized flower petal, and the banquet proceeded.

The next morning Ardrian reported that the Adjudicators, responding to pressure from Urd House, would sit during the afternoon. The Urd grandees felt that Asrubal was suffering inconvenience by reason of irresponsible accusations and desired that all restrictions upon his freedom be lifted at once.

The Adjudicators convened as before, in the Grand Hall of the palace Varcial, which was scarcely less sumptuous than Ramy Palace. As before, Asrubal was brought out by the Regulators and conducted to the massive chair beside the wall. As before, Asrubal sat stiff and still, his bone-white face blank of expression. From time to time he fixed his round black eyes upon Jaro, to cause a curious squirming sensation in Jaro's viscera. If he closed his eyes the frightening old images appeared.

The Panel, after muttered interchanges, began its deliberations. Asrubal's counsel, Barwang of Urd, addressed the Panel: "Honorable sirs, I request that my kinsman Asrubal be discharged at once from this absurd situation. What we are seeing is an outlandish farce, hanging upon purported wrongs done to an off-world huckster. And how does he support these claims? By proudly calling upon his son, who has admittedly suffered brain damage. All of us have noticed his blinking and sniffing and his vacuous expression. He is obviously neither reliable nor alert. This trial cannot be taken seriously. Asrubal is guilty of nothing whatever; still he is excoriated for non-existent crimes! I ask you, is this the justice of Romarth?"

The Magister held up his hand. "To what crimes do you refer? Asrubal has been charged with misconduct of several categories."

"For a start," said Barwang, "I will deal with the charges of the first category." He read from a sheet of paper. "They include swindling, fraud, larceny, peculation, treachery, inveiglement, collusion and betrayal of trust." Barwang rapped the paper with the back of his hand. "All bunkum, of course. Even if true, the charges should be dismissed, so that we might expeditiously resume our ordinary pursuits."

After a glance toward Jaro, Barwang continued. "The allegations are based upon nearly illegible records kept slap-dash by—"

"One moment," said Morlock, Tawn Maihac's counsel. "The ledgers are totally readable. They were meticulously maintained by a painfully honest clerk."

Barwang bowed politely. "That, sir is a matter of opinion. The clerk is a well-known mooncalf, lacking the acumen which distinguishes Asrubal and which has guided his expert financial policies."

"So stipulated," said Morlock, "it goes to explain why Asrubal commands vast wealth and Yamb lives in poverty."

"Irrelevant, in all respects," said Barwang. "Asrubal has better things to do than to haggle over every tin of pickled fish. That is work for the pettifoggers, a term which will never be applied to my intrepid kinsman!" He turned to Asrubal. "Am I right, sir?"

"You are right!"

Morlock asked, "And is that your defense? The fact that Asrubal is not a pettifogger?"

"Of course not!" declared Barwang. "I was merely claiming the attention of the court. Our defense is simple. Asrubal cannot be convicted on grounds of larceny or peculation! Why not? Because such offenses are not cited in the criminal Code. How can this be? Simple enough. Over the centuries such offenses were unknown at Romarth. On this basis I assert that Asrubal has been charged with nonexistent crimes. I therefore ask that the charges be dismissed and Asrubal be awarded punitive damages."

"Not so fast," declared the Magister. "The Code is not encased in steel. We all know the nature of these crimes. Your arguments are disingenuous. To amend the Code will require at most ten minutes, and we will make the new statute a century retroactive, which surely will encompass the worst of Asrubal's crimes."

For a time Barwang stood disconsolate; then he said, "Sirs, it appears that Asrubal might have been a bit careless, preoccupied by his visionary schemes. I believe that the Panel in its wisdom should dismiss Asrubal with a caution, and perhaps a word or two of advice. Then no more need be said of these rather trivial faults."

The Magister said, "Your recommendation is noted. Tomorrow we will render a verdict and take up the subject of the murders. This is swift justice indeed, but the grandees of Urd House have asked for such despatch, and if it means the early conviction and execution of Asrubal, they have only themselves to blame. That is all for today. We will reconvene tomorrow at the same time."

On the following day Ardrian and his guests arrived early at the grand hall in Varcial Palace and took their places. At the appointed hour the Regulators brought Asrubal into the room and seated him in the chair by the wall. Barwang joined him, and the two spoke in murmurs.

Finally, ten minutes late, the Adjudicators appeared and settled themselves behind the table. The Magister called the session to order. "In the case of Asrubal, we cannot find him guilty of peculation or larceny, because the Roum never commit such crimes—until the advent of Asrubal, of course. But no matter; Asrubal has committed crimes against the public welfare, and so we find him guilty of baneful conduct. No, Barwang, we do not care to hear your outcries. Asrubal, we now proceed to your sentence. Please state the totality of your financial holdings."

Asrubal's face became even more stern and pinched than before. "That is my private business. I do not care to divulge these facts to anyone."

Barwang leaned close to Asrubal and spoke urgently. Asrubal's thin mouth sagged. He said, "I am advised that candor is my only option."

"Excellent advice."

Asrubal raised his eyes and stared thoughtfully at the ceiling. "I have on hand, here at Romarth, about two thousand sols. At Lorquin Agency I maintain a fund of about five thousand sols, for emergency expenses. At the Natural Bank of Loorie, I keep my basic balance, like all the others of Romarth. It amounts, so I suppose, to perhaps twenty or thirty thousand sols."

"Is that all?" asked the Magister.

"I may have some small accounts elsewhere of more or less negligible value."

"Just so. Which are the 'more negligible' and which are the 'less negligible'? Please explain in detail."

Asrubal made a gesture which was almost coy. "I can't remember the exact amounts. I am not a mercenary man."

"You have a list of these holdings?"

"Yes, I should think so."

"Where is this list?"

"It is in the security box in my private study."

The Magister addressed the Regulators. "Take Asrubal to his study, allow him to open his security box, then draw him aside. Bring the contents of the box here, at once. No, Barwang of Urd; you will remain here."

The Regulators pulled Asrubal to his feet. "Come."

A few moments later the Regulators returned with the contents of Asrubal's security box. The Adjudicators studied them for several minutes. Then they looked at Asrubal in something like awe. Asrubal's pinched white face remained expressionless.

The Magister said, "This is all very interesting. Your financial irregularities take on a new dimension. There are five accounts, in as many banks. These 'more or less negligible' funds appear to total over a million sols. The Lorquin Agency has been amazingly profitable."

"That is not all Lorquin money," Asrubal stated. "I made some fortunate investments."

"What were you planning to do with all this money?"

"I have not made firm plans."

The Magister chuckled. "Whatever they were, you might as well dismiss them. The money is confiscated. Further, you will no longer manage the Lorquin Agency. There will be other penalties, as well, depending upon the outcome of the more serious charges against you: to wit, that you attempted the murder of Tawn Maihac, that you murdered the child of Tawn and Jamiel Maihac, and the murder of Jamiel Maihac herself. How do you respond to these charges?"

"They are bold, reckless and nuncupatory nonsense. I have murdered no one."

The Magister said, "Asrubal, your response is so noted. And now," he looked to Justiciar Morlock, "you may present your case."

Morlock came forward. He gestured toward Maihac. "There sits Tawn Maihac, an off-world trader. Twenty years ago he came to Romarth, hoping to bypass Lorquin Agency and trade directly with the Roum, through a system that would facilitate trade and produce wealth for everyone concerned, not just Asrubal. Urd House naturally resisted his proposals, since it would end Asrubal's monopoly.

"After two years of litigation, Maihac secured permission to bring a cargo of tools here, to be sold to the civic bursar, and for distribution to the Seishanee. Maihac's price was a third of that quoted by Lorquin Agency. Asrubal was outraged by the program. To protect his interests he plotted a dastardly deed. When Maihac and Jamiel with their two children, Garlet and Jaro, tried to leave Romarth aboard a flitter, Asrubal brought a gang of Urd cavaliers masked as Assassinators. These persons have been identified and will testify, if need be.

"Responding to Asrubal's orders, this cowardly gang attacked

Maihac's flitter and attempted to seize Jamiel and her children. After a struggle, Maihac and Jamiel escaped, only to find that one of their children, Garlet, had been snatched from the flitter. As they watched in horror, Asrubal dashed the child to its death upon the rocks, after which he threw the corpse into the river.

"Maihac was horrified, but he had no other choice than to take Jamiel and Jaro to Flad, where they intended to take passage aboard the *Liliom* to Loorie. Asrubal forestalled him. He sent a radio message to Arsloe, the machinist at Flad, who arranged that a group of Loklor should attack Maihac and his family upon their arrival. The Loklor captured Maihac; Jamiel and Jaro escaped.

"Maihac survived for three years, and finally was left for dead after fighting a house-ghoul.

"During this time Asrubal tracked Jamiel to Point Extase on Camberwell, and there killed her. Jaro was six years old at the time. He remembers the coming of Asrubal to their residence on the outskirts of Point Extase. At his mother's command, he ran to the river and escaped in a boat.

"To sum up: Asrubal is guilty of two murders and the attempted murder of Maihac.

"Now then: how do I prove these assertions? I need only prove a single murder in order to secure the verdict of 'Guilty'; luckily, this is simple and straightforward. Maihac, six Urd cavaliers and a pair of Ratigo women directly witnessed the murder of the child Garlet. Their testimony will prove my case. As for the other two crimes, the evidence is circumstantial and indirect. Arsloe, the technician who arranged Maihac's capture by the Loklor, departed Flad many years ago, and his whereabouts is unknown. Nevertheless, Asrubal's guilt is a certainty. As to the murder of Jamiel, the evidence is real. Jaro saw him approach the house at Point Extase and look through the window. On this point his memory is absolutely clear. Later, Jamiel was discovered dead, her head battered to fragments. Asrubal ransacked the house, searching for the incriminating ledgers which Jamiel had obtained from Aubert Yamb at Loorie. Asrubal was also anxious to recover a bank draught of three hundred thousand sols which had been in Jamiel's possession. He found nothing and decided that the documents must be in the possession of Jaro. Asrubal notified Terman of Urd that Jamiel was dead and that Jaro was missing. Asrubal could not know of these facts unless he had been in intimate proximity to the murder. He ordered Terman to locate Jaro, and Terman finally traced the missing boy to Thanet on Gallingale.

"That, gentlemen, is my case. I ask a verdict against Asrubal immediately and without further delay." Morlock returned to his place.

The Adjudicators conferred for a moment in low tones; then all turned to inspect Asrubal, who sat leaning back in the massive chair, his expression sardonic and imperturbable.

Barwang strolled forward. "Morlock's arguments are nuncupatory. I will now demolish his case."

The Magister said testily, "Not so fast, Barwang of Urd! Asrubal sits yonder; let him do his own talking."

Barwang's face fell. "As you wish, sir." He hunched, discomfited, back to his seat.

The Magister spoke to Asrubal: "Sir, you have heard Morlock's cogent accusation. What is your response?"

Asrubal smiled thinly. "You have stripped me of my property but you shall not so easily snatch away my life. The charges are false. I have done no murdering. Bring on your witnesses, by the tens and the hundreds, and, if need be, by the thousands. The sum of one million zeros never exceeds zero. Guilt can never be proved when there is none to prove."

"All very well," said the Magister. "How do you account for the circumstances? Remember: even a dead child is considered a corpse."

"Bah! It is all a mistake. When the off-worlder thought to leave Romarth on the sly, I went with some friends to dissuade him. We intended a peaceful demonstration, but some mad women wearing Ratigo masks interfered, and tried to take the two children."

"Why should they do this?"

Asrubal smiled. "Who can know the mind of a Ratigo woman? Their creed is something called 'The Doctrine of Improbability.' It was a random act."

The Magister studied Asrubal, then asked abruptly, "If the act were random, why did they bring a pair of dummies to the scene?"

Asrubal's smile was as bland as before. "I am a logical man. The Ratigo doctrines are beyond my understanding."

"So that their appearance came as a startling surprise?"

"Of course."

"I see. Proceed with your account, if you will."

"There is little to tell. While Maihac and Jamiel were watching my little demonstration, the women took one of the children and left a dummy in its place, then attempted to seize the other. After a short struggle, Jamiel retrieved the second child, whereupon Maihac took the flitter into the air and the two departed, evidently assured that they carried both children.

"I saw the doing of the deed, and thought to recall the fugitives, so that they might retrieve their child. To attract Maihac's attention, I threw the second dummy high into the air; the child was of course safe and taken to a place of security, perhaps by the mad women. That was the end of it. Call your witnesses; they will corroborate my statement. The off-worlder continued to Flad, where the Loklor captured him. My complicity is pure speculation and can not be proved. Only Arsloe could supply valid testimony and he is ten years gone from Fader. It is slander to voice such charges when not an ounce of evidence can be provided!"

"The point is well taken," the Magister admitted. "Let us go on to other phases of the case."

Asrubal made a rather condescending gesture. "As for the murder of Jamiel of Ramy, again I must refute a tissue of lies. It is not right that so much scurrility and inconvenience should be visited upon me."

"Do not complain!" said the Magister. "The Panel allows you opportunity for rebuttal. In less wholesome communities, you would probably be hanged out of hand."

Asrubal made a contemptuous sound, then said, "I will take very little of the Panel's time. I traced Jamiel of Ramy to Camberwell in order to recover stolen documents. She resided in a small house on the outskirts of Point Extase. I went to this place, intending to ask for the purloined documents, which could be used to embarrass me. I intended to offer her a generous sum for their return. I went in company with Edel of Urd, a person of unassailable honor and rashudo. Together we arrived at the house of Jamiel. The time was sunset. Edel went to inspect the premises at the back of the house, while I waited at the fence. I saw the boy staring at me through the front window, so I knew Jamiel was at home. When Edel returned, we approached the house. I looked through the window. Again I saw the boy. Then I moved away and went to join Edel at the side of the house. We conferred for several moments, then we entered the house, to find that grisly deeds had been done. On the floor lay Jamiel, her head shattered. The boy was gone. I sent Edel to find the boy while I started to look for the ledgers. I found nothing. Edel returned and reported that the boy had apparently gone off in a boat. We went to look for him, but evening had come and we could see nothing distinctly. I concluded that the boy had taken the ledgers and the bank draught. Who had killed Jamiel? We had no clue then, nor do we now."

Barwang strode forward to address the Panel. "Your Honors, Edel of Urd sits yonder. As you must know, he is a respected gentleman of high rashudo; I call upon him now to testify as to his recollection of this terrible event."

Barwang signaled, and a middle-aged gentleman came forward. Barwang welcomed him with a slight bow. "Edel, you have heard the testimony of Asrubal. Can you inform the panel as to the truth or falsity of Asrubal's statement?"

Edel addressed the panel in a forthright manner. "Asrubal spoke the truth, in every detail."

"Did Asrubal kill Jamiel of Ramy?"

"That would have been impossible. He did not kill Jamiel, nor did I."

"Who, then, in your opinion performed the deed?"

Edel shrugged. "The culprit might have been a river bandit, or a thwarted lover, or perhaps a roving madman. The only witness would have been the boy, and he was gone."

"Thank you, Edel. That is all." Edel went back to his seat.

Asrubal continued his statement. "As I mentioned, Terman learned that the boy had been rescued by a pair of anthropologists and taken to Thanet on Gallingale.

"I was still anxious to recover the stolen ledgers. I sent Terman to Thanet where he made a careful investigation. He searched the house where the boy lived, but found nothing. While he was making his inquiries, Terman learned that the boy lacked all memory of the years prior to his arrival at Thanet. His classmates considered him timid and somewhat retarded, and used the word 'nimp' to describe him. Almost certainly he knew nothing of the missing ledgers. I abandoned interest in the boy, and never troubled him in any way. As I stated, I am not the murderer of Jamiel, nor of anyone else."

Again Barwang came forward. "It is now clear that the case against Asrubal is a mare's nest. Morlock's charges are no more than flatulence, of a particularly purulent sort. The panel must now dismiss these charges, since none can be proved, and we will expect Morlock to render a polite but explicit apology."

The Magister seemed to be amused. He said, "I am the Chief

Adjudicator; I am the conscience of Romarth. I perceive that evil deeds have been done; that, either by luck or by adroit design, the criminal has slid away from the consequences."

Barwang sprang to his feet. "Slander!" he cried out. "Most dreadful and injurious slander!"

The Magister regarded him impassively, then said, "Barwang, be so good as to control your outrage. Asrubal has little reputation left to protect.

"The statute against slander," the Magister continued, "does not prevent me from noting that Arsloe, the single witness to the crimes against Maihac, is missing. I find it wonderful that a reputable gentleman should testify to the innocence of Asrubal at the murdering of Jamiel, when all of us, including Barwang, intuitively recognize Asrubal's agency, either direct or indirect. In the case of the child Garlet, Asrubal regales us with such far-fetched claptrap that even Barwang must be taken aback. Asrubal tells us that in order to persuade Maihac to remain at Romarth, he arrives on the scene with six masked Assassinators, and two mad women. Instead of singing and dancing the dance of joy, they attacked Maihac and set about kicking his head, while the mad women stole his child. When Maihac escaped in the flitter, Asrubal thought to induce his return by throwing his child high into the air, then flinging its corpse into the river. Maihac did not know it was a dummy. To protect Jamiel and his other child, he flew on to Flad, where Arsloe, responding to Asrubal's order by radio, betrayed him to the Loklor, and where Asrubal was sure Maihac would dance with the girls and die.

"Asrubal was wrong, Maihac survived, and it appears that Asrubal was too clever for his own good. A question is weighing on us all, and now Asrubal must answer. He straddles the horns of a terrible dilemma: no matter how he responds, he cannot avoid a serious consequence. If the child Garlet is dead, he is a murderer. If Garlet is alive, he is a kidnapper. I will now put the question." The Magister turned to face Asrubal. "Hear this question and answer! Where is the child Garlet?"

Asrubal sat staring into space, as if preoccupied with private thoughts. The Magister leaned forward. "Asrubal, you have heard the question. Where is the child Garlet?"

Asrubal fixed his round black eyes upon him, then spoke in a soft voice, "I don't know."

"That is not a satisfactory answer," said the Magister. "The child was in your custody. How did you dispose of him?"

Asrubal shrugged. "At the time, and I freely admit this now, I was in a bad temper. I transferred the infant to my major-domo Ooscah, with brusque orders: I told him to take the infant from my sight, to keep it secure, until its parents came to claim it. In the meantime I did not want to be bothered with it, in any way, since the problem was not mine. Ooscah took the child off and the parents never returned; that is all I know."

In a gentle voice the Magister asked, "Surely the whereabouts of Garlet is known to you?"

Asrubal sat erect, his white face pinched. "After Ooscah took the child, I put the incident from my mind; it was not important, and I have not thought of it since. The child may be alive or it may be dead. Ooscah, obedient to my orders, has issued no reports. If the child cannot be found, I disclaim responsibility, since I ordered that it should be kept in secure and wholesome conditions."

"In that event, we must question Ooscah. Summon him here, at once."

Asrubal sat thinking for a moment, then slowly rose to his feet and departed the hall. At a signal from the Magister, a pair of Regulators followed. Jaro, sitting near the door, looked up into Asrubal's emotionless face as he stalked past and out into the entrance hall. Jaro rose to his feet and followed, as unobtrusively as possible. He passed through the door and halted beside a tall screen, carved intricately of honey-colored wood. Behind the screen were shadows; Jaro moved to where he could see but could not be seen.

The entry hall was much like that of Carleone, high-ceilinged, with a broad flight of stairs leading up to a balustraded gallery. Across the room a passage opened into an informal parlor; at a desk to the side of the passage sat a grichkin wearing black and white livery, a smart conical black hat, with a narrow brim, and black boots with curled toes. He was hunched and portly, with the wizened skin and compressed features of mature years; his function would be that of under-seneschal, with a status only slightly inferior to that of the major-domo. Asrubal imperiously waved the Regulators to stand back, and approached the grichkin's desk, with the Regulators watching from a distance. Asrubal bent forward and gave the grichkin terse instructions. The grichkin asked a dubious question. Asrubal spoke again, rapping his knuckles on the desk for emphasis. The grichkin bowed his head submissively. Jaro wondered why such forceful instructions were needed simply to summon the major-domo Ooscah. It was a curious proceeding, thought Jaro. He watched with growing curiosity.

Asrubal, finally satisfied that his requirements had been made clear, straightened and looked around. Jaro moved farther back into the shadows. Asrubal's attention, however, was fixed upon the Regulators. He seemed to be weighing his chances of escape.

The chances were clearly nonexistent. Asrubal slowly returned across the entry hall, past Jaro, back into the chamber where the Adjudicators awaited him. The Regulators followed.

Jaro watched as the grichkin picked up a telephone and spoke a sentence or two, evidently notifying Ooscah that his presence was commanded in the grand hall.

Jaro remained in the shadows. Asrubal's conduct had been most peculiar, and almost certainly directed to his own advantage.

The grichkin hoisted himself to his feet and trotted across the entry hall, around the stairs to a low stone archway, through which he disappeared. Jaro's suspicion was reinforced. He crossed the chamber on long strides. As he expected, the archway opened upon a flight of rough stone steps, leading down to the crypts below Varcial Palace. The grichkin had gone from sight. Jaro hesitated. The prospect of following the grichkin down into the crypts was most unappealing, but still—Jaro upbraided himself for his own cowardice. He looked over his shoulder. No one was in sight. There was no help for it; he screwed up his face in a grimace of utter distaste and followed after the grichkin, through the low archway and down the stone steps, lit by the dimmest of lights.

At the first landing Jaro paused and looked down the steps; these were the precincts of the white house-ghouls. He felt for the bulk of the power-gun at his hip; the contact was reassuring. He continued down the steps to the next landing, then around and down to the left, to another landing, and down again. Arriving at the first level, Jaro found it opened upon a small bleak chamber, furnished with a wooden table, a chair and a cupboard, all in a state of neglect. The chamber was empty. The air had become dank and smelled of ancient mold.

Jaro listened; the grichkin's footsteps still sounded in the dark. He drew a deep breath, touched his power gun once again and ran down the steps—down, down, down, past landings, and two more levels, each opening into a small sparsely furnished and deserted chamber. Passageways led away from these chambers, but to what purpose Jaro cared not to speculate.

The steps had become narrow and crude, as if the areas below were remote in every way from the upper world. Down flight after flight went Jaro, the dim bulbs casting wavering shadows ahead of him.

The grichkin's shuffling footsteps sounded more distinctly now and Jaro slowed his descent. The fourth level was close below. Suddenly the footsteps no longer could be heard. In their place was the sound of muted voices. Jaro moved quietly forward and peered around the last corner, into the fourth-level chamber. Like the others it was furnished with a table, chair, shelves, a sink and a cupboard. A grichkin wearing a gray smock and a dull yellow hat sat at the table. The grichkin who had arrived from above leaned over the table, much as Asrubal had leaned over his own desk. The grichkin in the yellow hat scowled at him resentfully, and muttered complaints under his breath. He was wrinkled and very old, with a gray skin, huge pouches under his eyes, a long nose hooking over the tiny gray bud of his mouth. He made an angry gesture and cried out in a shrill voice: "What about me? Has anyone thought for my convenience? Or is it to be the bin, for wasted old Shim."

"No matter! You have heard the orders."

The old grichkin rose to his feet and called: "Oleg! Come! Oleg? Wake yourself! There is work to be done."

From a side-chamber came a man of great size, with massive shoulders and torso, wide hips, and a big belly. A tuft of dirty brown hair raised above his scalp, a ragged beard surrounded his loose wet mouth. He halted in the middle of the chamber, yawned, scratched at his armpits and looked suspiciously at the grichkin from above. "What do we have here, all swivets and sashes? Speak, little twinkle-toes; did you bring down our laundry?"

The grichkin responded with dignity: "You may know me as Overkin Pood, assistant to the major-domo. I am here with important instructions, to be obeyed at once."

"Instruct away, then, and we will listen. Down here we do our duty!"

Pood prepared to speak, but was distracted by a sibilant sound from across the room. He looked over his shoulder and gave a sudden squeak of distaste. He pointed a long trembling finger. "Look yonder! Do you let them peer in at you like that?"

Oleg chuckled. "Why not? They are my little pets! Shim is never convivial and I must seek amusement elsewhere."

Shim, Pood and Oleg all looked across the room toward an iron-barred door which closed off a dark corridor. Behind the bars there was a stirring of dark shapes and a glimmer of white faces.

Oleg said judiciously: "Still, I allow no liberties." He took up a staff and thrust the end through the iron bars, to jab into one of the white faces. The house-ghoul gave a chittering sound of rage and seized the end of the staff. Oleg chortled and pulled the staff back. "That is a naughty trick, my poppin! Be grave; be kind! There is more to life than simple frightfulness!"

For a moment Oleg stood grinning at the house-ghoul, which in a sudden fit of energy shook the iron bars so that the door rattled in the frame. Oleg took up the staff and worked it energetically through the bars. The creature, hissing and moaning, retreated into the shadows, where it continued to make soft rasping sounds.

The grichkin Shim called out peevishly: "Come, Oleg! To the task!"

Oleg reluctantly turned away from the door. The two grichkins, followed by Oleg, set off along a corridor opposite to the iron-barred door. They disappeared from sight. Jaro brought out his gun, stepped down into the chamber and crossed to where he could look down the corridor. The dim light revealed the three forms where they halted, beside a heavy door with an iron-barred inspection window. Oleg glanced through the window, then unbarred the door and threw it open. He looked into the cell, and called out: "Are you awake, my dearie? I see that, as usual, you are brisk and dapper! Come out now; there are changes to be made! So it's hop, skip and jump, with far miles to travel! Where do we go? To the land of dreams; where else?"

Pood spoke impatiently, "Be quick; less foolish talk! Haste is a priority!"

Oleg ignored him, and continued in a soothing voice: "Why do you wait? It is not yet time for your glunk; you are far too avid for your luxuries, but then, who can blame you, since it is all so good! Ah, the tasty gruel! The tidbits which you relish so keenly. I am tired, and henceforth you must fetch them yourself. That will be the new way."

Once again Pood made a pettish protest: "Get on with the work; enough of this gabble!"

Oleg turned his head and spoke to the grichkin, "If you are so hot for action, go into the cell yourself and bring him out! You will find he is as agile as a spider; he jumps high; he walks around the walls; he is everywhere at once! If you had a beard, he would pull it well. As it is, he must content himself with your nose."

Pood responded sulkily, "That is not my job. You must do the work, and quickly! Those are the commands!"

Oleg shrugged and turned back to the cell. "Come now! Out with you! There is no time to waste!"

From within the cell came a mutter which Jaro was unable to make out.

Oleg called sweetly: "Will you come? I would enter your cell were I not dainty as to where I place my feet. So come, my good one! Up and away, to fly the far spaces and up to the moonpalaces, where wine flows from crystal spouts and the lunar damsels dance!"

Pood made further fretful sounds. Shim called through the doorway: "Come now, and out with you! No more sulking! Must Oleg go tinkly-tinkly-tinkly with the spanker?"

From within came a grumble. Shim called approvingly: "That's the way! Step by step; come along now! Faster still; we must hurry!"

Into the corridor shuffled a dark shape which Jaro could not see clearly.

Oleg gave a hoarse call of encouragement. "Forward now! It's goodbye to your beloved home, and all your favorite nooks and crannies. But no regrets, since it's all for the best! Oh what fine things await you!"

Jaro backed across the chamber and up into the shadows of the staircase; he watched with a pounding heart. Into the room came the two grichkins, followed by Oleg and a person of indeterminate age. A loose brown smock covered his thin body; dank buskins, improvised from rags, were wound around his feet. A tangle of black hair and a black beard concealed most of his face. Jaro searched for resemblance to himself, and saw a likeness in the spacing of the eyes and the shape of the nose.

"Now then," said Oleg. "Hold hard a moment; I must light the way!"

Oleg went to a shelf and fitted a tubular device to the end of his staff. Behind the iron-barred door black robes fluttered and a pair of white faces jerked and bobbed. Oleg approached the door and pointed his staff toward the bars. He touched a trigger; the tube spurted a long flame through the bars. Hissing, spitting, moaning imprecations the house-ghouls tumbled backward down the corridor while Oleg gurgled in glee. "So then, my good fellows! When Oleg speaks for patience, he expects close attention! Now, stand back! There will be time enough for your treat." Oleg peered through the bars. "No tricks or sudden starts; the flame is ready!"

Oleg unbarred the door and, with flame-staff ready, threw the door open on squealing hinges. He turned to the prisoner. "Now we must say goodbye, since we travel in separate directions. Your way is yonder, into the country of the unknown, where you will arrive after perhaps some small tribulation. So step lively now; in with you, and our good wishes go with you."

The prisoner stood motionless. The two grichkins each took one of his arms and urged him toward the open door. The prisoner held back, his eyes bulging. The grichkins pulled more insistently. "Come along with you! We all must obey orders!"

Jaro stepped down into the chamber and, aiming his gun, destroyed the legs first of Shim, then of Pood. Both fell screaming to the floor. Jaro waved his gun toward Oleg. "Drag them into the corridor; be quick with you, before I shoot again."

Oleg roared in mindless outrage. He flung the staff; it whirled through the air and struck Jaro on the chest, to send him reeling. Oleg lurched forward, seized Jaro and hugged him to his enormous chest. He grinned down into Jaro's face, his great maw hanging loose and wet. "This is a surprise! But you have hurt poor old Shim, and also the popinjay Pood. That was not nice, and you shall not gain by your cruelty! Make ready! You must walk in tandem with Garlet, down that avenue into the unknown! Now we will go. If you struggle I will squeeze your head." He started to drag Jaro toward the corridor. Jaro let his legs go limp, hoping to sag to the floor, but Oleg only hugged tighter and Jaro's ribs creaked. He tried to use his elbows, to kick and butt with his head; Oleg's great frame was sheathed with thick pads of fat and muscle and Jaro's efforts came to nothing. He tried to point the gun at Oleg's foot, but Oleg struck his wrist and the gun dropped to the stone floor. Jaro thought desperately of the months and years of Gaing's training, and the endless exercises. Now the reflexes built into his body would save his life. Even so it was touch and go, for Oleg was a behemoth and his great mass made most techniques useless.

But not so for one tried and true procedure. Jaro jerked up his knee with all his force. He felt the great testicles crush and squirm, and heard Oleg's instant howl of agony. Jaro dropped from Oleg's embrace, seized his gun and also the staff. He pointed the tube toward Oleg and pressed the trigger. Flame sprayed against Oleg's chest and he fell back, turning Jaro a look of plaintive surprise. "You burned me."

"I will burn you again," panted Jaro. "Drag those grichkins into the corridor beyond the door."

"They are thrashing about! They are howling in pain!"

Jaro pointed the fire-tube. Wheezing and sobbing, Oleg obeyed, ignoring the horrified protests.

"Now then," said Jaro. "You too! After them!"

Oleg turned him a frantic look. "They are waiting. They do not like me; I have burned them."

Jaro pressed the trigger. With bursts of flame he drove Oleg moaning and crying into the corridor, then slammed and barred the door. Strange sounds came from the corridor: cries of pain and clacking sounds of insane glee.

Jaro turned to the erstwhile prisoner, who sat in the corner, slumped against the wall. Jaro appraised him for a moment, struggling between disgust and pity. Garlet watched him with stony detachment.

"Garlet! I am your brother! My name is Jaro."

"I know."

"Come then; on your feet, and we will leave this awful place." Jaro reached to take Garlet's arm. Garlet gave a hoarse cry and, springing to his feet, hurled himself upon Jaro, who was totally unprepared for such an act, and was buffeted back against the wall. Garlet's hair was thrust into his face, choking him; the hair smelled of filth and Garlet's body was fetid. Jaro struggled, squirmed, ducked, turned his head away from the hair and gasped for air. Despite Garlet's clutching fingers, he tore loose from the rancid body and jumped back. He cried out: "Garlet! Don't fight me! I am your brother! I came to rescue you."

Garlet leaned against the wall, panting, his face convulsed. "I know of you and your life; for a time I could push myself into your soul. That was long ago and you cut me off to isolate me in the dark! It was a bad thing to do. You lived the life of a prince; dancing and basking and sucking sweet juices while I paid the price, moaning here in the dark! But you did not care. You would not listen! You stopped off my small glimpse of your wonderful life! You left me nothing."

"It could not be helped," said Jaro. "Come; let us leave this place."

Garlet stared blindly across the room. Tears formed in his

eyes. "Why should I go from here? Nothing remains for me. All my days are gone, and my golden hours! You cannot pay the debt! All that is precious and mine is gone! I do not care what happens; nothing is left."

Jaro tried to speak cheerfully: "From now on your life shall go nicely, and you will make up for the time wasted. So now, will you come?"

Garlet slowly turned his head. His eyes widened in unreasoning anger. "I will kill you, so that your blood flows across the floor into the drain! Then, and only then, will I be satiated!"

Jaro protested. "That is not a good thing to say!"

For response Garlet lunged at Jaro and seized his throat. The two toppled into a writhing heap. Garlet's thin body, under the stinking smock, was bony and harsh. He tried to pound Jaro's head against the stone floor. As he strove, he uttered gasping phrases: "I will put you into the cell and lock the door! Then I will sit outside where Shim sat. I have long envied him! Now I, too, can sit at my ease, free to walk either this way or that. I will turn the light off or on as I wish. At every meal I shall eat my fill of salt fish, and no one will interfere."

Jaro struggled to protect himself from Garlet's crazed strength. At last his patience wore thin and he cuffed Garlet smartly. Garlet sat back in shock. He tenderly massaged his cheek. "Why did you do that?"

"To bring you to your senses." Jaro rose to his feet. "Please do not attack me again." He reached down and helped Garlet stand erect. "Now we will leave this place."

Garlet made no further protest; the two climbed the steps.

At the second level Jaro called a halt to catch his breath. Garlet stood, fidgeting, peering first up the steps, then back down the way they had come. Jaro asked, "What are you looking for?"

"I am afraid that Oleg will find us here, out of our cells, and walk on us; this is his way."

"No fear as to that! Have you had enough rest?"

"I need no rest. In the cell I run across the floor and run up the walls. Someday I want to run up so far that my feet touch the ceiling."

The two continued up the steps—past the first level, and at last out through the archway into the entrance hall. Jaro noticed that Garlet was squinting. He asked, "Does the light hurt your eyes?"

"It is bright."

The two crossed the chamber, Garlet shambling behind, eyes half-closed against the glare. At the door into the grand hall, Jaro paused to look in upon the proceedings.

A grichkin in the splendid regalia of a major-domo stood before the Adjudicators, giving testimony. This, thought Jaro, would be Ooscah. Asrubal, as before, sat in his massive chair of heavy dark wood.

The Magister, leaning forward, addressed Ooscah: "Let me review your testimony. Listen carefully. If I speak inaccurately, correct me. Remember, the penalty for purposeful mendacity is the bin."

Ooscah bowed his head, smiling a small pursy smile. "Yes, Your Honor."

"Now then: back to the episode in question. Asrubal gave the child to you, with instructions to see to its safety."

"Yes, Your Honor." Ooscah spoke in a high clear voice, enunciating as if each word were a choice morsel to be savored. "He handed the child to me with care, as if he felt great pity for the woeful mite."

"At this time, so you aver, you were approached by one of the Ratigo holy women, who stated her readiness to care for the child. Since apparently she had come at Asrubal's behest, you obeyed her request. Am I correct?"

"Yes, Your Honor."

"And when next did you see the child?"

"Never, Your Honor. I assumed that perhaps its parents had returned to do their duty."

Maihac had noticed Jaro and came to the doorway. Jaro pointed to Garlet. "I found him on the fourth level of the crypts. They were about to give him to the house-ghouls. I arranged that they should not do so."

Maihac looked Garlet up and down. "I am your father. These many years I thought you dead."

"I don't know what to think," said Garlet. "The light hurts my eyes."

"You are in bad shape, no doubt about that," said Maihac. "But that's not your fault, and we'll set you right as fast as we can."

"I don't want to go down again."

"You need not worry. Yonder sits Asrubal, who put you down in the dark. Let us go look at him. He will not be pleased to see you." Garlet held back, shuffling his feet. Maihac took hold of his arm and led him across the hall.

Ooscah was speaking. "I can tell you no more. Time comes and goes; who knows what the future holds."

Maihac and Garlet halted in front of the Adjudicators. There was silence in the chamber. Asrubal stared aghast at Garlet. Ooscah called out in a high quavering voice of simulated joy: "Here he is now. The missing child, safe at last! Let us all cry out our glad welcomes!"

In a sharp voice the Magister demanded, "What has happened? Please inform the panel."

Jaro spoke, "I can tell you what happened. When Asrubal left this chamber, he instructed the grichkin Pood to go down to the fourth level, where he should ensure Garlet's disappearance. I followed him down the stone steps, to the dungeon where Garlet was imprisoned. The jailers brought Garlet from his dungeon and started to give him to the house-ghouls. I interfered and killed the jailers. Then I brought Garlet up the many levels. He has been in the dark dungeon for twenty years. Asrubal did not treat him well."

The Magister looked at Asrubal, who returned a blank stare. The Magister asked, "Did you treat Garlet well?"

"Adequately well."

The Magister turned to Garlet. "This is a court of justice. Do you know what that means?"

"No. The light is bright."

The Magister gave orders to the Regulators: "Find some dark glasses, and bring them here, quickly." Again he spoke to Garlet: "When people do bad things, they are brought to a court of justice; and if they have committed crimes, they are punished."

Garlet squinted uneasily from right to left. "I spilled water from the dish; for punishment Shim gave me no more water. Will you send me back down without water? Is that my punishment? I will try not to spill water again."

"You are not to be punished," said the Magister. "You have done nothing wrong, so far as I know. How long have you been down in the dark?"

"I don't know. I remember nothing else."

"Look yonder at the man sitting in the chair; do you know him?"

Garlet looked toward Asrubal. "I have seen him three times. He came to my place in the dark. Oleg brought me out and the man looked at me. Then he went away."

The Magister turned back to Asrubal. "Do you have anything to say? You have a right to speak in your own behalf."

"I will say this. The off-worlder and the Ramy woman victimized me terribly! They pillaged my fortune and ransacked my Lorquin offices. I kept the child as a hostage pending their return to Romarth. But they failed to come; they shirked their duty! They are trifling creatures, devoid of fortitude. In a word, they are disgusting! Examine them. Yonder sits the son of Tawn Maihac and a flighty woman of Ramy House. He is young and handsome, as a toy animal is handsome. He is the darling of Fortune, but he is flawed! He has a sour soul, like a thing molded of bad cheese. Those who know him best call him a 'nimp.'" Asrubal paused, smiling coldly. Jaro stared back, shocked and incredulous.

Asrubal went on. "Long ago, I suffered a great wrong. I was disheartened. An off-world trickster had come to cheat me, to pilfer my goods, meanwhile groveling and wheedling. How could I deal with this sly rodent? I maintained full rashudo and all the dignity of my sept! I am a straightforward man! I deviate never from the course! And in the end the thieves paid dearly for their thefts. I tasted a rich vengeance. The off-worlder's child was immured in the dark. The off-worlder was given to the Loklor. I found the Ramy woman at Point Extase and punished her severely, inflicting so much fear upon her that she chose death rather than confront me face to face, especially since she knew that I would strangle her child before her eyes.

"I have enjoyed my victories for many years; no one can take this joy from me. Even now my enemies cringe when I look at them! Kill me if you like; all men die. But in my case, not until equipoise was satisfied. And who is to blame? Who else but Tawn Maihac, the faithless father who never returned to claim his lost son. There is the answer: twenty years the child has waited in the dark to pay for the avarice of his father and the stealth of his mother. Such is the interplay of karma. I will impart a final irony: The child's dungeon lies directly below the chair where now his father sits in bloated pomp. The man is an off-worlder; he is detestable."

The Magister held up his hand. "Enough, Asrubal! You have ranted only to your own shame. Tonight we will all have bad dreams, I grant you that! Barwang, do you care to plead mercy for your kinsman?"

Barwang, sprawling in his chair, muttered, "I have nothing to say."

"In that case the Adjudicators will now adjourn. In a week we will announce the sentence to be imposed upon the criminal. Regulators! Shackle the prisoner, take him to a dungeon secure from the house-ghouls. Serve him bread and water; allow him no visitors."

Morlock asked, "What of Ooscah?"

The Magister gave the slightest of shrugs. "Ooscah is probably no more venal than any other grichkin; still, he is an accomplice to a hideous crime. Regulators! This very moment, take Ooscah to the Foundance, apply a wire noose and drop him into the corpse-bin."

Ooscah melted into his chair as if he were molded of warm wax. A pair of Regulators gripped his arms and pulled him to his feet; sagging on uncoordinated legs, Ooscah was led from the hall.

The Magister said, "Proceedings are at an end; they have been taxing; they weigh upon us all. In a week the final judgment upon Asrubal will be pronounced. That is all for today."

NINETEEN

1

Jaro brought the flitter down from the sky and with Skirl and Garlet aboard, flew across the city of Carleone. Ardrian, with Maihac, Morlock and others, trooped back through the evening.

Garlet sat stiffly on the seat and looked wildly in all directions, but made no protest. Skirl tried to soothe him: "There will be many things new to you, and some will make you nervous. But you'll soon adapt, and suddenly everything will seem familiar. Think! You'll be just like Jaro."

Garlet made a rasping sound which Skirl took to be a sardonic chuckle. Clearly, any program involving Garlet would require both patience and unremitting good humor. If she were to be involved, she could only do her best, though she was not sure that her patience would be adequate to the task. Covertly she studied the huddled bad-smelling creature with hairy face and glittering eyes. She shifted her gaze to Jaro, then back to Garlet: incredible that these two were the same stuff! She spoke, trying to sound confident. The eyes in the hairy face swung around to fix upon her. Despite all efforts for control, her voice trembled. "If anything happens which you don't understand, ask, and we will explain as best we can."

Garlet's eyes gleamed at her through the thicket of hair. He blurted: "Who are you?"

"My name is Skirl Hutsenreiter; I am not a Roum. I am what they call an off-worlder."

Jaro told Garlet: "You and I both are half Roum and half off-worlder. It doesn't seem to be a bad combination."

Skirl pointed to the eastern sky, where the immense shape of the galaxy was pushing above the horizon. "If you look closely, you can see some of the individual stars." She pointed. "Out there to the left is the Gaean Reach. The world Gallingale is out there. My home is at Thanet on Gallingale. When we leave here, perhaps we will return to Gallingale, at least for a time."

Garlet showed scant interest in the stars. He continued to stare at Skirl. He said at last, "You are different from Jaro."

"Yes, quite different."

"I like the difference. But I can't understand what you are thinking."

Skirl laughed uneasily. "That's just as well. I'm different because I'm female. Jaro is male, like you. Can you understand what he is thinking?"

Garlet gave an ambiguous grunt. "It is not the same now." Garlet turned his head to the window and peered off toward the luminous shape in the east. He asked, "You said you are leaving this place?"

"As soon as Asrubal is properly dead. Then we will fly back to the Gaean Reach—the sooner the better." Skirl looked from the window. "We've arrived at Carleone. You'll soon be bathed and dressed in new clothes, and you'll feel much better."

Garlet said nothing. Skirl wondered if he had comprehended anything she had told him.

The flitter landed upon the Carleone terrace. The three alighted and Garlet watched half-suspiciously as Jaro sent the flitter aloft. Ardrian and Maihac arrived and the group entered the palace. Ardrian summoned his major-domo Fancho and gave instructions. Fancho turned to Garlet. "Come, sir! We'll make all well with you."

Garlet shrank back. "Is it to be the crypts?"

"No more crypts," said Maihac. "Only a bath and some general sanitation which you badly need. Fancho will find decent clothes for you, and you will feel a new man."

Fancho called winningly, "Come, sir! There is a nice perfume in the bath, just for you."

Garlet still hung back. He pointed toward Skirl. "I want her to come with me."

"Not this time," said Maihac. "Skirl will be busy elsewhere."

Jaro said, "I'll be with you, and you need fear nothing."

"I know you well," muttered Garlet. "You are as bad as the others."

"Come along, sir," called Fancho. "We'll have you as handsome as any fine cavalier, and you won't know yourself."

Garlet made a soft whining sound, but followed Fancho without further complaint. Apathetically he allowed himself to be bathed, barbered, shaved, manicured, pedicured, anointed with a perfumed lotion, then rubbed with a towel moist with an astringent spirit. Garlet scowled and winced at every stage of the proceedings. Jaro was often amused, but took care that Garlet should not notice.

Finally Garlet had been groomed, scented and sanitized to the best of the servants' abilities. Fancho laid out new clothes; Garlet, standing hunched, still looked graceless and miserable, like a scrawny plucked chicken. Jaro thought soberly: there, but for the caprice of the mad Ratigo women, stood himself, and Jaro smiled no further.

Under Fancho's direction, the Seishanee dressed Garlet in dark blue trousers, a striped blue and green blouse, a green jacket, and soft green leather ankle-boots.

The transformation was complete. Fancho asked, "Is everything suitable?"

"Very suitable," said Jaro. "You've done a good job. Garlet, what do you think?"

"These boots don't feel right."

"They look well on you," said Jaro. "You'll get used to them."

Garlet was not so sure. He looked uneasy and awkward in his new clothes. No surprise, thought Jaro. For Garlet every experience was a novelty of questionable value. Jaro studied him dispassionately. The two were similar in the general cast of their features and stature, though Garlet hunched his shoulders, so that they appeared thin and narrow. He held his bony arms bent at the elbows, with fingers clenched. His skin was notably pallid; his face showed hollow cheeks, deep eye-sockets, a bony chin and jaw. Jaro divined something of Garlet's miserable state of confusion, and tried to soothe him with words of cheerful encouragement. "You are absolutely a changed man! The difference is remarkable! Do you feel the change?"

Garlet responded in a surly mutter, "I have not thought about it."

"Would you like to see yourself in a mirror?"

"What is a mirror?"

"It is a bright glass which reflects your image. It shows what you look like to other people."

"It is the wrong choice!" Garlet complained. "The grichkin put me into water and cut away all my hair; then he put me into these clothes. Let the people look at the grichkin; he is responsible."

"It's not the grichkin who interests them; it is you!"

Garlet made a sardonic sound. Jaro asked patiently, "What of the mirror? Do you want to see yourself?"

Garlet said dubiously, "I might not like what I see."

"That is a chance we all must take," said Jaro. He led Garlet to the mirror. "There: look."

For a moment Garlet stared at his image, then turned away.

Jaro asked: "What do you think?"

"It is as I feared. I look like you."

Jaro had nothing to say. He took Garlet to the drawing room where Ardrian sat with Maihac, Skirl and others of his household.

At the door Garlet stopped short. All present rose to their feet, that they might offer Garlet a polite greeting. Garlet looked from face to face, his mouth drooping. He drew back a step and started to turn away, but Jaro took his arm and led him into the room. "Here is my brother Garlet," said Jaro. "As everyone knows, he has suffered mistreatment beyond our imagination, and as you see he has survived while retaining his manhood—for which I respect him tremendously. This is a new life for Garlet, and I hope he can forget the past. I will not introduce you all by name at this time, since it would serve no purpose."

Maihac came to stand beside Jaro and Garlet. "These are my two sons and I am happy that they are together again. You will notice that they are much alike. Garlet obviously will be the better for some good food and time in the sunlight. Jaro and I have a hundred things to teach him, and no doubt Skirl will help. But there is no hurry. We shall remain at Romarth until we are sure that Asrubal has been dealt with as he deserves. I might mention that the funds which have been confiscated from Asrubal belong to the Roum and, at your option, are sufficient to buy a pair of passenger packets, in good repair. You may then travel the Reach as you like; no longer would there be any reason to sequester yourselves out here beside Night Lamp."

Maihac took Garlet's arm, and led him to a couch. Garlet gingerly settled into the cushions. Fancho immediately served him a goblet of effervescent pink liquid. Garlet looked at it askance. "Drink without fear," said Ardrian. "You have been served an inoffensive potion known as 'Fairy Dew.' It induces only cordiality and a mood of creative tranquility."

Garlet lifted the goblet to his nose, smelled the contents and put it aside. Maihac raised his eyebrows. "Taste! You may like it!"

"And what if I don't?"

"Then don't taste again."

Garlet gave a curt nod. "I will think it over."

An hour passed. Garlet spoke little, though he was treated with formal courtesy by the others in the room. He was asked gentle questions, to which he responded in monosyllables. Presently, in an adjoining refectory the group was served a light supper.

It was an uncomfortable meal. Garlet sat staring at the table, showing no disposition either to eat or to talk. Skirl prompted him: "Garlet, you are not eating!"

"I know."

"Why not?"

"I don't see anything I like."

"In that case, try something new—for instance, one of these little pasties. They are filled with all manner of good things. And look at these lovely green grapes? Surely you like grapes?"

"I've never had one."

"Try one now; you can't help but like it!"

Garlet gave his head a shake. "I'm not so sure."

"But aren't you hungry?"

"Oh yes," said Garlet airily. "I'm hungry. I've never been anything else."

"Then try this nice ragout," Skirl coaxed.

"What are those white floating things?"

"Those are dumplings. They are light and fluffy and very good."

Garlet explained in a reasonable manner: "It is new to me. When I am not sure, it is best to go carefully. It may be the yaha will tell me what to do."

"Indeed? What is a 'yaha'?"

"It helps me decide in wise ways—especially about new things."

"Try one small taste; then it won't be new anymore when next you see it. You'll know what it's like and you won't need the yaha."

Garlet grudgingly admitted that Skirl's advice was sound, and gingerly tasted the ragout. "That is quite good," said Garlet. "I will have more."

"Of course! You shall have as much as you like. But first, try some of these other things. Then they won't be new either, and you will have a variety of choices."

"There is nothing here I want." Garlet looked up and down the table. "Does no one eat gruel for their glunk? Is there no salt fish?"

"No salt fish tonight," said Jaro. "I should think that you'd never want to see gruel or salt fish again."

Garlet made no response. His silence had a sardonic quality.

"The past is a bad dream," said Skirl. "You should put it out of your mind and think only of the future. That's where the good things will happen."

Garlet glanced at her sidelong. "Where will you be?"

"In the future? Aboard the *Pharsang*, which means anywhere in the Gaean Reach."

Garlet made a disapproving sound. "I want you to stay with me."

Skirl gave an uncomfortable laugh. "You'll probably be on the *Pharsang* yourself."

Garlet gave his head a slow definite shake. "My plans are not yet ready—but I think not. I shall stay here, and you shall stay here, too."

"That is not possible. Let us talk of something else. This wine, for instance. Have you tasted it? No? Try just a sip."

Garlet looked at the goblet, but made no move to touch it.

Maihac, from his place across the table, took note of Garlet's passivity. He asked, "What's wrong?"

Garlet allowed his mouth to droop, but said nothing. Skirl explained: "Everything is new. Garlet is cautious about trying new things."

Maihac, half-laughing, said energetically, "Garlet, that is illogical! Everything from now on will be new, at least once! That is how your life will be: a series of new and pleasant experiences!"

"I must think about this," muttered Garlet.

"You don't need to think," declared Maihac. "Let us do the

thinking—at least for a time. Meanwhile, eat, drink, relax! Enjoy yourself! If anything confuses you, ask about it."

"I am not confused," said Garlet.

Maihac raised his eyebrows. "So much the better! Is there anything you want to know? Anything you want to say?"

"Not just now."

Skirl said, "I should think that you would find everything so wonderful that you could not stop talking for sheer excitement!"

"I am not so inclined."

"I see." Skirl reflected a moment. "Nevertheless, you are hungry and you should eat. The pasties are very good and so are these pepper puffs!"

Garlet glanced at the platters and shook his head.

Skirl almost pleaded with him. "Why not? All the rest of us are eating!"

Garlet's eyes seemed to narrow. "Is it not clear? If I eat, I make myself part of the cabal."

With an effort Skirl choked back an incredulous laugh. "Garlet, be serious! What you say is absurd! I am eating and I have joined no cabal. Far from it! I am Skirl Hutsenreiter, and a Clam Muffin; I am nothing else."

Garlet was unmoved. He twisted the wine goblet between his fingers, watching the swim of golden shades and lights in the liquid.

Skirl opened her mouth, then closed it again. Garlet was impervious.

Maihac spoke gently, as if musing: "You are intelligent, Garlet, and you want to make the most of your life. Am I right?"

"My plans are not firm."

Maihac, taken aback, said, "Listen carefully, Garlet. The sudden transition in your life has caused you psychological shock. At the moment you are not in control of yourself; like Jaro, you have a strong mind. Still, the puzzles and uncertainties are too much for you."

Garlet watched Maihac stonily, but said nothing.

Maihac went on. "At the moment you don't know how to deal with your surroundings, so you have retreated into total caution, which is sensible. But you must relax and trust us; we are your family; this is your grandfather's home. You must live passively: watching, talking, listening, absorbing the feel of the environment. We will help you learn useful habits and before long they will become familiar. Do you understand what I am telling you?"

Garlet continued to twirl the goblet. In an offhand voice he said, "Of course."

Maihac went on somberly. "It is an uncomfortable position for all of us, and there is no predicting how things will go. Still, if you do as I suggest, you will avoid much distress. And soon you will feel happy with yourself and the world."

Garlet twisted the goblet so rapidly that the wine spilled out upon the table. Skirl cried out, "Garlet! That is not proper etiquette! You are soiling the tablecloth!"

Garlet said, "I was trying to swirl the wine up to the very lip of the goblet without spilling it."

"Regardless of that, it's not polite to play games at the dinner table; at least, that is how I was taught. I will teach you the same things, if you will permit me."

"Whatever you like." Garlet spoke, raising his eyes and looking across the table to Maihac, "I know nothing of psychological shock. I think of one item at a time and fit it into the frame. I am careful to think only my own thoughts, since there are no others which will fit into my plans."

Maihac smiled a rather perplexed smile. "You want no advice and no interference: is that what you are telling me?"

Garlet reached to swirl his goblet, but Skirl moved it aside.

Maihac said in a dry voice, "Whether you want advice or not, I suspect that you will hear a great deal. You would be foolish to ignore it."

"I will try to deal properly with advice."

"First of all, you should not starve yourself for irrational reasons."

"You are right in one respect, at least," said Garlet. "I must transcend shadow-play, and I will need all my strength." He reached out to a bowl of fruit, selected and ate a grape. "That is enough for now."

Without ceremony, Garlet rose to his feet and left the room. Skirl made an uncertain movement, as if to run after him, but Jaro was first and Skirl settled slowly back into her chair.

Jaro found Garlet on the terrace. He stood leaning on the balustrade, looking over the garden, silver and black in the light of the two moons. Jaro went to join him. Garlet paid him no heed.

Minutes passed. As Jaro leaned on the balustrade, enjoying the scented night, he could feel a building of tension in Garlet.

Garlet's patience at last snapped. He glanced sidewise at Jaro, his mouth compressed into an angry line. He demanded, "Why are you here? I came to be alone!"

"It's not safe to wander alone through the dark."

"Hmmf. Is that why you followed me from the table?"

"Partly. Why do you want to be alone?"

Garlet spoke in a surly mutter. "The drone of advice hurts my head. Everyone stares at me from round foolish eyes. I do not like the flavor of their thoughts."

In the light of the moons Jaro studied Garlet's face. He asked, "How do you know what they were thinking?"

Garlet shrugged. "Sometimes I know. I could look out from the dark, into your mind. I felt how you lived your life. I called to you; I told you of my despair. You refused to listen and held me away, so that I would not disturb your pleasure."

Jaro clenched his hands upon the cold marble balustrade. "That was not the way of it. As soon as I could, I set out to find you."

Garlet made a scornful sound. "You did nothing."

Jaro tried to speak, but the dull voice went on. "I am up from the dark, and nothing is the same. The yahas that gave me wisdom are gone; they may never return. What remains? A trifle. Faintly, faintly, I read the coming and going of thoughts. Tonight I looked into faces and I saw morbid glee, so I left."

"You are wrong," said Jaro. "What you saw was sympathy. There was no morbid glee."

Garlet spoke without interest. "Think as you like."

"Garlet, listen to me! I am not trying to enforce my opinions upon you; I want to help you adapt to a new life. To do so I must correct your mistakes; and you must heed me, because I know best what is proper! Do you agree?"

Garlet spoke without intonation: "I am not sure that you know best, nor that you want to help me. I judge by what has happened in the past. You were lacking before; why should you not lack now?"

"Everything is different. It is too complicated to explain."

"No matter. I need no help."

"What of advice?"

"I need no advice."

Jaro laughed shortly. "You need help and advice—very badly. Reality is pitiless. You will surely come to grief unless you change your attitude."

Garlet said softly, "I am my own reality, and I too am pitiless. What needs to be done shall be done."

Jaro looked at Garlet in blank perplexity. Garlet spoke on, in a soft monotone: "Yaha supersedes destiny. I know little and I know much. From where I sat in the dark, I sent myself into your mind. You cared nothing; you betrayed me, and failed to listen, to heed, to feel. You hated me; you enjoyed your freedom while I huddled in the dungeon. I ate husks; you ate good things. Sometimes I thought to see glimpses of what you saw, and I tried to feel what you felt. I called to you; my cries were in vain and you blotted out my voice." He looked over his shoulder at the sound of footsteps; Skirl approached. "Ah well, we shall see."

After a few moments Garlet allowed himself to be led to the chamber which had been set aside for his use. Standing beside a table of carved jade, he ate chunks of bread and cheese, then went to the far corner where he crept under a table and slept.

2

Asrubal had been taken to a cell in the basement of the Justiciary, where he was guarded by a platoon of Regulators. Within the week, a formal judgment would be pronounced. Execution of the sentence would follow immediately, so Morlock assured Maihac. The *Pharsang* remained aloft; on the ground the ship would become vulnerable to the attack of masked Urd Assassinators or any other band of bravos. Additionally, the *Pharsang*'s radar continually monitored the air-space above Romarth. If Asrubal were liberated from the dungeon and attempted to flee by flitter, he would instantly be detected.

During the week of waiting, Maihac, Skirl and Jaro spent much time with Garlet, trying to ease through the barriers of his suspicion.

Garlet's moods were proof against analysis. In order to simplify his own life, he obeyed a few instructions in matters of dress, and behavior, but otherwise isolated himself into his own mind, ignoring conversation and questions, though sometimes putting questions of his own. From the first Garlet indicated that he preferred Skirl's company to that of either Maihac or Jaro. Maihac's conversation bored him, and he listened to Jaro with blank indifference.

Skirl tried to teach Garlet the conventions and courtesies of ordinary existence. Garlet listened to her with apparent patience, and dutifully participated in her demonstrations. Sometimes he seemed to be smiling a secret smile, which always disappeared when she looked at him, and she wondered how much of her instruction, if any, had penetrated his mind.

Jaro, meanwhile, attempted to teach Garlet the first principles of reading and enumeration. He explained the function of words, the Gaean grammatical system, and the alphabetical basis of orthography. Garlet listened passively. When Jaro put pencil and paper in front of him, and instructed Garlet to copy the alphabet, Garlet created a few desultory scribbles, then dropped the pencil and sat back in his chair.

Jaro said, "There is no easy way. If you want to learn, you must drill until the skills become automatic."

"No doubt but that you are right," said Garlet. "However, I have heard enough for the day."

"Not really," said Jaro. "We have accomplished nothing. If you want to learn, I will teach you. If not, I will waste no more time. Which is it to be?"

Garlet considered. "I am not sure that the skill is useful." He indicated the alphabet which Jaro had inscribed and placed before him. "These symbols, so you tell me, are the relics of deep antiquity, as is most of the material you want me to read. It is a game for pedants with nothing better to do."

"That is partly true, but not altogether. Reading is often a useful skill. When you decide to learn, let me know and we will resume the lessons."

One day Skirl told Garlet, "For someone with your background, you speak very well. Did someone teach you?"

Garlet curled his lips. "I taught myself, of course. Old Shim liked to talk, and when he chided me for a misdeed, I could keep him going for hours on end. I also learned from Oleg, who talked to the house-ghouls. He used a strange way of talking, as if they were his lovely friends. I remembered everything I heard."

"But no one ever taught you to read?"

"Naturally not! Why bother? I was to be there forever."

Skirl shuddered. "This is a frightening place, and I will be very happy to leave."

Garlet looked at her in frowning displeasure. "You don't like Romarth?"

"That is a hard question to answer. The palaces are magnificent, beyond any I have seen elsewhere. Perhaps on Old Earth there are places equally grand. As for the Roum—" Skirl paused to analyze her feelings. "I don't like them very much; in general they seem humorless and vain. I don't feel easy here. At night I can't sleep for fear of the house-ghouls. In short, I can't leave Romarth too soon."

Garlet made an impatient gesture. "This is not well spoken. You must make changes in your thinking."

"Indeed!" Skirl was both amused and annoyed, as was often the case during her dealings with Garlet. "Why do you say that?"

"The reasons are surely clear. I do not care to leave Romarth, and you must stay as well, since there are things I want you to teach me. I am especially interested in the differences between 'male' and 'female.' You may show me your body."

Skirl shook her head. "That is not proper etiquette. You must put such ideas out of your head. In any case, we will not be staying at Romarth. That is definite. You will enjoy visiting other places on other worlds."

Garlet's mouth drooped. "Other places are different. I have learned something about this place. It is starting to become real."

"That's good news! It means that you are adjusting to your new life."

"Possibly so. There is something else at work of greater import."

"Really? What is this 'else'?"

Garlet deliberated. "I can tell you this: the force I command in the Great Surround is starting to flow back."

Skirl looked at Garlet in puzzlement. His most inscrutable statements sometimes yielded a peculiar logic, when she troubled to examine them carefully. She said, "You've gone past me. What is this force? What is a 'surround'?"

Garlet groped for words. "In the dungeon, I was acquainted with every item: every square inch, every surface, every knob and fissure. It was the 'Dark Surround,' and with the advice of the yahas, I was the master. When I came up here, the 'Surround' of the dungeon was left behind, and I was master of nothing. Up here is a new 'Surround' of large dimensions. To control this 'Great Surround' I need new strength. It is starting to return because I have made such a decision."

"That is an interesting idea," said Skirl, and now she violated her own rule against argument. "Unfortunately, Garlet, you are quite wrong! You cannot now or ever control anything, except your own conduct—which is enough. Specifically, you cannot control me, or Jaro or Tawn Maihac. It is best that you understand this. So do not waste time and energy deluding yourself!"

Garlet jumped to his feet. "It is you who are wrong! You feel nothing and you know only what I tell you!" He spoke in sudden decision. "I have heard enough talk for a time. Now I want to walk out and look along the avenues and see what is to be seen."

Skirl was not sure how to react to Garlet's sudden burst of willfulness. She said cautiously, "That can be arranged easily enough."

"We need no arrangements!" declared Garlet. "Let us go now."

Skirl reluctantly rose to her feet. "So long as we are back for lunch."

They left the Carleone terrace, walked along the avenue to the bridge and over into Gamboye Plaza. Instead of walking further, Garlet decided that he wished to sit at one of the cafés, that he might watch the passersby. Skirl made no protest and the two went to a table in the shade of a laburnum tree. They were served tea and a platter of crisp pastries. Garlet, however, seemed more interested in the persons strolling across the plaza. After a moment he pointed to a young gallant and a pretty young woman. "I am a bit puzzled," said Garlet. "Why are they dressed differently?"

"It's a long-standing custom," said Skirl. "The reasons are mysterious but you will always find it so, wherever you go."

"The woman is good to look at," said Garlet. "She fascinates me with her graceful movements. I would like to touch her. Please attract her attention and signal that she is to approach."

Skirl laughed. "Garlet, you are absurd! What you have in mind is not polite; the lady would be surprised and annoyed. Do you recall what I said about etiquette? If you wish to be known as a gentleman, you must restrain such impulses."

Garlet turned Skirl a critical glance. "I like to look at you, as well. There is something definitely appealing about both you and the woman yonder. It is a feeling I cannot define."

"The feeling is normal," said Skirl. "It is the procreative instinct, and results in the birth of children."

"How so?"

Skirl supplied a general non-explicit overview of the reproductive process. "The subject is very large," she told Garlet. "There are many variations but all are controlled by strict rituals."

"I know nothing about these rituals," Garlet grumbled. "Shim never mentioned them."

"I don't expect that he would have. The process usually starts when a man and a woman feel an attraction for each other; this is called 'affection,' or sometimes 'love.' When these emotions are present, the man and the woman may unite in a social contract called 'marriage,' or perhaps they may join in a less formal union. This is the case with Jaro and me. Under such conditions, society allows them to use their sexual apparatus in a process called 'copulation.' This is not a dignified act and is done in private."

Garlet leaned forward, eyes gleaming. "Describe this 'copulation' in detail! How is it done?"

Skirl sat up stiffly in her chair and looked off across the plaza. Speaking with care, she briefly outlined the copulative process, using broad and impersonal terms. Garlet made no effort to disguise his interest, and his eyes never left Skirl's face. "That," said Skirl, "is the ordinary system of reproduction, for many living creatures."

"The activity sounds interesting," said Garlet. "Let us try it out now. Here seems to be as good a place as any."

"Wrong!" declared Skirl with fervor. "The act is attempted only in privacy!"

"Then we shall return to the palace; we will be alone in my chamber. If necessary, we can call in Fancho to help us."

Skirl shook her head. "The activity is subject to the rules of convention. Jaro would be annoyed to learn that I had been copulating at random, even under Fancho's supervision."

Garlet stared at her. "I care not at all for Jaro or his preferences. They mean nothing! You may put them aside and we will attempt these interesting acts at once."

Skirl, torn between amusement, irritation, and pity, tried to hold her voice even. "It is not all so easy. Jaro and I are joined by a bond, which is equivalent to marriage. The conventions are strict."

Garlet threw himself back in his chair. "As always," he muttered. "Jaro is the obstacle."

"It is time we were returning to Carleone for lunch," said Skirl. She rose to her feet.

"I want no lunch. I will remain here."

"Suit yourself. You know the way back."

Skirl set off across Gamboye Plaza. Garlet glowered after her, then changed his mind and ran to join her. The two returned to Carleone in silence.

3

After lunch Garlet took Jaro out on the terrace. For half an hour they stood by the balustrade engrossed in earnest conversation. Jaro finally threw his arms into the air, indicating defeat and frustration. He returned into the refectory, leaving Garlet to stare moodily across the garden.

Jaro rejoined Maihac and Skirl at the table. "Garlet has seen some pretty girls and now is excited, though he doesn't quite know why. Skirl taught him a smattering of biology and now Garlet wants to visit the Foundance."

"The Foundance?" Maihac was perplexed. "Why the Foundance?"

"Garlet has an active mind. During lunch he noticed the Seishanee girls who served us, and he was curious about their sexual habits. He wondered if Roum gentlemen copulated with them. I said I had heard no rumor or scandal; perhaps such things happened, but on the whole I thought not."

"Correct," said Maihac. "The Seishanee sexual equipment is vestigial and doesn't work."

"I told Garlet that the Seishanee were not sexually active, but he told me I was wrong. He said that the Seishanee copulated in the Foundance to produce new Seishanee: Skirl had assured him of this, and they were planning to visit the Foundance in order to inspect the activity."

"What?" cried Skirl. "This is totally imaginary!"

Garlet appeared in the doorway. Skirl told him, "I have no intention of going with you to the Foundance, for any purpose whatever!"

Garlet looked at her a moment, then shrugged. "In that case, I will go by myself."

Maihac said, "That is not a good idea. You will get into trouble, one way or another." He rose to his feet. "If you want to visit the Foundance, I'll come with you."

Garlet turned to Skirl. "I intended that you should come with me, as you agreed."

"I agreed to nothing of the sort," said Skirl.

"You spoke no words to this effect," declared Garlet, "but I understood what was in your mind."

Jaro spoke politely, "You should not say such things! When you act this way you make everyone uncomfortable."

Garlet surveyed Jaro dispassionately. "I know what is in your mind as well. You betrayed me, and now you are anxious to thwart me, since I have grown in force, and you have become small. It is no wonder you are uncomfortable."

Skirl jumped up from the table. "It is foolish to quarrel over anything, much less something so trivial. I don't mind visiting the Foundance, since Maihac will be with us."

Jaro said grimly, "I will go as well. Let us start now, and make an end to the whole affair."

Garlet swung away abruptly. The excursion was not proceeding as he had wished. This, all things considered, was not surprising. The 'force' had not completely returned and the Great Surround had not yet molded itself to his will, as eventually it must.

The four left Carleone, crossed the bridge, turned into the Esplanade and walked beside the river to the lowering stone bulk of the Foundance. A ramp sloped at a slight angle down to the entrance: a wide open portal.

Skirl stopped short. "This is as far as I am going. There is nothing in there to interest me—only a very bad smell, which I prefer to avoid. I will wait here."

Garlet made an instant protest. "You must come with me! You yourself said it was where the Seishanee reproduce! The techniques will be interesting, and you can explain them to me."

Maihac, grinning, told Garlet: "We'll make a quick survey, then, if anything interesting is going on, Skirl might well change her mind."

"That is a good idea," said Jaro. "I'll wait up here with Skirl."

"This is not what I had planned!" stormed Garlet. "Must I always be thwarted by Jaro?" He turned to Skirl. "Leave Jaro here, and Maihac if he likes. Then you and I shall explore these rituals! We might learn some interesting details."

Skirl shook her head. "I am not interested in the breeding of Seishanee—nor of anything else."

Maihac laughed. "Come along, Garlet. If there are bad smells in there, we'll ignore them, like true scientists."

Maihac and Garlet walked down the ramp and entered the building. Watching from the street, Jaro and Skirl saw them pause, then turn aside and disappear.

Twenty minutes later the two emerged from the Foundance. Maihac showed no expression. Garlet's mouth drooped and he seemed thoughtful. When he reached the Esplanade, he turned back toward the plaza without acknowledging the presence of either Jaro or Skirl. Jaro asked Maihac: "What did you learn?"

"Much and little. The bad smell exists. We discovered no copulation, only six tanks of primordial muck. We stood upon a balcony which skirts the work area, in a precarious and improvised fashion, and surveyed the activity. Grichkin technicians tended the tanks, the contents of which appeared to work and ripen from one stage to another; in the process creating the malodorous environment. A jungle of plumbing and electrical equipment stretched everywhere, making it difficult to see the level below the tanks distinctly. There seemed to be rows of small vats, where—so I suspect—the new individuals develop. On this level the technicians were of a different sort. They might have been white house-ghouls, though I could not be certain." Maihac glanced back toward the Foundance. "The place is amazing."

Jaro called to Garlet. "And what did you think of the operation?"

"It was not what I expected. I saw no copulation, and I cannot understand how or where it could be managed. I want to return and study the processes. Skirl will come with me."

"No," said Skirl. "She will not come with you."

"Nor I," said Maihac. "Once is enough."

Garlet said, "In that case, I will allow Jaro to come with me."

"Thank you, no," said Jaro. "I would not like the smell."

"Just as you like. I will go alone."

"I must remind you again," said Maihac, "We are not popular at Romarth, and someone might injure you. In about three days we will be leaving, and I want to keep a low profile until then. For the time being, it is necessary to curb your interest in copulation. Do you understand?"

Garlet made no response and the group returned to Carleone.

4

The following morning Skirl's conscience overcame her caution and she took Garlet out on the terrace for his usual lesson in matters of general interest. On this occasion Skirl had decided to discuss the history of early man on Old Earth. She was interested in the subject and spoke with animation. Garlet seemed to become infected with her enthusiasm and moved forward in his chair. As she discussed the megalith-builders of northwest Europe, she suddenly became aware that Garlet was fondling her breasts and preparing to slide his other hand into even more private areas. For an instant she sat rigid. Then she jumped to her feet, and looked down at Garlet. His face was rapt in a fatuous grin.

Skirl spoke in her most chilly voice. "Garlet, your conduct is a breach of etiquette and cannot be tolerated."

Garlet's grin faded. "You are logically incorrect."

"Nothing of the sort!" snapped Skirl. She rose to her feet. "Logic is not involved."

"Wrong! Jaro is allowed to touch you as he sees fit. I am his twin brother; you are illogical to make artificial distinctions between us. Jaro realizes his debt to me and will be the first to agree that I should share his perquisites."

Looking across the terrace, Skirl saw Maihac and Jaro approaching. "Here he is now," she told Garlet. "Ask him yourself."

Garlet gave a moody shrug and looked away. Skirl spoke to Jaro. "Garlet feels that he should share in what I will call our connubial relationship; that it is only equitable, since you and he are brothers."

Jaro said, "Garlet, your logic is not sound. Please do not attempt any intimacies with Skirl, as it would seriously annoy both of us."

Garlet muttered, "I don't see what difference it makes. You are simply thwarting me, as usual."

"Not so! In a year or two, you will have learned the customs of your new life, and you will see that I am right. In the meantime, do not inflict your erotic impulses upon Skirl. You must understand that your conduct is impolite."

"I understand you through and through! I will say no more."

Jaro nodded. "The subject is closed. Maihac and I have a plan in mind. We are about to explore one or more of the abandoned palaces. Both you and Skirl may come with us, if you like."

"I shall come, with pleasure," said Skirl. "What is your plan?"

"You will see. Garlet, what of you?"

"No. I prefer to sit at a café on the plaza."

"Just as you like. But don't bother any women, or you will find yourself in trouble."

Maihac, Jaro and Skirl rode the flitter north into Old Romarth, where the tall trees of the forest encroached upon the gardens. Maihac landed the flitter in a courtyard beside a palace built of white syenite. The three alighted and all made sure that their guns were within easy reach, for fear of the white houseghouls. "You may not see them," said Maihac, "but they'll be near. By day we're safe, unless one of us wanders off alone. Once out of sight, something happens, and you are never seen again." Maihac spoke to Skirl. "Jaro and I intend a bit of discreet looting: specifically, books from the library. They don't belong to anyone—so we tell ourselves—and no one seems concerned about them, one way or the other. I suspect that they might bring very high prices back in the Reach, especially if we keep the mystery of their source intact."

"Hmf," sniffed Skirl. "It all seems rather undignified."

"Think of us as collectors of ancient art," said Maihac. "That is more dignified, and Jaro need not feel so much shame."

"What of yourself?"

"I am a spaceman and a vagabond. I don't know the meaning of 'shame.' "

The three entered the palace, to find themselves in a hall of majestic proportion, with furnishings still useful, except for the dust of ages. The three paused in the center of the hall to listen, but heard only the impalpable singing of silence itself.

To the side of the great hall was the library: a chamber of moderate size with a heavy table of polished hardwood at the center. Shelves supporting hundreds of large leather-bound books lined the walls.

Jaro selected a pair of books at random and brought them to the table. The black leather covers, supple and soft, were embossed with an intricate floriation and exhaled pleasant fragrances of wax and preservative.

Jaro blew the dust from one of the books, then carefully lifted its cover. The pages, so he discovered, were alternately text and richly detailed illustrations draughted with a fine pen and colored inks. The subject matter consisted of landscapes, interiors, portraits, persons engaged in various activities: all wrought with what Jaro considered an absolutely felicitous technique. The text, indited in archaic characters, was beyond his comprehension.

Maihac came to watch as Jaro turned the pages. "No one troubles to create these books anymore," said Maihac. "The practice ended with the Bad Times, which closed off the High Era of Roum civilization."

Maihac studied an illustration which depicted an elaborate garden where a youth in a white smock and blue pantaloons smiled down into the face of a dark-haired girl eight or nine years old. Maihac scanned the accompanying text, then returned to the illustration. He pointed to the youth. "This is the creator of the book. His name was Taubry, of Methune House now extinct." He looked back to the text. "The girl was his cousin Tissia. Taubry called her 'Titi'; that was his pet name for her. He worked the whole of his life upon this book, and no doubt Titi created a book of her own."

"It would be interesting to compare the two books," mused Jaro. He studied the face of Taubry with interest. "It seems a pleasant face. A bit delicate, perhaps."

"This is how he thought of himself. The image may be exact or it may be somewhat idealized; either way, it makes no difference. The book is Taubry's statement, the repository of his secrets and private theories. He asserts that he was born, that he lived his life, that he knew noble emotions and moments of high delight. You are looking into Taubry's soul—perhaps the first to do so since he closed the cover and clamped the seal for the last time."

Jaro turned pages, watching as Taubry the youth became Taubry the man.

"The book is about twenty-five hundred years old," Maihac told Jaro, "perhaps a bit older. Roum antiquarians can fix a date to within a year or so by looking at the clothes—especially the shoes, and of course the gowns of the women."

Jaro paused in his turning of the pages to study another drawing, even more complicated than the first. Taubry stood in a forest glade with one leg resting on a log. He played a stringed instrument: a rebec or a lute, while three girls, wearing short gowns of near-transparent white muslin, held hands and danced in a circle. Taubry was now a pale young man with thin features framed by locks of curling brown hair. The face he showed as he plucked his instrument was rapt in the pleasures of music. His face indicated a whimsical, somewhat astringent personality, introverted rather than forthright. To the adjoining page Taubry had included what seemed to be a protocol, or a statement of principle. Maihac squinted at the page and read:

" 'Here am I, Taubry of Methune: the one, the singularity who is I. My qualities are excellent; they encompass virtue, imagery, humor and bliss. Needless to say, there has never been another like me, and never shall the cosmos know my like again, since I stand at the apex of sentient life. How then have I transcended all others, across all of time? Have I performed prodigies? Have I solved the classic mysteries? How then? By my secret; why should I not yield the truth? No reason that would not label me an ingrate. So—what of this noble secret? It is tantalizing in its simplicity: I refer to my joy in being.

" 'So all you who come after: if you be beautiful maidens, sigh for a heart-sick moment; if you be gallant cavaliers, shrug a regretful shrug; alas! None of you may fall in with the rhythm of my gorgeous life, and this will be a pity, for all of us.' "

Jaro slowly laid aside the book of Taubry. "This one shall go."

"By all means," said Maihac.

Skirl said scornfully, "I hope you two are happy, looting this old palace like a pair of ragpickers."

"Quite happy," said Jaro. "In fact, elated."

Maihac attempted to reason with Skirl: "We can't leave these beautiful objects here to rot and moulder away. That would be a tragedy!"

Skirl refused to argue further. For want of anything better to do, she pulled a book from the shelf and started to turn the pages.

Jaro took up the second book. It had been created by Susu-Ladou of Sanbary House. For much of her life she had enjoyed great physical beauty, which she celebrated with artless abandon, and why not? No one would ever learn of her escapades. Her drawings, so Jaro thought, were fascinating and a source of perplexity. The verve of the erotic elements was balanced by an artless innocence, which made their charm almost palpable. For several minutes he studied one of the drawings. The girl Susu-Ladou, shamelessly nude, sat on the ledge of an arched window close beside the river. She leaned back against a marble column, clasping one of her knees and looking out over the tranquil river. The trees were rendered in exquisite detail, as were their reflections upon the water. The girl seemed to be daydreaming; her face expressed an emotion Jaro could not find words to describe. As he studied the picture, he noticed a vague detail in the shadows of the room behind the girl. Looking closely, Jaro saw the shape of what appeared to be a house-ghoul standing at the back of the room. The picture was intriguing in large part because of its ambiguity. Why the white house-ghoul? Why the girl's lack of concern? Was she aware of the creature? There was no answer to any of the questions. Jaro laid the book upon the "To go" stack.

Skirl pushed the book she had been examining across the table. "Since you are so intent on stealing books, steal this one as well. I find it interesting."

The three sorted books for an hour, discarding very few. Maihac brought the flitter as close as possible to the library and the three loaded books into the cargo space. They climbed aboard, flew up to the *Pharsang*, where Gaing Neitzbeck helped them to transfer their cargo. With that done, the flitter and its passengers dropped back down to Carleone.

Garlet had already returned from Gamboye Plaza and had retired to his room.

The three bathed, changed clothes and met Ardrian in the small drawing room. Morlock joined the group a few minutes later. "Rumors are flying around the city," Morlock told the group. "I think there is fire behind the smoke. Asrubal is scheduled to be executed at noon four days hence. I have heard that a dozen Urd Assassinators will don masks either tomorrow or the next day. A diversion is organized to occur on the plaza. At this time the Assassinators plan to liberate Asrubal from the dungeon and take him to a temporary retreat, until the Councillors can return to the Colloquary. If the off-worlders interfere, they do so at their own risk; and may well be killed in any event, to establish a precedent."

"And so?" asked Maihac.

"I am considering several measures."

Maihac rose to his feet. "The problem has an easy solution. Let us execute Asrubal now."

" 'Now'?" asked Morlock. "At this moment? It is barely dusk. I thought we would wait until midnight."

"Now is better. No one will expect us to act so briskly. We'll do the job immediately and have done with it."

"Very well," said Morlock, "though it is not the Roum way of doing things. We prefer to ponder and calculate every permutation."

"This time we shall act as Gaeans," said Maihac. "I am ready."

Jaro rose to his feet. "I'm ready, as well."

Maihac said, "I want you and Skirl in the flitter, to provide us support, in case of a 'permutation,' as it is known here at Romarth."

Jaro put forward no arguments. He went out into the garden, brought down the flitter. Maihac called to Gaing aboard the *Pharsang*, and notified him of the plans, and the two discussed possible emergencies and settled upon a means for dealing with any such event. Maihac armed himself and Morlock with heavy Model RTV guns from the flitter's armory; then the two set off on foot toward the Justiciary. Jaro and Skirl followed overhead in the flitter.

Dusk had not yet given way to night; the Roum were preparing for their social engagements, and the avenues were empty.

In front of the Justiciary, Maihac spoke by radio to Jaro, in the flitter, two hundred feet above the surface. Maihac said, "Everything seems quiet. The Regulators are on duty. We're going in."

Maihac and Morlock entered the Justiciary. A few minutes later Jaro received another message from Maihac: "Everything is orderly. We are in the downstairs service lobby. The Regulators are bringing Asrubal up from the dungeon."

Five minutes later Maihac spoke again. "Asrubal has come into the lobby. The Regulators have put him into a chair. He has not seen us yet. Now—the time has come."

The voice went silent. In the lobby Morlock went to a cabinet, unlocked the door painted black and white, withdrew a flask containing amber syrup. One of the Regulators brought water in a goblet, which he set on the table beside Asrubal.

Morlock poured half a gill of the amber syrup into the goblet, and stirred it with a glass rod. Asrubal looked on, his bone-white face expressionless. Morlock pointed to the goblet. "Your time has come. Drink. You will be dead inside half a minute, and we will not need to strangle you with a wire noose."

Asrubal looked at the goblet. His fingers twitched. Morlock stepped back, to protect himself in case Asrubal should think to throw the poison into his face.

Asrubal looked across the lobby at Maihac, then back to the goblet. He told Morlock, "You are early."

"True. We want to forestall trouble."

Asrubal showed a thin smile. "You have solved none of my problems."

"That was not our intent."

Asrubal nodded. With a slow steady motion he took up the goblet and without hesitation swallowed the contents. He put the goblet back on the table, and sat staring morosely at Morlock. Silence in the room was dense.

Asrubal spoke at last, in a voice of measured cadence: "You have your opinion of me, but never shall you say that I failed to confront destiny in other than proper decorum."

"That is true," said Morlock. "Your dignity is impeccable. It is a good basis on which to die."

Asrubal's lips twitched; his jaw sagged; his eyes moved strangely, so that they seemed to look in different directions. He slumped forward to lay face-down upon the table.

Morlock turned to Maihac. "He is dead."

Maihac nodded. "So it appears." He stepped around the table and using his light Ezelite-gun punched three holes into the back of Asrubal's head. With each shot the body jerked.

Maihac stepped back from the table. He told Morlock, "It is not that I do not trust you, but a man may drink liquid and live; a man with three holes in his head is dead."

"You are a practical philosopher," said Morlock. He turned to the Regulators. "See that the hulk is taken to the Foundance and put into the corpse-bin."

TWENTY

1

Maihac and Morlock returned to Carleone. Morlock notified the dignitaries of the city of Asrubal's death, and explained the rationale of the early execution. From Urd House came rumbles of discontent, but the bravos grudgingly abandoned their plans for either a foray upon the Justiciary or the extermination of the off-worlders. It seemed as if the early execution had achieved its purpose.

Maihac wanted to leave at once but Morlock prevailed upon him to delay a day or two. "I mention this on behalf of the Select Committee," said Morlock.

"What is their interest in me?"

"Nothing to alarm you. In the simplest terms, they want information."

"About what?"

"Let me describe the Select Committee," said Morlock. "It is not precisely a secret organization, though it meets in private and operates without publicity. There are ten members, including six Councillors, four highly-regarded savants, and myself. The committee is aware that Romarth and its civilization is in a state of decline. Sometimes we use the word 'decay.' We also suspect that the patterns of Roum life might unkindly be described as 'decadent'—though I, personally, find this usage debatable. There is one unassailable fact, however: the population of Romarth is declining, and if the trend persists, in two hundred years there may be no more than a dozen old men and women huddled in their grand halls, with only Seishanee to fend away the white houseghouls. The Select Committee is aware of this trend and by one means or another hopes to revitalize Romarth. No course of action has been ruled out. There has been talk of ending Roum isolation and undertaking new contacts with the Gaean Reach."

"This all seems sensible enough," said Maihac. "Why do they need me?"

"You are an off-worlder and you know the ways of Romarth. Your qualifications are unique. The Committee wants to hear your opinions. They will expect you to speak with full candor, even though one or two of the most conservative grandees are already grumbling as to the risks of what they call 'vulgarization.' "

"Sometimes it can't be helped," said Maihac. "Still, I'll talk with them. When and where? It must be quick."

"The time is two hours after noon tomorrow. The place is here at Carleone."

"Very well," said Maihac. "That is convenient enough. Directly after the meeting we will leave Romarth aboard the *Pharsang.*"

When Garlet learned of the projected departure, he wasted no time in expressing his disapproval. "I see no reason to leave this place," he told Maihac and Jaro. "I have learned the route from Gamboye Plaza to Carleone, and also down the Esplanade as far as the Foundance, which is adequate for my present needs. My rooms at Carleone are tolerable, as is the food. Jaro will be on hand to help me make social connections."

Maihac said gently, "Your ideas are impractical. In the first place, Jaro will be gone aboard the *Pharsang*. You would be alone, to fend for yourself. The Roum would not take care of you. They live by rituals which you do not understand. If you tried to stay here alone, you would be barely tolerated—perhaps not even that, if you interfered with the women."

Garlet gave his head a stubborn shake. "Jaro knows these rituals well enough. He can teach me; it is the least he can do."

"I shall be here only one more day," said Jaro. "That is hardly time enough to teach you anything."

"I did not specify one day," Garlet told him. "We will proceed at a suitable pace, as our life develops."

Maihac became impatient. "Listen, Garlet, and listen carefully! There is nothing for you to do here, nothing for you to learn. You would soon become unhappy."

Garlet said mulishly, "That is not necessarily so. At the moment, I am quite content to sit at a café where I can watch the Roum pass by on their promenades. Already I have seen several young women of haunting beauty, and I wish to become intimate with them. This is where Jaro's assistance will be valuable."

"It is not so easy, even for Jaro," said Maihac, grinning. "The young women may be polite, but none will become intimate with you. Like everyone else, the girls are constricted by convention, and the arts of Roum love-making are elaborate. In any case, Jaro will be aboard the *Pharsang* with the rest of us."

Garlet turned to Jaro. "It is your duty to stay!"

Jaro shook his head. "I can't leave this weird world fast enough."

Garlet muttered, "Once again I am thwarted." He jerked to his feet and turned to leave. Maihac called to him, "Where are you going?"

"To the plaza."

Maihac reflected. "The Urd bravos still think we have shamed their house, and they might decide to make an example of you. I would prefer that you remain at Carleone, but in the plaza you are probably safe—especially if Jaro is with you."

"Jaro may come," said Garlet judiciously, "but he must be helpful and not interfere with what I have in mind."

Maihac laughed sourly. "He might be forced to interfere, to save your skin, if I am guessing your intentions correctly." He thought a moment, then brought out his heavy RTV power-gun. He told Jaro, "Let's trade for today. You give me your Ezelite, and carry the RTV."

The exchange was made. "Now you are safe for sure," said Maihac. "At one puff the RTV will take out the entire House of Urd. The threat will end before it starts."

Garlet grumbled, "If I should speak politely to a beautiful young woman, I do not think that Jaro should be entitled to shoot her."

"He will be careful," Maihac assured him. "Still, to be on the safe side, do not speak to any women, beautiful or otherwise. They might misunderstand your interest."

"They'll understand, well enough," said Jaro, "which is worse."

Garlet said, "I would prefer to carry the gun myself. Jaro's judgment is not to be trusted."

Maihac shook his head. "You do not know how to use the gun. You might end up shooting your own foot, or Jaro, or some passing stranger."

"Bah. I am not so foolish as you think."

Jaro sighed. "One more day on Fader, then back to the tranquil routines of space—though, with Garlet aboard the routines might not be so tranquil as before." He rose to his feet. "Come. If we are going to the plaza, let's make a start."

As the two walked along the avenue, Jaro watched Garlet covertly sidewise. He wondered what would happen if Garlet insisted upon remaining at Romarth? Jaro suspected that Maihac would bring him aboard the *Pharsang*, either willingly, unwillingly and sullen, or drugged and unconscious. In any case Garlet would undoubtedly depart Fader with the *Pharsang*, and the hoped for tranquility of the voyage would be in jeopardy. Jaro sighed once more. What must be, must be.

The two arrived at the plaza. Garlet pointed. "That is the best café; the girls who pass there are prettier than those to be seen elsewhere."

"You are observant," said Jaro. "That is a good thing to know."

The two seated themselves and were served fruit punch. Jaro sat back to contemplate the Roum, perhaps for the last time. They were folk of intriguing characteristics, with virtues and vices, strengths and weaknesses, unique to themselves—not to mention an environment crammed with art treasures they took for granted, and white house-ghouls which they endured as elements of their ordinary experience.

For an hour Garlet sat silent, occasionally exclaiming as to the merits of a passing woman, sometimes in marvelling enthusiasm so earnest as to attract the attention of the woman or her escort, which in turn caused Jaro to grope for the reassuring bulk of the RTV. But Garlet's acts brought only supercilious stares from the Roum.

Jaro became bored. He suggested that they return to Carleone.

Garlet picked up a pastry knife, tapped it upon the table a few times, held it still, watching intently. He tapped the knife again, then looked up at Jaro. "Not yet."

Jaro shrugged and composed himself to wait.

The sun settled toward the tall trees of the Blandy Deep. Once again Jaro suggested that the time had come to leave.

Garlet frowned, craned his neck to look here and there around the plaza. "There was a most appealing woman who passed yesterday. I observed her carefully and we exchanged glances. I was hoping that she would pass today, when I planned to propose a more intimate relationship."

"Give up that idea," said Jaro. "The plaza is almost empty; the Roum are all dressing for their dinner parties. The woman will not be back."

"She might if she knew that I was waiting to speak to her."

"Not a chance. Come; the sun is dropping into the forest."

Garlet said coldly, "If you are anxious to leave, you may do so."

"It is not so easy," said Jaro. "If I left you here and by some chance you came to grief, I would be held accountable. The woman will not be back today."

"Perhaps not." Garlet searched the plaza. "We will try again tomorrow."

"Tomorrow morning, if you insist—though nothing can come of it. We will be leaving Romarth tomorrow afternoon."

"The others perhaps," said Garlet in an uninterested voice. "You and I will remain."

Jaro gave a curt laugh. "Wrong.. We are taking you back into the Reach for your own good." Jaro hitched himself forward in his chair. "Are you ready to go?"

"One moment. I will consult yaha once more." Garlet held the pastry knife an inch above the table. It twisted to the right and tilted down to tap the table. "I am advised to wait another ten minutes."

"Interesting," said Jaro. "The knife is your 'yaha'?"

Garlet gave a snort of confident superiority. "Not the knife, naturally. 'Yaha' is something I discovered years ago, while I huddled in the dark. It came upon me like the dawn of order upon a field of chaos. It was known as 'yaha.' Does the word carry meaning to your mind?"

"No."

"Not surprising, since it was I who formed the word. The idea is strong. I would not be the man I am today were it not for 'yaha.' "

Jaro looked from the knife to Garlet. "What do you do when no knife is available?"

Garlet gave another snort of disgust. "The knife is incidental. In simple words, it is the play of independent free will among choices. The ordinary mind does not control or even affect yaha, and this is the basis of the force. The conscious mind puts the question; yaha searches among the options and indicates a 'yes' or a 'no.' To the left lies the energetic, restless, daring principle; it also signifies 'negative.' To the right is 'affirmative,' and also the serene and restful. Imagine a circle. Outside is the 'left'; inside is the 'right.' "

"I must give the idea further thought," said Jaro.

"That is just the start. Yaha works another way, with no reference to 'left' and 'right.' Yaha becomes a vehicle of suspenseful wonder! It is a source of excitement; yet all is accomplished with the simplest of means—in fact, nothing whatever. In the dark dungeon I could always undertake a glorious adventure using the infinite scope of yaha." Garlet peered sidewise at Jaro. "Ha hah! You wear that blinking fat-cheeked face of stupidity which so ill becomes you!"

"Oh, sorry," said Jaro.

"Do you discredit what I am telling you?"

"No, certainly not! The idea is difficult to grasp."

"Listen then! Place four fingers flat on the table. They are like four little entities, each distinct from the other. They lie quiet; they are thinking. One of them will move. Which one? I don't know, nor do I know when. I wait. Then, from nowhere, comes yaha. By mysterious impulse, one of the fingers moves! The suspense bursts in a tingle of surprise. Now then, another time: I hold a finger close to my face. Will I touch my nose? Or my chin? A mystery! The future is inscrutable! The denouement cannot be guessed! I sit for minutes on end waiting for yaha to act. Here is the soul of high drama! And then—the finger moves! Where? I cannot reveal the secret. I will say this, however: the finger might touch neither nose nor chin, but move in a startling direction, as if impelled by a mischievous imp—to ear or forehead! Here is yaha in a playful mood, and sometimes very endearing. But enough; now you know something of yaha—but not everything; I assure you of this." Garlet sat half-smiling, lost in a reverie, thinking back across his years in the dark.

Jaro stirred himself. "Ten minutes has come and gone; it is time we were going."

Garlet made no protest; the two returned across the plaza, over the bridge, along the avenue to Carleone.

2

During the afternoon, while Jaro and Garlet sat at the cafe, Maihac and Skirl had visited another ancient palace. Skirl, abandoning all compunctions, worked energetically with Maihac to ferry three cargoes of magnificent leather-bound chronicles up to the *Pharsang*. After the third transfer, instead of returning to Carleone, Skirl had elected to remain aboard the *Pharsang*.

Jaro reported to Maihac that Garlet had reiterated his intent to remain at Romarth, and described Garlet's development of the 'yaha' principle.

Maihac was both intrigued and impressed. "We may be expecting the impossible from Garlet. He trained his brain to function in the dark dungeon. Up here in the sunlight, and a space of far perspectives, he has become disoriented, and now is probably quite mad. Tomorrow he will try to give you the slip, and hide until we are gone. That is my guess. If he decides to visit the plaza tomorrow morning, you must not let him out of your sight."

"He may simply refuse to return. I can't carry him back."

"Take a radio. If he gives you trouble, call for help and I'll bring the flitter. Don't forget your RTV."

In the morning Maihac and Jaro took breakfast with Garlet. They found him taciturn and preoccupied with private thoughts. He seemed not to notice the absence of Skirl and ignored Jaro. After breakfast he went out to sit on the terrace. Jaro joined him and tried to initiate a conversation. Garlet responded with curt monosyllables, and presently Jaro fell silent.

Half an hour passed. Garlet rose abruptly to his feet. Jaro, lounging nearby, asked, "Where are you going?"

"Out to the cafe."

"I'll come with you."

Garlet gave an indifferent shrug and set off along the avenue, with Jaro beside him. At Gamboye Plaza, Garlet halted and looked about the area. The hour was early and few folk were abroad. Garlet frowned in dissatisfaction and turned away. "The Esplanade is more interesting. The girls walk with an easier motion."

"You may well be right," said Jaro. "It's a nice distinction which I admit that I have not made."

Garlet deigned no reply. The two walked along the Esplanade almost to the Foundance before Garlet selected a cafe which exactly suited his purposes. The two seated themselves at a table overlooking the river. Jaro ordered tea and scones, which Garlet scorned with a sidelong glance and a sniff of contempt. He turned half-away, to stare out over the river. Jaro was content to sit in silence.

Time passed, while Garlet continued to brood across the water. Then, as if impacted by a sudden thought, he swung around to study the bulk of the Foundance. Purposefully he jumped to his feet. Jaro watched in fascination. An idea was developing in Garlet's mind.

Garlet glanced down at Jaro. He said, "I'm going to look into the Foundance. You may stay here."

Jaro frowned toward the heavy brown structure, which he had so carefully avoided on a previous occasion. He spoke disapprovingly: "Why go there? You've already seen it once."

"I want to see it again. You don't need to come."

Jaro reluctantly rose to his feet. "I'll come. Those were my orders."

Garlet turned his head sharply. Jaro thought that he might be smiling. Garlet set off along the Esplanade. At the ramp he paused and looked back over his shoulder. Jaro stared in wonder. Odd!

For an instant Garlet's gaunt hollow-cheeked face, with its gleaming eyes had become the face of a sly wolf. Jaro blinked and looked again. The peculiar illusion was gone.

Garlet spoke softly, "There are bad smells inside this place. When you were here before, you decided to wait outside. Do so again, if you like."

Jaro saw that Garlet was taunting him. The overt hostility was not unwelcome; his duty toward this intransigent person was becoming more and more nebulous. He said, "I can tolerate it if you can."

"Oh yes. I am used to bad smells. I hardly know one from another."

Garlet turned and loped down the ramp; Jaro hastened to catch up with him; together they passed through the open portal and into a wide corridor, which at one time had served as a reception hall. A row of dilapidated benches ranged the wall to the right. To the left windows overlooked a production area on a lower level. Garlet spared only a glance toward the windows and proceeded down the corridor. Jaro halted to survey the scene below. He was awed by the confusion of massive kettles, vats, tanks, tubs, tangles of glass plumbing and heavy banks of energy converters, peculiar archaic equipment—some suspended on rods from overhead girders, some balanced precariously on pedestals, some perched on staging close above the slurry tanks. Jaro turned to look after Garlet, who had passed through the archway at the far end of the corridor and no longer could be seen. Jaro's subconscious suspicions began to take definite shape; he could not dismiss the notion that Garlet might be pursuing a devious plot. Jaro uneasily felt for the RTV at his belt.

The archway at the end of the corridor opened into what evidently had been an administrative office: an area now scattered with hulks of old desks, storage compartments, broken chairs. Garlet was nowhere to be seen.

Another archway led into the room adjacent: a workshop cluttered with the wrecks of machine tools, gauges, meters and other equipment. Garlet stood by a door leading out upon the balcony which flanked the production area thirty feet below. The door was ajar; Garlet was on the point of stepping through the opening, out upon the metal mesh of the balcony deck.

Jaro called, "Hold up! Where are you going?"

Garlet looked back from the open door. "The breeding tanks are below. If you are interested in the bad smell, you must come out here."

"No need," said Jaro. "I can smell it well enough in here."

"Ah! But if you want to test the full strength, you will find it only out on the balcony, where the steam rises from below."

"Some other time," said Jaro. "I am not a connoisseur of such things."

Garlet pondered a moment, then asked, "Are you not interested in the breeding processes?"

"I saw all I care to see from the window in the hall. I am astonished that the system functions. The technicians are either masters of improvisation—or madmen."

Garlet turned to look around at the old machinery. "I don't understand these devices." He pointed. "What is that thing?"

"That is a positronic welder. It spurts positrons and where they strike, the heat of the reaction bonds materials together."

Jaro explained the function of several other mechanisms.

Garlet turned his attention to the workbench. "What are those things? Some are strangely shaped."

"They are hand-tools. That object is a pipe wrench. On the wall is a dimensional shaper. That long rod is an ordinary pry bar. Those are gouges, with blades of an artificial substance called 'gorgolium,' which never grows dull."

"And that thing yonder?"

"It is a meter, for measuring stress."

Garlet studied Jaro skeptically. "How do you know all these things?"

"I worked several years in a machine shop at the Thanet spaceport."

"No matter. Do you care to sit? I am about to reveal my plans."

Jaro leaned back against the workbench. "Speak on, but try to be brisk, since before long we must return to Carleone."

"I will speak to the point. The plans are firm, so please suggest no changes." Garlet's voice was calm and reasonable. "The ideas you are about to hear are not idle conjecture. I have built upon a foundation of indisputable first causes, so that the unifying force which controls the cosmos is revealed in full clarity. I refer, of course, to 'balance.' If a system ignores 'balance,' it will collapse. The laws of dynamic equity govern everything large and small, near and far. They may be applied to any appropriate phase of existence."

"Yes; very interesting," said Jaro. "We will take up the subject again some other time, but now we must be getting on back to Carleone."

"Not just yet," said Garlet. He stood stern and straight, shoulders thrown back, eyes gleaming in their deep sockets, a peculiar pink flush coloring his cheeks. "The topic has an immediate application. I refer to the system which includes you and me. Over the years the 'balance' has been distorted into an abnormal shape, and is now in an unstable condition."

"This is neither the time nor the place for dialectics," said Jaro. "In any case these ideas reflect your personal perspective, not mine; and certainly they represent no universal truth. However, we have no time to argue the matter. Let's be out of here; for a fact the stink is oppressive."

Garlet's eyes flamed. "Silence. Listen with care! The distortion exists: that is our premise. Let us develop the idea. Are you alert?"

"Of course! Get on with it."

Garlet paced back and forth across the workshop. "At the beginning, Jaro and Garlet were one, and 'balance' existed. Then came the schism, and everything changed. Both pity and shame were ground underfoot. Jaro was ordained the singular and preeminent 'I.' The miserable Garlet became a huddle in the dark, lacking even so much as a pronoun to indicate his identity. He was nothing: a barely sentient plasm, a thing of the dark depths, only just able to realize that he was alive. So the years passed. With glacial torpor the thing developed. The grichkin Shim talked incessantly; the thing learned of ideas and their transfer. From Shim he learned his name, and a few other oddments, since Shim enjoyed his boasts. He spoke largely of many things, whether he had certain knowledge or none. From Shim, Garlet learned hunger, deprivation and spite; from Oleg he learned fear and pain. From his own inner faculties came sentience. You and I are the same stuff, and there was resonance between us. I became able to watch from the dark! I began to know yearning; I began to crave what I sensed of your enjoyments and gluttonies. In my longing I called to you, but you only hugged your privileges more tightly.

"In the end Destiny has altered its face and suddenly an era of adjustment is upon us. We will stay at Romarth, and you must accept this plan with stoicism, even though you will now subordinate your joy to mine. Our first acts will be to engage the sympathy of the lovely maidens who saunter the streets in such profusion."

Jaro gave a painful laugh. "Garlet, be realistic! Your ideas are absurd. We are leaving Romarth this afternoon. You must adjust to this idea."

"Not so! You are wrong! You will stay here with me. Why? Because equipoise implies redress! I am entitled to solace! To this end you might wish to do a stint in the dungeons to show the sincerity of your grief. I will assume the function of Shim, which truly would please me, and we will continue in this fashion until we agree that equilibrium has been restored."

Jaro listened in awe. Garlet was not necessarily mad; by the tenets of his own universe he might be wise, but away from the fourth level dungeon, the mental tools he had fashioned so painfully were useless. Indeed, worse than useless.

Jaro spoke gently, "Garlet, believe this as fact: I had no part in your misfortunes and I will accept no guilt. I will help you to a reasonable extent—but, once and for all, I am not staying with you at Romarth. I want you to come away, perhaps to Gallingale, and start a new life."

Garlet laughed in delight. "Now! You must take counsel with yaha! There is a choice, or better to say a divergence in destiny! The choice you must make is this: will you abide here at my command or will you try to thwart me again? If so, it will be the last time, for I shall have lost patience."

"Garlet! Be reasonable!"

"The time of decision has come. It is a most important yaha. So—what is it to be? 'Left' or 'right'? 'Yes' or 'no'? 'Life' or 'death'?"

Garlet watched Jaro keenly. Then he cried: "The decision has come, and my patience is gone. 'Death' you have chosen; 'death' it shall be."

His posture stately and grave, Garlet walked to the workbench, picked up the pry bar, hefted it and found its length and mass to his satisfaction. He nodded, as if to say: "Yes; this will do admirably." Then he turned to face Jaro, who displayed the RTV.

"This," said Jaro, "is a most powerful gun. In a twinkling it will reduce you to flaring particles."

"Just so," said Garlet. "But I forbid you to use it in that manner. Give it to me." He stepped forward, hand outstretched.

Jaro backed away. He thought: If I put the gun away, I can probably subdue him, bar or no bar, and I will not need to kill him. Or so I hope. Jaro tucked the gun into his belt. "Garlet, put the bar down and let us leave this dreadful place."

"No. I shall abide here for a time. There are grichkin below; they will supply my gruel and salt fish." He advanced upon Jaro, bar ready to strike. Jaro prepared to feint, seize Garlet's arm and twist until the bar dropped from his fingers, and Garlet cried in pain. Garlet's smile broadened. "I know what you have in mind." He brought up his other hand and threw a stress-gauge into Jaro's face. It struck Jaro full on the mouth and nose, blinding him and breaking his concentration. Garlet struck with majestic force, but Jaro in desperation lurched aside and the blow crushed his shoulder instead of his head. Jaro reeled back, to fall heavily, half through the door to the balcony. Garlet strode forward, to stand straddling Jaro like a vengeful colossus. With deliberation he raised the bar, as Jaro clawed the RTV from his belt. Garlet kicked, and the gun slid out upon the mesh of the balcony. Up went the bar; down with all force, so that Garlet's eyes bulged with the effort. Jaro rolled frantically aside and the bar clattered down upon the mesh, jarring loose from Garlet's grip. Jaro scrambled after the gun, left arm dangling limp. Garlet flung himself forward, hissing and screaming, to snatch the gun away from Jaro's clutching fingers.

Garlet stood back in the doorway, pointing the gun down at Jaro, who lay on the mesh of the balcony. Garlet said, "So it comes to this: the ultimate yaha. I ask, shall I kill you at the count of five or shall I wait for the unexpected impulse?" Garlet reflected, half-smiling, torn between two delightful choices. "Let it come as it comes! That is the soul of yaha. First, a subsidiary question: shall I shoot at your head, or your chest? Or shall I let the gun decide? The indecision is thrilling; it is yaha."

The two stared at each other. Garlet said, "The tension swells! It is about to bubble, to burst!"

Jaro cried out, "Garlet, think what you are doing! I am your brother! I came here to help you!"

Garlet smiled. "Nothing avails! My pain knows no redemption. Now!" His voice rose in a catch of excitement. "My finger closes on the trigger! I shoot!"

Nothing happened. Garlet looked for a moment at the gun, puzzled. "Ah! Now I see; this is the way!" As he spoke, Garlet released the saftey and fired.

Jaro frantically rolled aside at the twitch of Garlet's finger. He saw the blue energy flash downward past his head to hit the pedestal supporting a tall copper tank. The tank toppled into an energy converter, which exploded on impact. Glass pipes fell tinkling and clashing to the floor.

Garlet seemed not to notice. Lips drawn back, he fired again as Jaro kicked at him. The bolt went wide and struck the work area. More converters exploded and burst into flames. Beneath the balcony screams rose from horrified grichkin and, perhaps, from white house-ghouls on the sub-surface level.

Garlet, with single-minded purpose, stepped forward and again fired down upon Jaro, who just managed to scramble behind a pillar. Now he watched the blue energy strike an enormous centrifugal separator that broke apart and fell into the slurry vats, smashing them and spilling their contents. Flames crackled and explosions sounded throughout the Foundance. Garlet at last became aware of the terrible destruction. He stared in surprise over the rail.

Jaro pulled himself to his knees, then staggered upright, grasping the pry-bar that his hand had fallen upon. Garlet turned about, serene and confident. Jaro jabbed the pry-bar into his face. Garlet gave a cry of outrage and fell back against the rail. He raised the gun. Jaro struck swiftly with the bar and Garlet, jerking back, lost his footing and tumbled over the rail. He fell whirling and flailing into a pool of flaming reagents, writhed for a moment, then became still.

Panting, Jaro looked down in horror and pity at the black corpse of his brother. It was over; there was nothing he could do. He turned, departed the Foundance, and ran at best speed to Carleone, while behind him tendrils of smoke rose into the sky.

3

Not until middle afternoon did the full impact of what had happened at the Foundance strike into the consciousness of the Roum. Even then, the implications of the event only gradually became clear. Gamboye Plaza thronged with the stunned folk of the city, who now realized that during the day, without warning or premonition, their lives had been irrevocably ravaged. Everywhere the same questions were heard: what had happened? How great was the damage? Was it definite that there would be no more Seishanee?

The reality was hard to grasp. Changes would be gradual, as the labor force dwindled by attrition and the quality of life became ever more austere. There would be no more splendid pageants, no more grand banquets, no more gorgeous costumes except what could be salvaged and repaired. In about twenty years, or at most thirty years, the last of the Seishanee would be gone and the glorious traditions of old Romarth would become a memory.

The options for the future were dismal. The Roum must either toil for sheer survival here on Fader, or they must emigrate to new homes somewhere among the worlds of the Gaean Reach. In fifty years all the palaces of Romarth would be abandoned, with only house-ghouls to stare by moonlight across the decaying gardens. The prospect was dreary indeed, and the folk in Gamboye Plaza became ever more oppressed as they considered the future.

Gradually it became known that off-worlders had caused the disaster. A great fury infected the Roum. Had Jaro or Skirl or Maihac been on hand, they would have fared badly. But the

Pharsang was already far off in space, fleeing back toward Yellow Rose Star.

4

Early in the afternoon, Maihac met with the Select Committee in the grand hall at Carleone. Jaro had returned to tell his terrible tale only half an hour before, and it became Maihac's painful duty to inform the Committee of the disaster. He did so in six crisp sentences.

The ten dignitaries showed shocked white faces to Maihac, but for a time were unable to make coherent utterances. There were inarticulate stammers and guttural rasps of dismay; then, as if reacting to a common impulse, all sagged back into their seats. The Foundance had been destroyed; there would be no more Seishanee, and the folk of Romarth must face a difficult and dreary future.

Maihac watched while the ten Roum assimilated the news. He wondered whether they still would want to hear his statement. His ideas were more cogent now than ever; he must speak, regardless of their probable disinclinations. A new thought occurred to him, and he wondered whether he dared express it to the company. The idea might well be resented, but even if they became furious, he carried the Ezelite handgun and was leaving Romarth within the hour; probably the worst they could do would be to revile him and call him a bumptious fool and a mischievous swine of an off-worlder. He had survived invective many times before.

Maihac held up his hand to fix the committee's attention upon himself. "Gentlemen, I sympathize with your distress, but since my time is limited and what I can tell you is important, I will ignore tact. Please do not expect to be soothed.

"Originally we were to discuss the gradual decay of Romarth and its discouraging prospects. As I understand it, you wanted constructive suggestions as to how you might best deal with these problems. After what has happened, these problems become even more urgent, since you can no longer hope for gradual solutions. Changes must be made at once. There will be dislocation and discomfort whether you like it or not.

"I am prompted to point out, and I do so very timorously, that what happened at the Foundance may not be an unmitigated calamity. Now you cannot indulge in long and stately deliberations; you have no choice but to act."

One of the grandees found his voice. "Action is easy to recommend, but more difficult to plan and organize."

"I agree," said Maihac. "Here are several constructive ideas.

"First, the entire Roum population might emigrate to other worlds of the Gaean Reach. This is an obvious concept, and probably the least appealing, since it is unpredictable and several generations might pass before a satisfactory standard of living could be achieved.

"Second, and equally obvious, is the notion that the Roum themselves undertake the work now done by the Seishanee. I realize that you are congenitally averse to physical labor, but it is not so irksome as you may believe, especially when you use modern agricultural methods and machinery, along with material synthesizers.

"Third, there is the possibility of expanding your export trade. Asrubal has demonstrated that there are profits to be earned, but you will need to develop business techniques. Your best hope might be to send a cadre of young men and women to Gaean business schools.

"Fourth is tourism. If some of the old palaces were converted into hotels, Romarth might become the focus of a profitable tourist industry. Under these conditions you would continue to live as picturesque aristocrats dedicated to the arts and rituals of Old Romarth. You would wear your splendid costumes and practice your exquisite etiquette. On the other hand, you would not be allowed to mistreat the tourists. Needless to say, such a scheme requires the investment of considerable capital."

"Unfortunately," said Ardrian, "capital of this magnitude is not at our disposal."

"You have confiscated over a million sols from Asrubal. That is a start, though it is not nearly enough. More capital is accessible through banks or, better, from private investors, who may be able to bring expertise to the project. Now then—and here is the nub of the matter. I know of at least one man who commands great wealth and who might be attracted to a project of this sort. This person is hard-headed, practical, self-willed. However, he is neither a thief nor a scoundrel, and he is susceptible to reasonable argument. I am leaving Romarth immediately. I will transport a deputation aboard the *Pharsang* so that they may meet this gentleman. If he becomes interested in the project, as I think likely, he will enter into a covenant with the folk of Romarth, each party defining its rights and privileges. He will want to make changes. For instance, he will bring in professional exterminators to eradicate the house-ghouls. As for the Loklor, you might decide that these nomad horrors contribute to the picturesque charm of Fader, and allow them the liberty of the Tangtsang, provided that they ask no tourists to dance with their girls.

"As to how you might replace your Seishanee and provide yourselves domestic service, I cannot even guess.

"That exhausts my list of constructive suggestions. If you intend to act upon Item Four, select a deputation at this moment. I repeat: they must be ready to leave at once, since I don't want to be on hand when the mob comes to call."

5

At Thanet, Maihac, by means of hints and mysterious allusions, induced Gilfong Rute to dine with him at the Blue Moon Inn. The two were served aperitifs, but Rute refused to look at the dinner menu until Maihac had explained the nature of his business. "My time is valuable; I am not here to exchange pleasantries, nor yet to revel in the Blue Moon cuisine. Get to the point, if you please."

"Be calm," said Maihac. "You will hear everything in due course. In the meantime, enjoy this tonic. It is known as the 'Toe-Clencher Number Two,' and I ordered it mixed to a special recipe."

Rute tasted the tonic. "Yes, most refreshing. And now, as to the revelations you were hinting at, please offer me some light instead of smoke and subterfuge. Speak on!"

"Oh very well," said Maihac, "if you insist. Personally, I was enjoying the suspense." Maihac opened a small valise and brought out a large leather-bound book, which he placed on the table in front of Rute. "Look into this book, if you will."

Rute glanced through the pages, at first casually, then with growing interest. "I can't make head or tail of the text, but the pictures seize upon the imagination. The detail is meticulous. In fact, it is a beautiful book!" He looked again at the first few pages, then looked up with a frown of puzzlement. "I see no mention of the publisher, nor any commercial advice."

"For a good reason," said Maihac. "The book is indited in a

special calligraphy and illustrated by the same person. Her name was Zahamilla of Torres House; the book is an autobiographical document and represents an overview of her life. There are no copies and no commercial production; in this sense it is unique."

Rute studied the pages. "Hmm." He glanced up sharply. "Is this place real? Or is it a fantasy created by the imagination?"

"It is real. I have been there myself."

Rute nodded and, in an elaborately offhand voice, asked: "Where is this place?"

"That is part of the mystery," said Maihac. "It is a lost world."

Rute turned more pages. "Strange and amazing. Why do you show this book to me?"

"It is a long story. Let us order our dinner and I will tell you what I know."

During the dinner and afterward Maihac spoke of his association with the world Perdu. "That is not the proper name," he told Rute. "But for present purposes it will do very well."

Rute listened with impassive interest, while Maihac spoke on.

"The city is very old. Many of the ancient palaces are abandoned, though structurally they are sound and could be converted into tourist hotels of the highest category with relatively little expense. There are other interesting aspects to this world, including—as you have seen—a unique civilization of an advanced and sophisticated culture. Tourists and tour groups from everywhere in the Reach would want to visit Perdu if they were able to do so."

Rute surveyed Maihac under hooded eyelids. "Why do you tell me all this, in such detail?"

"To develop Perdu for tourists would require considerable capital. You could supply this capital, and I thought that you might be interested in such a scheme."

Rute reflected a moment, then asked, "What is your personal interest in the project? In short, how do you gain?"

"So far as I can see, not at all. I have brought here a deputation from Perdu; you would deal with them exclusively."

"Hmmf. You are taking no percentage, or fee?"

"Nothing. The deal is between you and the deputation. I have no plans to return to Perdu."

"Hmmf. Most quixotic." Rute once again looked through the pages of the book. "Do these pictures accurately represent the condition of the palaces?"

"They do not do the city justice." There was a pause while

Rute studied pages of the book. Maihac went on: "I can think of three areas of possible difficulty. The inhabitants of the city are aristocrats and they will not allow what they call 'vulgarization.' They are proud of their traditions and you will need all your tact when you deal with them."

"No problem. What else?"

"Second, many of the abandoned palaces are infested with what are known as 'white house-ghouls.' They live in tunnels and crypts under the palaces and must be exterminated."

Rute grinned. "So long as I am not asked to lead the charge in person."

"Third, and not too serious—in fact, more of a picturesque adjunct than otherwise—savage nomads wander the steppes, and will need to be disciplined."

Rute nodded. "Anything else?"

"A multitude of minor problems, no doubt. If you are interested, you will want to visit the city in person."

"True."

"Then you are interested?"

"Yes, I think so. Enough to want to take a look."

"In that case, we will need to prepare an initial covenant, or contract, to prevent you from acting independently, once you learn the location of this world. Otherwise there would be nothing to prevent you from sending out an expedition to act strictly in your own best interests."

Rute showed Maihac a sour smile. "You seem to lack confidence in my integrity."

"You are wealthy," said Maihac. "Your money did not come to you because of your bonhomie. Along the way you must have left a number of disgruntled adversaries."

"That is an understatement," said Gilfong Rute. "In this case, you need not worry. I will try to behave in a civilized manner."

"That is reassuring," said Maihac. "Again I emphasize that the folk of Perdu can, at times, be tiresome. They consider themselves the elite of the universe and tend to think of off-worlders as ignorant louts and buffoons."

Rute waved his hand. "In my time I have dealt with both Quantorces and Clam Muffins. Now I am ready for anything."

Maihac agreed. "It is the same kettle of fish. You'll have an interesting time. Tomorrow we will take legal advice and draw up the preliminary covenant. After that, you are on your own."

6

Gilfong Rute, accompanied by the Roum deputation and a team of professional advisors, had departed Thanet, bound for Fader and the city Romarth. Maihac had counseled Morlock, Ardrian and the others to the best of his ability, explaining that in any final contract with Gilfong Rute, all parties would be well served by stipulating every phase of the development in minute detail, leaving as little as possible to interpretation.

Maihac advised that the final contract with Rute should be negotiated not at Romarth but at Thanet, where the Roum could employ competent legal representatives of their own.

Finally, Maihac recommended that the Roum protect the contents of their palaces with great vigilance. "The books, curios, art goods—they will disappear like snow in summer unless you take special care. Tourists can not be trusted; when they want a souvenir, honesty flies out the window!"

During the transactions Jaro and Skirl wandered about Thanet, where everything seemed at once familiar and strange. Merriehew had been razed to the ground; Sasoon Ayry housed a new family, high up the ledges of status, the gentleman a Lemurian and his spouse on the committee of the Sasselton Tigers.

While Jaro looked into the old offices of the Faths at the Institute, Skirl went off on an errand of her own. When she rejoined Jaro, she was bubbling with excitement. "I have studied the Clam Muffin by-laws and I have conferred with several of the committee members. They agree that I may nominate you into a special category of the Clam Muffins. This is a privilege accorded to members so that they need not feel embarrassed when they introduce their spouses in public. You would become an Associate Member, Provisional. The vote will be almost automatic—but first we must be formally married."

"What!" cried Jaro. "Am I to become a married man and a Clam Muffin at one fell swoop?"

"It may not be as bad as you think," said Skirl. "Also, it is what I want."

"Oh well, why not?" said Jaro.

"We shall be married tomorrow, in the Clam Muffin sanctuary," Skirl told him. "It will be a very important occasion."

At the wedding Jaro wore a formal dark suit in which he felt self-conscious. Skirl was dressed in a white frock and a tiara of white flowers. In Jaro's opinion she looked totally beautiful, and he thought that it was a great privilege to be married to her. He recalled Langolen School, where he had first noticed Skirlet Hutsenreiter. Smiling to himself he remembered the mannerisms which among her peers had caused such stifled outrage, jealousy and awe, but which now, in retrospect, seemed only quaint and charming. Imaginative, intelligent, daring little Skirlet Hutsenreiter! He had admired her from a distance, and now he was married to her! These were the marvels which sometimes accompanied the act of being alive. Jaro wondered if 'yaha,' in one phase or another, were involved. He would give the matter thought when he had more time.

Skirl had also been looking back over the years. "It seems so long ago," she mused.

Jaro smiled in wistful recollection. "The world was very different then. I like it better now."

Skirl squeezed his arm and laid her head on his shoulder. "Think of it! We've visited Old Romarth and we own the *Pharsang!* And so much is still ahead of us!"

The two celebrated their new status with Gaing and Maihac at the Blue Moon Inn. Before dinner, they sat in the lounge, drinking one of the soft yellow wines produced in the rolling hills to the east of Thanet.

Skirl made an announcement: "This is truly an important day for us, but for Jaro most of all, since he is now a Clam Muffin, and a person of great prestige! He deserves the honor, and I am proud of him!"

Jaro said modestly: "I don't want to exaggerate the honor. If you look at the fine print on the certificate, you will see where it reads: 'Associate Member, Provisional.'"

"That is a minor detail," said Skirl. "A Clam Muffin is a Clam Muffin, anywhere in the universe!"

"It is better than being a nimp," said Jaro. "Hilyer and Althea would also be proud of me, or so I suppose."

"I'm certain of it," said Skirl. "I'm not so sure about my own father."

"I'm somewhat proud of him myself," said Maihac.

Gaing, not normally demonstrative, reached over and shook Jaro's hand. "In my innocent way, even I am proud of him. In fact, I'm proud to be part of this rather distinguished group."

Maihac called for another bottle of wine. "Before we become even more proud, we should decide what to do next. We control a large sum of money, and we are carrying a cargo of valuable books, from which we should realize another large sum."

Jaro asked, "Where do you propose we sell the books?"

"The most active markets are the auction houses of Old Earth. That is where we will find the best prices, especially if we can surround the books in an atmosphere of romance and mystery."

"That seems reasonable," said Jaro. "But first we should settle our current accounts. The money we took from the bank at Ocknow represents repayment for the Distilcord; that should be divided between you and Gaing. The money from the sale of the books we can divide four ways; then everyone should be relatively wealthy. In fact, I still have my income from the Faths."

Gaing said, "At the moment I don't want the responsibility of so much money. Better that we put it into a safe account where it will earn interest, and which is open to all of us. This system has a great advantage. If one of us is killed, the survivors will find no difficulty in the transfer of his share."

"A grisly thought, but practical," said Maihac. "I agree."

"I'll also agree," said Jaro, "because I'm sure that there will always be enough money in the fund for all of us."

"I'll agree, on the same basis," said Skirl. "Also, because I'd be foolish not to. Though I hope that no one dies."

"Good," said Maihac. "Tomorrow we'll establish the fund at the bank. After that, so far as I know, there is nothing to keep us on Gallingale, so we'll be off to pursue our careers as traders and vagabonds."

"The *Pharsang* is ready," said Gaing. "I've checked out the systems and re-stocked the lockers. As soon as everyone is aboard, we'll be prepared to take off."

Skirl started to speak, but changed her mind and sat back to drink wine and listen while her companions spoke of unknown and barely known regions of the Reach. Skirl's mind wandered. Ahead of her lay an eventful life, crowded with adventure, color, the pageantry of strange customs. In the far saloons and markets she would find wines of novel flavor, strange spices, food she might not care to eat. She would hear music she had never expected nor even imagined: music sometimes haunting and soft; sometimes wild, fervent, compelling. There might be hardships or annoyances, such as the conduct of an obstreperous passenger; or the bite of an exotic insect; there might even be danger, if only the risks of a brawl in some remote saloon.

Jaro was watching her. "You are pensive. What are you thinking about."

"Different things."

"Such as?"

"All sorts of odd notions. I remember that at one time I thought I might become an effectuator, and earn a great deal of money solving crimes which had baffled everyone else."

"You still can do so—if we come upon any crimes you care to solve."

Skirl, smiling wanly, shook her head. "I might function as an effectuator on Gallingale, where I understand how people think, but on other worlds people behave in strange ways. After Garlet, I want no more abnormal psychology. Furthermore, I am now married and quite wealthy, so that I no longer need to earn my own living."

"That is always a pleasant thought," said Maihac.

Skirl went on. "Still, I don't want to be a vagabond forever—at least, not a total vagabond. Someday I want to buy a house in the country, perhaps on Gallingale, or perhaps on Old Earth, where we can raise our family, and where Gaing and Tawn can live when they are of a mind to do so. It will be a home base for all of us, so that whenever the mood comes over us, we can go off in the *Pharsang*, along with our children, and visit places we have never visited before. In this way, we'll only be semi-vagabonds and a good example for our children. Think of it, Jaro!"

"It sounds very nice to me. And now, shall we order another bottle of wine, or perhaps it is time to think about dinner."

Jack Holbrook Vance was born in San Francisco, California, in 1916. His early childhood was spent in San Francisco and then on a ranch near Oakley, in the Sacramento River delta, a setting which instilled a love of both the outdoors and of reading in him. Over a six year period he studied subjects as varied as physics, journalism, mining engineering and English at the University of California, graduating in 1942 – during this time he also worked as an electrician in the Pearl Harbour shipyards in Hawaii, which he left a month before the Japanese attack in 1941.

Despite his weak eyesight Vance joined the US Merchant Navy and served during the Second World War, after which he embarked on a varied career including work as a rigger, carpenter and surveyor, all whilst trying to establish himself as a professional writer. His earliest writing successes included the sale of one of the first Magnus Ridolph stories to Twentieth Century Fox, and his subsequent employment as a screenwriter for the 'Captain Video' television series.

His first published story, 'The World Thinker', appeared in *Thrilling Wonder Stories* in 1945, and a number of his science fiction stories were published in the pulp magazines over the following years. *The Dying Earth*, a series of linked fantasy stories, was published as a collection in 1950 (under the original title, *Mazirian the Magician*). In the professional writing career – including fantasy, science fiction, and thriller novels – which followed Jack Vance's novels went on to win the Hugo Award (for *The Dragon Masters* and *The Last Castle*); the Jupiter Award (for *The Last Castle*); the World Fantasy Award (for *Lyonesse: Madouc*, Jack Vance was also awarded the World Fantasy Award for Life Achievement in 1997); and an Edgar award (for his debut mystery novel *The Man in the Cage*). He died in 2013.

A full list of SF Masterworks can be found at
www.gollancz.co.uk